Searching for Sylvia

Joanna Stephen-Ward

Also By Joanna Stephen-Ward

The Doll Collector

Dedicated to:

Kerry Conroy my sister
Peter my husband

Praise For Joanna Stephen-Ward

I really enjoyed this book,had me gripped from beginning to end. A must read, I didn't want this book to end. **Karen S – Amazon Reviewer**

Best book I have read in a long time. This author is fantastic. I couldn't wait to see what happened next. What a brilliant ending too. I can't praise this book enough. Loved all the characters.....except Gloria of course ... but I did feel sorry for her too. What a good book. 5 stars for sure xx **Kylee – Amazon Reviewer**

Great read, couldn't put it down. Character depth was brilliant and the story built nicely to a unexpected ending. Will look for more by this Author. **Amazon Customer**

The Doll Collector exceeded all my expectations. It's different, it has some dry humour in it and I couldn't put it down. I read about 85% of it in one sitting. I loved it. **Nicola in South Yorkshire – Amazon Top 1000 Reviewer**

Part 1
Tordorrach

Chapter 1

Sydney 2010

When calamity struck Paul's life he had just finished dealing with two obnoxious clients. At first it had seemed strange that the son had been left with nothing, while his sister had inherited everything from their mother's estate. However, when Paul wrote to the sister to inform her that her brother and his wife were contesting the will, her solicitor had then sent him copies of documents that had changed his mind.

'Is it true that you sent back gifts and cards that your mother sent your children?' he asked the son and his wife on their second visit. He pushed a one-page letter towards them. 'And that you wrote this letter telling her that if she attempted to contact them again that you would take out an injunction against her?'

'Yes, because she was a nuisance,' answered the man's wife. 'Always phoning or calling round uninvited. But we made peace and did a lot for her before she died. More than her daughter, actually.'

'Was that after you discovered she had cancer?' Paul asked, keeping his tone neutral.

'Yes,' said the son. 'That's when we realised what she meant to us.'

What her money meant to you, thought Paul. He handed him a copy of a returned envelope addressed to one of the children. 'Is this your writing?'

'It's mine,' said the woman.

'Over a three-year period you returned all the Christmas and birthday presents and cards she sent you and your children – her grandchildren. You wrote threatening letters. In one you called her an "interfering old hag". I advise you to accept that your mother disinherited you because of your behaviour.'

'But we need the money – we've got children. My sister hasn't got any.'

'How old is your sister?'

'Thirty-one.'

'She's of childbearing age then. This will is valid –'

'But it's not fair,' protested the son.

'Fairness does not come into it. All that matters is that your mother was of sound mind, the will is not a forgery and there was no coercion.'

The woman leaned forward. 'Coercion? There would have been.'

Paul held up his hand. 'These letters and envelopes are damning. The originals would be submitted in court if you continued to contest the will. You will end up in debt – perhaps heavily in debt.'

When they left Paul prepared to brief his law partner about the encounter and defend his stance in not prolonging the contest. Tim would have encouraged Paul's clients to take it further because it would mean more money for the firm. When he entered Tim's office Tim looked serious.

'What's wrong?'

'This is hard for me,' he began. 'Paul, I'm sorry. Kathryn is leaving you. She's moving in with me. This will mean a lot of adjustments for you. I've found someone who will buy your share of the firm. They start here in four weeks time.'

Paul was so stunned he left without speaking. He walked to the bus stop praying that he would find Kathryn at home and that she would tell him Tim was lying or mistaken. There had been no indications that they had been having an affair. She was never late home from work and they spent every weekend together, either at the sailing club or playing tennis.

She was waiting for him. 'Has Tim told you?'

He nodded. 'Is it true?'

'Yes.'

'Why?'

'I love him.'

'How long has this been going on?'

'Three months.' Instead of looking guilty or sorry she looked elated. 'I've never felt like this – he's made me alive.'

'What about our children?'

'They're grown up – old enough to fend for themselves.'

'When are you going to tell them?'

'I'll leave it to you. I'm sure you'll make me look guilty –'

'You are guilty.' He struggled to keep his voice from breaking. 'I thought we were happy, that we had a good marriage.'

'We were. We did. But Tim is –'

'A philanderer. He's been divorced twice. He was too selfish to have children.'

'I know. But I don't care. I love him. It's nothing you've done, Paul. You've been a good husband and father. But . . . don't look like that.'

'How am I supposed to look?'

'Paul, you can keep the house –'

'It's in our joint names.'

'I don't want Holly and Bill to be homeless. And Tim's got everything I could ever want or need.'

'It won't last.'

Her expression was defiant. 'It will.'

'He'll have affairs.'

'He won't. My bags are packed. I'm leaving everything but my clothes, toiletries and jewellery. Tim's coming for me at seven.'

'Come on, Kathryn. You're too sensible to fall for someone like Tim.'

'Sensible,' she said as if the word was obscene. 'Sensible Kathryn with her sensible life, her sensible husband and her sensible children. Sensible is a euphemism for boring. Boring Kathryn with her boring life, her boring husband and her boring children.' She went into their en-suite bathroom.

He followed her and watched her putting her cosmetics and perfumes in a bag. He tried to look and sound calm. 'Where and when did you meet?'

'You introduced us years ago.'

'I didn't mean that and you know I didn't. When and where did you have your . . . assignations?'

'Lunchtimes. And we e-mailed each other. Sometimes I took a day off work.'

'He came here?'

'No. I wouldn't . . . not here. I went to his house.'

'And he had days off too – and they coincided with yours?'

She nodded.

Tim's extended lunchtimes were explained. So were his evasive answers when Paul asked him how he had spent his days off. Kathryn was the manager of a jewellery shop, which was a twenty-minute walk away from their office. She only had an hour and Paul was so busy he never had more than thirty minutes, so they had never bothered to meet for lunch. Now he understood why Tim had told their receptionist to stop booking in clients straight after lunch. Paul cursed his naivety in thinking that he was expanding his portfolio of properties.

When he heard Tim's Ferrari in the drive he went outside and sat by the swimming pool, praying that it was a nightmare, but knowing it wasn't.

Despite Kathryn's assurances that he could keep the house, e-mails arrived from Tim demanding that he sell the house and give Kathryn half. Reluctant to become embroiled in a costly battle that he knew he would lose, and never wanting to see Tim again, he agreed. Tim's offer of Paul's share of their law firm was reasonable, which meant that he could take his time in setting up another law practice.

Holly and Bill, already shocked and distressed by their mother's behaviour, were furious.

'You've lost everything and he's gained everything – Mum, your share of the law firm, and half the value of this house. You're left with nothing,' said Bill.

'You should have kicked him out of the firm,' said Holly.

'We were equal partners.'

'He should have left – not you.'

'Tim started the firm – I joined him later. He was prepared – he knew what was going on. I didn't have a clue.'

'Did he offer to leave?' asked Bill.

'No.'

'Slimy –'

'Name calling's not going to make your mother come home,' said Paul. 'The law is on his side. Your mother owns half this house. Stop dwelling on what can't be changed and concentrate on the future. We've got a lot to do.'

'Why does the house have to be sold?' asked Bill. 'Mum's living with Tim – she doesn't need it. She was the one who left.'

'Your mother told me she didn't want her half, she wanted you to still live here. Tim must have persuaded her to sell.'

Holly and Bill exchanged worried looks.

'What about us? Where are we going to live?' Bill asked.

'When this house is sold we could move somewhere else – smaller,' Holly said, looking as if the thought was repugnant. 'We could still have a cleaner and a gardener. We'll get heaps for this house.'

Paul had been thinking the same, but her use of the word 'we' changed his mind. 'No. Make your own way. It's time you were independent. Cook for yourselves and do your own washing, ironing and cleaning. You've had everything too easy, and so have I.'

'*Easy*? You deserved it,' Holly said angrily. 'You worked hard to buy this house – and Mum did too. It's not as if you inherited it or anything. You got your law degree – that wasn't easy.'

'It was. I didn't work hard at it – I found law easy. I went travelling for two years. Because I'd got honours Mum and Dad paid my airfare and gave me a lot of money – that was their reward. I married the first girl I fell in love with. We had a good marriage. You were good kids. Life was easy. Life was great. We were all happy.'

Bill was looking as irate as Holly. 'And that's bad? You're sorry you had such a good life? Would you rather have been born in a slum with drunken parents, been ugly, dim and unemployable?'

'No, but now it's all fallen apart I've got to make drastic changes, and so do you.'

'What are you going to do?' asked Bill more reasonably.

'I haven't got a clue.'

Paul bought newspapers with the intention of applying for a job with a large firm, rather than setting up on his own. Then he saw an article that jogged his memory. 'Cobar,' he murmured.

A week later on a Saturday, when they were having breakfast, he said to Holly and Bill, 'I'm moving to Cobar.'

They looked at him blankly.

'Where's that?' asked Holly.

'Five hundred miles north-west of here. In the outback.'

They gaped at him in astonishment.

Then Bill laughed. 'You're joking.'

'I'm serious.'

Holly pushed her cereal bowl away, opened her iPad and typed in *Cobar*. 'Is there an opera house?'

'Doubt it.'

She glared at the screen. 'I didn't think there would be.'

Bill stood behind Holly and peered over her shoulder. 'Dad, you're having a midlife crisis.'

'Yes, I am,' he agreed. 'There's plenty to have a crisis about. I need to seek new opportunities.'

Holly frowned. 'Have you ever been to Cobar?'

'No.'

'It's a mining town,' said Bill as if it was a jungle full of pythons and crocodiles.

'And agriculture – sheep and wheat and –'

'Populated by people who've never been to an opera,' said Bill.

'And probably don't know what an opera is.' Holly closed her iPad. 'Dad, you always advise people to take their time and make thorough investigations before making a major decision. How can you ignore your own advice?'

Bill pulled a face. 'Cobar is sure to be packed with exciting opportunities. Come on, Dad. Let's have some coffee and go through things sensibly.'

The kitchen was full of gleaming gadgets, including a coffee machine chosen by Kathryn, but left behind because Tim had a better one.

Holly went to the machine. 'Latte, espresso –'

'Espresso, please,' Paul said.

They were silent while the machine ground the beans.

'What do you know about Cobar?' Holly asked when the noise stopped.

'Not a lot.'

Bill looked satisfied. 'According to the website there's no opera house or concert hall. It doesn't say so specifically, but if there were, there would be photos of them.'

Paul shrugged. 'So what? I can listen to CDs and watch DVDs.'

Holly handed him a mug of fragrant coffee. 'Do you know anyone who lives there?'

'I'm not sure.'

To Paul's irritation they frowned in consternation. He could see them trying to decide on the next tactic as they sipped their coffee. 'When I was at school, one of the boarders lived in Cobar,' he told them. 'The school fees for day pupils at Scots College were high, so his parents must have been rich to be able to afford the fees for boarders. His father was a mining engineer. Ralph was always happy when it was time to go home for the holidays, and miserable when he returned. It would take him a week to cheer up. He talked about his friends in Cobar and how they ran wild and free in a way that Sydney children never could. He always stayed with us at Easter –'

'Why?' Holly looked triumphant, as if the fact that he didn't go home at Easter was proof that Cobar was a terrible place.

'Because the five-day holiday was too short for him to fly from Sydney to Cobar and back again.'

'Does he still live there?'

'I don't know.'

Bill put his mug down. 'Dad, it'd be sensible to find out if he's still there.'

'I'll look him up when I arrive.'

'But what if he's not there?'

Paul shrugged. 'Then he's not there.'

Holly put her mug down. 'He might be on Facebook. Let's have a look. What's his name?'

'I'll look him up later. Stop fretting.'

'Won't you miss the harbour? What about the view? What about the sailing club?' asked Bill.

'I won't miss the empty feeling and the memories that were good, and the sense of loss and failure I feel now.'

Holly chewed her lip. 'If you want to get right away, why don't you go to Melbourne?' She sounded as if she was talking to a person on the verge of a breakdown.

'I don't want to go to Melbourne.'

'Brisbane, then.'

'Holly, I don't want to go to Brisbane or Perth or Adelaide or any other capital city. I'm going to Cobar.'

Chapter 2

Paul joined Facebook and looked up Ralph McLachlan. Five names came up, but only one lived in Cobar. He sent him a friend request and a message. He received a reply the following day.

Paul! My old mate! Sorry to hear about your woes. When you arrive you're not staying in a hotel – you're staying with me and my wife. We've got two sons, both afflicted by wanderlust and living in London. You guessed wrong – I'm not a mining engineer like Dad, although I thought that's what I wanted to be, but after doing four weeks work experience at the mine, I hated it. I went back to uni and guess what? I'm a solicitor like you.

Your arrival is timely. My partner has just left for Melbourne, so I'm snowed under. He's divorced and his new romantic interest lives there. She didn't like Cobar. So if you're looking for a job I'd welcome you. To add to the crisis my receptionist/secretary has had a baby and left. The good news is that my niece has broken up with her boyfriend and is coming home from Brisbane and is going to work for me on a trial basis. Tell me when you're coming. I can't wait to see you.

That Ralph was a solicitor came as no surprise to Paul. At school they had both followed important trials and read books about famous lawyers. Ralph was the captain of the school debating team and his team invariably won.

Holly and Bill started searching for somewhere to live. Paul sold his Jaguar and bought a four-wheel drive. Uncertain about the reliability of signals in the outback he bought a satellite phone. He contacted an estate agent and put the house up for sale. He left the furniture for Holly and Bill, who were having trouble finding a place they could afford in a decent suburb of Sydney.

Holly knew exactly what she wanted to do and was in her final year at university studying meteorology. Bill was directionless. He had no idea what he wanted to do, but knew what he didn't want to do. He didn't want to be a solicitor, a teacher or a public servant. He was working as a sales assistant in a large department store in the city. Because most of the other staff in the menswear department were filling in between university or on a gap year, he felt stuck in a rut and inferior. Paul hoped that being forced to leave home and be independent would help Bill make a decision about what he wanted to do.

A week later Paul was on his way to Cobar with his iPad, laptop, television, three suitcases full of clothes, and boxes full of CDs and DVDs, bed linen and everything he would need for the kitchen. He listened to his opera and classical music CDs to alleviate the tedium. He stayed overnight at a motel in Orange. When he got to Cobar Ralph's house was easy to find and he and his wife were waiting for him in their front garden. Apart from a few grey hairs Ralph looked just the same. He told Paul he hadn't changed much either. Neither of them had gone bald and their hair was still thick, even though they were both forty-four.

Ralph's house was modern, built with brick and comfortable, and Paul had his own bathroom. They picked up their old friendship as if they'd only been apart for a few years rather than twenty-six.

'I've got a mate who's an estate agent. Do you want to rent or buy?'

Paul knew the sensible thing would be to rent something until he was sure he wanted to settle in Cobar. 'Buy,' he said.

'New or old?'

Buying a new house like Ralph's would have been wise. 'Old,' but before he went completely insane, he added, 'and in good condition. I don't want to have to do any repairs – I want to be able to move straight in.'

'I reckon I know just the place. It's only down the road from here.'

The following day the estate agent took Paul to a Victorian weatherboard house that was painted white. The corrugated iron roof, the door and window frames were green. Whether it had been well maintained since it had been built or restored by the current owners, Paul neither knew nor cared. He decided to buy it as soon as he saw the front garden with its bottlebrush bushes, two olive trees, borders of lavender and the lemon trees heavy with lemons. There were verandas at both the front and the back. The interior was equally attractive, with gleaming hardwood floors. The two bathrooms were spacious with white suites and tiles. The kitchen looked old fashioned, but had a modern oven and dishwasher. The cupboard doors were painted sea-green. The atmosphere was comfortable and unpretentious. He even liked the colour scheme.

'Do you like the furniture?' the estate agent asked.

'Yes, why?'

'The owners are moving into a retirement home and are selling most of it. Is there anything you want? They are taking anything with a yellow sticker on it.'

He went into every room. The furniture suited the house. It was light oak, plain and classical, and had been well cared for. 'All of it.'

Because he was paying cash the sale would go through smoothly and take eight weeks. Until then he stayed with Ralph and his wife, who refused to let him give them money.

'How many times did I stay with you at Easter?' Ralph asked when Paul tried to insist.

'I don't know – I didn't count.'

'Well it was every Easter while we were at school – that must add up to a lot of weeks. Buy us the odd bottle of wine, if you must.'

Ralph took Paul to his office, which was a five-minute walk from his house. 'The cases are mostly routine – conveyancing, divorces, drawing up wills and powers of attorney and the financial woes of the farmers caused by the droughts. We try and save them from eviction and having their electricity and gas cut off,' he explained.

Paul thought about the quarrels over money when couples were divorcing with each party determined to get as much as they could. 'I reckon that sounds more worthwhile than what I've been doing.'

'Some of them can't afford to pay. I let them pay when they can, but if they can't,' he shrugged, 'I don't pursue it. They've got enough troubles without me harassing them.'

Such benevolence was rare in Sydney. 'That's fine by me, but how do you know they are in genuine difficulties?'

'This is a small town. Everyone knows everyone. The drought's driving some to suicide. Only last month a farmer who was about to be evicted killed himself. That's the tragic state of farming in the remote regions. When their livestock die because of the drought they can't afford more.'

Unlike the large office in Sydney with its thick carpets, panelled walls and luxurious furniture, Ralph's office had dingy cream walls and functional, cheap furniture. Linda, his niece, started a week later. Ralph complained that she was full of fancy ideas.

'Uncle Ralph, this place is dreary. Get the walls painted. Hang pictures. Ugh – the furniture's awful. Buy some new stuff. The Venetian blinds are hideous. They look as if they've been here for fifty years.'

'Our clients don't notice the decor,' argued Ralph. 'They come here because they want help with making out a will, or contesting a will, or making arrangements to get power of attorney for elderly relations who are going into a care home because they're frail or have got dementia. They come in worried and agitated because they're getting divorced or are in terrible debt – they're not interested in what the place looks like. They want honest advice and help at a reasonable price.'

'But it's depressing,' said Linda.

'Often the people who come in here are depressed,' said Ralph.

'This will make them feel worse.'

Paul thought it was time for a compromise. 'Can we afford to get the walls painted?'

Ralph looked affronted. 'Of course we can. Do you think this is a poor house?'

'It looks like one,' said Linda.

Chapter 3

A year later Paul became an associate in an office with freshly painted white walls, new furniture and carpets, and pictures on the walls. Smart wooden shutters replaced the shabby blinds.

Two years later Ralph asked him, 'Do you like Cobar?'

'Yes.'

'What do you like about it?'

'The genuine and friendly people and a real sense of community. Everybody knowing who you are and saying hello when they see you in the street or in a shop.'

'Do you like it enough to stay permanently?'

'Too right I do.'

'How about a full partnership then?'

Paul held out his hand. 'I accept. Thanks.'

In January 2014 they received an e-mail from an accountant who lived in South Kensington in London.

Dear Messrs McLachlan and Knight,

Tordorrach

I am purchasing the above property. Would you act on my behalf and do the conveyancing, please?

Yours sincerely,

Noël Carlyle

'You can deal with him,' Ralph said to Paul. 'You're used to city dwellers.' His tone was scathing.

'You make them sound like undesirables, Uncle Ralph.'

'Where's Tordorrach?' Paul asked.

'A two-hour drive from here. Most of the road is unsealed. It's been up for sale for over four years. It is – or was – a sheep and wheat station.'

'Was?'

'The sheep died in the drought and the wheat crops failed.' He got onto the estate agent's website. 'Take a look.'

The photos of the seventy-thousand acre property made the state of the homestead clear. It was falling down. The red earth was dry and there was scarcely any grass.

'Good news for Seamus,' said Ralph.

'Surely no one lives in that house?'

'No. Seamus Ryan can't afford the maintenance. He and his wife live in a caravan. They've got no electricity, and their phone was cut off years ago. The poor wretches are heavily in debt. But Seamus has made some stupid mistakes. He's an infuriating bloke. You'll see that when you meet him.'

'Why would anyone from England want to buy this place?' asked Paul.

'Why not?' asked Linda.

'I'll show you.' They swapped seats and Paul looked up Noël Carlyle's address on Google Earth. As he'd anticipated it was a large white house with five floors. There was no front garden and just a small back garden with gravel paths and bushes.

'Tiny,' said Linda. 'What's good about it?'

'It'll be big inside,' said Paul. 'And see the garden in the middle of the square – it's for the residents of the square only. The gate will have a key.'

Linda wrinkled her nose. 'Big deal.'

'If Noël Carlyle owns the whole house he's rich,' Paul told them. 'Even if it's divided into flats and he just owns the basement or the attic flat he'll be well off.'

Ralph looked puzzled. 'How come?'

'Have you ever been to England?'

'Hell no. I've never lived anywhere except here – apart from when I was at school and uni.'

Paul smiled. 'That part of London is exclusive. My house here would cost less than a garage there.'

'You're kidding!'

He typed 'Rightmove' in the search engine and watched their expressions of bemusement when small mews houses in Bayswater and Knightsbridge came up with prices beyond two million pounds.

'That's four million dollars, isn't it?' said Linda.

Paul nodded and typed South Kensington in the location. A five-storey house had a price tag of twenty-four million pounds.

Ralph stared wide-eyed at the computer screen. 'Are my eyes going funny? Twenty-four million dollars?'

'Not twenty-four million dollars.'

He looked alarmed. 'My eyes are going funny?'

'Pounds. Twenty-four million pounds. Forty-eight million dollars.'

Ralph shook in head. 'This whole town wouldn't go for that much! Why does someone that rich want to buy Tordorrach?'

'Maybe he doesn't own it – he might just rent it,' said Linda.

Paul typed 'rent' instead of 'buy' in the preferences.

Ralph looked even more amazed. 'Ten thousand pounds a month?' he said slowly.

Paul couldn't help laughing at their incredulity. 'Yep. Twenty thousand dollars.'

'Why? Why does anyone want to live in London, let alone pay those crazy prices?'

'It's got a lot – cinemas, theatres, museums, two opera houses –'

'Bah – opera,' scoffed Ralph. 'Who wants to listen to that rubbish? A whole lot of women squawking and dying.'

'I like opera.'

Ralph shook his head. 'You were always going on about some bloke – Wagging?'

'Wagner.'

'Have you ever been to London?' Linda asked.

'I lived there for two years. It's an enthralling city.'

'How could you afford it?'

'I didn't live in a place like that. I rented an overcrowded, damp flat, with four friends.'

'And you call that "enthralling"? You need help.' Ralph looked at the copy of the e-mail. 'Surely accountants don't earn that much?'

'He might have inherited the house. His parents or grandparents might have bought it years ago, before property prices soared. How long has Seamus Ryan owned Tordorrach?'

'His father was the manager for Edward Halland, the previous owner who ran it with his son Charles. If things had gone the way they should have, Charles would be the owner now. By all accounts the place was in a prime state and profitable when it was sold to the Ryans in 1982.'

'Why did they sell it?'

'Two things happened. First Charles's wife walked out – wrote letters for him and their two little girls and just left. She had post-natal depression. That was a terrible blow for all of them. Then Charles was bitten by a snake – he died. His parents sold it to the Ryans and moved to Bowral. They took their granddaughters with them.'

'How old were they?' Linda wanted to know. 'The daughters I mean.'

'Eight and six.'

'Poor little things,' she said.

Chapter 4

aul emailed the forms to Noël. He was surprised when they came back with the buyer named as N. G. J. & Associates. There were five illegible signatures. He could only make out the N and the C of Noël's.

'He obviously knows about the dismal state of farming in the outback,' he told Ralph when he showed him Noël's email.

We intend to run Outback Experience holidays at Tordorrach where visitors will ride around the property on horseback and do walking tours. Could you please ask Seamus Ryan if he would be willing to be our manager? As soon as the sale is complete, work will start on transporting cabins to the site. A surveyor has been booked to see if the original homestead is worth renovating. A suitable place will be built for the manager, where, if Seamus accepts the position, he and his wife will live.

I will be arriving sometime in March.

Pleased to be able to tell Seamus and his wife Mary that they could still live on Tordorrach and earn money, Paul drove out to see them. The pretty garden, ablaze with flowers and bushes surrounding a battered caravan, struck him as incongruous. Fuchsia bushes with fat red and purple hanging flowers complemented the white and yellow roses. The white cast iron table with six matching chairs and a bird bath had obviously been moved from the old homestead and bought when they were well off. It was a hot day and a tattered umbrella shaded the table and part of the garden. The heat hit him as soon as he stepped out of the car.

Seamus and Mary looked at him suspiciously.

'Good news,' he said. 'You've got a buyer.'

Their poverty showed. A kettle hung on a frame over a small fire. Seamus's trousers were old and had holes in them, and his shirt was faded and frayed at the collar. His wife's jeans were torn and her T-shirt was in an even worse state than his shirt. Her greying hair was scraped back into a ponytail secured with an elastic band.

Paul had always been proud of his appearance and clothes, but now he was ashamed. Acutely aware of his expensive cream linen suit, dazzlingly white shirt, gold cufflinks, silk tie, leather shoes and briefcase he wished he had worn something more casual or at least taken off his tie and put his papers in a plain plastic folder. He pulled off his jacket and put it on the back seat of his car. As he got closer he could smell their body odour. Mary gestured for him to sit at the garden table and insisted on making him a cup of tea, which came in a blue and white china cup and saucer with a gold rim. He guessed that they had taken a few essentials from the ruined homestead.

'Stinking, filthy rich, English bastard,' Seamus snorted when Paul had finished telling them about Noël's proposal.

'Seamus!' said his wife.

Paul was taken aback. 'Mr Ryan, this is a very good deal for you. You won't get an offer like this again.'

'What's good about it?'

'Lots of things. One – you can still live here. Two – you're going to get a salary. Three – you're going to get a new house.'

'And be bossed around by a stuck-up Englishman who –'

Paul held up his hand. 'He's offered you the position of manager, and from his emails it sounds as if you'll be working together – he seems like a decent sort.'

'Why the hell did he buy this place?'

'I'm his solicitor, not his lifestyle guru. And it's just not one person buying Tordorrach, it's a group of five – an association. I get the impression that Mr Carlyle is the head.'

Seamus's scowl deepened. 'Five stuck-up Englishmen.'

'Are you interested in his proposal or not?'

'Yes, we are,' said Mary.

Seamus glowered at her. 'No. Find a proper buyer.'

'Mr Ryan, you are in no position to refuse to sell. Your property's been on the market for years. The sale will be complete in eight weeks. Mr Carlyle wants to get cracking. He's arranged to have cabins transported here the day after the sale is complete.'

'He can want.'

'Mr Ryan, in eight weeks time you'll no longer be the owner. If you are not going accept the position of manager you'll have to leave. Mr Carlyle will appoint another manager –'

'Yeah? Where's he going to find one so quick?'

'You must know there are other properties around here up for sale – suffering from the same plight as you are. I'm sure one of them would be happy to accept such a generous offer.'

Seamus grunted. 'Generous? With my wife expected to be a skivvy?'

'Mr Carlyle didn't say that.'

'No? Who's going to do all the cooking for the tourists? Who's going to do all the washing of the sheets and the cleaning of the cabins?'

'I don't know. The details –'

'You don't know, but I do.' He jabbed at his chest. 'Me and the wife – that's who.'

'I'm sure Mr Carlyle can afford automatic washing machines,' Paul said. 'It's not as if you'll have to wash sheets in the creek.'

'We haven't got a washing machine – I do everything by hand in the kitchen sink,' said Mary. 'Seamus, please accept the job of manager.'

'No. I'm not going to take orders from any Englishman.' Seamus glared at Paul. 'Don't you go telling me I'm lucky to get a buyer. Once the sale's gone through and they've taken my money for debts, I'll have nothing.'

Paul took advantage of Mary's discomfort to ask, 'Is that Mr Carlyle's fault? Did he get you into debt? He paid the asking price. Does he control the climate?'

Seamus didn't reply. Not bothering to hide his annoyance Paul stood up and walked away without saying goodbye. He was on his way to look closely at the wrecked homestead when Mary Ryan caught up with him.

'I'm sorry about Seamus,' she said.

'Is he always this negative?'

'You'd not believe it, but he used to be cheerful. When things started going wrong he couldn't cope.'

'I thought this would be good news for him.'

Mary sighed. 'It would have been if the owners had been Australian or anything other than English.'

'What's he got against the English?'

'His ancestors were Irish and they got transported for speaking out against the English.'

That Seamus held a grudge from centuries ago made him sink even lower in Paul's estimation. 'It might to useful to remind Seamus that there are far worse things to worry about now rather than dwell on what the English did to his ancestors hundreds of years before he was born.'

Mary looked at him blankly. 'We haven't got a TV or a radio, and we can't afford newspapers.'

Paul wanted to say that if Seamus had accepted the position of manager they would be able to afford newspapers, a TV and radio and new clothes, but he guessed that Mary knew that, and telling her would make her feel worse.

He gazed at the derelict homestead, which looked more dilapidated than it did in the photos. Even in its present condition he could see that it had once been an attractive house.

'There was a storm,' Mary explained. 'A bad one. Most of the roof blew off. We couldn't afford to get it fixed. It was cheaper to buy a second-hand caravan – we didn't have the money for a new one. We could only just afford this one.'

He guessed that they were not insured and thought it tragic that such a basic necessity had been beyond their means.

'Seamus is unhappy. He acts strangely when he's unhappy and says things he doesn't mean. I'll try and persuade him to take the manager's job.'

Although Paul pitied them, Noël Carlyle was his client and had to come first. 'I'm sorry, Mrs Ryan. I don't think he'd be the right sort of manager. One of the manager's duties would be driving a minibus to Dubbo to pick up visitors from the airport and drive them to Tordorrach. How do you think they'd react if they were met by someone so sullen? If he's as brusque to the visitors as he was to me, they'd demand their money back.'

'Please let me try, Mr Knight.'

Paul sighed. 'I'll only consider him if I can't find another manager. I've got to inform Mr Carlyle about his attitude.'

'The house might be a wreck, but come and have a look at the orchards and the vegetable garden,' she urged him.

He followed her. The vegetable garden was as well kept as the homestead was neglected, with compost heaps at various stages of composting. The orchard had apple, apricot, plum, peach, quince, lemon and orange trees.

'This is where we spend all of our time. There's plenty of fruit here for the visitors. We tried to get shops interested in buying our stuff, but it's too far out of town. If we took it in ourselves we wouldn't make any profit after paying for the petrol.'

'How do you manage to grow things in this drought?' he asked.

'Necessity,' she said with a wry smile. 'To save water we don't use the flushing toilet – not that it's much good anyway. We use chamber pots and put the urine on the compost heap and bury the other stuff. It works well. Take no notice of what Seamus says, I'd be happy to do the cooking, cleaning and washing and ironing. Can you give me your phone number?'

'I didn't realise you had a phone.'

'Seamus's mum gave us a satellite phone. She was worried about emergencies.'

'How do you charge it?'

'We can't. When she visits she gives us her fully charged one and takes ours home with her to charge up.'

Ralph was out when Paul got back to the office. He emailed Noël and recounted his meeting with Seamus Ryan.

The following morning he received a reply.

Thanks for the information, Paul. I'm flying to Sydney and staying in a hotel for two days. I'll fly to Dubbo on 2nd March, and catch a bus to Cobar. I've booked into the Great Western Hotel. Can I see you the next day? And I need to visit Tordorrach. Your idea about asking one of the other owners whose property is up for sale to be the manager, is a good one. Could you please do it as soon as it's convenient?

Please send me your account for the work done to date.

Ralph stared at Paul in disbelief. 'Seamus turned it down? The halfwit. He's made a lot of mistakes, but this is the worst.'

'What else has he done?'

'His troubles began when the manager's house burnt down ten years ago. Instead of waiting for a fire investigation, Seamus blamed the manager and sacked him, making him, his wife and four children homeless. It caused a lot of resentment in the district. One of the other station owners put up the manager and his family. The investigators found that the fire was caused by defective wiring, which was Seamus's responsibility. The manager sued Seamus and won. Seamus had to pay hefty compensation and couldn't afford to hire another manager or build another house.

'The manager found another job and Seamus, who was never popular, became even more unpopular. His manager had done all the paperwork. Seamus was useless at that side of things. He was fined because he didn't fill in tax returns, and bills went unpaid. I can't believe he's turned down this chance to get out of trouble.'

'What other owners might be interested in Mr Carlyle's offer?'

'Matthew and Coral Fulham are in the same predicament as Seamus, but through no fault of their own. They own Ravenscroft. It's been on the market for three years. They were the ones who put up Seamus's manager and family when they left Tordorrach. You could ask them.'

'Have they got an email address?'

'Yes, do you want to email them? They've got a phone – or they did have.'

The email Paul sent was returned as undeliverable. The phone number was not recognised.

'They must have been cut off,' said Ralph. 'You'll have to visit them.'

'It might be a good idea to ask if Mr Carlyle wants you to drive him to Tordorrach,' said Linda. 'He probably thinks it just outside the town.'

'He seems astute – the estate agent's website gave the location.'

'I bet he's got no idea that most of the road from Cobar to Tordorrach is unsealed,' said Ralph.

Paul replied to Noël's email and offered to drive him to Tordorrach. He attached the account and the firm's bank details. Two days later the money arrived in their account.

Ralph was pleased. 'Looks like we've got ourselves a wealthy client who won't need any reminders about payment.'

'He might not be wealthy.'

'He must be,' said Ralph. 'He's paying cash for Tordorrach.'

'With four other people. He may be in debt, and that's why he's selling up in London and moving here. He might be a victim of the financial crisis in the UK –'

'People like him aren't affected by things like that. It's the poor and the middle classes who suffer.'

Thanks for the offer of a lift to Tordorrach, Paul. I accept. We intend buying a plane when we get settled, so will need a runway on the property.

Ralph laughed when he read it. 'Buying a plane! I don't think he's having any financial problems. He's done his homework well – Google Earth I suppose. I wonder who "we" is.'

'His wife I presume. She's probably one of the associates.'

'But it looks as if he's coming out by himself.'

'She's probably coming later. The other associates might stay in London. Noël and his wife might live here and the rest of them could be sleeping partners with only a financial interest.'

'Right, Uncle Ralph,' said Linda. 'Give me some money. I'm going out to get some proper china – cups and saucers.'

Ralph looked exasperated. 'This is a solicitor's office, not a hotel.'

'You can't give someone posh like him a mug with a picture of a dog on it, can you, Paul?'

'No,' Paul agreed.

Ralph pulled out his wallet. 'Nothing fancy,' he said as he gave Linda the money. 'Plain – no flowers.'

She gave him an 'I'm not an idiot' look and left. She returned with four cups, saucers and plates and a matching sugar basin and milk jug. They were white with a silver rim. 'Okay?' she said in a tone that dared them to disagree.

'Perfect,' Paul said.

Ralph nodded. 'What are the plates for?'

'Biscuits. I'm not going to dump them on the desk in a packet. When I first moved to Brisbane I was a silver service waitress. I know how things should be done. And so will Mr Carlyle.'

Chapter 5

Ravenscroft was Tordorrach's nearest neighbour. Hoping the owners, Matthew and Coral Fulham, would be more civil than Seamus had been, Paul drove out to see them. After witnessing the dire poverty of Seamus and Mary he wore no tie, and a shirt that didn't need cuff links. Their house was freshly painted and had solar panels, so he assumed they had survived the hard times. Given the state of the two homesteads he was perplexed that Noël had chosen to buy Tordorrach rather than Ravenscroft.

A woman came onto the veranda carrying a basket full of washing. His spirits flagged when he saw her expression.

He smiled. 'Hello, I'm Paul Knight, a solicitor from –'

'Matt! Matt!' she shouted. Her voice was panic-stricken.

Before he could reassure her, a man came round from the back of the house holding a spade. His hands, face and arms were powdered with red dust.

'It's a solicitor!'

Before Paul could apologise for interrupting his gardening Matthew threw down his spade and rushed into the house. Paul's bemusement turned to fear when he came out holding a revolver.

He looked straight at Paul. 'Right, this is it then,' he said quietly. 'The end.' 'First I'm going to shoot my wife. Then I'm going to shoot myself. Do you like animals?'

Paul was too stunned to do anything other than nod.

'Good. Because we have two cows, three horses and some hens. I don't want them to suffer. You can shoot them yourself or call a vet. Or give them to the neighbours.'

Paul dropped his briefcase and held out his hands. 'Mr Fulham, why –'

'You ask me why? You know why. It's because of your type – you greedy lawyers and bankers, that we're losing the lot.'

'I'm not here to get money – it's –'

Coral's eyes shone with tears. 'Why then? More threats from the banks?'

'No. I've got good news – please will you listen?'

Matthew lowered the revolver. 'What good news? You're sure not here to give us money.'

'In a way I am.'

Coral's expression was dubious. 'What?'

'Tordorrach has been sold –'

The hope that had wavered in Matthew's eyes, dimmed. 'Well that's good for Seamus – I can't see that it's good for us.'

'How come he can sell that tip?' Coral burst out bitterly.

'I don't know – your house is much better – but it's still good news for you.' The wind blew a cloud of dry earth in his face. 'Can I come inside and explain?'

'No. Tell us what the good news is,' demanded Matthew.

'I don't think there is any good news,' said Coral. 'He's stalling. He's come to evict us and once he's inside –'

His eyes were gritty with dust, but worried that Matthew would raise his revolver again Paul got to the point. 'The buyers of Tordorrach want to employ a manager. Seamus turned it down so they asked me to offer it to you – or another near neighbour.'

They looked incredulous.

Paul picked up his briefcase. 'I've got all the papers in here. Are you interested in the proposal?'

Coral put down the washing basket and wiped away her tears. 'Come inside. Would you like some tea?' Her tone was more friendly, but they both looked wary.

Because of their hardship Paul was about to decline, but knew if they accepted Noël Carlyle's offer they would no longer be poor. He picked up his briefcase. 'Thank you,' he said. He took out his handkerchief and wiped his face. He wished he could splash water on his eyes, but owing to the scarcity of water, he didn't ask, just blinked.

The inside of the house showed no sign of poverty, which, given their desperation, confused Paul. Even Seamus hadn't been suicidal. On their way to the kitchen he saw a study with a flat screen computer that looked new, the furniture in the rooms he passed looked comfortable, the units in the kitchen were in good condition, everything was clean and tidy, and neither Coral nor Matt's clothing was threadbare, although it was faded.

'I tried to send you an email, but it was returned.'

'We changed our address. We were getting too much spam. Are you based in Cobar?'

'Yes. I'm with Ralph McLachlan.'

Matthew smiled. 'If I'd known that I wouldn't have been hostile. He's a good bloke. Kind – not like the banks.'

Paul handed the business plan, job vacancies and wages and contracts to Matthew. Coral stood next to him. Paul enjoyed their expressions of hope as they read.

Coral finished reading first. Her eyes widened in disbelief. 'Are you serious?'

'Yes.'

Matthew smiled. 'We accept. Seamus rejected all this?'

Paul nodded.

'He's a bigger nincompoop than I thought he was,' said Matthew.

Coral went to the sink and filled the kettle. 'Lucky for us that he is. Seamus never repaired his homestead and he was too useless to put the roof back on. His son went to Brisbane and only used to visit once a year. Now he never comes. He could have helped his dad put the roof back on and fix things up. It used to be a beautiful place when Edward Halland owned it and before Seamus let it fall apart. He's good with the gardening and the land, but no good with people. His dad was popular – a lovely man.'

'Even though he was born on Tordorrach, Seamus never fitted in here,' said Matthew. 'His mum and dad sent him to a Catholic boarding school in Sydney and that filled his head with the idea that he was better than everyone else. We're the same age, but he never played with me – I wasn't good enough.'

'Did your father own Ravenscroft?'

'Yeah.'

'But if his father was the manager and your father owned –'

'Seamus never thought like that. The manager's house on Tordorrach was grand – not as grand as the homestead, but it was bigger and better than this house. And Tordorrach is twenty thousand acres bigger than Ravenscroft. When the Hallands sold it and his dad bought it, Seamus became even more superior. Apart from Seamus we all help each other around here. If he hadn't been such a snob we all could have pitched in and helped him put the roof back on and patch up the homestead, but he never helped us. Most of the time he sneered at us, so we didn't bother. Anyway, he didn't ask.'

Coral took a bottle of milk out of the fridge. 'If he had asked we would have refused. He thinks he's too good to mix with the rest of us. He's always going on about his ancestors and how ill-treated they were by the English.'

'He says they were transported for saying things about the English, but I reckon they stole stuff or rioted,' said Matthew. 'Not that you could blame them – with lots of them starving.'

'I don't care who my ancestors were,' said Coral taking mugs out of the cupboard. 'I only know back as far as my grandparents. I don't know why Seamus is like he is. He's nothing like his dad, which is a pity.'

Paul put the documents back in his briefcase. 'Has Seamus got any other children?'

'A daughter,' said Coral. 'She got married and lives in Perth. She hasn't been here since. Our kids do all they can to help us. Last December a van arrived with solar panels for the house. We thought they'd got the wrong place, but it was a Christmas present from our son and daughter. No more electricity bills.'

'She's a dentist,' Matthew said proudly. 'And our son's a whiz kid with computers. He's with some big oil company at the head office in Sydney.'

Coral put everything on a tray and carried it to the table. 'I'll do whatever Mr Carlyle wants. I can cook –'

'She's a good cook,' said Matthew.

Coral beamed. 'This is so exciting. But we don't need a new house – we can drive to Tordorrach – it's only two miles from here. If they put a gap in one of the fences it'd only be a mile away.'

'Excellent. I'll get the contract drawn up with your details and send it to you to sign.'

Clearly unable to believe their luck and worried that any delay might make the offer disappear, Matthew said, 'We've got to go into Cobar tomorrow and get supplies. We'll call into your office, if that's okay.'

Paul agreed. 'Your house is lovely.' He hesitated, anxious not to sound inquisitive. 'What went wrong? Apart from the drought.'

They looked at each other. 'We were stupid,' said Coral.

Matthew looked mortified. 'We were short of money and didn't tell our kids – we were too proud and we didn't want to worry them. We weren't in debt, but we couldn't afford to do things that had to be done. The house needed painting, inside and out, the boards on the veranda were rotting and some of the water tanks were leaking. We took out a loan – this place had been owned outright by my mum and dad – they paid off the loan as quick as they could. We weren't as wise. The farming economy got worse, the drought got worse and we couldn't pay off the loan – of course it went up and up and the interest grew and grew. But now we'll be having a regular income we can start paying things off.'

'What you did wasn't foolish,' said Paul. 'It was sensible. Rotting boards are hazardous, and if the water tanks were leaking you could have run out of water. It was more bad luck than anything.'

When Paul left them they were smiling, and so was he.

Matthew and Coral arrived at Paul's office the next day with anxious expressions, which changed to relief as soon as the contract was signed.

'This morning when I woke up I wondered if it was a dream,' said Coral.

When they left Paul emailed Noël, and attached a copy of the contract.

Thanks, Paul. We're willing to advance their wages so they can pay off their debts. This will prevent them from gathering more interest. Can you find out how much they owe, and their bank details and we'll get the money to them immediately.

'Is this bloke too good to be true?' Linda asked.

Ralph looked worried. 'Do you reckon he's fishy, Paul? He hasn't even asked how much they need. That shows how rich he is. What if he's a drug baron?'

Paul smiled. 'I doubt it. It's an advance on their wages – he's not giving them anything. Anyway, money can be earned honestly – you're honest, so am I.'

'But we're not multi-millionaires,' Ralph countered.

'Would a drug baron be kind enough to pay off someone's debts?'

'It might be because he wants to bind them to him – make them do whatever he tells them,' Linda said.

'Have you two got anymore cheerful suggestions? You'll be thinking he's a mass murderer next.'

'I'm a solicitor,' said Ralph. 'I don't make a fortune. He's an accountant and he does make a fortune.'

'He might be an accountant to a drug baron,' suggested Linda.

Paul threw up his hands. 'He could have won the lottery. He could have made some shrewd investments. His aunt or his grandmother or his parents could have left him the money. Stop being so suspicious.'

'I don't want us getting involved in anything dodgy.'

Paul laughed. 'We're solicitors – we can wriggle our way out of anything dodgy.'

Matthew Fulham was astounded by Noël's offer, and reluctant to accept it.

'Ha! Even he's suspicious,' said Linda when she read his email.

'What's wrong with everyone?' said Paul in exasperation. 'It's an advance of their wages. I'll email Mr Carlyle.' He looked at his watch. 'He should still be awake.'

He received an immediate reply.

Tell Matthew and Coral that as their house is habitable and only two miles from Tordorrach we won't have the expense of building them a new one. I am aware how debts escalate, and what starts off as a small debt turns into a big one.

They agreed to this. Noël sent the money to their bank. Matthew called in to see Paul the day he went to the bank. He looked happy and relaxed – a different man to the overwrought person Paul had first met. 'Please tell Mr Carlyle we appreciate his thoughtfulness. I've just paid off all our debts and bought a satellite phone.'

$$\Omega$$

'You've had this gloomy face for too long, Mary. When are you going to speak to me again?'

'When you tell Mr Knight you'll accept the manager's job.'

He sighed and picked up the phone his mother had insisted on giving them. 'Have it your own way.'

She took the phone from him. 'No.'

'What now?'

'Drive into Cobar and go into their office. Be polite. Tell them you're sorry and you'll be happy to accept the job of manager.'

He looked at his watch. 'It's too late to go there now – they'll have gone home by the time I get there.'

'Go tomorrow. Wear a clean shirt. That one stinks. And wash properly before you leave.'

Paul had just finished dealing with a client about making a will when Linda came into his office. 'Mr Seamus Ryan wants to see you.'

'Did he say what it's about?'

'No.'

'Make him wait ten minutes.'

'Shall I ask if he wants coffee or tea?'

'No.'

'Hello, Mr Knight,' Seamus said politely, when Linda ushered him in to Paul's office.

Guessing what Seamus wanted, Paul smiled innocently. 'Yes, Mr Ryan, what can I do for you?'

'It's about the manager's job. I've thought it over. I'll be pleased to accept Mr Carlyle's kind offer.'

'I'm sorry, Mr Ryan, but someone else has accepted the position.' Before he could say any more Seamus stormed out of the office and slammed the door.

Chapter 6

Paul and his children kept in touch by emails and on Facebook. In desperation Bill had joined the public service in the education department. He hated it. Holly had finished her degree and was happy working for a radio station. Neither of them commented on the photos he sent them of his house, but they assumed he was renting it. Their messages became alarmed when he told them he had bought it. When they finally accepted that his move to Cobar was permanent they came to visit him. They arrived in February. As he had anticipated they made disparaging remarks about his house and the town. They declared that his house was too small.

'It's got three bedrooms and two bathrooms, what more do you want?' asked Paul.

'There's no en-suite,' complained Holly.

'No swimming pool,' said Bill, using the same tone Paul would have used if there had been no toilet or running water.

'I'm managing to live without a swimming pool.'

'You've lost weight,' said Holly. 'Are you eating properly?' When Paul didn't answer, she went on, 'What are you eating?'

'I miss your mother's cooking,' he admitted.

Bill grimaced. 'So do we.'

'What do you eat?' Holly insisted.

'Sometimes I eat with Ralph and his wife. Sometimes I have a big lunch in the café and don't eat in the evenings. Sometimes I have microwave meals.'

Kathryn had abhorred microwave meals and until he moved to Cobar Paul had never eaten one.

'We buy microwave meals too,' confessed Bill. 'More than sometimes.'

'Mum's not happy,' Holly said suddenly. 'She says she is, she pretends –'

'Is she still with Tim?'

They nodded.

'What makes you think she's unhappy?'

'She looks dejected. Her smiles aren't real,' said Holly.

'She's lost weight,' Bill added.

Paul found he didn't care, but not wanting to sound vindictive he said nothing.

'Come back to Sydney, Dad,' Bill pleaded.

They went into the kitchen and Paul put the kettle on. 'When your mother and I first became members of the yacht club, we met a mega rich bloke,' he told them as he got out mugs and milk. 'One day he said something to me that I'll always remember. "I've got the house, I've got the cars, I've got the plane and I've got the yacht. But my friends have got love, and I do not."'

Bill and Holly looked bored. Paul gave up, and they drank their tea in uncomfortable silence. Desperate to get some normal conversation going, he asked them if they wanted to walk around the town. Reluctantly they agreed.

'It's so parochial,' said Bill after five minutes. 'What a stupid town. There's an airport, but you can't land there – you have to fly to Dubbo and catch a bus. How crazy is that? What a waste of time.'

They went into a café.

'Call this a café?' muttered Holly looking distastefully at the lino floors, plain tables and chairs and white-washed walls.

To Paul's dismay Linda was sitting at a table with three of her friends.

She waved and said, 'Hi Paul.'

He waved back. He didn't want her to witness his children's sulky behaviour, so he chose a table as far away from her as possible. Holly and Bill didn't even ask who she was. After eating sandwiches and drinking chocolate milk shakes, which they grudgingly admitted were very good, they walked home.

While Bill wandered restlessly around the house, Paul wondered how he had managed to create such material children.

'Come on, Dad,' said Holly, 'Tell me one good thing about Cobar.'

'Sincerity,' he said. 'Cobar's got sincerity.'

'Look at this,' Linda said when Paul arrived at the office on Monday morning. 'Noël Carlyle is renting out his house fully furnished – listen – the house comes with,' she giggled, 'a butler and a cook, who live in the flat in the basement where the kitchen is located. And it's got a library,' she clicked on the picture of a large room lined with floor-to-ceiling bookcases full of books. She grinned. 'Sounds like *Downton Abbey*. He should buy a Kindle – he could use the room for something else. And the housekeeper lives in the attic flat. Cleaners come in everyday. Look at that gorgeous furniture.'

'I wonder if he's happy,' Paul said.

After giving him a quizzical look Linda asked, 'Did you have a good weekend with your kids?'

He was about to say that he had, but decided to be honest. 'No. I was pleased to see them leave.'

'What happened?'

'Nothing much.'

'Did they like Cobar?'

'No. They didn't think much of my house either.'

'You do like it here, don't you?' she asked anxiously.

'Very much.'

She looked relieved. 'Your son's handsome.'

'Is he?'

'He looks like you. Has he . . . got a girlfriend?'

To tell her that she was too good for him would have been disloyal. 'Not that I know of.'

She smiled. Paul went into his office. He hoped for Linda's sake that she never saw Bill again.

Ω

Kathryn cursed her stupidity in having allowed Tim to persuade her that her serene life with Paul was boring. It was only after she had married Tim that her life had become boring. Before their marriage Tim had been attentive and loving. He took her to glamorous restaurants, the theatre, opera and on expensive holidays. They went to New Zealand, Fiji and Tasmania where they stayed in luxury hotels. He always paid with his platinum credit card. He bought her jewellery for her birthday and at Christmas. He had a cleaner and a gardener.

It was only after they were married that she realised that his financial situation was precarious. As well as being a solicitor Tim also invested in property. He owned five houses that he rented out. One had been destroyed by fire when his tenants had a wild party. Another had water damage after someone had left a tap running when they had gone to work. He sacked all the staff at his office, but before his secretary left she took her revenge by cancelling the insurance policies for all his properties.

His two previous wives had demanded, and got, half the value of his house. His mortgage was huge and he needed Kathryn's wages. She pushed away the suspicion that the only reason he had married her was because he needed the money. He scoffed when she suggested they move to a smaller house in a less exclusive suburb. Point Piper was one of the most expensive suburbs in Sydney and Tim's house was even bigger than the one she had owned with Paul. He called her naive when she asked, 'Why do we need such a huge house?'

The money she got from the sale of the house in Kirribilli went into paying off his debts. He told the cleaner and gardener he could no longer afford them, and told Kathryn she would have to do all the housework and cooking. He complained that she didn't iron his shirts properly and told her she was pathetic when she argued that as she worked all day they should share the housework.

'You sound just like my other two whinging wives. My job is more important and stressful than yours. I have to use my brains. You don't. You just sell jewellery.'

Desperate to make the marriage work she tried even harder. She got up early and made his breakfast. Sometimes he thanked her, but more often he was silent. She cooked dinner for them when she got home from work. She stayed up late doing the ironing and cleaning. Instead of spending the weekends playing tennis or going sailing, she mowed the lawn and pulled up the weeds. Tim did nothing. He was rarely at home.

I made everyone unhappy for nothing, she thought as she sat in the house alone one night waiting for Tim to come home. *I'm probably even more unhappy than Paul now – although how he can be happy in that outback town I'll never know.*

Paul's prediction that Tim would have affairs looked likely. She wondered how she could catch him out. She considered writing to Paul and asking him to forgive her, but her pride rebelled.

Chapter 7

March 2014

Linda came into Paul's office looking startled and gleeful. 'Noël Carlyle is here.'

Assuming from her expression that he was handsome and young, Paul smiled and said, 'Show him in.'

'I can't.'

'Why not?'

'I can show *her* in.' She covered her mouth to stifle her giggle.

'Oh. Right. Give me a minute.'

'Do you want tea or coffee?'

'I'll have whatever she's having.'

Linda went back to reception. Paul composed himself and tried to look as if he'd known from the start that she was a woman. They had addressed each other as Paul and Noël in their emails, but he debated if in person this would be too informal. *I don't even know if she's married*, he thought. *Rings will tell me, but what if she's not wearing any? Miss – Ms?*

He hadn't consciously imagined what she'd look like, but when Linda ushered her in he realised he'd envisaged someone about fifty with grey hair and a stern expression. He stood up and shook hands with the attractive brunette, whom he judged was in her early thirties.

'Good morning,' he said.

'Paul, it's good to meet you in person.'

She was carrying a briefcase. Her face, although fine featured, was strong, although too thin, and her gaze was direct. With her olive complexion she looked more Greek or Italian than English.

Her eyes were such a vivid blue he wondered if she wore coloured contact lenses.

'Mrs Carlyle's going to have tea,' said Linda. 'The kettle's on – it won't be long.'

'Thank you, Linda.'

While they waited for the tea he asked Noël about her trip. Her voice was mellow, and although the accent was not plummy it was certainly upper-class English. She wore a silk shirt in emerald green with tiny navy polka dots, and navy trousers. Linda brought in the tea and the biscuits, which were on a matching plate. While she laid everything out he studied Noël who was watching the process. Apart from a pearl necklace and earrings her only jewellery was a wedding and engagement ring.

Kathryn had taught him about precious stones. Noël's engagement ring was a fine white diamond in a setting that looked antique. It was large enough to be impressive, but not large enough to be ostentatious. Her wedding ring was a circle of diamonds. Her big hands looked odd with her slender wrists and build. Her fingernails were bitten, and the cuticles were torn and inflamed. Kathryn's nails had always been perfectly manicured. She would have adored the rings, and despised the nails. He could imagine her saying, 'Why draw attention to her ugly nails by wearing sensational rings? There's nothing she can do about her mannish hands, but she could stop biting her nails and get them manicured.'

After all the documents had been agreed and signed Paul arranged to drive Noël to Tordorrach the next day.

'Take a picnic,' said Linda when Noël had left. 'You can take her to the billabong and have it there.'

'Billabong?'

'Yes – it's on the estate agent's photos.' She saw his doubtful expression. 'It's a two-hour drive to Tordorrach. You're going to be hungry and thirsty. Make sandwiches – take juice and a thermos of soup. And cake.'

'She might be a vegetarian.'

'So she might.' Linda rolled her eyes. 'So make one lot of cheese and tomato and another lot of egg and cress.' She smiled suggestively. 'She's very attractive.'

'And married.'

'I don't think she is.'

'Then why is she wearing a wedding ring and a great big diamond engagement ring?'

'She's divorced – it's just a feeling I've got. I can sense that she's had a lot of unhappiness – she's too thin.'

'Linda, if she's divorced she wouldn't wear rings on her left hand.'

'Why not?'

He didn't have an answer. 'Even if she is divorced she's too young for me.'

'She's older than she looks.'

'Another of your feelings?'

She nodded. 'I'm intuitive. And I'm usually right about this sort of thing. She's available, believe me.'

'Well I'm not.'

'Why not? You're divorced.'

He didn't have an answer for that either. He rang Matthew and Coral, who were startled to learn that Noël was a woman.

'I'm taking her to meet Seamus and Mary and she wants to meet you too.'

'Great,' said Coral. 'I'll bake a cake. Or will sandwiches be better?'

'She did eat the biscuits, so I'd guess she got a sweet tooth.'

'A cake it is.'

He rang Seamus. His phone went to messages. 'Mr Ryan, I'm bringing the new owner out to Tordorrach tomorrow. We'll leave Cobar at eight in the morning so should arrive around ten. Also, Noël Carlyle is a woman, not a man, as I thought.'

$$\Omega$$

Even though Paul had given no indication that he was surprised she was a woman, Noël had known as soon as she saw the secretary's amazed expression, that they had thought she was a man.

'Would you like some music?' Paul asked as they drove out of Cobar. 'There are some CDs in the glove box.'

Not knowing what to expect, she opened the glove box. 'Opera!' she exclaimed. She picked out *The Flying Dutchman*. 'I love Wagner.'

'Did you go to the opera much in London?' he asked as she took the CD out of the box.

'All the time. Both the Royal Opera House and the English National.'

'Yet you're moving out here – no opera house. Won't you miss all that?'

'No. I've seen all the operas. It's getting silly with directors thinking up outrageous ideas – dragging opera into the present time or even the future. Some work well – most don't. They call it being innovative, but there's classy innovation and trashy innovation. We'll have a cinema in the new homestead so we can watch DVDs of any opera we want.'

She put the CD into the slot and music filled the car. Nostalgic memories of her husband filled her mind. It was Wagner that had brought them together. She and her cousins Grace and Juliet had been at the Royal Opera House in Covent Garden. During the interval of *Tristan and Isolde* they bought wine and had been moving away from the bar when an elderly man fell against Noël. Her glass broke and a piece had slashed a vein in her hand. She'd known from the alarmed reactions of his companions that the man was critically ill. Grace and Juliet had helped them lower him to the floor. Noël had pulled off her jacket and put it over him. One of the young men had comforted an older woman who he called grandma, the other concentrated on getting help. When the ambulance men arrived they took one look at Noël's bloodstained white dress and her hand, which was dripping with blood, and insisted that she also go in the ambulance.

The rest of the night passed in a haze. Grace and Juliet went to the hospital with her, in spite of her protests that they should stay and see the rest of the opera. As soon as they arrived at the hospital the elderly man was rushed off on a stretcher followed by his fraught family. Noël's hand was stitched and bandaged. It was only when they got back to their flat that she realised she was without her jacket and handbag. When Grace rang the hospital her they had not been handed in. The loss of her jacket didn't matter, but the loss of her wallet, pocket diary, account cards and money did. The next evening they received a phone call. The two young men had Noël's jacket and handbag and had found her address in her diary. Juliet, who had answered the phone, arranged for them to visit. They arrived at their flat with the jacket and handbag, a bouquet of flowers, three tickets for the best seats in the opera house for the following night and the news that their grandfather was out of intensive care. They introduced themselves as Adam and Friedrich. They were cousins, and the man who had had a heart attack was their grandfather.

They stayed for coffee and then invited the girls out to dinner at the Savoy. Juliet and Friedrich married twelve months later in 1997 and Adam and Noël married later the same year. Noël had never foreseen that seventeen years later she would be on the other side of the world, driving along an unmade road through the outback.

Tears blurred her vision. She turned her face to the window.

Seamus was looking even more belligerent. He stood outside his caravan with his arms crossed. 'What do you want?'

'Didn't you get my message?' asked Paul.

'What message?'

'I left a message on your phone.'

'I never bother about messages.' He looked at Noël. 'Who are you?'

'This is Mrs Carlyle – the new owner of –'

'Not till the end of next week she's not. You're a girl,' he said accusingly. 'He said you were a man.'

Paul was embarrassed, but Noël looked amused not annoyed. 'Well, girlie, what –'

'Mr Ryan, you can call me Noël or you can call me Mrs Carlyle. Do not call me girlie.'

He snorted and looked at her left hand. 'And what does your husband think about you gadding about the outback with another man?'

'I'm a widow.'

Paul was shocked by Noël's revelation and disgusted that Seamus didn't have the empathy to apologise or look sorry. *Linda was right about the unhappiness*, he thought.

His wife came out of the caravan. 'Seamus, you'll have Mrs Carlyle thinking Australians are uncouth and rude,' she said sternly. 'Would you like a cup of tea?' she asked them.

Noël's smile was strained. 'No thanks, Mrs Ryan. I just wanted to chat to you about your future plans and tell you what I've arranged. The owner of one of your neighbouring properties has accepted the position of manager. He has experienced the same misfortunes as you have, but has been unable to sell his property.'

'Yes, we know.' Mary looked as if she was about to cry.

'Which property?' asked Seamus. 'Lots of them are for sale around here.'

'Ravenscroft,' said Paul.

Seamus grunted. 'Matt Fulham's a useless man. You'll be sorry you had anything to do with him.'

'Seamus, shut up,' Mary said wearily. 'Are there any other positions available, Mrs Carlyle?'

'Yes, a lot,' said Noël.

'We're not interested,' muttered Seamus.

'I am – you can do what you like. Go to Cobar and live with your mother, for all I care.'

Seamus gaped at her. 'Now look here, woman, if I say –'

'We're finished, Seamus. I've stuck by you, but you've ruined the one chance we had of getting our happiness back and staying on to live here.'

Seamus looked astounded. Paul had no desire to witness the disintegration of a marriage, and judging from her expression neither did Noël.

'Mrs Ryan,' she said, 'you can stay here and we can discuss what job would be suitable. We need cooks, cleaners –'

'My wife's not going to be a cleaner! We own this place and you expect her to be a skivvy?'

'Be quiet, Seamus,' snapped Mary.

Noël's dark green chinos worn with a pristine white cotton shirt tied at the neck with a royal blue silk scarf patterned with green leaves, made Mary's clothes look even more threadbare.

Her clothes probably cost more than their caravan, Paul thought.

Noël's voice was firm when she said, 'Mr Ryan, I'll give you a week to decide what you want to do.' She took a large envelope out of her briefcase and gave it to Mary. 'Here are the details of the staff we need and their duties and the wages. There is also a list of what work is going to be done and a projected timetable. Let me know what you think. I'll ring you in a week.'

'Maybe I was a bit hasty,' said Seamus desperately.

'Maybe you were,' said Noël. Her expression was as frosty as her voice.

After leaving Tordorrach they drove to Ravenscroft to meet Coral and Matthew. To Paul's relief the rapport between the three was instant. The ginger cake with lemon icing that Coral had made was delicious. When they arrived they were on formal terms of Mr and Mrs. By the time they left an hour later it was Noël, Matt and Coral.

Paul and Noël stopped for lunch at the billabong. Paul spread a rug on the ground. Linda, not trusting him to pack a picnic, had taken it upon herself to do it for him. The insulated bag contained sandwiches wrapped in foil, a thermos of vegetable soup, mugs, paper plates, paper serviettes and two buns that smelled of cinnamon.

'This is great,' said Noël. 'Thank you.'

Her dark brown hair gleamed in the dappled light shining through the trees. There were so many questions Paul wanted to ask her, but most of them were intrusive. How long had she been a widow? How did her husband die? How did he make his money? How old was she? He tried to think of subtle ways to ask.

He poured the soup into mugs. 'I apologise for thinking you were a man.'

She smiled. 'That's okay. Men get taken more seriously. Yes, even in these days when we've had women Prime Ministers.'

'I'm glad you're not annoyed.'

'How could I be annoyed with a man who loves opera?'

After the picnic Noël said she wanted to go and look at the homestead.

'It's in a terrible condition,' said Paul. 'Worse than the photos.'

'I want to see if it's possible to restore it.'

'I doubt it. Did you have a survey?'

'Yes. The surveyor said it would be possible to renovate, but that he wouldn't advise it because it would cost a fortune.'

From a distance the homestead looked in a reasonable condition. It was only when they got closer that the extent of the devastation was evident.

'I'm sorry Seamus was so rude to you,' Paul said as they stood looking at it. He hates the English because –'

'I'm not English.'

'Oh, What are you?' he asked thinking she must be Scottish or Welsh.

'Australian.'

'Eh? You don't sound it.'

She looked amused. 'I was born on Tordorrach. Edward Halland was my grandfather.'

Chapter 8

When Noël and Paul arrived back in Cobar Paul debated whether to invite her to his house for coffee. He wanted to ask her out for dinner, but didn't want to embarrass her or make a fool of himself. It was so long since he'd dated anyone he was clueless about modern dating etiquette. He drove her to the hotel and watched her go inside. They had spent seven hours together, but already he wanted to see her again. He had no idea if she wanted to see him in a non-professional situation.

After the revelation that she had been born on Tordorrach, he had bombarded her with questions. *Probably too many questions*, he thought dismally, although she had seemed happy to answer them. He hoped she wasn't being polite. She could have resented them. He went into the office, where Linda and Ralph were waiting expectantly.

'Well?' they said together.

'Thanks for the sandwiches, they were –'

'Forget the sandwiches. Tell us about Mrs Carlyle,' said Ralph.

'She's not a drug baron or a serial killer.'

'What is she?' asked Ralph.

'An accountant.'

'Duh,' said Linda.

'We know that,' Ralph said impatiently.

Paul looked at Linda. 'She's a widow.'

She winked at him. 'I told you she was available.'

'She's Australian.'

'Australian?' they echoed.

'She was born on Tordorrach.'

'What?' they said.

'You sound like a chorus.'

'Paul! Tell us,' demanded Linda. 'Why was she born at Tordorrach?'

'Her mother was there at the time.'

'Obviously,' said Ralph. 'Why was Noël's mother at Tordorrach?'

'She and her husband were spending Christmas 1975 with her parents and her brother Charles. Noël arrived three weeks early on Christmas Day – hence the name.'

'She's a Halland?' Ralph looked astonished. 'Why didn't she tell us in the first place?'

'I don't know.'

'So *that's* why she bought Tordorrach.' Ralph's expression became perplexed. 'But in her emails she said, 'we'. If she's a widow, who is she buying it with?'

'Her cousins, Juliet and Grace.'

'Ah, the other two associates. But there were five signatures –' Paul nodded. 'Their husbands.'

'Juliet and Grace – Charles Halland's daughters?' said Ralph.

'Yes.'

'Was he the one who was bitten by a snake?' asked Linda.

'Yes.'

'Where are Juliet and Grace now?'

'In England. They're coming out later.'

Linda shut down her computer. 'How come they all went to England?'

'Noël lived in Sydney. When she was twenty her parents were killed in a car accident.'

'God, how awful,' said Linda. 'What an unlucky family – snakes, car accidents, depressed mothers.'

'Grace and Juliet lived in Bowral with their grandparents. Their grandfather died the day after his daughter's funeral and their grandmother died three months later.'

'And that's why they went to England?' asked Ralph.

'Not entirely. They wanted to find Juliet and Grace's mother – she was English. Their grandparents had tried, without success, to find her in Sydney.'

'Did they find her in England?'

'No. They have no idea where she is, or even if she's still alive.'

'Talk to Wendy Jenkins – she was their governess,' said Ralph. 'When the Hallands left Tordorrach she moved into town and taught at the local school. She might know something.'

'She was my teacher,' said Linda. 'She was fabulous. When I was in her class I loved going to school.'

Ralph gave Paul Wendy Jenkins's address and he rang and arranged to visit her. This gave him a good excuse to contact Noël who was surprised that Miss Jenkins was still in Cobar.

'I think she was originally from Sydney. She was probably only twenty when she became Grace and Juliet's governess. She came when Grace was four – Juliet would have been two.'

'Did you spend much time at Tordorrach?'

'All the school holidays.'

'Do you remember much about their mother?'

She shook her head. 'Grace and I were only five when she left. My strongest memory of her is that she just sat around in a daze. She cried a lot, but on the days she was normal she was fun. Miss Jenkins was more of a mother to them than Aunty Sylvia. It's not till we grew up that we understood what was wrong with her. Grace and Juliet were fearful that they might suffer from postnatal depression like their mother, and that's why they only had one child each. Juliet had slight postnatal depression for a month – nothing serious, thank God.'

He wanted to ask Noël if she had any children. She had never mentioned any, but then he hadn't known her long.

Wendy Jenkins lived in a house similar to Paul's, but smaller. She looked younger than fifty, and her smile when she saw Noël was rapturous.

'Please call me Wendy,' she said when Paul introduced himself.

Her living room was comfortable and there were photos of children on every surface. She had made tea and sandwiches and they sat opposite each other with a coffee table between them.

'I remember the day Sylvia left,' she began. 'I'd taken Grace and Juliet to the billabong to paint. I'd packed a picnic and we spent most of the day there. Grace was an excellent artist, much better than Juliet, who enjoyed painting, but got more paint on her clothes than on the paper.'

'You're a good judge. Grace is a successful artist now,' said Noël. 'It's how she met her husband – he owned an art gallery in London and he loved her work.'

'Wonderful,' said Wendy. 'I'd like to buy one.'

'I'm sure she'll give you one – we often talked about you.'

She gestured to the wall. 'I've got one – pride of place.'

Paul stood up and looked closely at it. It was a collage and he recognised that it was of Tordorrach. 'It's very good. How old was she when she did this?'

'Not sure. It was after their mother left – I was with her when she did it – I was trying to distract her. When she painted she was absorbed – it's was as if she was somewhere else.'

'She's still like that. You go into the room where she's painting and she looks as if she's never seen you before.'

'What's Juliet doing?'

'She's a photographer – she does weddings, portraits and school groups mainly.'

'I wish I could see them again.'

'You will. They're coming out as soon as Grace's exhibition is over. Juliet's got two weddings booked – both at the end of March. They'll be here in the middle of April.'

'Is Juliet married?'

'Yes, she married Friedrich, my husband's cousin. He's an architect and he's drawn up the plans for the new homestead and applied for planning permission. Anyway, you were saying that you'd been at the billabong.'

'Yes. When we got back to the homestead their grandmother was in a terrible state. She gave me the letters and I read them. I tried to keep calm for the children's sake. I just told them that their mummy had gone away for a while, but would be back. They kept asking why she hadn't kissed them goodbye. When their father came in and read the letters he went white. The children started crying. Somehow we managed to get through the evening. We had dinner, and kept trying to convince ourselves that she would be back. I put Grace and Juliet to bed.

'The next morning I met Mr Ryan on his way to the homestead. The poor man had had an accident the day before – he fell out of a tree when he was pruning it. His face was a mess. I was taking Grace and Juliet to the paddock to try and distract them with the horses. He saw they were upset and asked them what was wrong, probably thinking they'd been punished for being naughty. Grace told him that their mother had left and gone to Sydney. Then Juliet started crying. He was very kind and told them she'd be back. Grace told him that their mother had left a letter . . . she had seen their father put it on a shelf and she got out of bed at night and read it.' Wendy smiled slightly. 'Grace told him that Sylvia had a fog in her head and thought she was no good.

'Mr Ryan was horrified. He asked me if it was true. I nodded. He still couldn't believe it and asked if she had packed a case, plainly expecting me to say she hadn't. I told him that she must have because all her clothes were missing. He was perturbed. But then he was such a lovely man. Generous – he'd do anything to help anyone.'

'Unlike his son,' Noël said.

'Seamus was always uppity. The last time I saw him was in 1983 when your grandparents left. He didn't bother to say goodbye to me – I probably wasn't important enough to speak to. And now his father owned Tordorrach he was way above me on the social scale. I must admit to a feeling of satisfaction when I heard he was in terrible debt.

'Anyway Mr Ryan said he had to go and tell his wife and she would be happy to help look after the children. He ran off. Later he and his wife came to the homestead to say how sorry they were and if there was anything they could do. Bernadette – that's his wife, looked shaken. She was shy – she never said much, but she was nice. But after she started helping me with Grace and Juliet she became more confident. Seamus was at boarding school in Sydney and I suppose she was lonely and missing him. He only came home for the holidays. Grace and Juliet gave her something to do and children to love. She filled a void in their lives and they filled a void in hers.'

Ω

Bernadette Ryan bought two lamb chops from the butcher for Seamus and Mary, wishing she could buy more. Because their caravan didn't have electricity she could only buy them meat for one meal during the summer, which Seamus would cook on the barbecue.

When she arrived home she packed everything in a box. She would have bought more, but having to depend on her for basics humiliated Seamus. If she bought jam, marmalade or biscuits he would refuse to accept them. It had taken a lot of persuasion to make him take anything. She used Christmas and birthdays as an excuse to buy them clothes and little luxuries like shampoo and good soap. He hadn't even wanted to accept these because he was unable to give her presents in return. It was Mary who came up with the idea that she and Seamus would give her fruit and vegetables in exchange. It had taken weeks to persuade him to accept the satellite phone she had bought them. Only she and Mary insisting that he must take it in case there was an emergency made him accept it. Their plight worried her. They had lost a lot of weight and she could see through their pretence of managing. She hoped the rumour that someone had bought Tordorrach was true.

But if it was, she thought, *surely Seamus would have rung me?*

She put ice packs around the milk, butter, cheese, eggs and lamb chops and put the bread, tea, jar of Vegemite, coffee and toilet rolls on top. During the drive to Tordorrach she hoped that when it was sold they would come and live with her. She liked Mary and they got on well. When she pulled up in front of their caravan Mary was hanging a kettle over the small fire. It saddened Bernadette that they were forced to live as if it was a hundred years ago.

'Bernadette, it's great to see you,' said Mary, taking the box from her mother-in-law. 'And it's not just that you bring us food and stuff. We're indebted to you. If it wasn't for you we'd have to live off fruit and vegetables.'

Bernadette kissed her. 'There're two chops for your dinner tonight. She gestured to the box. 'And Seamus said he needed matches for the barbecue – they're somewhere in there. Is it true that you've got a buyer?'

Seamus came from the orchard with a basket full of vegetables, apricots, oranges, plums and apples. 'Yes, it is,' he said.

'Wonderful. I'm so happy for you.'

He handed Bernadette the basket. 'It's not wonderful at all. A bloody English woman bought it.'

'Oh, Seamus,' said Bernadette.

'She paid the asking price,' Mary said quietly.

'Well that's good,' said Bernadette, disconcerted by the distinct antagonism between them. 'Your dad didn't hate the English and neither do I – I can't understand where your hatred comes from. Your grandmother was English.'

'And she had the sense to emigrate to Australia,' said Seamus.

'The new owner offered Seamus the position of manager,' Mary said. Ignoring his glare she continued. 'He turned it down.'

Not wanting to berate her son, Bernadette said, 'What are you going to do? You can come and live with me if you like.'

'I'm staying here. There are lots of jobs on offer,' said Mary. 'Seamus can do what he wants.'

'I'm sorry there's trouble between you,' said Bernadette.

Mary sighed. 'So am I. Seamus is so stubborn. If we stay here we'll get a cabin – with electricity and a washing machine. And we'll get paid. The owners are rich and are getting solar panels.'

'If that's the case I think you both should stay,' said Bernadette. 'I'd hate to see you separate. You used to be so happy.'

'I'll think about it,' said Seamus.

Chapter 9

Mary sat at the table in the garden reading the list of positions Noël had given her.

Seamus looked over her shoulder. 'Housekeeping duties,' he read aloud. 'You're not doing that.'

Mary sighed. 'It's not arduous work. The new homestead's going to have a big laundry. When the visitors are here there'll be temporary people to clean and do the laundry and the ironing. The housekeeper will supervise and make sure everything is done properly.'

'Going into town and getting supplies, it says. What for? I grow everything here.'

'Do you grow soap, washing up liquid, washing powder, shampoo, olive oil, rice –'

'There's no need to rave on.'

'I don't rave. You do.'

'Look,' Seamus continued. 'Overseeing the cleaning of the apartments in the new homestead. What a lazy lot. Why can't they do their own chores?'

She thrust the papers at him. 'Take a look at the salary, Seamus. It's at the top of the page.'

He looked. 'Oh.'

'Does that make a difference?'

'No. You'll just be a –'

She shoved back her chair and stood up. 'A paid employee. With a full-time job. Living in a brand new cabin with electricity, instead of a cramped, scruffy old caravan that's ready for the scrap heap. With four weeks holiday. *Paid* holiday.'

'Not to be taken during April, May, June, July and August, when the guests will be here,' he read. 'What if you want to take your holidays then, Mary?'

She snatched the papers back. 'I won't. It's years since we had a holiday – or had you forgotten?'

'I suppose that's my fault.'

'Yes, Seamus, it is. I've given up making excuses for you. When we got married we lived in a beautiful house. We had a manager. We had cleaners. We went on holidays. Now we live in a tiny caravan.'

'The drought's not my fault.'

'No, but everything else is. The homestead is in ruins because you forgot to renew the insurance and were too incompetent to do the repairs. Other homesteads in the area were damaged by the storm, and they've been repaired because their owners kept their insurance payments up to date.' She threw the papers at him. 'Make up your mind what job you want. If you're not going to do anything you can't stay here.'

He looked at the list of jobs. 'Have you decided which of these menial tasks you're going to do?'

'Assistant cook.'

'Who's the cook?'

'Coral.'

'You'll be sweeping the floor and doing all the dirty work for her.'

'Make up your mind, Seamus. So I can ring Mrs Carlyle and tell her.'

'The head gardener.'

'I didn't see any head gardener on the list.'

'That's because it's not on the list.'

'Then you can't be the head gardener. You'll have to be a gardener.'

'I'll be the head gardener or nothing.'

'You'd be hopeless – you'd bully the others. What's your gripe? If you're a gardener you'll have lots of others to help.'

'Seeing you're a mine of information, do you know who's going to live in the other three cabins?'

'The full-time odd job person –'

'What's he going to do?'

'Repairs, maintenance, cleaning the windows, and anything else that needs doing – feeding the chooks and pigs –'

'Pigs?'

'Yes, they're going to raise pigs.'

'What for?'

'So they can entertain the visitors with their singing and dancing. To eat –'

'Stop being sarcastic. Who else is going to live in the cabins?'

'Vasco –'

'Who the hell's Vasco?'

'The groom.'

'What sort of a name is "Vasco"?'

'His dad's Spanish and his mum's quarter aboriginal.'

'Can he speak English?'

'Of course. He was born here. His dad works at the mine.'

'Have you met him?

'No.'

'Then how do you know?'

'Coral told me.'

'When does he start?'

'The day the cabins arrive.'

'So who'll be in the other cabin?'

'Xavier, the other full time gardener. I wish there was another staff cabin.'

'Why?'

'For me, so I could get right away from you.'

'Right – that's it,' Seamus threw one of the chairs at the caravan. 'I'm cancelling.'

'What?'

'The sale. I'm not selling.'

'You can't do that.'

'I can. This place is in my name only. And it's not sold yet.'

'Bad news,' said Ralph when Paul came back from lunch. 'Seamus just phoned. The sale is off.'

'What? Why?'

'He didn't say.'

'Do you think he's got another buyer?'

'I doubt it. He would have told me and started haggling.'

Paul grabbed his phone and punched in Seamus's number. 'It's Paul Knight,' he said calmly.

'That's got you rattled.'

'You are just delaying the inevitable, Mr Ryan. Your financial circumstances are so bad that you're in danger of repossession.'

'I haven't been repossessed so far.'

'Wait and see, Mr Ryan.' Paul disconnected the call.

Ralph was frowning. 'How come you're so composed? What's Noël going to say?'

'The sale will go through – it will just be delayed.'

Paul's phone rang.

It was Seamus. 'You hung up on me.'

'It's pointless talking, Mr Ryan. You're just running up your phone bill. You don't want to sell. That's fine. Mrs Carlyle will buy another property – there are plenty of them around.' He disconnected the call.

'Paul, what the blazes are you doing? They want Tordorrach.'

'We know that, but Seamus doesn't.'

'Do you think he's bluffing?'

Paul shook his head. 'He's serious. He doesn't want to sell Tordorrach to Noël, but it will be repossessed eventually and it will be cheaper than ever. The money doesn't matter to her, but it matters a lot to Seamus. He's got debts and the less he makes on the sale the less, if anything, he'll have after his debts have been paid off.'

Ralph's doubtful expression was mingled with admiration. 'You're cunning.'

Paul laughed. 'I'm from Sydney. I'm used to tough negotiations.'

The phone rang again. Paul looked at the caller identification. It was Seamus. He didn't answer. 'Let him sweat.'

Linda looked at him with approval. 'You're cool.'

'Are you going to tell Noël?' Ralph asked.

'I'll have to. The refusal to sell will have to be formalised – they were so near completion.'

The phone rang. It was Seamus.

Linda laughed. 'He's getting frantic.'

'He's dim,' said Ralph. 'That's one of the reasons Tordorrach is in such a terrible state.'

Paul rang Noël and asked her to come to the office.

Noël was dismayed. 'What should we do?' she asked when Ralph and Paul explained the situation with Seamus. 'Juliet and Grace are going to be shattered.'

'Dissemble,' said Paul. 'Let's get Matthew and Coral in on the act.'

'What good's that going to do?' Ralph asked.

'Trust me.'

'I'm panicking,' Noël told them as Linda came into the office with a tray.

As she set their cups, coffee pot and biscuits on the desk, Paul rang Matthew and told him that Seamus had decided not to sell. Matthew swore.

'I suggest that we call his bluff,' Paul said when Matthew had stopped cursing. 'Let him think that Noël and her family are going to buy Ravenscroft instead.'

Matthew laughed and then said, 'But what if he's okay with that?'

Paul's confidence in his plan faltered. 'Do you think he will be?'

'Anything's possible with that mad sack of snakes.'

'Okay, Matthew, leave it with me. I'll discuss it with Noël.'

Noël rubbed her head. 'What would be the first step in your plan?'

'Write to Seamus formally, saying the agreed sale is off and tell him that as he has withdrawn from the agreement so near completion a hefty fine will be imposed.'

She nodded.

'Second step?' Ralph prompted.

'Let him think that Noël is discussing the purchase of Ravenscroft with Matthew and Coral.'

'Will the delay in the completion seriously disrupt your plans?' asked Ralph.

'No. But I'm worried that Seamus will cancel the sale permanently. What if he finds another buyer? What if he's got one already and that's the reason why he's cancelled the sale?'

'Unlikely. Tordorrach's been on the market for years,' said Ralph. 'It's not as if the drought's broken and made the place more attractive.'

Noël took a deep breath. 'Right, let's do it and see what happens.'

Mary burst into tears of fury and distress.

'It's not that bad,' said Seamus without conviction. 'They might offer us more money.'

'It is that bad, you imbecile – don't you understand?' She threw the letter at him. 'They are going to buy Ravenscroft instead! I'm warning you, Seamus, the day they buy Ravenscroft is the day I leave you.' Ignoring his devastated expression she continued, 'I'll work for them. Everything that they were going to do here they'll do there.'

'Mary, they might not want us.'

'Not us, Seamus, me. They won't want you, but they will want me. You can stay here alone in this revolting caravan and rot. I'll have nothing more to do with you. As you told me Tordorrach is in your name only, so all the debts are yours, not mine. When you're evicted you can go and live with your mother.'

'I'll ring them –'

'You've tried ringing them – they don't answer. They know it's you and they want nothing more to do with you. Go and see them.'

'I don't know if there's enough petrol in the car to go all the way to town.'

'Then walk!'

'But –'

'Drive as far as you can and if you run out of petrol get out and walk!'

'And how do I get back? I can't walk over a hundred –'

She pushed him towards the car. 'When you get to Cobar borrow your mother's car.'

Linda came into Paul's office. 'Guess who's here?'

'Seamus Ryan?'

'Yep.'

Paul grinned. 'Tell him to make an appointment.'

'For tomorrow?'

'No – next week.'

She left and returned a few minutes later. 'He's flustered. And apologetic. He's begging to see you now.'

'Ask him what it's regarding.'

She giggled and left. 'The sale of Tordorrach,' she said when she returned.

'Tell him I'll see him next week.'

'Phew, you're so cool.'

Hope I'm not being too cool, Paul thought.

She came back moments later.

'His car ran out of petrol two miles away. He walked the rest of the way.'

'What does he want me to do about it?'

She grinned. 'See him now, I presume.'

Paul buzzed Ralph and asked him to come into his office. 'What do you reckon? You know him better than I do. Is there a risk that he might realise we're bluffing?'

Ralph shook his head. 'He's in a panic and he doesn't think clearly at the best of times. But it might be best to see him today. Make him wait till the last. At least we'll get this sale over sooner. Ring Noël. See what she says.'

'See him today,' she said. 'It looks as if your strategy's working.'

'Have you told your cousins about the delay?'

'No, I don't want them fretting. Coming home means everything to them.'

'Okay, Linda, tell him I'll see him at five,' said Paul.

Seamus went to see his mother, who sympathised, made him a mug of tea and a sandwich, and gave him money for petrol. After he had eaten, he bought a can of petrol and she drove him to where he'd left his car. He poured the petrol into the tank and drove into Cobar where she gave him enough money to fill up the tank.

Just before he left to see Paul she made him take some more money. 'Buy some food.'

'Thanks, Mum. I'll pay you back when we get the money from the sale,' he said, grateful that she didn't tell him she thought Mary was right and he was wrong.

'Things will be better then.'

'I doubt it. I bet that snobby English woman knows nothing about horses and has never ridden one. She'll probably beat them and sack me when I protest.'

'Congratulations, Noël,' said Paul when she walked into his office. 'NGJ and Associates are now the owners of Tordorrach.'

Linda, followed by Ralph, came in carrying a tray on which were four glasses. 'I hope you like champagne.'

'I do. This is lovely. Thank you very much.'

Although Paul had bought the most expensive bottle the shop in Cobar had, he hoped it would not fall too short of Noël standards. *Maybe we should have celebrated with tea and cake*, he thought. But she sipped it, and looked as if she approved.

After Linda and Ralph left his office Paul asked Noël if she would like to have dinner with him. He was delighted when she said she would.

Chapter 10

'Are you a vegetarian?' Paul asked when Noël ordered a nut roast.

'No. But unless I know where the meat comes from I don't eat it. In London our cook bought meat from an organic free-range butcher. When we stayed in Yorkshire we bought our meat from the farm shop on the estate. We knew that the animals had been well treated during their lifetime and had died humanely. The butcher lived on the estate and the slaughtering was done by him. None of the animals had to endure being transported. That's what we are going to do on Tordorrach.'

Paul thought it would be impossible to get a butcher to live on Tordorrach. 'Isn't Tordorrach too far away from the town to make such a venture viable? Surely it would be more profitable for him to have a shop in the town?'

'I can fly him in and out when the animals are ready to slaughter. We'll have a shed and he'll have a stun gun. He'll take the dead animals away, skin them, and cut them into joints. Then I'll collect them.'

Paul admired her ethics, but doubted they would work in such a remote area. 'I've got you a house-warming present,' he said not wanting to dampen her ideas. He gave her the package.

'Ah,' she said, looking in delight at the polished wooden sign with TORDORRACH carved on it. 'It's beautiful. We'll have to get a new gate to do it justice. Thank you, Paul.'

'Are you going to tell Seamus who you really are?'

'No. If he's crazy enough to hate someone because of their nationality rather than because of their character, that's up to him. I never liked him much. One day – Grace and I were about five – I asked him if he'd play hide and seek with us. He scoffed and said he didn't have anything to do with little girls. He was a hypocrite. Always nice to us when his parents or other adults were around, but he snubbed us when we were alone. He never teased or bullied us, but he was haughty.'

'Why did you offer him the manager's job?'

She shrugged. 'He was there. He knew the land, and his father had been a brilliant manager. I thought he might have changed. He was only seventeen the last time I saw him.' She finished her glass of wine and the waiter came over and refilled it. Paul had only taken a few sips of his.

'Have you still got Sylvia's letters?' he asked her when their main course arrived.

'Grace has. Why?'

'I'd like to see them. I may be able to help.'

Noël was silent.

'I mean it would be good for Grace and Juliet if they could find their mother and good for her too. Wouldn't it?' he asked when she said nothing.

'It depends.'

'On what?'

'On what sort of state she's in. Where she is. What she's doing.'

He saw that her glass was almost empty again. He wanted to warn her not to drink too much, but knew that his comment might be judged as interference. She looked and sounded sober. He imagined her response if he dared to broach the subject with, 'Noël, it's none of my business, but you're drinking a lot.' She might tell him it was none of his business, or worse, might leave the restaurant and refuse to have anything more to do with him. 'Do Grace and Juliet want to find their mother?'

'Yes. They don't have any of the reservations that I do. They think that if they find her everything will be perfect. They think that even if she's still suffering from depression, now they're rich they'll be able to buy some miracle cure.'

'Are they moving here permanently?'

'Yes. Once the cabins have arrived and have been connected to the water tanks and had solar panels installed we'll move into them while the new homestead is being built.'

'When are the cabins being delivered?'

'The first four are being delivered tomorrow. They looked great on the website. I'll be there to make sure they are okay. If they are I'll order the rest.'

He wanted to advise her not to be too hasty. She was so optimistic that their venture would be a success, but he wondered what they would do if it failed.

'You look doubtful, Paul.'

'I was thinking about the possibility of very few people, or perhaps no one, booking. You'll be stuck with all these cabins.'

To his surprise she smiled. 'One of the best things about being rich is that you can afford to take risks, as long as the profit and loss is calculated correctly. If it does fail the only loss will be the money we paid for the cabins, and we can always sell them. It's not as if we intend to make a huge profit. Our main aims are to give people an unforgettable holiday, encourage them to buy free range organic meat, and to help the stricken farmers in the area. Also, Grace and Juliet will be back home, which is what they've always longed for.'

'I've known a lot of rich people, Noël, but never anyone like you. What sort of people are you targeting?'

'Mainly people who either ride or want to learn. Riding will be the main activity, but new riders will only have half-day lessons, or else they'll end up aching all over. We'll also have tennis courts and provide racquets and balls.'

'Children?'

'No. Adults only. Children are, or can be, a liability. Their parents' fault, of course. They bring them on holiday and then dump them, and want someone else to take responsibility for them. Some children behave atrociously. This will be a holiday place free of screeching brats.'

'Don't you like children?'

She smiled. 'Do I sound like a mean child hater? I love them. It's the idiot parents that I detest. Juliet and Grace and their husbands were brilliant parents and their children are delightful . . . they've always been delightful.'

He wanted to ask if she had children, but suspecting that she didn't because she would have mentioned them by now, he didn't want to hurt her or have her feel she had to explain. 'Would you like a lift tomorrow?' he asked instead.

'I've bought a car – a Land Rover. I pick it up in the morning.'

He felt apprehensive that now she was independent their meetings would cease. *Don't be a dag*, he told himself. *She wouldn't be having dinner with you if she didn't want to see you again.*

'And I've ordered a plane – a Cessna 172. When it arrives, would you like to go up for a flight?'

His spirits revived. 'I certainly would. How many passengers does it take?'

'Three. Two seats in the back and two at the front – one for the pilot. We'll get a hangar built on Tordorrach.'

'Are you going to rent a hangar at Cobar airport?' he asked hoping her trips to Cobar would be frequent.

'No, I'll only be in the town briefly. The airport has got a parking apron with tie downs.'

'Tie downs?'

'To anchor the plane so it won't blow over in strong winds.' She looked hesitant. 'I've got a favour to ask. Juliet and Grace and their husbands will be arriving in two weeks, and that's before I get the plane. They're going to catch the coach to Cobar, but with all their luggage it's going to be an uncomfortable drive to Tordorrach. If you're free, would you be willing to come too?'

His spirits soared. 'I'll be delighted.'

'I must warn you that Juliet will be in a foul mood. She hates flying – since the Twin Towers attacks she's been worse, and she also gets bad nose bleeds on take-off and landing. When we first flew to England, by the time we got to Heathrow she looked as if she'd been in a massacre. Now she takes a change of clothes and plenty of tissues. She gets seasick too, otherwise she and Friedrich would have come by ship. I'll pay you for your time, of course.'

So, I'm just a business associate, Paul thought. 'Don't be daft. She's not that bad is she?' he managed to joke.

'She a joy when she's happy and ghastly when she's in a mood.'

'How does her husband cope?'

'Friedrich's brilliant. He's just the right type of chap for her. He's calm, but refuses to put up with any nonsense, which forces her to back off. He's sympathetic when she's ill or frightened, so he's an ideal travelling companion for her.'

'Is he German?'

'His father was Swiss. When his mother was killed in a skiing accident his father married a year later and his step-mother was unkind to Friedrich – it sounds as if she was jealous. He spent the school holidays at Shuttleton Court with Adam and his parents and grandparents, and asked if he could stay. From what I've heard, his step-mother was pleased to get rid of him. Adam and Friedrich were like brothers. Adam insisted that Friedrich was an equal beneficiary in their grandparents' will.'

'Unlike some wealthy families who quarrel about money,' said Paul. 'How did they make their fortune?'

'Cotton mills.' She opened her phone and handed it to Paul. 'That's a photo of Shuttleton Court.'

He gazed at the photo of the mansion. 'Wow. It looks like a palace. How many rooms?'

'About ninety.'

'Do the family still have the cotton mills?'

'No. They converted them into flats and sold them in the seventies.'

'What about the house? It would make a fantastic hotel.'

'Apartments – twenty of them. Some one bedroom, some two and three and some that we call grand apartments have four bedrooms. We sold most of them and made a fortune. Adam's parents live permanently in a three-bedroom one, and Juliet and Friedrich and Adam and I had two-bedroom ones that we stayed in at weekends and when we had holidays. We always had Christmas and Easter there. Now we're all going to live in Australia we've let them out as holiday lets.'

The wine bottle was empty. Noël had drunk most of it. Paul debated whether to order another bottle. If he didn't she might think he was mean or short of money. *It's not as if she's going to drive anywhere tonight*, he thought. 'Would you like another glass of wine?' he asked.

She looked at the bottle. 'Empty.' Her expression became pensive. 'Yes, but no.'

He raised his eyebrows.

'I'd love another one, but I shouldn't. I'm drinking too much.'

'Probably because I'm slow.'

'No. I've got to stop it. I'm not an alcoholic or anything –'

'I know.'

'When Adam . . . my husband . . . was diagnosed with pancreatic cancer I drank to dull the pain. That type of cancer is a death sentence. I knew that, and so did he.'

He reached over and took her hand. 'Did it work?'

'Yes. And when he died I drank to ease the loneliness and the loss of the future that we'd planned. It became a habit.' She picked up the drinks list. 'I'll have orange juice.'

He squeezed her hand. 'So will I. What would you like for dessert?'

When Paul got home he went to his computer and put *Farm Stays NSW* in the search. Several came up. Their websites were detailed with plenty of photos. The one he most liked the look of had saunas, massage, a recreation room with pool tables, table tennis and darts. There were cycling tracks as well as all the things Noël had mentioned. They also catered for children. He was about to send it to her but thought this might be construed as interfering.

He told Ralph and Linda about his misgivings the next morning.

Linda reacted immediately. 'If all the other places cater for families, that makes Noël's idea unique.'

'I agree with you about the need to have lots of activities other than horse riding,' said Ralph.

'But I read the business plan – she's doing that – tennis courts, plane rides, walking tours. You men! No imagination.'

'I think you should suggest having a recreation room with a billiard table and dart board,' said Ralph.

Linda threw up her hands. 'The main thing is horse riding. After a day in the saddle most people will be too knackered to do anything other than eat their dinner and go to bed.'

'It's not just that, Linda,' Paul said patiently. 'It's that Tordorrach is so remote. If people drive from Sydney –'

'But they don't have to drive from Sydney,' she argued. 'They can fly into Dubbo and get collected in the minibus – that's what I read.'

'What if they want to drive?' Ralph asked.

'That's up to them. It's their choice. I know what I'd rather do – fly into Dubbo and get driven to Tordorrach in a comfortable minibus.'

'It's a four-hour drive,' said Ralph.

'Better than a twelve-hour drive from Sydney,' said Linda. 'You two are so pessimistic.'

Chapter 11

'Seamus.'

He was sitting in the branches pruning one of the pear trees. He looked down and saw Matthew. 'What do you want?'

'Mrs Carlyle wants to know what job you want – if any.'

'She can ask me herself.'

'She has asked you, but you haven't told her yet.'

'I want to be the head gardener.'

'There's no head gardener. Just two full-time gardeners and four seasonal assistants. Did you read the duties on –'

'I know what a gardener does. I don't need you to tell me.'

To Seamus's fury, Matthew was relaxed and confident. 'Upset are you?' he asked, wanting to provoke him.

Matthew looked puzzled. 'Why would I be upset?'

'Mrs Carlyle's bought my place not yours.'

'Oh that. No, I'm relieved and so is Coral. I'd much rather be the manager of this place – it's bigger, and the bonus is that you won't own it – someone nice will. One of the blokes whose property's been repossessed is the other full-time gardener – he's a similar age to you. Xavier's a good bloke. His wife died a few years ago. He –'

'I'm not interested.' Seamus dropped the branch he had just cut off, narrowly missing Matthew's head. 'Tell Mrs Carlyle that I'll be a gardener. Tell her that Mary and I will move into one of the cabins.'

'Poor Mary,' said Matthew. 'Being married to you must be tough.' He smirked. 'She's nice and so is Xavier. You might have some competition. His parents were Irish – that makes him more

Irish than you. You've never even been to Ireland. It's strange that he doesn't have the same hostility to the English as you do. Mary's parents were Irish too, weren't they? It'll be nice for her to have something in common with him. Who knows – their parents might have known each other or come from the same place.'

Every morning Seamus woke to new activity. Furniture and appliances and solar panels had arrived for the staff cabins. The five cabins for the visitors had been delivered and put in place. More solar panels and water tanks would be arriving tomorrow. Two tennis courts and a runway were under construction. Today, heavy diggers were on the site where the new homestead would be built. His hopes that planning permission would be refused were dashed. So the work could be completed without delays there were caravans for the builders, which would be sold when the work was complete. Seamus envied their size.

He and Mary were having breakfast in silence. Because their caravan was so tiny they ate outside most of the time. These days she seldom spoke to him. Remembering what Matthew had said about the other full-time gardener, he tried to make amends.

'Mary, do you still love me?'

'No.'

Her curt reply stunned him. 'Why did you marry me?'

She spread butter on her bread. 'Because I loved you.'

Forgetting his desire for them to be reconciled he asked, 'Or was it because I was the only child of a rich grazier who would inherit everything? Did you look at the homestead and imagine yourself living there? Did you see all the hired hands my parents had? Did you think how good it would be not to have to do any cleaning, washing or ironing?'

'I loved you so much I would have lived in a tent with you,' she said quietly.

'A caravan's better than a tent, isn't it?'

Mary brushed their crumbs onto one plate and tipped them onto the bird table. 'I'm too old to live in a cramped place where, if I don't look where I'm going, I fall over something. It didn't happen suddenly, Seamus.'

'What didn't?'

'The death of my love for you. It started dying when you made Don and – '

He looked at her blankly. 'Don?'

'Don Overton. Our manager.'

'Oh him. What's he got to do with anything?'

'You threw him and his family –'

'I thought the fire was his fault.'

'But it wasn't. Your mum told you to wait, I told you to wait, but you didn't listen. If the fire had happened when your dad was alive he would have let them live in the homestead with us – there was enough room. Even if the fire had been Don's fault your dad wouldn't have sacked him – he would have had a new house built with the insurance money and told him to be more careful in the future. Your callous act to an innocent man and his family was the start of my love for you unravelling. Your behaviour since then has killed it completely.'

'You're making excuses. It's poverty that's killed your love.'

'And who is responsible for our poverty?'

'The drought.'

'You, Seamus. Just you. The insurance money you got for the manager's house went to paying Don when he sued you. Because you sacked him you had to do everything he used to do – except that you couldn't. If Don was still our manager he would have kept the insurance policies renewed and the homestead would have been repaired after the storm.'

'And Don would have stopped the drought, would he? He would have made it rain?'

'No, but we'd still be living in the homestead. And even if we had to sell, the place would be worth more than it is now.'

Later that morning Seamus was in the orchard checking the fruit was free of pests when he heard a car. As he went to investigate he heard Matthew's voice. He ran towards the cabins and saw Matthew and Coral taking plastic boxes out of the boot.

'What do you think you're doing?' he shouted.

Coral jumped and almost dropped the box she was carrying.

Matthew stared at him. 'We're delivering food and supplies to the cabins.'

'You should have told me you were coming. You can't just –'

Matthew ignored him and carried the box onto the veranda of one of the cabins. He put it down and opened the door. 'I'm the manager of Tordorrach. I've got permission from the new owners,' he said, emphasising the 'new owners' with a sly smile. 'They're moving here tomorrow. Coral and I are getting everything ready.'

To Seamus's annoyance, Mary joined them. 'Do you need any help?'

Matthew grinned. 'That's mighty good of you, Mary. If you'd take some of the lighter boxes into the cabin, that'd be a real help.'

Seamus wanted to drag his wife away, but restrained his fury. 'Nice little set of slaves they've got themselves. Not even moved in yet and they're bossing you around.'

'It's what we're paid to do,' said Coral, going into one of the cabins with an armful of bed linen still in its packaging.

Seamus followed Mary into a cabin and watched while she unloaded tea, eggs, milk, cream, two loaves of homemade bread, butter and a jar of marmalade onto the kitchen counter. He wanted to order her back to their caravan, but, unwilling to make a scene in front of Matthew and Coral he inspected the rest of the cabin. It was the first time he'd been inside any of them, and it was where he and Mary would live when the homestead was finished and the new owners moved in. It was spacious, clean and simply, but well furnished. The bedroom had built-in wardrobes and bedside tables. The shower room was bigger than the one in their caravan and had ample towel rails and hooks for dressing gowns. He was standing in the bedroom when Mary pushed him out of the way and began to open the package containing the quilt.

'Take the plastic off the pillows, please.'

Seamus scowled. 'Do it yourself.' He went back to the kitchen where Matthew was putting things in cupboards.

'Coral made that marmalade herself,' he said. 'The eggs are from our chickens and the milk is from our cows.' He checked to make sure the fridge and washing machine were plugged in, and tested the oven. 'All good. Want to help, Seamus?'

'No.'

'I didn't think you would.'

Coral carried a large casserole dish into the kitchen and put it on the counter. She pulled a pen and notebook out of her pocket and wrote – *Chicken casserole in the fridge – just needs heating. Bowl of strawberries in the cupboard.*

Seamus sniggered. 'You're really fawning over them. What a pair of crawlers.'

Matthew's gaze was steady and without rancour. 'Mrs Carlyle and her family have been good to us.'

'Rather you than me. They'll expect you to be eternally grateful.'

'We will be eternally grateful,' said Coral. She smiled. 'To them, and also to you for turning down the position of manager.'

Matthew slapped him on the shoulder. 'Too right. Thanks for that, Seamus. You did us a big favour.'

Seamus snorted. 'You'll be sorry.' He saw the paper plates and plastic glasses and stainless steel cutlery. 'That's a bit meagre. How come you didn't rush out and buy fine china, silver and crystal for them?'

'This is what they asked for. They'll get proper stuff when they move into the homestead. Lots of it is being sent from England. It's due to arrive before the homestead's finished.'

Coral put a bowl on the table. 'I'll fill that with fruit,' she said. 'What's in the orchard, Seamus?'

'You're not taking any of my fruit.'

'No she won't,' said Matthew. 'She'll be taking the *new owner's* fruit.'

Seamus nearly knocked Mary over as he stormed out of the cabin.

She ran after him. 'Where are you going?'

'They're taunting me.'

'You asked for it.'

Desperate to escape he walked past the orchard. Half an hour later he came to the glade of trees his father had planted in 1980. He put his head against the trunk of a gum and wept. The tears made him even more irate. He had lost everything. 'My wife hates me, I've lost my land, I hardly ever see my children.' He banged his head repeatedly on the trunk, not caring about the agony to his temple or the blood that flowed from the lacerations. When he saw Matthew's car drive away he went back to the caravan.

'What have you done to your head?' Mary asked.

'Do you care?'

'No. I'm just curious.'

Not long ago she would have fussed over him. She would have bathed the gash with antiseptic and given him painkillers and a cup of tea.

Chapter 12

Grace threw herself into Noël's arms and cried.

'We haven't been parted all that long,' said Noël as she returned the embrace.

Grace's tears stemmed from relief. When they had seen Noël off at Heathrow eight weeks ago, she had been pale, listless and too thin. Her nails had been bitten to the quick and the cuticles were puffy and inflamed. Now she had put on weight and her old enthusiasm had returned. Her nails were short, but the cuticles had healed.

'This is Paul,' said Noël. 'He's kindly offered to help drive us and the luggage to Tordorrach.'

Her emails had frequently mentioned Paul. Now Grace had met him she hoped that he was the reason for the improvement in Noël. Juliet was moody, which, in the presence of a stranger, who might also be a love interest, embarrassed Grace. The long journey from London to Sydney had been a torture for Juliet, who'd had severe nose bleeds every time the plane had taken off or landed. Even the overnight stay in a hotel in Sydney had done little to shake her out of her bad mood.

Juliet put a peppermint in her mouth and sucked it. 'The flight to Dubbo was almost worse than the flight from London,' she complained. 'It was a small, noisy plane.'

'She was sick on the coach,' said Friedrich. He put his arm around her. 'We'll soon be at Tordorrach.'

When Grace was miserable she could, if she had to, disguise it. Juliet never could, and her inability to do this had caused Grace anxiety on many occasions. It was something she and Noël had learned to accept. Noel called this trait in Juliet a misery gene.

'Grace, you and Guy go with Paul in his car,' said Noël.

Paul looked at Juliet. 'There's a cafe nearby. Do you want to have a drink and something to eat first?' he asked sympathetically. 'You must be feeling hungry.'

Juliet's scowl faded. 'Thank you.'

To Paul's surprise Grace and Juliet looked nothing alike. Juliet's golden blonde hair fell in soft curls around her face, her eyes were slate grey and her complexion was alabaster with pale pink cheeks. She wore a black jumper over a white blouse with a ruffled collar. Grace was statuesque with wavy auburn hair done in a French pleat, olive skin and brown eyes. The amber-coloured polo neck jumper she wore suited her hair colour. The family genes had been well distributed. The only things the three of them had in common were clear skin, even teeth and they were all the same height. And they were all attractive. That they were wealthy was evident from the way they all dressed. Guy and Friedrich wore tweed jackets over expensive looking shirts – one white, the other pink and white striped. Grace and Juliet's jumpers looked like cashmere. Their engagement rings, like Noël's, were impressive and looked antique. Grace's was a round sapphire surrounded by diamonds. Juliet's was a brilliant cut diamond surrounded by rubies. They had enough luggage for ten people, but, as Paul reflected, they were not here on holiday they were moving their lives.

Because Noël had warned him that Juliet would be in a foul mood Paul had been sympathetic rather than embarrassed. He was pleased that Grace and Guy were in his car. Both were talkative and friendly.

He felt comfortable enough to say, 'You and Juliet don't look like sisters, and Noël doesn't look as if she's even vaguely related to either of you.'

'Juliet takes after our father and I'm like my mother. Only one of us resembles the Hallands – Noël looks like her father – he was Italian. He came to Australia when he was three, so apart from his surname you wouldn't have known he was Italian.'

'Grace, your paintings have come to life,' said Guy when they arrived at the gate to Tordorrach.

The four cabins were rustic but solid. From the outside they suited the landscape. Inside they were spacious and comfortable with divan beds that could be single or pushed together to make a double, fitted wardrobes and chests of drawers. They had one bedroom, a lounge and a kitchen big enough for a dining table and four chairs.

'The visitors' cabins won't have a kitchen or lounge,' said Noël. 'Just a bedroom and shower room. The visitors will eat outside in the courtyard of the new homestead.'

'What if it's raining or windy?' asked Guy. 'Not that it looks as if it rains much here.'

'Then they'll eat inside. Friedrich designed a long room just off the kitchen for that purpose, but from the look of the parched earth it won't be used much – if at all. The four cabins will be for the permanent staff.'

Juliet and Grace wanted to see the old homestead immediately, in spite of Noël's warning that it was in a worse state than the photographs showed. It was a five-minute walk from the cabins. As they approached it a cat ran inside. They stood in silence for a few moments looking at the remains of the homestead.

Grace ran her finger in the dust on one of the unbroken windows. 'Our life's journey has brought us back to the place we never wanted to leave,' she said softly. 'What are we going to do with this?'

'Bulldoze the lot,' said Guy.

Juliet and Grace looked regretful, but nodded.

'But not until I've had a chance to paint it,' said Grace. 'Twin paintings . . . beauty and dereliction.'

'No,' said Noël. 'We should leave it.'

Friedrich cautiously stepped inside and looked around. 'Ahha.'

'What?' said Grace.

'Kittens.'

Grace stepped inside, and then came out smiling. 'The mother cat's very thin. We'd better get some food for her. Don't go in – the floorboards are dodgy. Come out, Friedrich.'

'Just from the small bit I saw,' said Friedrich when he was back outside. 'It's going to cost more to renovate than rebuild. And who would live here? We've got a new homestead under construction.'

Noël pointed to one of the mud nests that some species of bird had made. 'Leave it. It's home to wildlife – feral cats and –'

Paul shuddered. 'Venomous snakes.'

'Not if there are cats around,' said Grace.

Paul thought that the presence of cats meant that the snakes had not killed them, until Grace told him that it was the cats that kill snakes.

'But it's an eyesore – we can't just leave it,' said Guy.

'Plant trees around it. Evergreens. Peppers, pines, gums, maybe a few deciduous ones. Rebuilding it or pulling it down would disturb the wildlife.'

'It was a beautiful house,' whispered Grace. 'How could anyone let it go to a ruin?'

'A moron,' said Guy.

'Let's get some food and milk for the cat,' said Noël.

Back in the cabin they cut up some bread and poured milk over it.

'What about taking some chicken out of the casserole Coral made,' Paul suggested.

Juliet shook her head. 'Too rich.'

They took the saucer over to the homestead and put it inside the door.

'Noël said you wanted to see our mother's letters,' Grace said to Paul as they walked back to the cabins. 'I brought them with me. I'll ferret them out and you can read them next time you're here.'

They invited him to stay for dinner. Paul wanted to accept, but thought it wise to let them all have time together in their old home. No doubt they would have memories and stories of their exploits to tell Friedrich and Guy.

'I hope you'll be happy,' he said as he got into his car. He saw Noël's pensive expression and realised that 'happy' was the wrong word.

Chapter 13

'Happy,' whispered Noël as she lay in bed that night. 'I doubt I'll ever be happy again. All I wish for is peace. And I want tragedy to stop following me like a hungry dog.'

When Sylvia had left Tordorrach in 1980 it was the start of the school holidays and Noël's parents were getting ready to drive to Tordorrach the following day. Noël's case was packed and she had books, comics and puzzles to keep her occupied during the twelve-hour drive. She remembered her mother answering the phone and a few minutes later telling their father that Sylvia had left. That holiday was more sombre than the others Noël had experienced on Tordorrach. Every night she prayed with Grace and Juliet that Sylvia would come back. When it was time for them to go back to Sydney, Juliet was furious with God for not answering their prayers. By the time the next holiday came everyone had got used to Sylvia's absence and the atmosphere was more cheerful, but Grace and Juliet still prayed every night for their mother's return.

When Charles was bitten by a snake three years later it was during term time, so Noël's mother could only take two days off to go to his funeral. They never went to Tordorrach again. The house their grandparents bought in Bowral had a large garden, but Noël, Grace and Juliet longed for the vastness of Tordorrach and the horses. It was then that the three girls had begun to fantasize about going back to live on Tordorrach.

'When we are grown up we will buy it back,' declared Grace.

'The years in England were an interlude,' Noël whispered. 'A long interlude. We are all back where we belong. We went to escape from the trauma and tragedy of death, and to search for Sylvia. We failed in that, but we all found love and success.'

Unable to sleep, she thought about Paul. She hoped that turning down their invitation to stay for dinner was because he didn't want to intrude on their first night back at Tordorrach, rather than him feeling their association had to be only professional. Paul was the only man to have aroused her interest since Adam's death. She thought of ways to contact him without it being too obvious that he meant more to her than just her solicitor. She got out of bed and opened her laptop.

Dear Paul,
We are so grateful for all you have done for us and the trouble you went to. Could I take you out for dinner to thank you?
Noël.

Before sending it she hesitated, wondering if she sounded over eager. She reasoned that he had taken her to dinner and had bought champagne to celebrate when the purchase was finally complete. 'But was that simply good professional interaction? Is his interest in Sylvia's whereabouts because it's an intriguing mystery?' she whispered. He had never mentioned that he was involved with someone, but that didn't mean he wasn't. Her finger hovered over the send key and then moved to delete. Annoyed with herself for being so uncertain she pressed delete and went back to bed.

When she showered and dressed the next morning she went over to the old homestead and looked at the saucer. It was empty. 'We'll have to buy you some cat food,' she said to the wary-looking cat.

Grace and Juliet emerged from what had once been the kitchen and was now a mess of cobwebs, rusty appliances. It smelt of decay.

'What are you doing in there? The floorboards are rotten. It's dangerous.'

'We were careful,' said Grace. 'It's not as bad as it looks. No snakes that we could see.'

'I should hope not.'

'Paul's very pleasant,' said Juliet failing to sound casual.

'I thought so too,' added Grace.

'Well?' asked Juliet when Noël stayed silent.

Noël picked up the saucer. 'Well what?'

Juliet nudged her. 'Stop being so infuriating. Do you like him?'

'Yes.'

'Is anything going on? Does he like you?'

'If you mean are we romantically involved – I don't know.'

'Why don't you know?' demanded Grace. 'Would you like to be romantically involved?'

Noël nodded. 'We've got to get some food and fresh water for the cat.'

'What's the problem, Noël?' insisted Grace.

'I don't know if he feels the same way.'

'Oh, I'm sure he does,' Grace said slowly. 'What do you reckon, Juliet?'

'Definitely. So what are you going to do about it?'

Noël shrugged. 'I don't know. Now let's get stuff for this poor cat.'

'We'll think of something,' said Grace as they walked back to the cabin. 'He's interested in the letters Mum left for us. So that's a good excuse to contact him. I'll ring him – it'll make it look less obvious.'

Ω

Grace attributed her success as an artist to Noël, who, although hellishly untidy and undomesticated, was an excellent organiser. In 1995 it was Noël who had booked their flights to London and their stay in the YWCA. It was Noël who had insisted that they buy a flat as soon as they arrived rather than wasting money on rent. Every day she would write a list of what they were going to do. She wrote a list of their criteria. 'If we look at a flat and two of us like it and one doesn't, we won't buy it.' They went to estate agents and looked at flats. It only took a week for them to find something they all liked.

Noël's inheritance from her parents had been large. With the money she got from selling their house she was well off. Their grandparents' house in Bowral had five bedrooms and a swimming pool and tennis court, and with their life insurance and sale of their house Grace and Juliet were also well off. Their combined finances made them wealthy enough to buy an attic flat in Chelsea. Because it needed renovating the price was reduced. They were able to pay cash, and had money left over for a new kitchen and bathroom. While the new kitchen was being installed in the summer they lived on salads or ate out.

It was when they were in a wine bar that had just opened that Noël looked thoughtfully at the bare walls. After the waiter had taken their order she asked him if she could speak to the manager.

'I'm sort of the manager,' he said. 'The owner's not here. When he's here I'm not the manager.'

Noël smiled. 'You need something on the walls,' she told him.

He looked embarrassed. 'Well, there's not a lot of money left, so the owner's gone for the minimalist look.'

'Right,' said Noël. 'Can we make an appointment to see you tomorrow?'

'What's it about?'

'Your bare walls.'

'Well the owner –'

'It won't cost him anything.'

'Okay then.'

The following day Grace, Juliet and Noël carried some of Grace's paintings to the wine bar.

'Do you like them?' Noël asked.

He looked trapped. 'They're great, but we can't afford to buy them.'

'No, you just hang them on the walls with a notice saying they are for sale. The artist gets free exhibition space and you get free pictures on your walls.'

He beamed. There was a picture rail, and they helped him hang them. Noël had printed out a flyer saying the pictures were for sale and stating the prices.

'Those kangaroos look like they're moving. If I was rich I'd buy them all,' said the waiter.

'I'll do you one as a thank-you present,' Grace promised.

Three days later the waiter rang. 'Got anymore pictures? The first lot are all sold and the walls are bare again.'

Grace achieved her ambition to paint all day. She painted from memory and many were of the Tordorrach landscape. Every painting had either a person or an animal in it. During a two-week holiday in Cornwall, she painted the villages and the sea. When she had finished four paintings Noël and Grace took them into a local restaurant where the manager was delighted to hang them on his walls. He bought the one with children building a sandcastle for himself.

Six months later when they went into the wine bar for dinner, the waiter pounced on Grace. 'Here she is. Grace Halland. Grace, this is Guy Ashcroft.'

Guy held out his hand. 'I own an art gallery in Mayfair. I'd be interested in exhibiting your paintings.'

Chapter 14

Glad that Grace had rung him, Paul drove to Tordorrach to have lunch with her, Juliet and Noël and to study Sylvia's letters. While Grace and Juliet prepared lunch he read what their mother had written.

My darling Grace and Juliet,

I'm not leaving because I don't love you, but because I do love you. You deserve better than a crazy mother who keeps crying all the time. When you grow up I hope that you will understand and forgive me. I love your father too, and he also deserves better. I am a burden on you all, not a blessing. A mother should be good at mothering, and I am useless. If it wasn't for your grandmother we would all starve. If we didn't have a cleaner the house would be dirty.

One day, when I am better, I will come back. I want to get well.

Your loving Mother

Darling Charlie,

The fog in my mind is getting worse. I can no longer fight it. I wake in the mornings with dread. I go to bed at night thankful that another day, when I achieved nothing and brought no one any happiness, is over.

You and your father and mother work hard all day. I try, but I end up staring into space and doing nothing. I should be helping your mother. I should be happy, but I find it impossible.

I doubt that I will ever get better and that is why I am leaving. I am going to Sydney. I will try and get treatment there.

I love you and always will. You are a patient, kind and wonderful husband. I have been a worthless wife.

I love you,

Sylvia

To Paul these were the despairing words of someone who was desperate, so trapped in depression she felt she had no choice but to leave. He had the impression that if she had recovered she would have returned. Even if she hadn't, surely she would have written to her children? He concluded she was dead, but didn't want to drown their hopes.

When lunch was ready they sat at the table.

'What do you think, Paul?' asked Grace. 'It'll be interesting to get your opinion – we've gone over this countless times with Guy and Friedrich.'

He thought carefully before replying, 'If she had recovered I'm sure she would have come back.' He looked at Guy and Friedrich. 'Do you agree?'

They nodded.

'Let's examine all the possibilities,' he continued. 'When your grandparents left Tordorrach, did they leave their new address with Mr and Mrs Ryan?'

'I don't know. We could ask Seamus,' said Juliet.

'We moved into a guest house in Bowral. Our grandparents bought a house after that. But when we left Tordorrach we didn't have a permanent address,' Grace said. 'When they bought their house they may have written to Mr and Mrs Ryan.'

'If they didn't, your mother might have got help from a specialist in Sydney and recovered. She could have come back and found you all gone. Your grandparents were so distraught about your father that they may not have thought to leave an address so she could find you. How long were you in the guest house?'

'Not that long – I can't remember – a few months?' said Grace.

Before they got too optimistic, Paul continued, 'But even if she had been looking for you, it shouldn't have been too difficult. Presumably your grandparents were in the phone book?'

They nodded.

'She may have remarried,' he suggested.

'But how could she?' asked Guy. 'They weren't divorced. She had no idea that her husband was dead.'

'Was his death written up in the local paper?'

'I don't know,' said Grace. 'But even if it had been, she wouldn't have thought of looking.'

'Did she have any friends in Cobar – in the town?'

'People often visited Tordorrach,' said Grace. 'Our grandparents and parents were friends with the Fullhams.'

'I remember when we went to the Cobar Show one year, lots of people stopped and chatted,' said Juliet.

'Then if she had returned and found you gone, and Mr Ryan didn't have a forwarding address, she could have gone to the town and asked someone? Wendy?'

'Maybe,' said Grace. 'You think she's dead, don't you? Guy does. Friedrich's not sure.'

'She could have got worse and decided to end it all, but there are other possibilities. Where did you look in England?'

'We had her parents' address from letters –'

'Where did they live?'

'Acton. But they'd moved away – we expected that,' said Grace. 'I was five when Mum left and twenty when we went to England and started looking. We rang lots of Dales in the phone book, but none of them were our grandparents.'

'Did you go to a search agency?'

'No. We did it ourselves. Do you think we should have?' asked Juliet.

'They've got experience – they know where to look. But if you couldn't find your grandparents they could have died.'

'We went to the Family Records Centre and looked at all the death records on microfiche. It took weeks to go through them all. We searched backwards till we got to the date of their last letter.'

'How old were your English grandparents?'

'We don't know. We'd never met them.'

'Did you check through the birth records?'

'No.'

'Did you do any searches in Australia?'

'We didn't, but our grandparents did.'

'Maybe you should hire a private detective. I can help.'

Grace looked thoughtful. 'When we looked in London, we'd just arrived. We didn't think of private detectives, and we wanted to spend our money on buying somewhere to live. Now we can afford it maybe we should hire someone. As you say, private detectives know where to look. And she may be still in Australia.'

After lunch they looked up detective agencies on the internet. The one they chose specified that he did not spy on spouses, but specialised in missing persons and finding the birth mothers of adopted children. On his website were seven stories written by his clients about reunions between mothers whose children had been forced to emigrate to Australia in the fifties.

It was dusk when Paul walked back to his car. Noël came with him. Not bothering to be subtle, he asked, 'I hope I'll see you again soon.'

She put her hand on his shoulder. 'Kiss me, Paul. Please – just kiss me.'

The private detective found Sylvia's parents in Wales, but they had not seen or heard from her since she left Tordorrach.

Sylvia was one of five children – four girls and one boy. Her parents said she was different from all the others, did not get on well with her siblings or with her parents. They said she was rebellious and moody. Her contact with them, once she arrived in Australia, was infrequent – mostly postcards and a letter once every few months. She told them she was getting married and sent wedding photos and photos of her daughters.

Attached is a copy of the letter Charles Halland wrote to them after she left. Her parents, although horrified that she had deserted her children, seemed unconcerned about her whereabouts. They have fifteen other grandchildren who all live in England or Wales, and I surmise that they were not interested in the two they had in Australia.

There are no records of her anywhere in Australia under the name of Halland or Dale. I think it strange that she is on no electoral roll or census records either in Australia or the UK. Her name does not appear on any shipping or airline passenger lists and there was no record of her leaving Australia, but I found a record of her entry into Australia in 1969 at the age of seventeen. There was only one British passport and that expired when she was twenty-seven and it was never renewed. There is nothing under the name of Sylvia Halland.

There are no death records. She may have used another name. If she only rented flats or shared houses on a casual basis with friends it is possible that her real identity was never known. In 1980 she would not have needed proof of identity to get a job or medical treatment. It is possible that she met a man and took his name, even though it would not have been possible for them to marry.

The only other thing I can suggest is that I put an advertisement in the papers with a photograph.

Grace and Juliet sent him two photographs. One was her wedding photo. The other was with Grace and Juliet taken about three weeks before she left. The photos were clear. His reply was promising.

A friend of mine is a reporter on *The Sydney Morning Herald*, and he is interested in doing a story around your mother.

The photos are good and if anyone knew her they would be sure to remember. Also this will cost you nothing, whereas a large eye-catching advert would be expensive.

The story ran to one page. Grace, Juliet and Noël were sure that someone somewhere would know something.

'She might see the article herself and contact us,' Grace said excitedly.

'Don't get your hopes up too much,' Paul cautioned.

'But if she's not dead and she didn't leave Australia, she must be somewhere,' Juliet maintained. 'Someone must know something.'

But no one came forward. Their disappointment was profound.

'Could your mother speak any languages other than English? asked Paul.

'No, why?' asked Grace.

'I thought she might have gone to Europe.'

'But she didn't have a current passport.'

'No, but she might have stowed away on a ship.'

'But she'd still have to get through immigration in the UK,' Juliet pointed out.

'There are ways of getting a passport under another name,' Paul said.

'But why would she go to all that trouble? It's not as if she was a criminal or escaping from a violent husband,' said Grace.

'Maybe she was escaping from a violent boyfriend,' Paul suggested. 'Someone she met in Sydney.'

Their spirits were raised again when the detective emailed them to say that newspapers from Melbourne, Brisbane and Adelaide had seen the story and wanted to write about it. A month after the stories had been written up, no one had responded. Paul was mystified. If Sylvia hadn't left Australia and she wasn't dead, where was she?

Chapter 15

Anxious to prove her cooking skills, Coral rang Paul. 'It's only fair that they should judge for themselves if I'm capable of cooking for a crowd, so I was thinking about inviting people here for dinner. The new owners and their husbands, you, but that's not enough seeing I'll be cooking for a lot more than that when the visitors arrive for holidays. Any suggestions? Not Seamus.'

Paul laughed. 'I wouldn't dream of suggesting him. I'm sure Ralph and his wife and Linda would love to come. Hang on – I'll ask them . . . Yes,' he said seconds later.

As soon as they arrived, delicious smells wafted from the kitchen. In spite of cooking for eleven people Coral was calm. Two tables had been pushed together so when they were all seated it was not crowded. The cauliflower and blue cheese soup, served with bread rolls she had baked herself, was delicious. The pastry on the rabbit pie was golden brown and light, and the accompanying carrots, runner beans and potatoes complemented the flavour of the rabbits that Matthew had shot.

'What gun do you use?' asked Noël to Paul's amazement.

'Depends on what I'm after. A ·22 calibre for rabbits and a ·222 for kangaroos.'

'You can shoot?' Paul asked her.

'Yes.'

'Wow,' said Linda.

'She's a crack shot – a steady hand and a good eye,' said Juliet. 'Grace and I would be more likely to shoot anything other than the target.'

'It's a bit of a coincidence,' said Matthew. 'But Charlie Halland had two daughters – Juliet and Grace – and a niece called Noël Moretti who lived in Sydney and came here for the school holidays with her mum and dad. Grace and Juliet would be beside themselves with excitement the day they were due to arrive. They'd be waiting at the gate. Noël would leap out of her parents' car when she saw them and they'd hug each other shrieking with excitement.

'Now this little Noël begged her Uncle Charlie to teach her to shoot. Her parents and grandparents were against it, but she was insistent. So one day Charlie Halland and his dad took her out. I came too. We thought she'd be bored. Her uncle spent ages explaining the workings of first a revolver, a pistol and then a rifle to her. She was fascinated. Then he told her how to hold the rifle and showed her the target.' He laughed. 'She almost hit the bulls-eye with the first shot – she hit it smack in the middle with the second. Bit of a coincidence that.' He raised his eyebrows. 'Or is it?'

Juliet smiled. 'We wondered if you'd remember.'

'I didn't make the connection at first – when I met Noël for the first time. I didn't recognise you at all – posh English accent and all that. Grace and Juliet – names from long ago – but I still wasn't sure – English accents and you were only kids when you left. But I did wonder. I told Coral and she said it must be a coincidence.'

Coral nodded. 'It was because we thought you were English. If you'd had Aussie accents we would have sussed it.'

'We remember you well,' said Grace. 'You were nicer than Seamus. You used to let us play games with you.'

Matthew beamed. 'Welcome home, girls. Welcome home. I'm that pleased to see you.'

He bombarded them with questions. He was visibly upset to hear about Noël's parents.

'I've had an idea,' said Coral when the memories had been raked over and Matthew's questions about what they had been doing since they left Tordorrach had been answered. 'I don't know what you'll think.'

'Tell us,' said Grace.

'These horse treks – four hours total with a one-hour break for lunch, have I got that right?'

Noël nodded. 'From ten till midday, then one till three then back to the homestead to have tea or coffee and get ready for dinner.'

'What about stopping here for afternoon tea? I can make cakes and sandwiches. They get here at three, stay for an hour, then head back to Tordorrach.'

'It's a good idea,' said Noël thoughtfully. 'But you'll have so much to do, what with cooking the breakfasts and dinners and preparing the lunch boxes. Won't you need a rest?'

Matt laughed. 'Coral's no good at resting. The more she's got to do the happier she is.'

'And I'll have an assistant.'

'More than just one,' said Noël. 'Mary Ryan is willing to be your full-time permanent assistant. Unlike Seamus she's happy to do anything. We're not getting dishwashers – well, not mechanical ones. They use too much water. Person one will clear the table. Person two will scrape the dishes. Person three will wash and rinse them. Person two will dry them. Person one, who will have finished clearing the table by then, will put them away.'

Matthew grinned. 'Sounds as if you're going to have a big kitchen.'

'We are,' said Noël. 'Coral, would you like to come into town and we'll go shopping together – you can choose what you need for the kitchen. Don't ask me to help – I can't cook.'

Grace grimaced. 'She can't do anything domestic. When we moved to London we bought a flat. It had one big bedroom and one small one. Juliet and I made Noël sleep in the small one, because neither of us could stand her untidiness.'

'In the beginning we had a rota for cooking, but she'd either burn the food or undercook it, so Grace and I did it.'

Paul knew it was banter between cousins and Noël was smiling, but nevertheless he felt compelled to defend her. Careful not to sound confrontational he smiled when he said, 'Lots of people can cook, lots of people are good at housework, but not many people can fly a plane, shoot, or ride a horse. I can't cook or fly a plane.'

'Can you ride?' asked Coral.

'I'm going to teach him,' said Noël.

As if feeling his remark had been a rebuke, Juliet said, 'Grace and I couldn't have survived in London without Noël. For someone so untidy she's amazingly organised.'

'And we wouldn't have bought Tordorrach if she hadn't arranged the whole thing,' Grace said.

$$\Omega$$

Bernadette opened her front door before Wendy reached it.

'Hi, Wendy, I saw you from the window. Cup of tea or coffee?'

'Tea would be great,' said Wendy following her into the kitchen. 'Actually, I came to pick your brains . . . well, your memory really. You know the day Sylvia Halland left Tordorrach?'

Bernadette turned to the sink and filled the kettle. 'Vaguely.'

'Did she ever say anything to you about where in Sydney she was going?'

'No. She rarely spoke to me. Not because she was a snob or anything like that, but she was depressed.'

'So you can't give me any clues?'

Bernadette shook her head. 'Why?'

'It's just that her children want to find her. They've hired a private detective.'

'Grace and Juliet? Why now?'

'They've bought Tordorrach with Noël . . . didn't you know?'

Bernadette was bewildered. 'I don't think . . . but Seamus said the new owners were English.'

'They lived in England for a long time. It only just occurred to me – did Sylvia ever come back to Tordorrach when the Hallands left?'

Bernadette shook her head. 'Why do you think she might have?'

'She might not have known that her husband was dead and that his parents had sold Tordorrach to you. Don't worry, it was just a thought. Are you okay? You look pale.'

Bernadette dropped tea bags in their mugs. 'I'm worried sick about Seamus. There's a lot of conflict between him and Mary. It's so sad.'

'I thought they would have been happy that they've finally got a buyer.'

'His pride is wounded. He's going to be a gardener. Mary's going to be the assistant cook. She's pleased about it, but Seamus isn't.'

'From what I can see he's lucky,' said Wendy. 'He's been saved from getting evicted.'

The kettle boiled and Bernadette poured water into their mugs. 'Yes, but he doesn't see it like that.'

When Wendy left, Bernadette was going to ring Seamus and tell him who the new owners really were. Then she hesitated. 'It won't make him happy – nothing makes him happy these days. He's so perverse he might hate them even more if he knows they're Hallands because they didn't tell him,' she said to herself. 'He'll think they deceived him.'

Wendy sent Paul an email.

I asked Bernadette if Sylvia had ever returned to Tordorrach after the Hallands had left. She was too distracted about the strife between Seamus and Mary to be of much use, but I think we can discount Sylvia returning, as Bernadette would have seen her.

Chapter 16

The following Saturday morning Paul had just showered and dressed and was about to hang his washing on the line when the doorbell rang.

It was his ex-wife. 'Hello, Paul.' Her smile was as fake as it was brittle. 'You don't look pleased to see me.'

'I'm not. Why are you here, Kathryn?'

'I wanted to see you.'

He felt a moment's alarm. 'The children?'

'No. They're –'

'What then?'

She had lost weight. He was pleased to see that it made her look haggard.

'All gone wrong, has it?' he guessed.

She gave a gasp. Tears overflowed, making trails in her make-up. She brushed them away, smudging her mascara.

'Kicked you out because he had someone else, did he?'

'I left him. He had affairs.'

'You knew he had affairs. You knew that's why his two wives before you divorced him.'

'I've left him.'

'So? Are you expecting sympathy?'

'Please let me come in.'

He flicked the catch on the fly-screen door.

'Thank you,' she said as she tried to open it.

'It's locked,' he said.

'I can't talk to you through this door. Paul, please.'

'I don't want to talk to you.'

Just as a neighbour walked past she began to sob. He let her in but said nothing. Anxiously she glanced around, and he was pleased the cleaner had been in the day before. She stood awkwardly in the hallway. Paul folded his arms. She reached out to touch him. He stepped backwards out of her reach and hoped that Noël would not arrive or ring.

'Can we talk, Paul? Please.'

'What have we got to talk about? The money's all been divided – do you want more? Because if you do I'm not giving you any.'

'It's not money I want – it's you.'

He couldn't resist a satisfied smirk.

'Can't you forgive me, Paul? I made a mistake. I'm sorry. I know I hurt you. It's only when you've lost something you realise –'

'You didn't lose it, Kathryn, you threw it away. Your boring life, your boring husband and your boring children.'

'I didn't mean it. Tim convinced me that my life was dull.'

'That makes you spineless and gullible. You were happy before he got his hooks into you and you allowed him to make you think your life was boring. You made the choice to break up our marriage.'

'He promised me a thrilling, exhilarating life. I was . . . I don't know . . . enticed. Please forgive me.'

'I might have been able to forgive the betrayal.'

She looked hopeful. 'I can let you think about it – I know this must be unexpected –'

'It's not unexpected. I knew he'd have affairs. I knew your marriage would end.'

'Then . . . you'll forgive me?'

'The adultery perhaps. But I can't forgive you the restaurant.'

'The restaurant?' she asked in bewilderment.

He nodded. 'The restaurant.'

'What restaurant?'

'It was my mother's birthday.'

'Oh.'

He stared at her. 'Remember? Understand?'

'I remember. Understand? Not really.'

'It was a calculated act of spite.'

'He –'

'Stop blaming Tim. I was there. I saw your expression. For the first time I realised how malicious you were.' He gestured to the door. 'Now leave.'

She gazed at him in the way that once had touched him. 'I wanted to show you we loved each other, because you told me it wouldn't work – that he would be unfaithful.'

'I was right.' He went to the front door and pulled it open. 'I've got important things to do – and I can't waste time arguing with my ex-wife. I no longer love you. I seldom think about you. Now excuse me. I'm off to have a flying lesson.'

'A flying lesson?'

'Yes. There's no sailing here, but I'm learning to fly.'

She left with tears running down her face. Paul was unmoved.

He pulled the washing out of the machine and went into the garden to hang it on the line. He tried think of Noël not Kathryn, but the scene in the restaurant dominated his thoughts.

He shoved aside the memory, finished hanging the washing out and went to Cobar airport to have his first flying lesson. It was Noël who had suggested it and had offered to give him lessons, but recalling his fraught driving lessons with his father, he'd decided that an impersonal instructor would be best.

A week after Kathryn's visit Paul's children arrived unannounced. They both looked sullen.

'We can only stay the weekend,' said Holly. She stalked down the hall to one of the guest bedrooms. She dumped her overnight bag and made for the kitchen where Bill joined her.

Holly shivered. 'It's freezing here.'

'It's June,' said Paul.

'I thought the outback was supposed to be warm, even in winter.'

'Mum told us that you –' began Bill.

'Ah, so that's why you're here.'

'Mum's sorry. She's very upset. She wants you back. Her marriage to Tim is over. Why can't you leave this dump and move back to Sydney? You can start again.'

'I don't want her back. I don't want to start again.'

'You must still love her.'

'Why must I? She betrayed my trust. She betrayed our marriage vows. She said I was boring. She left me. She was unfaithful.'

'Stop being judgemental – you sound so old fashioned,' said Bill.

'I began a new life here. I'm happy.'

Holly looked exasperated. 'Dad, how can you be happy here? Cobar's got nothing.'

'People are born here, get married here, have children and grandchildren here and die here.'

'So what?' said Holly. 'It proves that they lack the courage to leave. They lack adventure. They stagnate.'

'Is there someone else?' asked Bill.

Holly rolled her eyes as if finding an appealing woman in Cobar was an impossibility.

In spite of his irritation, Paul smiled. 'I am interested in someone – yes.'

'Who?' asked Holly. 'Is she from Cobar?'

'Yes – she was born here, but –'

'Be careful, Dad,' said Bill. 'She might be after your money.' He laughed.

Dad,

You should have told us you were interested in someone else and you should have told Mum. It would have saved us a wasted trip to that dump you now call home. Serves you right if she's after your money.

You don't care how all this has disrupted our lives. You weren't the only victim. While all was great with Tim,

Mum hardly saw us. Now it's all gone wrong she keeps phoning, calling round and emailing us, and trying to make us feel guilty. You've taken off to the outback and you're not interested in us. We used to be such a happy family, but you and Mum have wrecked our lives. All we want is our parents back together again. It's not much to ask.

Mum's engaged in a battle with Tim about money. Stupidly she did as he asked and put all the money from the sale of our house into his account, not a joint one. She's been reduced to renting a small flat in Manly. I bet you're pleased about this – you've been proved right. Mum will never get her money back as he was heavily in debt and used her money to pay it off.

Have you forgotten the brilliant weekends at Kirribilli when we had our friends round for swimming and tennis parties? But of course, now you've got someone else you don't think about us. We tried to warn you that your girlfriend might be interested in your money and you laughed – that shows how much you value our opinion.

Holly and Bill

Paul read the email feeling sorry that he was estranged from his children, and furious that Tim was denying Kathryn money that was rightfully hers. He delayed replying until he had calmed down. Holly and Bill seemed to be more upset about the loss of their social standing in the eyes of their friends than in their mother's predicament. He had never noticed their mercenary side. Their mother, in particular, had made them aware from an early age that they were fortunate to live in an affluent country. He remembered their sad expressions when she'd told them that some people from poor countries had no clean water and very little food. Those memories dissolved most of Paul's resentment. She had been an excellent mother and wife until she had ended their marriage. He wished he had been kinder to her when she visited, but the memory of her behaviour on his mother's birthday had rankled.

Just after Kathryn had left him for Tim he'd taken his mother to a restaurant for lunch. To his dismay Kathryn and Tim had come in. He thought they would leave when they saw him, but they didn't. They chose a table where he could see them. Kathryn took Tim's hand. He kissed it. She kissed his hand. He shot Paul a triumphant look. If Paul and his mother had not just started their main course they would have left.

His mother was appalled. 'How could she? If I wasn't a lady I'd get up and slap her face.'

Paul had wanted to get up and punch Tim, but restrained himself.

He wondered if he should have told Holly and Bill about this incident when they visited, but he had no desire to make his children more alienated from their mother than they already were.

When his anger about their email abated he looked at the situation objectively and managed to see things through Holly and Bill's eyes. They had been loyal to him and had refused to go to their mother and Tim's wedding. Their lives had been uprooted too. Although they had lived at home they had their privacy and independence. They could bring friends home whenever they wished. Holly's boyfriends and Bill's girlfriends were allowed to sleep in their rooms. They paid more board than their parents had asked for and then they had been forced to leave their secure and happy home.

Dearest Holly and Bill,

I do care about you very much and so does your mother. I am sorry that she is having problems with the distribution of money from her marriage to Tim. Please tell her that I will be willing to negotiate with him on her behalf.

Paul didn't negotiate. He sent an email.

Tim,

Do you understand the power of social media? Unless you give Kathryn the money that belongs to her I will use it against you. If your finances are tight, sell your house and buy something smaller. I'll give you two days to reply.
Paul

Tim did not respond. Paul imagined his sneer when he read it. He looked him up on Facebook. Tim hadn't put any privacy controls on his entry, which, considering he was a solicitor, was reckless. His new law offices were near their old ones and his new business partner was a woman. He had put his status as single. He advertised their law firm in his posts. He was also on Twitter.

Paul tackled Facebook. On his own page and Tim's he wrote :

Tim Morris is a thief, an adulterer and a liar. He has been married and divorced three times. He is denying his latest ex-wife money that is hers.

Holly and Bill shared what he had written and also wrote their own damning posts, not just on Tim's page, but on those of his two hundred friends. Tim sent Paul an email threatening to sue. Paul replied that he looked forward to seeing him in court. Kathryn received her money two weeks later. She sent Paul a thank-you card.

Dad,

Thanks for getting Mum's money for her. She's buying a flat in Manly, and is happier. Can we come up one weekend soon? We're sorry we were so negative about Cobar and your house – it's just that it's so different from Sydney. We look forward to meeting your friend. What's her name?
Holly and Bill

Chapter 17

Paul was apprehensive about their visit. He was used to being introduced to their boyfriends or girlfriends, but now Noël would be under their scrutiny.

Should I tell them she's rich before they meet her? he asked himself. *The last thing I want is for them to suspect she's after my money. Her English accent will puzzle them.*

He tried to anticipate their reaction to the fact that she owned a plane, had a pilot's licence and a gun licence. He didn't want them to quiz her about her finances, nor did he want to tell them too much.

Hi Holly and Bill,

Yes, we got off to a bad start – my fault too. When you come for the weekend you shall meet my friends and Noël. We haven't been going out for long, but we are serious about each other. She's a widow. She's Australian, but has lived in London since she was twenty.

The reason I was amused is because she has plenty of her own money. She and her two cousins have bought a 70,000 acre property for cash. It's a two-hour drive from Cobar.

Paul told Ralph he was concerned about his children's visit.

'No worries. How about me and the wife throwing a barbie? We'll invite lots of friends – Linda and her mum and dad and all the neighbours – Matt and Coral too. More people will make things easier.'

When Holly and Bill arrived on a Saturday evening in July the barbecue at Ralph's place was underway. There were people on the front lawn, in the house and all over the back garden. As Ralph had said, introducing Holly and Bill to strangers was easier among a crowd. The guests greeted them with genuine friendliness and Holly and Bill were on their best behaviour. Although tense at first they soon lost their inhibitions, and when Paul introduced them to Noël their greetings were warmer than Paul had expected. He was amused when Linda approached Bill, and pleased when they talked for a long time. Later when Ralph put on a CD and people began to dance, he was pleased to see Bill dancing enthusiastically with Linda. People were interested in Holly's career as a meteorologist and someone asked her if she could predict when the drought was going to end. She entertained them with stories about forecasts that had failed to eventuate.

Holly and Bill helped clear everything away when all the guests had left. While they walked home he wanted to ask them what they thought of Noël, but knew better than to question them. It wasn't until the following morning when they were having breakfast that they both said cautiously that Noël seemed a good sort. Holly asked questions about her and Paul was happy to answer them.

'It was a bit noisy and I'm not sure I heard right. Did she say she's got a plane?'

'Yes. And she can fly it.'

'Wow.'

Bill was lost in thought. Later he disappeared.

'Did he say where he was going?' Paul asked Holly.

'No, but I think it's something to do with Linda. How are your flying lessons going?'

'Very well. The hardest bit is taking off and landing, but both are easier than hand-break starts on the Sydney hills. Once you're airborne it's easy – there's no traffic to worry about.'

'Are you going to buy a plane?'

'Not yet. Noël said I can borrow hers.'

'It's serious then.'

'Yes.'

'Any plans to . . . get married?'

'Too early. She loved her husband very much – she always will love the memory of him.'

'Move in together?'

'Maybe. Not for a while, though.'

On Sunday evening when Paul drove them to Dubbo airport, they both hugged him.

'Thanks, Dad, fantastic weekend,' said Bill, who looked happier than Paul had seen him for a long time.

'Bill's troubled,' was the first thing Linda said when Paul arrived at the office on Monday.

He had seemed happy at the barbecue so her statement perplexed him. 'Did he say why?'

'No, but I could tell.'

'Ah, another one of your feelings.'

'Yes, but I felt that even before he told me he hated his job.'

'You're probably right.'

'Is it to do with your divorce?'

'Partly. But Bill wants the unattainable – a perfect job and a perfect life.'

'He told me about the house you had in Sydney. It sounds grand. Do you miss it?'

'It's not things that I miss. It's people and the life.'

'But you must have had a fantastic life.'

'I did once – then I didn't. I'm happy here.'

When Linda had gone home that evening, Ralph came into Paul's office.

'What's up, Ralph? You look gloomy.'

Ralph sat down. 'I'm not sure the barbie was a good idea.'

'Why not? It went brilliantly. I was afraid Holly and Bill would be surly, but they enjoyed themselves.'

'Linda's keen on your son.'

'What's so bad about that?'

'He's not going to move to Cobar, is he? So we might lose our secretary – the best one I've ever had.'

'She's the best one I've ever had too,' Paul agreed, recalling that in their Sydney office he and Tim had had a secretary each. Their receptionist had been too superior to do anything as lowly as make tea or coffee, so that task had fallen to the office junior.

'Her mum and dad are pleased she's come home from Brisbane. They'll be upset if she takes off to Sydney.'

'Come off it, Ralph, it's too early to think about romance. Bill and Linda just enjoyed each other's company over a weekend.'

'It's not that I don't like your son – I do.'

'Ralph, stop worrying.'

'I can't help it. Everything was going so well.'

'It's still going well.'

'You worry me too.'

'Why?'

'If you and Noël get really involved I suppose you'll go and live on Tordorrach and I'll lose you too.'

Paul laughed. 'The way you're going you could give up law and start a dating agency.'

'Come on, Paul, what will happen if you go and live on Tordorrach? You're not going to want a two-hour drive there and back, are you?'

'No.'

'See what I mean?'

'It's unlikely that I'll ever live on Tordorrach, but if I did there are two alternatives. I could do a lot of work from Tordorrach via the internet and come into Cobar two or three times a week.'

Ralph brightened. 'Would you sell your house or rent it out?'

'Haven't got a clue. Heavens, I haven't thought that far ahead.'

'Either way you could stay with us.'

'Or I could ask Noël if I can use her plane to fly me here and back. I'll have my licence by then – I hope. If she doesn't trust me not to wreck her plane she might be willing to fly me here and back.'

'Why is it unlikely that you'll live on Tordorrach? You live with Noël every weekend. You seem to get on well. You love her, don't you?'

'Yes, but she's a respectable widow and I'm a divorcee.'

'A respectable divorcee. It wasn't your fault.'

'No, but it's still a failure. Her husband was a better man than I could ever hope to be.'

'In what way?'

'He was an ophthalmologist. He believed passionately in the National Health Service, worked as a consultant at some big hospital in London, and refused to have a private practice or see private patients. He was rich, but he had morals and ethics and used his money to help others.'

'You're not immoral. Neither am I. You pay your taxes and don't cheat.'

'No, but I'm not as good as him –'

'You never knew him. You're both individuals with strengths and weaknesses. He must have had a good salary from the hospital. She wouldn't be going out with you if she didn't like you. Do you think she worries that you might be after her money?'

'No.' Paul smiled. 'She wouldn't be going out with me if she thought I was like that.'

'My point exactly.'

Part 2
The Outback Experience

Chapter 18
January 2015

The day the homestead was completed Seamus watched as Noël, Paul, Grace, Guy, Juliet and Friedrich stood and looked at it. The cream timber walls glowed and the white gloss on the window sills and frames shone as if it was still wet. The doors leading to the three apartments were painted in different colours – scarlet, royal blue and emerald green. The corrugated iron roof was the same colour blue as the sky.

Earlier, when no one was around, Seamus had explored the interior, which smelt of paint and new wood. The apartments were identical in layout and flooring, but even without furniture they all looked distinctive, with different wall colours and kitchens. Noël had chosen white wooden slatted shutters throughout, while Juliet and Grace had opulent curtains in velvet, chintz or brocade.

As he planted hydrangeas, bottlebrush bushes and ferns in the courtyard he listened to them exclaiming over the beauty of the building and the way it fitted into the landscape.

You'd think they built it themselves instead of strutting round giving orders to the builders, carpenters and painters, he thought.

'Seamus is doing a terrific job on the landscaping,' he heard Guy say.

Yes, and what are you doing a terrific job on? Talking, spying on the workers to make sure they're doing what you asked, and drinking coffee and tea with your posh English wife, he thought. Through the open windows of the kitchen he could hear Coral and Mary exclaiming.

'It's the best kitchen I've ever seen,' said Coral. 'Even on TV they're not this good. I'm looking forward to working here.'

'Me too,' said Mary. 'So much space and everything you could need.'

'Look at that juicer,' he heard Coral say in delight.

'And the fridges. I've never seen them so big.'

The ground floor of the south wing housed the kitchens where food would be prepared for the guests, the laundry, a games room with a billiard table and dartboard, and a long dining room where the visitors would eat when it rained or was windy. The office and Grace's art studio were upstairs.

'I've never lived in a new house,' he heard Paul say.

'Neither have we,' said Juliet. 'Whereabouts did you live in Sydney?'

'Kirribilli. The house was built in 1900.'

Seamus grudgingly admitted to himself that when it came to gardens they all had the right idea.

'Just because something is functional doesn't mean it can't be beautiful,' said Grace, taking him and Xavier to the area where the three rotary hoists for the washing were located. 'Could you landscape this area and plant it with lavender, rosemary, mint and thyme – nothing elaborate – just attractive and scented.'

'Sure,' said Xavier. 'And plants will stop it becoming a dust patch. Leave it to us.'

'We'll move in at the end of the week,' Noël told Seamus. 'The carpenters said they'll be finished all the cleaning and sweeping up by tomorrow. You and Mary can move into the cabin whenever you like. Our furniture is due to arrive from Sydney the day after.'

Seamus nodded, knelt on the ground and pressed the earth down on the newly planted bush. 'We can't expect you lot to get your hands dirty,' he muttered when she walked away. 'If any of you had to do any manual work you'll fall over. So would I – from shock.'

His jealousy increased with the knowledge that from the moment they moved into the new homestead, they would have a fleet of people doing their bidding. A full time odd-jobber had been employed to clean windows, wash cars and floors, get rid of rubbish, wash dishes and help in the kitchen, gardens and stables. During the holiday season he would have an assistant. Even at the height of his and his parents' financial success, they had never had as many staff. They had seasonal shearers and jackeroos and a full-time gardener. His mother had done all the cooking, but their manager's wife was the cleaner and she also washed the dishes and did the washing and ironing. As soon as he left school Seamus helped the gardener and looked after the horses. When he married Mary he was pleased that his mother and his wife liked each other. When his father died the prosperity continued. As soon as his son and daughter were old enough he sent them to Catholic boarding schools in Sydney.

The prolonged drought had killed most of the sheep, and the wheat crops had failed. They borrowed money they could not repay and went from being wealthy to heavily in debt. He was unable to afford the school fees and the children came home and went to the local school in Cobar. They were unhappy and moaned constantly about missing their friends in Sydney. As soon as they left school they moved to Sydney and seldom came home. When the manager's house burnt down their financial troubles multiplied. After the destruction of the homestead his mother moved to Cobar, and urged Seamus and Mary to sell Tordorrach, but Seamus was loath to sell the place where he had been born and kept telling himself that the rains would come and eventually everything would be back to normal. When he finally capitulated and put it on the market no one had been interested. The fact that none of the other stricken landowners had been able to sell their properties either gave him no consolation.

Mary was in the laundry ironing when Noël came in. 'Mary, can I have a word?'

Mary, thinking that Seamus had done something awful and that Noël was sacking them, felt a sense of dread.

'It's all right . . . there's nothing to worry about.'

'I thought it was something to do with Seamus – I'm sorry he's so rude.'

'It's not your fault. Do you want us to leave all the bed linen and towels in the cabin you'll be moving into? Otherwise they can go in one of the visitors' cabins. We're getting everything for the homestead delivered from Sydney.'

Mary thought about their thin towels with frayed edges and the bedclothes with rips in them. 'That would be wonderful, Mrs Carlyle –'

'Call me Noël.'

'How much do you want for them?'

'Nothing.'

'That's very generous of you.' Relief made her emotional. 'I thought you were going to sack me.'

'No, Mary. We like you and you are an excellent worker. You more than compensate for Seamus's . . .'

'Rudeness?' said Mary, blinking away her tears.

'More resentment. Thanks for doing the ironing till the housekeeping staff arrive.'

'Have you got a housekeeper?'

'Not yet. We've advertised, and had a few replies.' She looked at Juliet's blouse on the ironing board and the row of shirts and blouses hanging on the rail. 'Beautifully ironed – thank you.'

'It's a pleasure to iron such beautiful clothes.'

'Are you happy?'

'Yes. I can't wait to move into the cabin.'

Seamus hid his enthusiasm that he and Mary would be moving into one of the cabins, with derisive remarks. 'Look at that. Noël's carrying something. She's doing some work. Where's my camera?'

'In the old homestead rotting away, with all the nice furniture we bought with the money my grandparents left me,' Mary said as she picked up their breakfast things.

'Stop going on about it.'

Mary said nothing.

Seamus pointed towards the runway. 'What's that thing?'

'A wind sock.'

'Who wants a wind sock?'

'The pilot of the plane. It's so they can see in what direction the wind is blowing.'

'How do you know?'

'Xavier told me.'

'What would he know about it?'

'More than you. Help me get the caravan emptied so we can move straight into our cabin.'

'Do it yourself. I've got trees to plant.'

Vans from department stores in Sydney had arrived the previous day with furniture, rugs, lamps, curtains, bedding, glassware, tablecloths and serviettes for the homestead. The china, silver and crystal had arrived from Shuttleton Court and their London houses, and Seamus had to help unpack it. They bought most of the things for the visitors from the Cobar shops.

Noël, Grace and Juliet and their husbands were moving out of the cabins. Later that morning Seamus was planting trees around the old homestead. He had planted an ash sapling and was digging a hole for a sycamore when Matthew came up to him.

'Seamus, we need your help to get everything moved from the cabins into the homestead.'

'I'm not a removal man.'

Matthew glared at him. 'Do it.'

Seamus wiped the sweat off his brow. 'I've got to get this tree in the ground – do you want it to die?'

'When you've planted it come to the cabins – and hurry up.'

In spite of his protests, Seamus looked forward to being in the air-conditioned homestead and looking around now the apartments were furnished, but when he saw Noël's large rooms with her furniture, paintings and rugs, his bitterness, envy and fury intensified. He carried two suitcases into her bedroom and dumped them on the floor. Even her bathroom was beautiful with a Victorian style bath, basin and toilet and burgundy and cream floral tiles and pictures on the walls. Thick towels hung from the towel rails.

The mahogany furniture was offset by pale grey walls, a burgundy and cream rug and white woodwork. Coral was straightening the white quilt cover on the king- sized bed. *Won't be long before Paul moves in with her*, he thought. It looked welcoming, with photos on the dressing table and chest of drawers and original paintings on the walls.

'Funny colour scheme, he said. 'Grey walls – they must remind her of England. A colour would have been better than this dismal grey,' he said.

Mary put a suitcase on the floor, glared at him and left. Coral shook her head and followed her. He went over to one of the paintings and was surprised to see that it was of the original homestead. 'Where did she get that from?' he muttered. He peered at the initials GH on the bottom right hand corner. 'Must have bought it in Cobar. It's been a long time since the grass was green.' He heard footsteps and turned around.

'Hurry up, Seamus,' said Matthew. 'Stop gawping. There's lots more stuff to get from the cabins. And once you've moved into the cabin, get rid of that eyesore of a caravan.'

'Get rid of it? How?'

'Hitch it to your car, drive into Cobar and take it to the scrap yard.'

Seamus went into the cabin they had used as an office, picked up a swivel chair and carried it to the homestead. There were three computers and four laptops. In spite of the computers, the office in the new homestead had old-fashioned desks and bookcases, and the swivel chairs were upholstered in leather. The other modern touches were whiteboards and white-slatted wooden shutters at the windows.

When all the cases and boxes had been moved from the cabins into the homestead, Seamus and Mary took their clothes into the cabin vacated by Juliet and Friedrich. They had so few possessions the move didn't take long. Their television had broken years ago so they left it in the caravan. The first thing Mary did was to have a shower and wash her hair. Because of the scarcity of water and money she had only washed her hair in the sink with cheap soap once a week. Since they'd left the old homestead they had never bathed or showered. They had splashed water on their faces and rubbed a sponge over their bodies. A week ago, when they had gone into town, she had splurged on shampoo, Pears soap and deodorant.

The kitchen, dining area and lounge were open-plan. Two sofas were upholstered in dark green cotton fabric. The kitchen cabinets and dining table and chairs were painted green, which went well with the roughly plastered cream walls. The green theme was repeated in the striped bed linen. The shutters were white. In the bedroom and shower room a faint trace of Juliet's perfume and Friedrich's aftershave lingered.

Seamus watched Mary rearrange the kitchen to her liking. She was humming and he could see she was enjoying using the new saucepans that Juliet and Friedrich had left for them.

'It's good to be in a bigger place, isn't it, Mary?'

She ignored him.

He tried again. 'It's better than the caravan. But we got used to it.'

She put two lamb chops under the grill without speaking. His other attempts to start a conversation were met with a grunt.

'Can I pick the mint for the mint sauce?' he offered.

She pointed to the mint on the worktop.

'Do you want me to chop it up for you?'

'No thank you.'

He sat on the sofa. 'It's a long time since I've sat on a sofa this comfortable.'

He watched her drain the potatoes and hoped she wasn't thinking about Xavier. 'It's good to have new stuff,' he said desperate to get her talking. She looked impatient so he gave up.

She put their dinner on the table and sat down.

He took her hand. 'Mary, I'm pleased to be here. Are you?'

She snatched her hand away. 'No. I'd much rather be in the caravan. I hate having a washing machine. I'd much rather slave away and do it all by hand. Next time we go into Cobar we can buy an iron and an ironing board and some new clothes. I'm fed up with wearing rags. Am I pleased to be here? What do you think?'

Disconsolate that moving to their new home hadn't changed her attitude toward him, he ate his dinner without speaking. When he finished he pushed his plate aside. 'Delicious,' he said, not expecting her to respond. She didn't even look at him. 'Mary, please can we start again. I'm sorry. I was wrong. I've been bad tempered and unreasonable. I know I'm useless. The only thing I'm good at is gardening. And from now on it's my job.'

Her expression softened. 'You're not good at gardening, Seamus, you're brilliant at it. The courtyard is going to look spectacular when everything you've planted grows.'

The unexpected praise brought tears to his eyes. He wiped them away.

'Oh, Seamus,' she said her voice full of regret.

'It's so long since we've . . . well since you've said anything nice to me – I just . . .'

'I only realised when Matthew became the manager how you isolated me. You hated him, so instead of being friends with Coral I had no friends. I was lonely, with only your mum for company. We got on well, but that wasn't the same as having a friend my own age. You didn't like any of the other neighbours either. Now that I know your hatred of Matthew is unreasonable, Coral and I are getting friendly. I regret the years that passed without knowing her. She's nice and so is Matthew.'

'I'm sorry, Mary.'

'I know why you hate him now – you're jealous and resent him giving you orders. But why did you hate him before? He's not English – his ancestors came over for the gold rush. Why did you lie and tell me he was nasty?'

He didn't have a reasonable answer. 'We never got on when we were kids. It's a hangover from that.' He knew that to gain her respect he had to twist the truth. 'He taunted me about going to a boarding school and teased me because his dad owned Ravenscroft and my dad was only the Tordorrach manager,' he lied.

'That's in the past. You were both young.' She sighed. 'Okay, we'll try again. We're not in debt anymore. We haven't got much money, but we're both earning. I lost faith in you – it was just one thing after another and most of it was your fault. We'll see how things go. At least we can be polite to one another. But you've got to stop saying spiteful things about the new owners. It's to our advantage to help them make a success of this venture. And they're good people. Hating them because they're English is madness. I bet your ancestors killed a few aborigines. And your mum said your granny was English – you kept that quiet.'

'Okay. If that will make you happy.'

'It will.'

But he knew that she would never forgive him for turning down the job of manager. He wished that Paul Knight had not told him the new owners were English.

'We'll take the caravan into Cobar tomorrow,' he said.

'I can't. I'll be working. You take it. I don't suppose you'll get any money for it, but I hope they don't charge you for taking it off your hands. It's a shame about the garden though. I might ask Noël if it's all right if we transplant some of the flowers and bushes from there to in front of this cabin. And now we're both getting money we can pay Ralph McLachlan.'

'Pay him? What for?'

She sighed. 'Representing you over the tax form you didn't fill in. If it hadn't been for him the fine would have been a lot more. And he represented you when the manager sued you. Have you forgotten?'

'Yes. It was years ago.'

'Funny how you forget when someone does you a favour, but you remember a grievance forever.'

'Okay. I'll take the money to him tomorrow,' he said depressed that Mary was finding fault with him so soon after their truce.

'Did you get anything for it?' Mary asked when Seamus came back from taking the caravan to Cobar.

'Not much, but better than nothing. I used it to pay Ralph McLachlan. I wouldn't have had enough cash otherwise.' He was pleased when she smiled.

'I asked Mrs Carlyle if we could transplant some of the bushes from in front of where the caravan was, and she said no, because when the other cabins come one can go where it was.'

His good mood withered, but unwilling to incite Mary's wrath by condemning Noël he said nothing.

'But, she said she'd give us money to buy plants so we could start another garden in front of our cabin.'

'That's good news,' said Seamus. He was rewarded by Mary's smile.

'Now we're living in a bigger place, how about getting the rest of the china and cutlery we left in the homestead?'

'It's not ours anymore,' Seamus said. 'I'm sure Noël will claim it as their property.'

'Don't be silly, Seamus. I'm sure they've got real silver cutlery and wouldn't want our silver plate stuff. Our china's good, but I bet theirs is better.'

'Ask first. We don't want them claiming we're stealing.'

'Of course, Mary,' Noël said when she asked. 'Do you need any help?'

'Thanks, but Seamus and I can do it.'

Seamus drove the car to the old homestead and parked near the door. 'Where did we put the stuff?' he asked when they went inside.

'We didn't put it anywhere,' said Mary. 'We left it where it was – in the china cabinet and the sideboard in the dining room.'

He had wanted his mother to take all the china with her when she moved to Cobar, but because it had been a wedding present from Mary's grandparents, she had refused, saying, 'One day, things will come good – the rains will come, your luck will change, and you'll move back into the homestead when you get it fixed.'

He shuddered.

'What's wrong?'

'I hate being here. I've got too many memories of how it used to be and how happy we were.'

The dining table that had once gleamed with polish, was coated in red dust. The stuffing was coming out of the chairs. They had laughed and talked and made plans. Even after his father had died the future had looked good. His mother still lived in the homestead and had insisted on moving into the section where Seamus and Mary were, to let them have the main part of the homestead. 'It's only me now. You and Mary have the rest. It's only right.'

'I wonder what Dad would say if he came back.'

'He'd be very annoyed with you,' said Mary. She put on a thick pair of gardening gloves and gave him a pair. 'Be careful of spiders.'

The china was in the glass-fronted cabinet. The hinges on the doors were so rusty they were difficult to open and the glass was dirty and strung with cobwebs. Surprisingly the six-piece china set, although coated with dust, was intact. The drawer containing the cutlery was so warped Seamus had to break it open. 'It's black,' he said when he saw it.

'I bought some silver polish the other day – it'll look as good as new when we clean it.'

Back in the cabin Seamus, trying hard to make Mary love him again, helped her wash the china and put it away. After soaking the cutlery in the silver dip it shone.

'Just like new,' he said.

Chapter 19

Now she was living in the homestead Grace was itching to start painting again. Deciding to do a still life, she wandered round the apartment looking for inspiration. She remembered the old journal that Adam had found in the attics in Shuttleton Court in Yorkshire. It had arrived in a crate, along with the china and silver that Friedrich and Juliet had packed up and sent before they left England.

'The journal . . . open. An old inkwell, a quill pen and an old typewriter,' she murmured.

She went into their apartment. Friedrich was up a ladder banging a nail in the wall.

'Friedrich, have you unpacked that old journal?'

'Yes.'

'Is it handy?'

He climbed down the ladder. 'It's here somewhere – do you want to read it?'

'No, I want to paint it. Have you read it?'

'I tried. It made my eyes ache. But maybe you or Juliet could try, or Noël.'

'Let me paint it first.'

'Juliet!' Friedrich called. 'Do you know where the journal is?' he asked when she appeared.

She frowned. 'I'm not sure – it's somewhere here, I think. Or did it get taken to the office?' Her eyes widened. 'If you want to read it –'

'No thanks – Friedrich said it was –'

'I know. Difficult to read –'

'More like impossible,' he said.

'It'd be interesting to type it up,' said Juliet.

'I'm not going to read what some boring old Victorian wrote. I just want to paint it.'

'Boring? The first lines are, "Today is the happiest day of my life. My father is dead." 'What's boring about that?' Juliet remonstrated.

'The writer sounds vile,' said Grace.

'Maybe he was ill or suffering,' said Juliet. 'His father I mean.'

'I don't think so,' said Friedrich. 'The next line said something about him having power.'

Grace grimaced. 'Sounds like a gruesome read.'

Friedrich found the journal.

Grace opened it at the first page. 'You're going to need a magnifying glass.'

Juliet peered at the writing. 'Maybe we could do it together.'

'I'm not interested in what's in the journal. I just want to paint a still life with it as the centrepiece,' Grace said impatiently.

Juliet, Friedrich and Guy watched Grace put the journal on the old desk Noël had bought from an antique shop in Sydney. They had carried it from the study to Grace's studio.

Interested as to how Grace, who had only ever painted landscapes or people and animals, was going to set up her still life, Juliet wondered how her first attempt would turn out. 'What mood are you aiming for?'

'A mixture. A through-the-centuries sort of thing. Old – the open journal and a quill pen and ink stand, newer – an old manual typewriter . . . do you think a computer would be overdoing it?'

'Not overdoing it, but there's nothing evocative about computers. It would be too sterile,' Guy said. 'Where are you going to get a quill pen and an old typewriter?'

Grace tapped her head. 'From memory.'

Friedrich looked at the writing in the journal. 'This wasn't written with a quill pen – he probably used a pen with a steel nib.'

Grace nodded. 'Yes . . . I'll paint a quill pen and one with a steel nib.'

Juliet studied the desk. 'A candle – alight. Maybe two candles.'

Grace nodded. 'With wax running down – lots of wax.'

'Posh atmosphere?' asked Guy. 'Or impoverished writer-in-an-attic atmosphere?'

Grace bit her lip. 'This desk's too posh for an impoverished writer, but I prefer that idea.'

'Can you make the desk scruffy? Put scratches in the leather and dents in the wood?' Guy suggested.

'Noël's not going to agree to me vandalising –'

'Not the real desk – in the painting.'

'Sorry, yes, I can.'

Juliet adjusted the light meter on her camera. 'Open it in the middle somewhere so there's writing on both sides.' After she had taken the photos she looked at the digital image. 'I know you can imagine things, Grace, but to get an idea of how the painting is going to look we need an old typewriter and the rest of the stuff.'

'Did your grandparents have an old typewriter?' Guy asked. 'If so, there might be one in the old homestead.'

Grace shook her head. 'I can't remember. I think they wrote everything by hand. Let me work on the painting and see what comes out.'

'Okay,' said Juliet. 'When you've finished the painting, I'm going to type out the whole thing.'

Grace frowned. 'Good luck.' She pointed to the writing. 'How are you going to decipher that?'

'I'll help you,' offered Friedrich. 'The first lines are intriguing. It makes me want to know why he was happy when his father died,' said Friedrich.

It took Grace three days to finish the painting. She was happy with it, but wanted other opinions. When they were all assembled in her studio she performed the unveiling and waited for their reactions.

Paul stared at it in awe. 'How do you do this so fast?'

Grace shrugged. 'It just happens.'

'But you did so much from memory. That cobweb hanging from the ceiling – I swear I saw it move.'

Guy nodded. 'That's one of the things that makes her a great artist.' He grinned. 'Even your still life is moving. You'll have to call it "moving still life".'

'What are you going to call it?' asked Noël.

Grace shook her head. 'Any suggestions?'

'The writer's attic,' said Paul.

'Good, but I think poet's attic would sound more poetic,' said Juliet.

'Are you going to sell it?' asked Friedrich.

Grace nodded.

'Can you do me one like it?'

'I'll do one for your birthday. That's the great thing about being an artist. I never have to think about what gifts to give people – I just paint them a picture.'

'The visitors' cabins,' Juliet said. 'We want them to look homely – not like stark hotel rooms. Could you do paintings for those?'

'Great idea,' said Grace. 'I'd better get cracking.'

The Poet's Attic sold a day after Guy had posted it on Grace's website.

Ω

'Linda's cousin is interested in the housekeeping job,' Paul told Noël.

'How old is she?'

'A bit younger than Linda. I've met her – she a nice girl. She works in the hotel as a waitress. Do you want to interview her?'

'Has she seen the job description?'

'Yes. She likes the sound of it. She lives with her parents.'

'She'll be happy to live here?'

'More than happy. She wants some independence. Her mother babies her.'

'Okay. Tell her she can start as soon as she works her notice at the hotel.'

Chapter 20

Noël was reading up on the Australian tax laws and Friedrich was helping Juliet decipher the writing in the journal.

He held the magnifying glass over the first lines. 'Horrible chap, whoever he is. And to think he's one of my ancestors.'

'What makes you think the writer's a man?' asked Juliet. 'It could be a woman.'

'The line – "Now I have power". Females didn't have power in 1850.' He saw Noël frown. 'Sorry, Noël, are we disturbing you?'

'Nothing disturbs her concentration.' Juliet giggled. 'Not even if World War Three broke out below her window.'

Noël smiled. 'I've forgotten too much about the Australian tax laws. You're not disturbing me. I like having people in the office, so talk as much as you need.'

Juliet began typing.

Shuttleton Court
Yorkshire
1850

My father died yesterday. It was the happiest day of my life. Now I have power. I never have to please my father again. Never again do I have to endure his derision. I will never have to go hunting. I cried at the first hunt I attended. I cried in anguish as the dogs ripped the fox apart. I vomited as the fox's tail was cut off and I was lifted from my horse and my cheek was blooded. When we got home he beat me. I heard my grandparents pleading vainly on my behalf. On future hunts I prayed that the fox would escape. One day when I laughed after an abortive hunt my father beat me.

When my sister was preparing to attended her first hunt I told her to pretend she was enjoying it. The fox got away, and she delighted in galloping through the woods and over the fields. On the second she couldn't pretend when the fox was caught and torn to pieces. She screamed and cried and ran away when they tried to wipe the bloody tail on her cheek. The beating my mother administered was so severe Imogen was in bed for a week. There were explosive rows between my parents and grandparents. My grandparents called my parents evil, and my parents called them stupid and soft. Between icy silences and rows my grandmother cried. When I learnt to shoot I stayed as far away from my father as possible so he would not know I deliberately missed the pheasants. I was lucky that the gamekeeper was fond of me and lied to my parents about the number I had shot.

Most of my childhood was spent with stinging buttocks from the leather strap or the cane. The scabs from the cane would be barely formed when I was beaten again. On the occasions my father was not at home, my mother beat me. She was worse than my father and most of the time I had no idea what I had done wrong. Going to Eton was bliss. I was rarely beaten, but when I was the pain was nothing compared to the beatings at home. I worked hard at my lessons, was obedient and good at sport and music. It astonished me that some boys cried because they missed their parents. The people I missed were my sister, her nanny and our grandparents. My grandfather died when I was at school. When the news reached me I was able to shut myself away and cry. My grandmother died three months later. At the end of that term I dreaded going home more than ever.

I don't need to make plans. I'd started to write down everything I would do the day my father took me to a house to break the news to the mother of one of his mill workers that her son had been caught in some machinery and killed. He called it 'toughening me up'. The front room of her house was the size of one of the cupboards in Shuttleton Court. He warned me that her house would smell terrible, because these people were dirty and lazy. It was clean. It was also freezing. I could see my breath. She had been blackening the grate. Her face was grey. She was emaciated. When my father broke the news, tears ran down her face, but she made no sound.

'She won't miss him. She'll miss the money, but she's got so many other children she probably had to think hard about who I meant,' he said as we got back into our coach.

I didn't argue. At sixteen years old I was still young enough for him to thrash me. I am now twenty. I had been my father's deputy at the mill for two years. He put the manager, Victor Deaville, in charge of me. My father only came to the mill three days a week, so for the other three days I only had one brute telling me what to do. I got through the days by thinking about all the changes I would make when I was the owner. In my pessimistic moments I thought I would be in my thirties when that day came. Mercifully it has come much sooner. In the two-and- a-half years since becoming his deputy there have been so many deaths from illness and accidents I have lost count. My father and the manager saw each death as an inconvenience. Replacements could be found immediately, but they had to be trained.

I knew that if the working conditions were safer and the workers had more nourishment there would be fewer deaths, but when I broached the subject my father was disgusted. 'You sound like your ridiculous grandfather. If that is how you are going to run things after my death I shall write you out of my will.'

I knew his threat was empty because I was his only son, but angering my father would mean humiliation and scorn. 'I apologise, Papa. I was only thinking it might save money,' I said. I never raised the subject again.

I knew little about the working of our household, but guessed that if conditions were as bad as they were at the mill I would have many changes to make. Before my father's funeral I went to the attics where the kitchen and scullery maids slept. Two rooms each had twelve beds. The sheets were coarse and the blankets were thin. Uniforms hung on rails. I touched one, appalled by the thin fabric. The rooms were damp and cold. The house maids were of slightly higher status and only eight slept in each of the two rooms. The blankets were still thin, but there were two on each bed. Gertrude, my sister's governess, had a small room to herself with a brass bed and a thick eiderdown. I knew that if my parents could have got away with housing the governess in the same mean conditions as the kitchen maids, they would have done so, but governesses were well educated and came from good homes. Some were vicars' daughters, but Gertrude's father had fallen on hard times.

Because footmen and coachmen were seen by the family and visitors they had smart uniforms made of good quality fabric. The housekeeper wore black dresses with a white lace collar and cuffs. The butler's uniform was similar to the clothes my father wore, but plainer. Without telling the manager I asked the foreman of the mill to organise the making of new uniforms in thick cotton, and flannelette petticoats for all the maids. I ordered dozens of new blankets for their beds.

When I visited the kitchen the maids froze in terror. The girl scrubbing the floor scrambled to her feet, looking as if she would faint. For a moment I was too appalled to speak. The maids collected their wits and bobbed a curtsey.

'Please,' I said, 'don't curtsey.'

The housekeeper came into the room. Her eyes widened in alarm when she saw me. 'Sir, what is wrong? If any of these girls have offended you they shall be punished.'

'No,' I said quickly. 'No one has offended me. I wanted to see how you all are.'

The housekeeper looked suspicious. The girls looked bemused.

The cook hurried into the kitchen with a basket of eggs, which she almost dropped when she saw me. Realising that my presence was causing consternation I left without informing the maids that they would have thicker blankets and new uniforms. I was walking up the basement steps when I registered how thin and pale the maids were. I returned to the kitchen and asked the housekeeper if I could speak to her. She took me into her comfortable sitting room. Unlike the maids she and the cook looked well fed.

Keeping my voice conversational rather than accusing, I said, 'I intend to get involved in the running of the household.'

'There's no need for that, Sir, her ladyship-'

'There is every need. What do ...' I looked into her cunning eyes and stopped. She was well fed. The maids looked as though they were starving. I had been about to ask her what the maids ate, but knew that she would lie to me. I stood up. 'It does not matter,' I said and left. I would ask the maids themselves.

I visited the places I had never been to on the estate. We had two hundred servants. Because of the separate passages and staircases used by the indoor servants, most of them were never seen by the family. The maids in the dairy looked healthier, probably owing to their access to milk, cream, butter and cheese. I knew that they were forbidden to eat or drink anything other than what they were served at mealtimes, but if there was no one watching there was nothing to stop them from helping themselves. I hoped they did help themselves. The laundry maids were as thin and exhausted-looking as the kitchen maids.

I approached two maids who were hanging sheets on the line. They looked alarmed when they saw me.

'Good morning,' I said.

They looked down, and with their hands hanging onto the sheets they managed a wobbling curtsey, but said nothing.

'Please, don't curtsey. I can see how busy you are. I just want to ask you what you eat.'

They gaped at me.

Their fear depressed me. 'What do you have for breakfast?'

'Porridge or bread and milk,' said one. 'And a mug of tea, Sir.'

'Anything else?'

They shook their heads. I saw their chapped red hands. One had a split along her knuckle. 'What about lunch?'

'Bread and cheese, Sir.'

'And a mug of water, Sir.'

I thought about the delicious three-course lunches I ate. 'Is that all?'

'Yes, Sir.'

'What do you eat for dinner?'

'Bread and a mug of milk, Sir.'

'Is the bread buttered?'

'No, Sir. It's got dripping on it.'

'Do you ever eat meat?'

'No, Sir.'

'Fish?'

'No, Sir.'

'Fruit?'

They looked guilty and I guessed they sometimes went to the orchards.

'If any of the fruit is bruised or has been got at by the birds, the gardener gives us some – not a lot.' They blushed.

I bid them goodbye, and as I walked away I heard one of them whisper. 'You should never have told him that – the gardeners will get into trouble now – the spoilt fruit should go on the compost.'

I was grieved that two hungry servants were terrified because they had been given bruised fruit. I walked to the gardens. The gardeners were housed in a long barn. Their mattresses were on the floor. Their blankets were a little thicker than the maids. Two enormous doors would be pulled shut at night, but in cold weather the wind would blow through the many gaps. Our stables were better than this. The head gardener and his wife lived in a cottage with two bedrooms. His two deputies had cottages with one bedroom. I looked at the sagging roofs and added their repairs to my list of urgent tasks.

The gardeners, although dressed in shabby clothes, looked healthy. Being outside would have added colour to their skin and they must have taken some fruit and vegetables. Who was going to count the fruit on the trees, the tomatoes on the vine and the leaves on the cabbages and lettuces? I hoped that they also managed to catch fish from the stream.

Our servants were trapped. If they left there would be no reference. If they were sacked there would be no reference. The workhouse loomed. At the many house parties and banquets our parents had hosted, I had noticed that the servants from some of the other households looked happy and well fed. Some, however, looked as miserable and undernourished as ours. Imogen and I vowed that under our guardianship the Shuttleton servants would be the happiest in Yorkshire.

My father's death had also freed me from the marriage my parents had arranged, which was to take place in six months time. Plans for the wedding had to be postponed for a year, but I had no intention of marrying the plain, spiteful girl from an impoverished, but noble, family. My father had declared it an ideal match. We had wealth. They had titles. I had plotted how to avoid the marriage. My ideas had jumped from making myself so ill on the day I would be unable to get to the church, to bribing someone to make sure the girl was so ill she would be unable to get to the church. My father had told me he expected me to have many children. I dreaded kissing her, let alone doing what was necessary to beget children. The day she and her parents called with their condolences I left the house and only returned when I saw their carriage leave. My mother was livid, but I no longer feared her anger.

A week after my father's funeral I informed the manager of the mill what I had planned. I knew he would be horrified, but I was not prepared for him telling my mother what I had said. She tackled me when we were having breakfast.

'You can't do this. I forbid it.'

My fourteen-year-old sister looked at us anxiously, too frightened to speak.

'Yes, I can. I have the power. I thought you would approve of increasing the working hours. Having the mill operational twenty-four hours with two twelve-hour shifts will make more profit.'

'I do.'

'Then what are your objections?'

'All the other nonsense.'

'Such as?'

'Giving them breakfast –'

'Why shouldn't they have breakfast? We do.'

'They are rabble.'

'Really? It is our mill workers, Mama, who provide us with the money to live in this mansion, have servants, horses, stables, coaches, good food, wine and fine clothes.' I stood up and went to the sideboard where silver dishes were laid. I lifted the lid off one. 'Kedgeree.' I picked up other lids. 'Scrambled eggs, kippers, sausages, mushrooms, tomatoes, bacon.' I slammed down the lid on the bacon and gestured to the toast racks and dishes of butter, jam, marmalade and honey. The footman was looking at me in astonishment. 'All this, and you want to deny the people who work hard for us a bowl of porridge with milk, a slice of bread and butter–'

'I suppose you want to put jam on it.'

'No. I hadn't thought of jam, but that's an excellent idea.'

'I was not serious.'

'But I am, Mama. A well fed workforce will have more energy–'

'Tell me if I heard the manager correctly. You not only want to give them breakfast, but lunch too – what sort of lunch?'

'A stew with meat and potatoes and vegetables, followed by a fruit pie.'

'You are actually proposing to let them have an hour-and-a-half break in their working day to consume all this food?'

'No. Half an hour for breakfast, half an hour for lunch, half an hour for dinner–'

'Dinner?'

'Yes, dinner. We have dinner, so why shouldn't they? They will also have fifteen minutes for morning tea and another fifteen for afternoon tea, where they will be given a mug of tea. That's two hours.'

'Are you going to lower their wages?'

'No.'

'Are you going to deduct the cost of the food from their wages?'

'No.'

'You're mad. Insane. I will have you committed.'

'You can't. If you try I will have you committed. You are a woman and you have no power. I am the owner of this house and the mill. I am the one with the power, like my father.'

My sister giggled.

'Go to your room,' my mother snapped. 'And wait for me.'

I'd heard that tone so many times and I knew what it meant. 'What are you going to do to her?'

'Give her a thrashing.'

'Thrash her and I'll hit you so hard it will take you a week to recover,' I said slowly.

My sister's eyes widened in disbelief and gratitude. 'Thank you,' she whispered.

'Keep quiet,' said my mother.

'No, Mama, you keep quiet.'

'I know where your bad blood has come from – your grandparents.'

'Good. I was devastated when they died. It pleases me that I am nothing like you or my father. My grandparents were kind–'

'They were absurd. If it had not been for your father stopping all their preposterous schemes we would not be as wealthy as we are today.'

I had been ten when my grandfather died, and when I came home at the end of the term my father had shut down the school house where the children of our servants and mill workers were taught reading, writing and arithmetic. The schoolmaster was sacked. Even though I was only ten I thought that a literate workforce would be more useful than an illiterate one. When I voiced my opinion he thrashed me.

I finished my breakfast in silence and stood up. The footman, who was standing behind my mother, smiled at me. 'I'm going to the mill. Tell me if she beats you,' I said to my sister.

I left the table. At the door I turned back. My mother was smiling. I knew I was in danger.

Chapter 21

A dozen more saplings to plant around the old homestead were ready. Seamus dug a hole and filled it with compost and water. He had just put down the watering can when he heard a noise. He crept closer to the sound. *A cat*, he thought. He stepped inside. On a rug was a cat with kittens. He was about to rush back to his cabin and get some milk when he saw two dishes. Someone had been feeding them. A ginger kitten came towards him on unsteady legs. He picked it up. The mother cat snarled.

'It's okay. I'm not going to harm your baby or you.' He gently blew the kitten's fur. As he suspected it was full of fleas. He put the kitten in his pocket and hurried towards his cabin. On the way he saw Juliet with a large camera slung around her neck.

'Hello, Seamus, she said. 'How's the tree planting coming along?'

She thinks I'm skiving, he thought. 'I've just found some kittens in the old homestead.'

'Ah, yes. We've been feeding them. We found some when we first arrived, but they've all disappeared and she's had another lot. We were going to catch her and take her to the vet to get her spayed, but she was scared and the next time we came we couldn't find her, even though she's been eating the food – or something has.'

'The kittens are flea-ridden – well this one is.' He took it out of his pocket.

Juliet looked surprised. 'She let you pick up one of her kittens?'

'She snarled, but didn't try to scratch me. The thing is, I know you're getting horses and I thought they could be stable cats – neutered and spayed, of course. They would keep rats and mice down and they kill snakes too. Mary and I love cats.'

'Would you like to have one of the kittens, Seamus?'

'I sure would. I was just going to my cabin to get some milk and meat for them.'

'Come with me – we'll get stuff from the kitchen. Next time we go into Cobar we'll get some flea powder.'

'A flea comb's better. Plunge it into water when there's a flea in the teeth and they drown. Flea powder can be toxic and the cats hate having it put on them, whereas they love being combed.'

When they reached the kitchen, Coral gave them milk and tins of cat food and she filled a bottle with fresh water. Juliet went to the old homestead with one tin of cat food and water. Seamus took the kitten back to his cabin where Mary was folding up the washing. Her look of delight pleased him.

'I think it needs a bath the poor little thing,' she said.

She filled the bathroom basin with warm water and added baby shampoo. Seamus gently lowered the kitten into the suds and rubbed the shampoo into its fur. 'It's okay, Ginger,' he said as it mewed and tried to escape. 'Just getting rid of all your dirt and fleas.'

Mary grimaced. 'Lots of fleas and lots of dirt.' She pulled out the plug, rinsed the basin and filled it with water again.

'Just one more wash and then we'll rinse you and you can have some milk,' Seamus said.

When they were sure all the fleas had gone Mary poured water over the fur to rinse out the shampoo. 'Lovely clean kitty,' she said. 'Lucky I didn't chuck all our old towels away. I was keeping them for polishing rags, but we've got another use for them.' She went to the cupboard, pulled out a ragged towel and wrapped it round the kitten.

As he filled a saucer with milk Seamus felt happy. He and Mary were doing something together with no animosity or tension. When the kitten was dry they were amazed at the difference. His bib and paws were snowy white instead of grey.

'Hello.'

Seamus looked up and saw Juliet standing in the doorway.

'We thought you'd want something for it to sleep in,' she said handing him a cardboard box. What are you going to call it?'

'Ginger,' said Seamus. He saw Mary frown and realised that he should have consulted her.

'I rang the vet,' said Juliet. 'He's going to give us something to put in the food to sedate the mother so we can get her to the vet to be spayed and cleaned up. She'll still be wild, but at least she'll be healthier.'

'We're going to have to put the mother cat down,' the vet told Noël. 'She's riddled with worms and she's had a lot of litters. We'll give the kittens worming tablets and clean them up before we spay and neuter them.'

When Noël flew all the kittens back to Tordorrach she had cat baskets and baby blankets, flea combs, bowls and twenty tins of cat food. Xavier took the black kitten and the other two were put in the stable where they slept on beds of hay covered with babies' blankets. Seamus took charge of feeding them and giving them water and milk.

'It was good of Noël to give us the cat basket and baby blanket,' he said to Mary in an effort to make her think his attitude had softened towards the new owners.

She just nodded. Later he heard her asking Xavier what he had called his kitten.

'I don't know. I thought of Jet. What do you reckon?'

'It's nice to be asked,' she said. 'Jet suits him. Seamus is calling ours Ginger.'

'It suits him.'

Thanks, Xavier, thought Seamus.

'The horses are arriving tomorrow, Seamus,' said Matthew. 'You're going to help me unload them.'

If Mary hadn't been within earshot Seamus would have claimed that he was too busy, but he loved horses and forced himself to say, 'Great. Can't wait. It'll be good to have horses around again. And good for the garden – all that manure.'

Matthew looked surprised.

'What time?'

'I'm not sure. They said they'd ring when they're getting close. I'll come and get you, okay?'

Seamus nodded. 'See you then.'

The fifteen horses arrived in horseboxes. A separate lorry brought bales of hay and their tack. Matthew exclaimed over the brand new saddles, which Seamus had to agree were the best he'd ever seen. Seamus presumed that it would just be him and Matthew, but Noël, Grace, Juliet and Friedrich were there, all dressed in jodhpurs and riding boots. Guy watched. Seamus was astonished when Noël put her arms around the first horse that came out and kissed it. 'Hello, what a handsome chap you are.'

'Thanks,' said Matthew.

Even Seamus laughed. All the horses had glossy coats. As they led them into the stables Seamus realised that Noël, Grace and Juliet were not the prissy city types he had thought them to be. The horses followed them into the stables Friedrich had designed. They had indoor troughs so the water would be under cover and not evaporate in the sun. So the horses could escape if there was a fire, both ends were open and there were no doors on the stalls. Each horse had its own stall to ensure that its food was not eaten by another more greedy horse. There were solar panels on the roof and water tanks at each corner. When all the horses were munching hay or drinking water, Seamus shovelled up their droppings and put them in a wheelbarrow.

'Can we call this one Winston?' Grace said, stroking a chestnut mare.

Seamus remembered that the Hallands had a horse called Winston. *English name*, he thought. *Winston Churchill and the English didn't win the war – the Americans did.*

The next day when he saw Noël put a saddle on one of the horses he could not hide his surprise.

'Thought she was a city miss, did you?' said Matthew.

'Saddles are heavy – it's a man's work.'

'I bet she can ride better than you can.'

'Doubt it. Dad put me on a horse before I could walk. She might be able to ride better than you.'

Matthew grinned. 'She probably can.'

Seamus said nothing as he watched Juliet, Grace, Noël and Friedrich ride out of the stables. Grace's black horse was high spirited, but she controlled it easily. None of them had whips. If they had, he would have lectured them or kept quiet and hidden the whips when they returned from their ride.

'They had a place in Yorkshire,' Guy told him. 'Horses, cows, sheep, chickens and pigs.'

'I thought they lived in London,' said Seamus.

'We all had houses in London, but we spent a lot of time in Yorkshire.'

Seamus guessed that Guy couldn't ride and wanted him to be embarrassed about admitting it. 'How come you're not riding with them?'

'I can't ride,' said Guy not looking embarrassed. 'They tried to teach me, but I didn't like it much. I'm more of a city type.'

Seamus pulled a face. 'You're in the wrong place here then.'

Guy shook his head. 'I like it . . . the space, the pure air – the silence. I was getting fed up with London – all the noise. Things here are more real – and safe. There aren't any extremists planting bombs and threatening to murder westerners.'

Seamus was sceptical. He doubted Guy's enthusiasm would last. 'What did you do in London?'

'I owned an art gallery.'

Seamus was sure Guy would return to London in less than a year. He wondered if Grace would follow.

Ω

Mary gave Seamus a bowl of vegetable and fruit peelings for the pigs.

'Come with me, Mary. They're the sweetest things.'

'No.'

'Why not? You'd love them.'

'That's why. Because one day they're going to be killed for meat. I don't want to get friendly with them, and I don't think you should either. You know what you're like about animals.'

'I know. I don't think about it.'

He took the bowl and went to the spacious enclosure where the pigs were kept overnight. He just meant to put it in their trough and walk away, but they squealed with joy when they saw him. It was not only the food they wanted, it was him as well. The females who were breeding stock were safe from slaughter, so he went to them, but the others demanded his attention and he found it impossible to ignore them. He stayed with them for an hour.

'Why is it that you're kind to animals and horrible to people?' Mary asked when he returned.

'I'm not horrible to you. I've never hit you –'

'True. But you're nasty to so many people. The first time you met Noël you were rude to her. I can't understand you. Your dad was charming. You're the opposite. Where does all your hate come from? Not from either of your parents.'

He sighed. 'The hardship – I can't cope with it. I never expected it.'

'This is the outback, Seamus. Droughts happen in the outback. It's a hard life.'

'It wasn't for my parents.'

'They were lucky – and they had a good manager,' she could not resist adding.

Chapter 22

The mystery of Sylvia's whereabouts was never far from Paul's mind. When Wendy Jenkins came to see Ralph about changes to her will, he asked her to come and see him afterwards.

'I was thinking about Sylvia's car,' he told her when Linda had brought them coffee. 'Do you know if it was registered in Sylvia's name?'

'I assume so. It was always referred to as "her car". Why?'

'She would have had to change her address on the registration papers. I was hoping I could at least discover a Sydney address for her. I guess it's too much to ask if you remember the registration number?'

She shook her head. 'Sorry. The only thing I can tell you is that it was an ordinary number plate, not personalised.'

'Do you know how old it was?'

'Quite old. By that I mean not new. Nine years, maybe. It was a Holden.'

'What colour?'

'White. Do you think you'll be able to trace it?'

'I hope so. I doubt she'll still be living at the same address, but it's a start.'

'It's too long ago.' She sipped her coffee. 'I've just had a thought. Why don't you contact *Find My Family*?'

'Yes,' said Paul. 'I should have thought of that. I've never watched it –'

'Neither have I. But some of the teachers at school say it's excellent.'

Grace and Juliet were excited about the prospect of *Find My Family* doing an episode about Sylvia. Neither of them had seen the programme, but the next time it was on they watched it. The sensitive and enthralling programme impressed them. A week after emailing their story with photos of Sylvia and Tordorrach, together with the copy of the private detective's email, the producers contacted them saying they would be interested in trying to find her.

> If we can't find her and arrange a reunion, we would still be interested in doing a slot about her in the hope that she will see it and get in contact with you.

Find My Family were unable to trace Sylvia, so they produced a ten-minute slot entitled *Have you seen Sylvia Halland?* As well as photos of Sylvia and her husband and children when they were young there was an interview with a psychiatrist who specialised in postnatal depression. There were shots of Grace's paintings and the new homestead. Grace and Juliet ended the programme with a plea to their mother, which Juliet had filmed and sent to the programme.

'Mum,' said Grace. 'You've got two granddaughters who live in England who would love to meet you.'

'Please come home, Mum,' was all Juliet was able to say, before emotion overtook her.

When the programme was shown Grace, Juliet, Friedrich, Noël and Paul were optimistic that Sylvia would either see it herself or hear about it and get in touch.

Guy was more pessimistic. 'If she'd found out that her husband was dead and she was a widow, she might have remarried and had another family. She might not want to be found,' he told Paul.

The thought that Sylvia would come into the office and introduce herself thrilled Linda. 'If she does, I'll be so excited I'll probably jump up and hug her.'

Weeks passed, but there were no phone calls, emails or letters from Sylvia or anyone who knew her.

Grace and Juliet were so despondent that Paul felt guilty for suggesting the programme and raising their hopes.

Chapter 23

'Noël,' said Matthew. 'I've just heard that a bloke whose property is near Willcania can't afford to keep his manager.'

'Do you know him – the manager?'

Matthew grinned. 'Very well. He stayed with us after Seamus sacked him from here.'

'Ah. Do you need or want an assistant manager?'

'Not really. He said he'll do anything.'

'He used to do all the accounts, didn't he?'

Matthew nodded.

'He can be my assistant then. Do you think he'd be okay with that?'

'Too right he would.'

'What's his name?'

'Don Overton.'

'Is he married?'

'His wife died a few years ago. Their kids are grown up and live in Brisbane. Seamus is going to be put out.'

'Tough,' said Noël. 'Can Don wait until we get another cabin for him?'

'He can live with Coral and me till then. We've got plenty of room. Better keep him out of Seamus's way, though. Where are you going to put his cabin?'

She frowned. 'I don't know. The obvious place would be at the end of the row next door to Xavier, but I don't want him unsettled by Seamus. Putting it anywhere else might make him feel isolated. Do you think there will be any animosity between him and Seamus?'

'Only from Seamus. Nothing's ever his fault. It's everyone else's. Don won and Seamus had to pay him compensation. That will rankle.'

'If it wasn't for Mary I'd sack Seamus. He's a terrific gardener, but he's aggressive. Is he worth the hassle?'

'I doubt if Mary would care if you did sack him.'

'Really?'

'As long as she could stay here.'

'Something about Seamus worries me. He's not . . .'

'Right in the head?'

Noël nodded. 'There's no telling what people like that will do. I don't want any animosity. Do you think he would turn to violence?'

'It's hard to say. Mary controls him – she keeps him calm – well, calmer than he would be without her.'

'Ask Don to come and see me for an informal interview. Normally I wouldn't bother as he comes highly recommended by you, but as we'll be working together it's best to make sure we like each other.'

'You'll like him, Noël, he's a great bloke.'

Matthew was right. Don was friendly and courteous and he came with a written letter from his employer praising his administrative skills and efficiency. They chatted over cups of tea in the office.

'You won't be working with Seamus, but you'll probably see him around. How do you feel about that?'

'Naturally I'd rather never see him again, but when I do I'll be polite – after all I won the case and he had to pay me compensation. I don't know how he'll react to me.'

'I'll tell him you're going to be working here. I don't want him accusing you of trespassing. How long were you his manager?'

'I was his dad's manager first. Seamus was nothing like him. I knew things would be more difficult when old Mr Ryan died, but I didn't know how bad they'd get. He's got a high and mighty attitude. His mum and dad treated me and the wife and kids like family. Seamus treated us like the lowly hired help and he looked down on us because we weren't Catholics.' He sipped his tea. 'Getting thrown off here was a nightmare. Seamus flew into a rage and said the fire was our fault. At the time I thought it was the worst thing that could happen, but it turned out to be the best. I knew Matt and Coral, but when they gave us a home we became close friends. And getting the manager's job with Oliver Fletcher was good. He's the opposite to Seamus, he treated us well.' He smiled. 'Thanks for giving me the chance, Mrs Carlyle –'

'Noël.'

'Noël. I'm looking forward to working here.'

'Tell Oliver Fletcher that if he's forced to sell or is repossessed, to come and see me and we'll try and work something out.'

Paul rang Noël on Friday afternoon. 'Linda wants to see you. Can you call into the office when you come to pick me up tonight?'

'Sure. What's it about?'

'She reckons her cousin let you down resigning from the housekeeping job.'

'Nonsense.'

'I've told her that. They've had a big row and Linda refuses to speak to her.'

'Okay. I'll come to the office this afternoon.'

Linda looked up from her computer when Noël came into the office. She flushed in embarrassment. 'Noël, I'm so sorry about –'

'There's no need to apologise, Linda.'

'But I was the one who told her about the job and encouraged her to go for it. Now you're without a housekeeper.'

'Your cousin was a very nice girl – we all liked her – she didn't let us down. She simply decided that the job didn't suit her and she missed her boyfriend too much.'

'She shouldn't have taken the job in the first place.'

Noel pulled up a chair and sat in front of Linda. 'Have you ever tried something and found it didn't work? Paul said you used to be a silver service waitress.'

'Yes, well. That was with a big hotel. I thought I wanted to get into the catering industry . . . own my own restaurant eventually, but there were too many things I didn't like about it.'

'Such as?'

'There were so many demanding and unreasonable customers.' She smiled. 'But I did like the tips.'

'There you are then. Your cousin thought she might like being a housekeeper, but she didn't. Do you really think she should have stayed doing something she hated?'

'Well . . . I suppose not.'

'Paul said you're not speaking to her. This is not worth falling out over. She did everything the right way. She worked her notice – it's not as if she walked out after an argument or everyone hated her because she was obnoxious. So make it up to her. Be friends again.'

'Thanks, Noël. Shall I make some coffee while you're waiting for Paul?'

Noël debated how to tell Seamus about Don. She could make a general announcement to all the staff to let them know about the new employee. But would that make Seamus more irate? she wondered.

'If you do it that way,' said Paul, 'Seamus might think you don't know anything about their past. It might dilute his anger. He could crow about Don losing his job, but as he's going to be your assistant, and therefore ranked higher than him, that will rile him.'

'Talk to him,' said Friedrich. 'Warn him off confronting Don. Tell him that if he causes friction he'll be sacked.'

Noël decided to make it official. She asked Seamus to come to the office. In an attempt to make the meeting seem friendly and casual she gave him a cup of coffee.

'I just wanted to let you know first, Seamus, that Don Overton will be working here.' Disregarded his expression of outrage she continued. 'I know that he was the manager here and –'

'He was careless and the manager's house burnt down.'

'The investigators found it was because of defective wiring.'

'Who have you been listening to? There was nothing wrong with the wiring.'

'Then why did the investigation find there was?' *Let him find an answer to that*, she thought.

'It was a put-up job.'

'By whom?'

'The house was burnt to the ground. How was anyone going to discover the cause?'

She filled her mug with coffee. 'Fire investigators are trained to find the cause. Seamus, I refuse to argue with you. I simply wish to inform you that he will be working here as my assistant.'

He sniggered. 'That'll be the end of this place then.'

She stood up. 'That will be all, Seamus. Thank you. And if you cause any friction or are aggressive to Don we will sack you.'

Seamus knew he would get no sympathy from Mary so he tried to tone down his fury when he told her.

'Good,' she said.

'Good? What's good about it?'

She turned her back on him.

'Shame about the housekeeper leaving,' he said keeping the satisfaction out of his tone. 'Nice kid she was.'

'She was. A bit young, though. I think they need someone older with more experience.'

'I don't think there are many housekeepers round here,' he said glad she was talking to him.

'No, but they need someone who has been married and run a house and looked after kids – someone used to organising things. They've put an advert in the local paper.'

'Have they? How do you know?'

'I talk to people. They talk to me. I smile at them. I don't scowl.'

'Here you go again, Mary. Always finding fault with me.'

'Just stating a fact, Seamus.'

Noël and Matthew interviewed three women for the housekeeper's position.

'All nice. All seem capable,' Noël said when the last one left. 'A hard decision. What do think, Matt?'

'I'd go for the one who's the most desperate.'

'Olwen.'

He nodded. 'And it'll help her and her husband to hang on to their property. They're not in debt, so hopefully her wages will help them to survive. By the look of her they scarcely eat. She lives a half hour drive from here and won't need to live in.'

'I'm amazed her car made it this far. If she accepts the job –'

'I reckon she will. She's probably praying all the way home.'

'I was thinking we could provide her with a car – a new one.'

'What about the other two?'

'I was just thinking about them. Do you think it would be insulting to offer them cleaning jobs?'

'You could write and tell them it was a hard decision and ask if they'd be interested in anything else. You could send them a list of what's available, and the duties involved and the wages. They both live in Cobar so they'd need to live in.'

Olwen burst into tears when she came off the phone. 'I've got the job!' she said to her husband. 'And – a car!'

Her husband hugged her. 'Well done. When do you start?'

'Whenever I want. How about Monday?'

Seamus was incensed that Olwen was given a new car, but he knew better than to grumble to Mary about how unfair it was.

Chapter 24

Noël had not anticipated the extent of the enthusiasm their plans for the Outback Experience holidays would cause. With the exception of Seamus everyone wanted to help. 'I'll do anything,' was a frequently heard statement. Coral and Matthew's son offered to design them a website.

Send me photos, a sample menu and daily schedules. Anything you want potential visitors to know I'll put it on your 'About Us' page, he wrote in his email.

He refused to accept payment. 'It's my hobby,' he wrote. 'And Mum and Dad were in a hell of a tight spot when you came along – it's the least I can do to thank you.'

Seamus felt even more sidelined when he was not invited to the first meeting. Mary was invited and so were Matthew and Coral and Xavier, the other full-time gardener, Vasco, Olwen and Don.

'They hate me,' he said to Mary.

'Can you blame them?' she said, tipping the water from the washing up bowl onto the garden.

He crumbled crusts of bread and put them on the bird table, along with a bowl of fresh water. 'I used to own this place.'

'But you don't anymore. It's time you got used to the fact.'

'Why do we have to have a meeting?' moaned Grace.

'So we can discuss things in a business-like atmosphere,' said Noël.

'Why can't we chat over dinner or lunch?'

'Because someone has to take the minutes. We've got to have a record of what is discussed and agreed,' she went on when Grace frowned impatiently.

'Are you taking the minutes?'

'No. I'm chairing the meeting. You're taking the minutes.'

Grace looked horrified. 'Me?'

'Yes, It'll will stop you drifting off to another planet, and you'll be too busy to get bored.'

'The only item on the agenda is about the website that Matthew and Coral's son has generously offered to design and maintain for us,' Noël began when they were all present in the office. 'I've drafted a few points for the 'About Us' page. Please add anything you wish. I need your feedback.' She picked up a sheet of paper. 'How does this sound? The Outback Experience holidays will run for one-week periods during April, May, June, July and August. Our priority is the safety of our visitors and the welfare of our horses. Snakes hibernate during the cooler months and this means our visitors can walk around and have picnics without worrying about being bitten. The summers get extremely hot and riding on horseback will be exhausting for the horses who will work hard during our holiday season.'

'Good,' said Matthew. 'This shows them that they'll have a fun time and be safe.'

Grace nodded. 'And animal welfare is an important issue.'

'People who love horses will be pleased to know we treat them well,' said Vasco. He frowned. 'Some people are cruel to animals. Should there be a warning on the website that the visitors must treat the horses well?'

'A crucial point. Thanks for raising it,' said Noël. 'As you'll be leading the rides, we'll have a separate meeting about what to do if a visitor ill-treats a horse.'

'Yes,' said Grace. 'And what we can do to prevent it.'

'Everyone agreed?' Noël asked, pleased that Grace was contributing.

They all nodded.

'You've all got a copy of Coral's sample menu. Any comments?'

'I protest,' said Mary. 'It's making me hungry.'

They all laughed.

'Me too,' said Friedrich.

'Are we all agreed that this is the sample that should go on the website?'

They nodded.

'It good that you've included a vegetarian choice, Coral,' said Juliet. 'It's tempting enough to make me want to go veggie.'

'Don't you dare,' said Friedrich.

'On the booking form we should ask visitors to state if they have any allergies,' said Guy.

'Ah, yes, thank you. Let's discuss the photos for the website, which Juliet will be taking. I thought external and internal views of the cabins. Pictures of the horses and saddles. And we can set the courtyard up as it will be for dinner. Anyone got anymore ideas?'

Xavier raised his hand. 'Can I suggest that we photograph the cabin with the garden in the front?'

'Yes, thank you. Would you be willing to plant similar gardens in front of all the other cabins?'

He grinned. 'I sure would. And maybe window boxes?'

'If you've got time.'

'I'll make time. Plants and flowers improve the look of things.'

'A photo of the minibus. Just so they know it won't be a basic truck, or worse, a cattle truck,' said Friedrich.

'Yes, good suggestion.'

'As you're offering rides on the plane, how about a photo of it?' Grace said.

Noël nodded.

'I'll take photos after the meeting,' said Juliet. 'And of the tennis courts.'

'It's important to put what will be included in the price in a prominent place – plane rides and borrowing jodhpurs, hats and riding boots, the transfer from Dubbo airport to here – as well as all their meals, so they'll know there won't be any hidden extras,' said Don.

'Thanks, Don. I agree,' said Noël.

'Make sure we emphasize that the food is fresh and the juice is from our orchards,' said Matthew. 'Should we say that the pigs, lambs, cattle and chickens are raised and slaughtered here, or will that upset people?'

Noël thought for a moment. 'They'll be able to taste the quality. Hopefully they'll think it's the best meat they've ever eaten. Perhaps only mention the details if they ask. And those who opt for a walking tour can be told all about it then.'

'About animal welfare,' said Coral. 'I'd stress that when the cows give birth to a calf it stays with them till it's weaned and not taken away to be slaughtered for veal if it's a male. I think a whole page should be devoted to our animals and how they are treated. And I think we should say that the animals are killed here so that they don't have to endure long journeys in trucks.'

Noël was pleased by Coral's use of the word 'we'. 'Thanks, Coral. Can we vote on it? Those in favour of Coral's suggestion?'

Everyone raised their hands.

'Passed,' said Noël. 'Has anyone got anything more they want to raise? No? Good. Meeting concluded.'

Seamus watched them come out of the meeting. Mary and Xavier stopped and chatted for five minutes. When they parted they smiled at each other.

When Matthew arrived home that evening, there were flowers on the dining-room table and a bottle of champagne in the fridge.

'I bought it when I went into town yesterday – to celebrate our new life,' said Coral.

He kissed her. 'Something smells good.'

'Chicken casserole with baked potatoes and a pear and almond tart for afters.'

She had set the table with the white damask tablecloth an aunt had given them for a wedding present. They only used it on special occasions.

'I was thinking about Seamus,' she said as she spooned the casserole onto plates. 'I think we should be nice to him.'

'Why? He's not nice to us.'

'I know, but we don't have to be like him.'

'We're not. We're only unfriendly to him – he's rude to everyone. The first time he saw Don he glowered at him. I've never seen anyone look at anyone with such hate. If I hadn't been there I think he would have said something foul.'

Coral took the plates into the dining-room. Seamus disturbed her and she suspected that Matthew's attitude towards him was making things worse. Since Don had begun working Seamus had been silent but smouldering.

'Matt, we should try and neutralise him.'

'How?'

She chose her words carefully. 'Instead of giving him orders –'

'I'm his boss. It's my job to give him orders.'

'I understand, but first ask him to do something. If he objects or refuses, tell him to do it. It's difficult for me because Mary is lovely and from a few things she's let slip I'd say their marriage isn't happy.'

'Could anyone be happy married to Seamus?'

'They used to be. She tells me a lot about the old days before the drought and the fire in Don's house. I don't think she loves him any more and when I see them together it's as if she despises him.'

'Actually I felt a bit sorry for him today,' Matthew admitted. 'He was watching Mary and Xavier talking and he looked worried and agitated. Maybe you're right. To treat him the same as he treats us drags us down. And he was helpful and willing when the horses arrived.' He raised his glass. 'Here's to us and our new life. I never thought things would turn out this good.'

Coral chinked her glass with his. 'Neither did I.'

Ω

The first lot of pigs were ready to be slaughtered. Noël flew into Cobar and returned with the butcher. The shed where the slaughter

158

would take place was clean, divided into separate compartments, airy and had beds of straw.

Seamus went up to Noël as she was leading the first pig into the shed. 'Noël, please don't do this,' he begged. 'Let them live.'

Paul wanted to interrupt. He knew that Noël was dreading the slaughter, but he guessed she could deal with Seamus better than he could. The pig ran to Seamus with joyful squeals.

He watched her put her hand on his arm. 'Seamus, I hate doing this,' she said quietly. 'But this is why we've raised them. They've had a good life and their death will be painless. They'll know nothing about it. I'm staying with them the whole time to make sure.'

'How can you stand it?'

'It'll be harrowing. But I'm the only one who is willing to be with them till the end. You can come with me.'

'No, I'm not as hard as you. How do you know the butcher will send you back the ham and bacon and pork from these pigs? It'd be easy to cheat you.'

'The taste,' she said, 'and the colour. Free range meat is far superior in taste and quality to meat from animals that come from factory farms and die in pain and terror.'

Seamus stumbled away. Noël went into the shed. The pig followed her happily. Paul saw that, even though she was talking to it, she was pale and tense. The second pig followed Matthew into the shed. He came straight out looking fraught. Paul had seen him with the pigs which he treated as if they were pets. Noël stayed in the shed. Paul didn't know how either of them could bear it. Grace and Juliet couldn't stand to be anywhere near the place and stayed in the homestead.

Paul swallowed. 'I wish I was brave enough to do this bit for her.'

'I'd stay with her but . . . I've got to get the next one.' Matthew took a deep breath and walked away.

When the pigs had been slaughtered Noël walked unsteadily out of the shed with tears running down her face. Paul held out his arms and she went to him.

'You must think I'm crazy or horrible,' she whispered, lifting her head off his shoulder.

'I think you're marvellous.' He took out his hanky and wiped away her tears. 'Noël, will you marry me?'

Chapter 25

'A quiet wedding?' said Juliet in dismay. 'They can't have a quiet wedding, can they, Grace?'

'They could, but I don't think they should.'

Like Grace and Juliet's, Noël's wedding to Adam had been elaborate with five hundred guests and a reception at the Savoy. She had thought that her cousins would agree with a quiet ceremony. 'We've both been married before.'

'Is there a rule that you have to have a quiet wedding if you've been married before?' Juliet demanded.

'No, but . . .'

'Noël, people here are going to be thrilled that you and Paul are getting married,' Grace said reasonably. 'You're both popular.'

Paul grinned. 'Not with Seamus.'

Juliet frowned. 'No one's popular with him.'

'Seriously, you can't deprive everyone here of a wedding,' said Grace. 'It will give them something to celebrate – to look forward to.'

'They can look forward to the success of the riding holidays.'

'One of the reasons we want to keep it small,' said Paul, 'is that we don't want any presents. If we have a big wedding they'll feel obliged –'

'Rubbish,' said Juliet. She turned to Friedrich and Guy. 'What do you think?'

'I agree,' said Guy, 'that it would give people something to celebrate and get excited about, but if Paul and Noël want a small wedding it's up to them.'

'We haven't got time to organise a big one – we want to get married in March.'

'Come on, Noël,' said Grace. 'If you told Coral the Queen was coming and gave her two days notice, she'd get it all organised in time.'

'You're the first people we've told,' said Paul.

'Oh. So your children don't know yet?' said Grace.

'No.'

'How do you think they'll react?' asked Friedrich.

'It's impossible to tell with Holly and Bill.'

'When are you going to tell them?'

'Sometime tonight. I'll try ringing them. If they don't answer, I'll email and say I want to Skype them.'

'Then it would be wise to wait for their reaction before deciding on what sort of wedding,' said Guy.

Holly and Bill were pleased. 'We'd given up hoping that you and Mum would get back together. As soon as we met Noël we knew there was no hope,' Holly told him when they Skyped.

He received a card from Kathryn congratulating him and wishing him well.

'That's gracious of her,' said Noël. 'Shall we invite her to the wedding?'

'No.'

'I thought you'd forgiven her.'

'I've more than forgiven her. I'm grateful to her for leaving me.'

'But you were happy together.'

'Yes, but it was a selfish life. I didn't think of it like that at the time, but looking back . . . fantastic house, plenty of money and I was happy. We never did anything for anyone else. We did donate to charity, but giving money you can afford is easy. I ate meat never thinking about the animals or their welfare. You've taught me that. At work we made money. Yes, Ralph makes money, but he cares about his clients. All the years I was a solicitor in Sydney there were only two clients I cared about. Here, I care about most of them. Their problems are real and caused by fate and the climate – in Sydney they were mostly caused by greed and bad behaviour. The number of people we had who fought over wills was sickening, but it didn't bother us because it meant money. Now if someone came into our office I'd advise them not to contest it – unless I thought there was something fishy.' He put Kathryn's card on the bookcase. 'You've changed me. I'm a better person than I used to be.'

Paul debated what to do about buying Noël an engagement ring. Given Linda's astuteness he decided to ask her. One evening when there were no more appointments booked, he asked her into his office. She came in with her notepad.

'You won't need that – it's personal – I need your advice. You've seen Noël's engagement ring.'

'Fabulous,' she said. 'And you want to know if you should buy her one.'

He smiled. 'I knew you were astute. Yes.'

'You're bothered that she might not want to get a new one?'

He nodded.

'Her first husband was in her past. You're her present and future. Buy her one – not diamonds . . . something else. Sapphires to go with her eyes, but not the normal design . . . make it unique.'

'Her favourite colours are navy and green.'

'Emerald green?'

'Yes.'

'Right. A central sapphire surrounded by emeralds. She's got big hands, so it has to be large – nothing small.'

'Linda, you are a genius.'

She grinned. 'Ah. How about having it made up with coloured glass first – to show her, in case she doesn't like it?'

Paul contacted the jeweller he had used when he had bought Kathryn presents. When the package arrived at the Cobar office he opened it. He liked it, but would Noël? He showed it to Linda.

'Gorgeous. Better than plain diamonds. Diamonds are uninteresting – not her diamond ring though, it looks antique.'

'It is antique.'

When he got back to Tordorrach he waited till he and Noël were getting ready for bed and, feeling apprehensive, gave it to her. 'It's only glass – I had it made to see what you thought. It doesn't matter if you don't like it. If you do, I'll get the real one made up. If you don't –'

She opened the lid and stared at the ring. 'It's superb,' she whispered staring at the oval faux sapphire surrounded by faux emeralds.

He didn't have to ask if she was only saying that so as not to hurt his feelings – her expression was rapt. 'I'll get the real one made up. I'll need your ring size.'

'Large.'

'I'll order the wedding ring at the same time. What would you like?'

'Gold. Plain gold.'

As soon as the sapphire and emerald ring arrived she took off Adam's ring and put it on her right hand. 'I know what I'm going to do with this.'

'It would be a beautiful brooch or a pendant.'

'No. I'll give it to Juliet's daughter.'

'Not Grace's?'

'No. Juliet's daughter is – was Adam's cousin. She used to call him Uncle Adam. There's no rivalry between them – they're very close. She can do whatever she likes with it. She probably won't wear it as a ring, but as you say, it would make a beautiful brooch or pendant.'

Everyone, except Seamus, was delighted by the announcement. 'Some people have all the luck,' he grumbled.

'Some people deserve luck,' said Mary. 'Don't you think Noël does? She and her family have turned this place into something worthwhile.'

Mary's tone was confrontational. Conscious of her growing friendship with Xavier and the fact that there were more men his age on Tordorrach than women he tried to sound reasonable. 'What I mean is she's a widow and it didn't take her long to find someone else. As soon as she gets here she meets her next husband. And it's not proved to be a success yet – wait till the visitors arrive and then judge.'

'Do you know when her husband died?'

'No.'

'So you don't know how long she's been a widow. Stop being cynical, Seamus. Be happy for her and Paul.'

'If I died – would you marry again?'

'Probably,' she said immediately.

'Xavier.'

She blushed.

'You and he are good . . . friends.'

'So what? Are you accusing me of –'

'You don't love me anymore.'

'No.'

'If you left me for him I'd kill you both.'

She looked contemptuous. 'Don't be mad, Seamus.'

'If you goad me enough –'

'I don't goad you. You goad me!'

Chapter 26

Coral offered to make Noël's wedding outfit. They searched the internet for patterns and fabric. As it would take place in the early autumn Noël chose a long dress in royal blue silk.

'That will look picturesque in the photos,' enthused Grace.

Juliet rode around the property on horseback, scouting for the best locations for the wedding photos, and came back with a list. The vicar was booked to perform the ceremony and the marquee and caterers were ordered. The invitations were sent either by email or given out personally. They wanted to keep it casual. There were no attendants. Grace and Juliet and Ralph were witnesses. Four of Noël's friends in London accepted.

Seamus looked scornfully at the wedding invitation. 'They don't want a present – that's the only good thing about it. The ceremony is at the billabong! That's not a proper wedding – it should be in a church.'

'I'm going,' said Mary. 'I don't care if you stay away.'

'I'll go,' he snapped. He didn't add that he was going because he wanted to make sure Xavier didn't get close to Mary.

'They wanted it to be a small wedding, but it doesn't look like they'll get their way,' she said. 'Juliet and Grace's daughters are coming from London and so are Noël's first husband's parents. Coral said Noël was fretting about how they'd react, but they're pleased.'

'It's extra work for you. Why did you offer to help Olwen make up all those beds in the cabins and homestead?'

'It's hardly difficult.'

'Then why can't she do it herself?'

'Because the temporary cleaners aren't starting work till April and Olwen's got to make an inventory of all the bed linen and –'

'Why? Do they think the visitors are going to steal stuff?'

'No. It's so they can order soap and everything before they run out. And if anything gets ripped or stained they can replace it.'

The next days were a flurry of activity. Mary helped Coral organise the kitchen for the caterers. Juliet and Grace's daughters arrived and exclaimed about how divine everything was and how wonderful it was to see such a blue sky.

Seamus hated them as soon as he heard their English accents. *Stuck-up little bitches*, he thought. *Bet they don't work – just live off their trust funds.* He was confounded when he learnt that Grace and Guy's daughter ran her father's art gallery, and that Friedrich and Juliet's daughter was an engineer. There was no trust fund. Their parents didn't believe in them. But it didn't make him feel any warmer toward them. 'How can they afford clothes like that?' he said to Mary, careful to keep the hate out of his voice.

'Probably because they've got good jobs,' she said in a tone that made him realise he had sounded critical.

Four days before the wedding Adam's parents arrived. They were younger than Seamus expected, although both had grey hair. His hope that they would dislike Paul died as soon as he saw them all together.

'We're delighted you've found happiness again,' he heard the man tell Noël.

Paul's parents were cheerful about the wedding and their son's new life.

When Mary wasn't busy in the kitchen with Coral she and Olwen made up beds in the cabins and the homestead and hung towels in the bathrooms and put liquid soap dispensers on the basins.

'It's too much work for you,' said Seamus. 'Why can't they –'

'I'm enjoying it,' Mary snapped. 'It's better than when we were sitting in that tiny caravan worrying about money and dreading getting evicted.'

'I bet Matt and Coral are unhappy with all these interlopers,' he said.

'Interlopers?'

'Juliet and Grace's daughters, Noël's in-laws and her friends.'

'Why would they be?'

'They're no longer the centre of Noël and family's universe.'

Mary put her hands on her hips. 'That's not true. They, like me and everyone else here, are pleased to see Noël so happy. They, like me, are thrilled about the wedding and looking forward to it. Coral and I are going to Cobar tomorrow – we're going to the hairdressers . . . it's years since I've been –'

'Don't rub it in.'

When she returned from the hairdressers the next day she looked fifteen years younger. The grey streaks had gone and her hair was light brown and cut to just below her ears.

When the rest of the guests from England arrived, Coral cooked a three-course dinner. It was a fine, still evening so they ate in the courtyard. Matthew lit a bonfire, and Mary and Coral set the table and served the food.

'You having to wait on them . . . it's demeaning. You're not a waitress.'

'Seamus, shut up.'

Mary was perturbed when she finally accepted that not only did she no longer love Seamus, she disliked him. His constant harping on about the past, despite his promises to change, angered her. His threat to kill her and Xavier unnerved her.

'Xavier,' she murmured, as she stood under the shower. In spite of his property being repossessed, he was cheerful and grateful to have found employment on Tordorrach. He was enthusiastic about the plans and worked hard to help them achieve success. 'He's everything that Seamus isn't.' She made herself think of Seamus's good points, but the only things she could come up with was that he was an excellent gardener and loved animals.

'Xavier loves animals too. He's a good gardener, but not as good as Seamus.'

She heard Seamus come inside and stepped out of the shower. She was shocked to realise that she wished she was living with Xavier. 'I'm too old for these thoughts,' she scolded herself.

On the morning of the wedding Seamus put on the new suit Mary had told him to buy. The last time he had worn a suit had been for his father's funeral, but he had lost so much weight since then the suit looked ridiculous when he tried it on, and Mary said that Coral would be too busy to make the alterations. He looked in the mirror as he straightened his tie. *I'm better looking than Xavier, even though I'm going grey. He's going bald – I've got all my hair – well most of it.*

Mary wore the new dress Coral had made her, and the high heeled shoes she had kept for years that had come back into fashion. Because she had seldom worn them they looked new. She had bought makeup and perfume. When she came out of the bedroom Seamus gaped at her. It had been at least ten years since she had last worn a dress, stockings and makeup. Her nails had polish on them and she wore her diamond engagement ring. He stood up and kissed her. 'You look grand,' he said.

'Don't mess up my lipstick.'

He wished she would smile at him. He took her arm.

'You look good too, Seamus,' she said. But there was no warmth in her voice. He wondered how Xavier would feel about her transformation.

Seamus had only seen Noël, Juliet and Grace in trousers, jeans or jodhpurs. He grudgingly told Mary how attractive they all looked.

'They do,' she agreed. 'Coral's a wonder. Making all our dresses took her no time at all.'

'Nice to see women's legs. But yours are the best.' He was depressed when she didn't respond. *But at least she didn't scowl at me*, he thought.

Paul's children looked happy and their attitude towards Noël was affectionate. Seamus had been hoping for some discord. *Why can't they hate her?* he thought. *Or at least disapprove of their father marrying again. My kids never visit now – I'm not divorced. I've been a faithful husband. The drought wasn't my fault. What's Paul done to deserve such devoted kids?*

During the wedding ceremony at the billabong Seamus thought back to the day he and Mary had married in the Catholic Church in Cobar. Mary had looked radiant and beautiful in a white satin dress and sheer veil. A two-week honeymoon cruise to Fiji followed. Back at Tordorrach they moved into the homestead with his parents, who had converted a section of the house into a self-contained flat for them. Their presents had been lavish. Mary's parents had given them a new car. They both had good clothes. Money was plentiful. He wished he could go back in time and do things differently. *But there was nothing I could do about the drought*, he thought. *That wasn't my fault. Mary's right though – everything else is.* He saw Wendy Jenkins among the guests. Her presence puzzled him. *What the hell is she doing here?* he wondered.

While Juliet rushed around taking photos after the ceremony, he watched Xavier. He was pleased to see that Mary was avoiding him. Ordinary wedding photos were not part of Juliet's repertoire, he discovered. Paul and Noël were photographed with horses, goats and cats, in the orchard and in front of the new homestead. When they wandered to the glade of deciduous trees his father had planted in 1980 Seamus remembered coming home from school and finding dozens of small trees in pots placed in the garden near the manager's house.

'I want to create a forest that we can see from the lounge windows,' said his father. 'Will you help me plant them, Son?'

Seamus, then fifteen, had helped take the trees to the place his father had marked out. He had carefully positioned them so that when they reached maturity they would not crowd each other. It took them all day to dig the holes, plant the trees and water them. Over the years he had watched them grow and counted their planting as one of his great achievements.

'Ah, just look at the colours,' Juliet exclaimed.

My trees, he thought. *Not yours. Mine. You didn't plant them. You didn't buy them. You didn't water them and nurture them. Me and my dad did.*

They were at their autumnal best – some were still green, others were gold and red. The royal blue of Noël's dress made a stunning contrast. Juliet took dozens of photos and looked in satisfaction at the digital images, before declaring that she had all the external photos she needed.

When they all assembled in the marquee Seamus was alarmed to find that not only were they seated at the same table as Xavier, Mary was next to him. There were no speeches. There was a disco and he and Mary danced. She looked flushed and happy. He saw Xavier watching them. *Bet he can't dance*, Seamus thought. He was wrong. Xavier asked Coral for a dance and was as good a dancer as Seamus. When he asked Mary for a dance she looked at Seamus. Not wanting to appear possessive he nodded. The three-tier wedding cake Coral had made and iced was cut.

He was talking to the vicar when he overheard Grace say to Juliet's daughter, 'This is Wendy Jenkins – she was our governess.'

Juliet and Grace, he thought. *But it can't be them. They're English. The Hallands were Australian.* The vague memory of two little girls crying, and his father promising he would take care of their ponies, returned. He had been so excited about moving into the homestead and being the heir to Tordorrach that he hadn't taken much notice of all the crying. He looked carefully at Juliet, who, from what he could remember, resembled Charles Halland. Grace looked like Sylvia, although not as beautiful. He remembered that Noël was their cousin. *That Noël could shoot*, he thought, aggravated with himself for not realising sooner who they really were. *This Noël can shoot.*

'What's the matter, Seamus?' Mary asked. 'You look as if you've been bashed on the head.'

'I'll tell you later.'

Mary looked at Seamus in astonishment. 'Are you telling me that you didn't connect the names?'

'Why should I? They were all English – the Hallands were Australian.'

'They only sound English. Noël, Grace and Juliet – not the most common names. It not as if their names were Anne, Jane, Sue or Mary. How could you not realise?'

'Well you didn't make the connection either.'

'I didn't know them. The Hallands were long gone when I met you. I knew about Charlie Halland, but I never knew his daughters' names. I'd heard that their mother deserted them.'

'Sylvia. She was mad.'

'In what way?'

'Useless. She cried all the time.'

'That sounds more like depression to me, Seamus.'

'That's what it was. She was okay before she had kids. Then she went off her head.'

'Postnatal depression is not going off her head, neither is it madness,' Mary said disapprovingly. 'So now you know they are Australian and not English, are you going to stop hating them?'

'They should have told me.'

'Why? You were so rude to Noël when you first met her, why should she tell you anything? I bet if you'd welcomed her and had been polite she would have told you.'

He wanted to argue that in going to England they had betrayed their Australian roots, but was desperate to get his marriage back to what it had been. He nodded. 'Yes, they're back where they belong. I'm happy about that,' he lied. 'I just wish I'd known sooner – from the beginning.' He gave her a hug.

Mary didn't respond, but she didn't push him away.

Ω

'Seamus, I want to have a chat with you and Xavier about what you'll be doing when the visitors are here. Xavier's made coffee so we'll go to his cabin.'

He knew Matthew was making an effort to be friendly, and determined not to give Mary any reason to end their marriage he put down his spade and followed Matthew into Xavier's cabin. The inside was full of family photos, and was the same layout as his, although not as tidy. They sat at the kitchen table. The coffee was weak and there was no cake or biscuits.

Useless, he thought. *Even when we were in the caravan Mary made better coffee than this.*

'Apart from keeping everything in the garden and stables shipshape like you're doing now, your main task when the visitors are here is to keep the kitchen supplied with fruit and vegetables and milk.' He looked at Xavier. 'What do you reckon is the best way to get them to the homestead?'

Xavier looked thoughtful, so Seamus answered. 'A wheelbarrow or a truck.'

'A truck would be faster,' said Xavier.

Duh, thought Seamus. 'Or we can pack them in boxes or baskets and load them into one of the station wagons.'

'Yes,' agreed Matthew. 'Good idea. The chap who milks the cows will make sure you get the milk and cream at the right time. We'll do it that way. Mary and Coral will talk to you about what fruit and vegetables are the most plentiful before the visitors arrive, so they can plan the menus.' He opened a folder and took out some sample menus. 'You'll need to provide fruit for stewing and juice for breakfast. In the evening vegetables for the soup of the day, and to go with the main course. Coral and Mary want a variety of coloured vegetables, and they'll let you know if they want fruit for the dessert course. Are you both okay with that?'

Although Seamus thought it was too fussy and that he and Xavier should just give the kitchen what was available, he agreed.

'Sure,' said Xavier with enthusiasm. 'All the visitors will be good for the compost heaps.'

'Are you going to throw them on the heaps then?' Seamus could not resist asking, but he smiled so they wouldn't know he was being sarcastic.

Xavier laughed. 'Nah – just the fruit and vegetable peelings.'

Chapter 27

Noël checked the emails. 'We've had a cancellation,' she said. 'Two sisters – their father's died.'

'Hell,' said Paul.

'It's okay – we've got a waiting list.'

'No one's going to want to come at such short notice.'

She smiled. 'Want a bet?'

'No. If you can't get anyone, what are you going to do?'

'Refund their money.'

'Not all of it.'

'Yes, all of it. Their father's died.'

'Noël, you can't refund all of it if you can't get a replacement. It's bad business –'

'It's excellent for business – for our reputation. It's ethical.'

'But if you can't get a replacement –'

'One cabin will be empty. We refund the money and write and say we were sorry to hear their news.'

'No other holiday organisation does that.'

'Exactly.'

The next day she said, 'No cabins will be empty. I've found replacements.'

'How's this for an idea?' Coral asked at the final meeting before the visitors arrived. 'Christmas is hot, so Matt and I never have a hot meal. When the children were young we used to have a winter feast on the nearest weekend to the shortest day – turkey and Christmas pudding. What if we do that here with the visitors? I can make two lots of puddings – one with nuts and brandy and one without – in case anyone's allergic to nuts or doesn't drink alcohol. And I'll make oranges covered in dark chocolate for those who don't like Christmas pudding.'

'Or are vegetarian,' said Grace.

'I use vegetable suet – it makes it much lighter. My daughter hated mixed peel so I used lemon and orange zest instead.'

'Coral, you are full of great ideas,' said Noël.

With only two days to go before the first visitors arrived Noël was surprised by Coral's tranquillity. As she had never done anything like this before and had a lot of responsibility, Noël had been prepared for nerves and a crisis in confidence, but she was calmer than everyone else as she sat at the computer studying booking forms on the website.

'We've got two vegetarians and one nut allergy,' she told Noël and Mary. 'Good – that's easily managed. But we have to be aware that some people don't read things, so we've got to be prepared for more allergies and vegetarians. I'll check when they arrive, just to make sure.'

Noël shook her head.

'What's wrong?'

'Nothing,' said Noël. 'I was just thinking you could have earned a fortune as a crisis manager – except if you were in charge there wouldn't be any crisis.'

Coral laughed. 'When you bring up kids in the outback, you learn to plan ahead to avoid trouble.'

The day before the visitors were due to arrive, everyone was asked to attend a gathering. Seamus thought he would be left out and tried not to show his relief when he was included. He knew from Mary that it was more of a thank you to the staff for all they had achieved, and that there was a celebration lunch afterwards that was being catered for by a cafe in Cobar.

'How come they haven't asked you and Coral to do the catering?' he asked Mary.

'Because they want it to be a treat for all the staff and it wouldn't be for Coral and me if we had to do the cooking.'

'They must have heaps of money if they can afford caterers. They haven't made any money on the holidays yet,' he said careful not to sound critical.

'The trips have all been paid for in advance. Noël's an accountant – she knows what she's doing,' Mary said as they walked to the office.

'Before we have lunch I want to show you the website that Matthew and Coral's son designed,' Noël began. 'Not only are all the tours for this season fully booked, most of the ones for next year are as well. This, I'm sure, has a lot to do with the excellent website.'

Now follows a sermon on the wonders of the Fulham clan, Seamus thought.

Noël clicked the mouse and a photo of the cabins came up on the screen. 'This has been a group effort. Juliet took all the photos.'

That must have been exhausting, he thought. She would have needed a week in bed to rest.

'Xavier and Seamus have worked like mad through the year to landscape the courtyard and the area surrounding the cabins. The result is spectacular.'

More me than Xavier, Seamus thought, although pleased and surprised by the acknowledgement.

The next picture was of the orchard and vegetable garden, and captioned with *Where all our fruit and vegetables are grown*. The photo of the tables in the courtyard set for dinner with a bonfire and huge candles in glass domes made the place look magical.

All the staff were praised and given satellite phones.

'Keep them with you at all times in case there is an emergency,' said Noël.

Thank you gifts were presented. Seamus and Mary received a television. His softening antagonism towards Noël was halted when Coral and Matthew's gift was a new car.

'You have all done a splendid job and this would not have been possible without you,' Noël finished. 'Now it's time for lunch.'

It was a warm day and the trestle tables in the courtyard were laden with food and covered with muslin to keep insects off. The caterers went around with trays of champagne, apple and orange juice.

'I wasn't expecting any presents,' Mary said to him. 'It's wonderful to have a new television.'

'A new car would have been better.'

'Seamus,' she said warningly. 'Coral and Matthew have to drive here. We don't. If you'd been cooperative from the start we might have got a new car too. And we haven't had a television since our old one broke. Who turned down the manager's position? You promised me you'd stop –'

He touched her arm. 'You're right. I'm pleased about the TV.'

'They care about all their workers so much they've given us satellite phones.'

'We've got the one Mum gave us,' he reminded her.

'Well now we've got one each. You can have the new one – it's more up to date. If you fell out of a tree you were pruning you could lie there for hours if no one was near. We're lucky to have such good employers.'

In spite of his envy that Matthew had a new car, Seamus was enjoying himself. The food was delicious, with sandwiches, flans, salads and cheese. A Pavlova and a chocolate cake were brought out from the kitchen when the rest had been cleared away.

Even Matthew made an effort to be friendly. 'Well done, Seamus. You and Xavier have transformed the area, with all the trees, bushes and flowers. No wonder the trips are fully booked.'

Keeping his promise to Mary he went up to Noël. 'Thanks for the TV. It was generous of you. We didn't expect anything.'

'I'm pleased you like it, Seamus.'

We're better off than we were a few years ago, he thought. *The cabin's comfortable and we're both earning money. I must put my resentment aside and be pleased that we're not in debt anymore. Maybe if I suck up to them like Matthew and Coral do, I'll get a new car one day.*

He was chatting to Juliet and feigning interest in her photography when he saw Mary and Xavier deep in conversation. His contentment was replaced by fear. He knew he would never get over his grief and humiliation if Mary left him.

Chapter 28

Apart from socialising with the visitors, Noël found that she had little to do. Olwen was a dedicated housekeeper and was cheerful and willing. Paul confessed that he felt guilty that Olwen had to clean and tidy his and Noël's apartment, but when he apologised she had looked in admiration at Noël, who said, 'It's my fault – I'm chronically untidy.'

'You can fly a plane. I may be able to cook and sew and keep things tidy and clean, but I can't fly a plane. I can't do accounts either or shoot.'

The staff were so well organised that from the moment the visitors arrived everything ran smoothly. After they had settled into their cabins Olwen checked to make sure that they had everything they needed.

'She's a marvel,' said Noël. 'It's as if she's been a housekeeper for years. She's better than the one we had in London, and she was good.'

No one fell off their horse or had an allergic reaction to their food. The visitors raved about everything. They were so tired after their horse riding most of them went to their cabins straight after dinner. The tennis courts were seldom used. Only those who had not ridden or done the walking tour had enough energy to play tennis.

It had not been their intention to make money from the holidays; they just wanted to break even. Juliet's framed photos, calendars and postcards sold well over the Internet, and she had two weddings in Cobar booked. Grace's pictures were selling well in local shops and over the Internet. Don was efficient and thorough and helped with the accounts, staff wages and tax returns. He made sure the insurance policies, car and bus licences were up to date, so Noël had plenty of time to read the journal. Juliet printed out the pages as she finished typing them, and gave them to Noël.

It was like reading a novel, except that she'd lived at Shuttleton Court and knew the rooms and layout rather than having to imagine what they looked like.

As I walked to the stables I tried to put myself in my mother's mind. In spite of my assurance to her that she had no power she would have many allies. The rich and powerful men who made up the judiciary would have no hesitation in agreeing that my proposals were mad, and that to even contemplate them meant that I was insane. A groom was waiting outside the stables with my horse. I thanked him and mounted Firebrand. Ideas swirled in my head as I rode to the mill. If I lost I would be committed to a lunatic asylum. Without me to protect her, my sister's life would be purgatory. I regretted my haste in revealing my plans so soon.

When I arrived at the mill I went straight to the manager's office. His veiled look of contempt made me even more determined that I would win. If I had been my father he would have leapt to his feet.

I resisted the urge to sack him and kept my tone neutral. 'Mr Deaville, can we discuss my proposals when you are free?'

He sat back in his chair and folded his arms. His smile was more of a sneer. 'Certainly.' He glanced at the clock on the wall. 'I can give you ten minutes.'

I pulled up a chair and sat down. 'Do you understand my objectives in wanting to provide food for our workers?'

He was so transparent I could see him thinking, *Because you are mad and soft.* 'No. It's an expense we do not need,' he said harshly. 'If you are going to give them all this food their wages must be cut.'

'No. Wait and see. I think it will improve productivity and our resulting profits will far outweigh the cost of the food.'

'Exactly how do you think productivity will increase?'

'The workers will have more energy to–'

'Plot revolutions,' he interrupted.

'The French peasants were starving and that's why they plotted a revolution that ended the monarchy in the bloodiest way. Injustice is the cause of revolutions. Well fed workers who feel they are valued will have no desire or reason to revolt. I recommend that we put what I've suggested in place for a trial period of six months, while productivity and expenses are monitored, and then evaluate the outcome. If profits increase the scheme will stay. If they stay the same or go down I'll abandon it and things can go on as they did under my father's regime.'

'A one month trial would be better,' he said.

'No. Six months will provide us with a truer indication.'

'They won't be grateful.'

'I don't want their gratitude. I want an increase in productivity and profits.'

This hint of ruthlessness seemed to please him, and he regarded me with more respect. Nevertheless, determined to modify my ideas, he asked, 'You said something about dinner. What do you plan to give them?'

'Bread, butter, cheese and an apple.'

He looked relieved. I almost asked him if he'd thought I would give them a three-course meal with wine, but I couldn't be bothered. When my scheme proved a success I would sack him. I stood up.

'If there is an increase in productivity and profits,' he said, 'It won't be anything to do with the food.'

'No?'

'It will be because of the increased working hours.'

'You approve of that?'

'Naturally. However, because of all the breaks you are giving them, each shift is actually shorter than before.' As if to emphasize my stupidity he went on, 'They will work fewer hours.'

'Good,' I said, knowing that he arrived at eight in the morning and left at six in the evening. 'But overall the mill will be open for twenty-four hours a day, excluding Sundays, rather than twelve. That will be certain to increase productivity.'

'It will not be operational for twenty-four hours – not with all these breaks you will be giving them.'

'The workers will take their breaks in shifts – not all at once. So the mill will be operating for twenty-four hours.'

'But not at full strength during their breaks, and we will need a second foreman for the night shift.'

His determination to have the last word incensed me. I stopped myself from retorting by reminding myself that I was the owner of the mill.

'You told my mother. Why? You had no right.'

'I have every right. I was your father's trusted manager. It won't be just you and your sister who will end up in the workhouse when your regime destroys the mill and makes you penniless. Your mother will be an innocent victim and so will your servants and the mill workers.'

'No one will end up in the workhouse. When we get more money, everyone will get an increase in wages – including you.'

Two days after the food breaks began, the foreman knocked on the door of my office. He declined my offer to sit down and stood in front of my desk looking like a nervous school boy.

'I just wanted to tell you, Mr Carlyle – Sir, that the workers are grateful for your generosity.' He scuttled out before I could reply.

I smiled. It was going to work.

Unlike my father, I made a point of going to the mill every day, patrolling the floor and talking to the workers when they were having their breaks. I learnt their names, which for my father had only been lists in the register. Although overawed by my presence, every person expressed their thanks.

Later in the week I went up to the loft area of the mill where the twenty workers who had been in the orphanage slept. There were eight girls and twelve boys. Mattresses were arranged on the floor. There were no sheets, just thin blankets. A strong draught rose from the gaps in the floorboards. I could see my breath. I imagined the horror of having to sleep in such a dire place. It was small wonder that so many of them got pneumonia and died.

That night when I arrived home I raided the linen closets where the sheets and blankets for the guest rooms were kept. The next morning, instead of riding to the mill, I took the carriage that I had filled with the bed linen. The foreman helped me carry the thick blankets upstairs and put them on the mattresses.

Now I owned the house, I invited who I wished to dinner or to play billiards. Excluded were the people from other wealthy families who used social occasions for advancement. Although we were new money we were rich, and money broke down most barriers, especially with the aristocratic families who had financial problems. Old and titled families might disdain us, but it was to their advantage to mix with us. Several of them were heavily in debt, including the parents of the girl I was supposed to be marrying. Her ancestry was noble, but her grandfather had been a gambler and they had been forced to sell much of their land. Their ancient house was crumbling and doing the repairs had been part of our marriage agreement. The only people who came to my parties were friends I had made at Eton. Two brought their fiancées and one brought his wife. We mainly talked about serious issues, although sometimes we were frivolous.

Chapter 29

Paul read the first review posted on their website, with trepidation. It was headed – *Misleading Information*.

I didn't want to go on this Outback Experience holiday, but my girlfriend dragged me along. Reading the website made me feel like cancelling the trip. I'm a chef in a top Sydney restaurant. Plain food well cooked translated meant bland and overcooked to me. Tough steaks and tasteless vegetables. My girlfriend tried to get me to look at the sample menu, but certain I would hate it, I declined. Only her teasing made me relent and come along. As she said, it was only for a week.

Paul wished he could delete the review. As there were no others it would be bound to put people off and he worried visitors would cancel and want their money back. He continued to read.

They were wrong about the plain food. Since when has leek, parsnip and ginger soup, followed by kangaroo stew with vegetables, and a dessert of pears in orange liqueur, been simple? I was wrong about its quality. The meat was tender and full of flavour. The vegetables were perfect. There was freshly baked bread to go with the substantial soups. We were there for seven days and the menu was different every day. The pastry in the apple pie was the best I've ever tasted.

Interested in the working of the kitchen, I asked if I could have a look. I was immediately taken into a clean kitchen where all the staff were working happily. I asked the cook where she had trained.

'At my mum's side,' she said.

Unlike most cooks she wasn't secretive, and she gave me her recipe for the best Christmas pudding I've ever eaten.

Christmas pudding in April? Yes. They've got the brilliant idea of having a winter feast with Christmas food in the cold weather. I'm going to suggest that we do the same when I get back to Sydney.

The kitchen was huge, with modern appliances and juicers and much more comfortable to work in than the one in Sydney. There was no stress, although our Sydney menus are long, while the Tordorrach ones were three set courses with a vegetarian choice.

We rode for two hours in the morning and then stopped for lunch. We rode for a further two hours and then went to the manager's house for afternoon tea. I assumed we would have tea and biscuits. There were biscuits, but they were homemade. There were scones, jam and cream, a sponge cake and sandwiches.

Even if I wasn't interested in riding horses I'd come here again for the food alone.

Ω

'Grace, Vasco just rang me – we've got a problem with one of the riders,' said Noël.

'Where?'

'They're at the billabong. Will you come with me?'

'Shall I come too?' asked Guy. 'Is it serious?'

'No one's hurt or anything. One of the girls is distressed.'

'Bet it's the girl that's with the thuggish bloke,' said Grace.

They got into the car and drove to the billabong, where they found Vasco and a girl standing apart from the rest of the group. The girl was crying.

'What's wrong?' Noël asked her sympathetically.

'Zara's boyfriend's angry with her because she is finding it difficult,' said Vasco.

The girl wiped her eyes. 'I can't ride. I don't want to.'

Grace put an arm round her. 'That's okay. Not everyone likes riding.'

'I don't,' Guy told her. 'I tried, but it's not for me. It's nothing to be ashamed of.'

'Her boyfriend says she's wasted the holiday and he's sorry he's brought her with him,' said Vasco.

'There are other things you can do,' said Guy. 'Can you play tennis?'

Zara blew her nose. 'Yes.'

'Then how about a game of mixed doubles,' suggested Noël. 'You, me, Guy and Friedrich. I'll ride your horse back to the paddock.'

Zara nodded. 'Thank you.'

They went to the car and Vasco went back to the riders. As she mounted the horse Noël saw the boyfriend scowling. As she rode back she realised that if Zara's boyfriend was bullying her, something more would have to be done.

After a game of tennis in which the girl proved herself to be an excellent player, Noël asked her, 'As it's only the start of the holidays, do you still want to share a cabin with him?'

'Not really, but where else –'

'Plenty of places,' said Grace. Matthew's got spare bedrooms or you can stay in one of the guest bedrooms with us or Noël.'

'I'd hate to put you to any trouble.'

'It's no trouble at all. I've got to collect my husband from Cobar in an hour. You can stay with us. We'll go and collect your luggage from the cabin now.'

'Will your husband mind?'

'Not at all. In fact he mentioned that he didn't like the look of your boyfriend and that you looked cowed. How long have you been together?'

'Three months. We don't live together – I still live with my parents. I didn't realise what he was really like till now.'

At dinner that night Vasco sat with Zara. Her boyfriend behaved like a changed man. He smiled at her, asked how she was, and begged her to come back to share the cabin. Noël had feared that his charm would work and was pleased when she refused. Already she seemed more confident. She spent the rest of the week going on the walking tour with Matthew and going up in the plane with Noël or playing tennis. She chatted to Coral and Mary and they accepted her offer to help in the kitchen. Every evening she and Vasco sat together. When it was time to go home she had tears in her eyes when she said goodbye to Vasco.

'She didn't sit next to the boyfriend – or ex-boyfriend I should say,' reported Matthew in the evening when he returned from taking them to the airport and collecting the new lot of visitors.

'I reckon it's because of him that she couldn't ride,' said Vasco who looked relieved. 'He made her take his camera – a big one and was constantly ordering her to take his photo. How was the poor girl expected to ride when she had to juggle with an expensive camera? It's odd that he was gentle with the horses and nasty to her. I think when she comes next time she'll be okay on a horse. No camera. No domineering boyfriend.'

Noël smiled. 'Just you, Vasco.'

Outback Experience? Terrible experience. The staff are vultures. One of the grooms seduced my girlfriend. A warning to all men. If you go on this holiday, don't take your wives, girlfriends or fiancées. The food was inedible, the cabins were rough, and the horses were too frisky. The wardrobe door fell off and the furniture in the cabins was cheap and shoddy. The water pressure was so poor it was just a trickle, but that's the outback for you. I'm never going again.

'Good,' said Noël . 'I've blacklisted him anyway.'
Matthew scowled. 'I'll get my son to delete it.'

'No . . .' She was helpless with laughter.
'What's funny?'
'Read the comment under it.'

You are a liar. The cabins were comfortable, the furniture solid and the water pressure was only slightly less than in Sydney. What did you do to the wardrobe door to make it fall off? If it did fall off, which I doubt. I suppose you kicked it in a temper when your girlfriend went off with the groom who is a lot more handsome than you. The other groom was better looking than you too. Most men are.

Matthew grinned. 'What a blow to his ego. Is the wardrobe door okay or did that narcissistic half-wit break it?'

'Olwen didn't report any damage when she inspected the cabins, so I guess he was lying. I can imagine him at his computer typing in a fury. I hope he sees the reply – that'll get him even more steamed up.'

The treks continued to go well with more people posting rave reviews and glorious photos on their website. One typical review read:

I wasn't sure what to expect from this holiday – it couldn't be all that the website claimed. The reviews were so glowing I was sure they must be fake.

On arrival my wife and I were shown to our cabin by the owners. I was surprised to find it was as described, comfortable but basic. What they failed to say on the website was that it had atmosphere and rustic charm. Everything was clean.

The three-course dinners were excellent. My wife is a vegetarian, and she and the other vegetarian in the group raved about their food. The next morning began with a hearty breakfast, which is just what we needed to set us up for the day ahead. The owners and their staff made sure we had horses suited to our abilities. The saddles were so comfortable I felt I was in an armchair. The horses were well behaved. After two hours we stopped for a picnic lunch. It was winter so we could sit on logs or rugs without worrying about snakes.

Most evenings we ate dinner outside. The sight of the stars and the moon was enchanting. For those who wanted it there was a one-hour plane ride, included in the price. There was a day spent walking round the station exploring the land. For those like me who love photography it was wonderful to see billabongs, kangaroos, wild goats and emus.

After a week we felt fit and well fed and sad that it was time to leave. We will certainly come again and will recommend it to our friends. Not only was it the most enjoyable holiday I've ever had, it was excellent value for money, which considering all you get, is actually cheap.

An amusing review read:

I'm a single girl, and I was looking for an adventurous holiday. As a keen horse rider who lives in Sydney and had only ridden in Centennial Park, I wanted the freedom of riding in the country without worrying about traffic. I got all this, plus yummy food and a plane ride with a brilliant bird's eye view of the outback. But the best thing was that I met the man of my dreams! Hopefully we'll return to Tordorrach for our honeymoon.

Some were technical:

Hardship in the outback? Not on Tordorrach. The owners have found ways to get around the drought. There are water tanks all over the place. The men are asked to relieve themselves on bales of straw, which is used as compost. The main homestead and all the holiday cabins have solar panels. No electricity bills is only one of the advantages. The en-suite shower room was small, but the water pressure adequate considering it was the outback. To save water the shower goes off after five minutes – there is a warning alarm after four.

One made Noël laugh.

Want to lose weight? Want to have a great time? Want to meet lots of men? Come on this holiday. In seven days I lost weight and ate more than I've ever eaten!

I didn't know if I'd like horses or riding. After this holiday I know I hate riding and I don't like horses. My fault – nothing to do with the people who run the place. I managed to have an okay time. The food was great. There were other things to do. I played tennis, went on a plane ride. The walking trek was educational. I learnt lots about meat and its production. I used to think organic was a con, but having tasted the delicious bacon, pork, lamb, chicken and beef I know it's not.

'It's all going so well,' said Grace. 'Life's perfect.'

'Not quite,' said Juliet. 'Mum never came back. I was so sure she would after the *Find My Family* on TV. What else can we do? There must be something.'

Grace shook her head. 'We've done everything we can.'

Chapter 30

Yorkshire 1850

I was so busy at the mill I had no time to organize the changes I planned to make in the house. The mill was closed on Sundays, although cleaners went in and repairs were carried out on the machines. One Sunday after we got back from church and I was feeling energized by the progress at the mill, I sat in the dining room with my mother and sister and thought about the lunch most of the maids would be having. Our soup course contained more nourishment than all the food they would eat in a day.

My mother had refused to speak to me since our argument, so I was surprised when she said, 'Have you any more schemes that will plunge us into poverty?'

'No.'

'Thank goodness for that.'

I should have stayed silent, but provoked by her arrogance I said, 'My plans involve getting our servants better conditions.'

'So you are planning to plunge us into poverty.'

My sister's lips curled in a smile, but she gazed at her plate.

'No, I am going to make the lives of our servants more bearable.'

'Have they complained?'

'No. I imagine they are too frightened. Mama, have you any idea how much they eat?'

'Too much.'

'Too little. Much too little. Have you seen how thin they are?'

'I have no interest in any of them.'

'They are hungry. You are never hungry. They are exhausted. You are never tired because you never do any work. The servants do it all.'

'That is how it is. That is how it should be. And you are absurd if you think otherwise.'

Our roast beef arrived, but the thought of the maids' meagre rations robbed me of any appetite. I excused myself, picked up my plate, ignored my mother's demands as to where I was going, and went down to the kitchen. The housekeeper was in her sitting room having lunch. The door was open so I went in. One of the maids was clearing away her soup bowl. Another was putting a plate of roast beef and vegetables in its place. She didn't say thank you or acknowledge their presence.

Before the maid left the room I said, 'I'm glad that you are all eating well.'

The housekeeper hadn't seen me and she leapt to her feet. 'Sir? Is something wrong?'

'No. It is one of my aims to ensure that all the servants are well fed. It pleases me that you are eating meat and vegetables.' I looked at the maid. 'Are you having the same?'

She looked in terror at the housekeeper, who obviously decided that I would find out if she lied.

She stood up. 'No, Sir. They have something different.'

I pretended to be surprised. 'Oh? What will they be having for lunch?'

'I'm not sure, Sir. You will have to ask the cook.'

I gave my plate of roast beef to the maid. 'Share it with some of your friends.' I gestured to the three other chairs at the housekeeper's table. 'Sit down and eat. Give me the names of two of your friends.'

She looked at the plate and blinked as if she expected it to dissolve. Astonishment made her incoherent.

I took the plate from her and placed it on the table. 'Go and get two of your friends and bring them in here.'

She scuttled off. I faced the housekeeper. 'From now on, the maids and all the servants will eat the same as you do.'

'Yes, Sir.'

'You will see to it?'

'I will make arrangements with cook.'

'As soon as you have finished your lunch.'

'Yes, Sir.'

The maid came back accompanied by two other skinny maids. They all looked uneasy.

'You shall have new meal arrangements,' I told them. 'Sit down. Share that plate of food. The housekeeper will explain. Won't you?'

'Yes, Sir.'

I knew that by now my mother and sister's empty plates of roast beef would have been cleared away and that soon a pudding would be served. In the kitchen there was a menu board listing the meals for the family. The cook and her assistants were putting the Apple Charlotte onto plates. They put them into the dumb waiter and pulled the ropes that would take them up to the servery where they would be taken into the dining room by the footmen.

A week later I went to the kitchen to make sure my orders regarding the new meal arrangements were in place.

'Clumsy girl!'

I pushed open the kitchen door and saw the housekeeper shouting at a trembling maid. 'What is going on?' I snapped.

'I'm sorry, Sir, but this girl is lazy and incompetent.'

'What is your name?' I asked the maid.

She looked at me in terror then fainted.

'Get up!' The housekeeper looked as if she was going to kick the prostrate girl.

I pulled her away. 'Leave her alone. She's not lazy, she's ill.' I bent down and helped the girl to her feet. She swayed in my arms. I picked her up and was appalled by the feel of her bones and the lightness of her weight. I addressed the maids standing wide eyed at the preparation table. 'One of you, come with me.'

The maid nearest to me hurried to my side. I carried the girl to the door, which was swiftly opened by the housekeeper. I walked along the dank stone corridor, up the steps, and kicked open the green baize door.

'I can't come in here,' whispered the maid who was following me.

'You can – you are with me – you have my permission.' I reached one of the smaller guest rooms and laid the maid on one of the beds. Her eyes were closed. The other maid was looking around the room in awe.

'Stay here,' I told her. 'Help her undress and get her into bed.' I went back to the kitchen where work had resumed.

I addressed the housekeeper. 'I gave orders that the servants were to be given proper meals. By the look of the girl I've just taken upstairs you have disobeyed my orders.'

'No, Sir. Your mother–'

'Does not own this house – I do. Starting from today, my orders that the servants will eat the same meals as you do will be carried out. Do you understand?'

'Yes, Sir, but we need to prepare. It will take time to–'

'Tomorrow, then. I will come here tomorrow morning and if your maids are not eating a proper breakfast you will no longer work here.'

'Yes, Sir.'

'Now get me two bowls of soup.'

Her face was scarlet as she picked up a ladle and put the soup in bowls.

'Cut two slices of bread and butter them. Put everything on a tray and give it to me.'

She handed me the tray.

'Thank you. I will see you tomorrow morning,' I reminded her as I left the kitchen.

The girl in the bed was awake, but so debilitated I had to spoon the soup into her mouth while the other maid devoured her own bread and soup.

'What are your names?' I asked when the bowls were empty.

'Eliza and Jane, Sir.'

'Which one is which?'

The girl curtseyed. 'I'm Eliza.'

'Well, Eliza. I want you to look after Jane.' I pointed to the other bed. 'You can sleep in here with her, until she recovers.' I went to the dressing room and pulled two nightdresses out of the linen press. Eliza's expression when I gave them to her pleased and saddened me. I take fine linen, comfortable beds and warm clothes for granted. Neither of these girls who slaved away for my comfort had ever experienced such luxury. They prepared delicious food they would never eat and they served people who were unworthy.

Chapter 31

August 2015

It was the last week of the season when Noël saw a familiar name on the visitor list.

'Something wrong?' asked Paul.

'I'm not sure.'

'You look worried.'

'I'm not worried, just . . . it's probably not the same person. Edwin Blake's not an unusual name, but not that common either.'

'Who is he?'

'He was my first boyfriend.'

Paul left his desk, stood behind her chair and put his arm round her. 'Need I be jealous?'

She laughed. 'Certainly not.'

'Do you want to tell me about him? You don't have to if you'd rather not.'

She pushed aside the accounts she was working on. 'We'd been going out together for nearly two years when my parents were killed.' She took a deep breath. 'Their brakes failed and their car ran off the road. The police report said that the brakes were faulty – the car was only six months old. The company paid me a lot of compensation. Mum and Dad both had life insurance. I had all this money coming at me, but all I wanted was my parents.

'Edwin called himself a free spirit – he was never going to marry or have children and kept reminding me that our relationship was temporary. Whenever we went to a wedding he'd tell me not to get any romantic ideas.'

'Did you love him?'

'I thought I did. He was glamorous, handsome and had lots of girls after him. I was flattered that he wanted to be with me. He was also . . . clean. He didn't take drugs and detested people who did. He didn't smoke – he did drink, but not much; just a few glasses of wine with dinner and the occasional brandy. He sneered at my parents' house – so suburban he called it. Sneered is too harsh – he said it was a nice middle-class house in a nice middle-class suburb. It wasn't what he said, it was the way he said it.'

'Did your parents know how he felt?'

'No. His manners were flawless. With hindsight I realise he was a hypocrite. He rented a flat that he shared with friends – he said he was never going to get tied down with a mortgage – renting meant freedom. He could move when he wanted to. He was an actor – went to drama school and did very well. He got the leading roles in all the drama productions. He was outraged when the auditions he attended after he left drama school only offered small roles, but he took them anyway. He thought something bigger and better would happen. He was going to be a famous film star. He was going to be a millionaire. He was going to travel the world. He was going to flit between Hollywood and London.' She grinned. 'I don't think any of that happened – I've never heard of him.

'Juliet hated him. She said he flirted with her. When I said that was just his way, we had a huge row and didn't speak to each other for a month. She said I was a dimwit – she was right. Grace didn't like him either, but she didn't show it. She was more subtle. I think Edwin relished Juliet's condemnation of him. It meant he'd made an impression. He had the gall to tell me that he thought she was attracted to him and was jealous of me.

'When my parents were killed he changed. Their ghastly suburban house was good enough for him to want to move into. I was so numbed by their deaths I let him. He said it was so he could protect me – a girl living alone would be prey to burglars and rapists. I thought it was temporary, until he began to really settle in – he moved all his books and clothes to my house – he didn't have much else. Then he said we should get married. He didn't ask me – just told me. After everything he'd said previously I was suspicious. He said I needed him to look after me. I was a junior accountant and could look after myself. I was earning more money than he was.

'Once I recovered my wits I realised that our marriage would mean he had a house with no mortgage in a decent suburb within walking distance of the beach. It would give him the freedom to buy good clothes, a brand new sports car and travel. I knew it wouldn't mean faithfulness – not for him, but he'd expect it from me – he was that type of bloke. I didn't need Juliet, or anyone else, to tell me that it was my inheritance that was attracting him. I asked him what he would do if we got married. He answered as I predicted – travel overseas first class and buy a Porsche. It wasn't the money or lifestyle he despised, it was having to work for it. I told him to get lost.'

'How did he take your rejection?'

'He was irate and vindictive. He said if he didn't do me the favour of marrying me no one would.'

Paul tutted. 'Pompous drongo.'

Edwin Blake sat in the comfortable minibus reading the schedule Matthew had given out.

Matthew's voice came over the speaker. 'For those of you who have never ridden before or have done very little riding I recommend you break up your riding days with a walking tour and a trip on the plane – a four-seater Cessna 172. The walking tour lasts all day and sets off at the same time as the horse riders. We'll all meet up at the billabong for lunch, and then at my house two hours later for afternoon tea. We'll be stopping in Cobar soon for sandwiches and tea or coffee. Then it's another two hours to Tordorrach.'

'Are you going on the walking tour?' asked his horse-mad girlfriend.

He nodded. 'Don't suppose you are.'

'No way. Unless all the horses are on their last legs.'

He hadn't told her that he'd known the owners. It would be embarrassing if they didn't recognise him. No matter how much Noël had changed he knew he would recognise her. He had never met anyone with such distinctive eyes. They were darker than royal blue, but not as dark as navy.

He had never recovered from her refusal to marry him. She was amusing, intelligent, passionate, loved classical music and opera and the theatre. Unlike many of his previous girlfriends she didn't simper or agree with everything he said. Although he considered accountancy to be one of the dullest jobs around, she found it easy and earned a lot more money than he did. She knew where she was going every day and her weekends were always free. She had none of the uncertainty and frustrations that he experienced. He admired her independent attitude and secretly considered her to be more of a free spirit than he was. He was always short of money, but when they went out she always paid for herself. Just before her parents were killed she had been looking for a flat with two friends. Certain that the break that would set him on the road to stardom was imminent, he'd overused his credit cards, and was in debt when Noël's parents were killed.

He knew she would inherit their house and all their belongings, but the amount of money she received in compensation and insurance policies astounded and pleased him. Six months earlier Noël had told him she loved him. In a moment of madness, he had regretted ever since, he'd told her not to get too keen as he wouldn't be around for long. It wasn't only his lack of money and her wealth that made him want to marry her. In spite of his talk about being a free spirit he was insecure. His parents had divorced when he was a child, and they both became so involved in new liaisons they had little time for him. Despite his derogatory speeches about permanent relationships the thought of being married to Noël appealed to him. He thought his free spirit persona made him attractive to women, and he feared that if he confessed his true feelings, her love for him would fade.

Noël's devastation when her parents were killed made him protective towards her. He moved into her house and said he would look after her. For a month she had needed looking after. It was when he had said that they should get married that she had pulled herself out of her emotional dependence on him. Later he realised he had proposed too quickly and made her think it was her money rather than her that he wanted. It was true that he would not have married her had she been poor, but it had taken him ten years to stop comparing every girlfriend to Noël.

He had tried to get over her by seducing a string of girls, but memories of Noël possessed him. A year later he went to her house, only to find it had been sold and the owners refused to give him her forwarding address. He rang her number at work and was told that she had gone to England. His dream of becoming a film star faded completely when he started losing his hair. By the time he was thirty he was bald. Unable to find enough work as an extra he applied for, and got, a job as a location finder. He was surprised to find it fulfilled him.

His latest commission was to find a location in the outback. Immediately he remembered Noël and her cousins telling him about Tordorrach. Not expecting a result, he put the name in a search engine and saw that it was now a holiday venue. He was surprised to see photos of Noël and her cousins. Rather than send an email he had decided to visit. He put the trip on expenses and asked his girlfriend, who was a stuntwoman, to go with him.

When they reached Tordorrach he tried to hide his apprehension. Juliet and Grace and three men who introduced themselves as Paul, Friedrich and Guy, were waiting for them. He wondered why Noël was not one of the welcoming party. They were escorted to their cabins. His girlfriend was in raptures over the location and the cabin and was eager to see the horses. Edwin was pleased that there was a good Internet connection. The first thing he did on entering the cabin was to plug in his laptop.

'Is it him?' Noël asked Juliet and Grace when they returned to the homestead.

'It's hard to tell if it's the greatest actor since Laurence Olivier or not,' said Juliet. 'Grace thinks it is. I don't know. He's bald.'

'I'm sure he recognised us,' said Grace.

'If it is him he might remember the name Tordorrach. We were always talking about it,' said Noël.

'I think he was looking round for you. I wonder if he'll say anything at dinner,' said Paul.

'I doubt it. He'll be too embarrassed to admit he hasn't made it as an actor. He's probably had so many women since we parted that he doesn't remember me.'

'If it's him, he'll remember you. Your eyes are unforgettable,' said Paul.

'And you haven't changed that much,' said Grace. 'If he recognised Juliet and me, he'll recognise you.'

Chapter 32

At dinner that night Noël gave no indication that she recognised him, and neither did Juliet or Grace. Edwin wondered if she had deliberately sat as far away from him as she could. Even when they had been going out together she had dressed classically and disregarded fashion. It was one of the things he respected about her. Tonight she wore a red polo-necked jumper with black trousers. Her pearl necklace and earrings looked real.

Funny how losing your hair makes such a difference, he thought. *I knew who they were straight away. I was expecting to see them and they weren't expecting to see me, but they should have remembered my name. She can't have forgotten me. The years have been kinder to Noël and her cousins than they've been to me.*

He had only ridden a horse once, and had hated the experience, so he decided to talk to Matthew about the chance of using Tordorrach as a location. He was reluctant to approach Noël, fearing that she would reject the proposal if she recognised him.

'This is divine,' said his girlfriend.

He'd been more interested in looking at Noël and her cousins than at his surroundings. He now recognised Grace's artistic style. She had been vigilant about creating atmosphere. He remembered her saying that it wasn't just the food that was important, it was also the way the table looked. Her table settings in winter had always had candles.

Nothing's changed there, he thought as he scrutinised the courtyard and table. The bonfire added warmth and light as well as ambience. The plastic-coated tablecloth looked like a Victorian print and the stainless steel cutlery was good quality and reflected the flames from the candles. The serviettes were green damask.

Paper ones would have been more practical, but the use of material showed that the visitors were trusted to behave well.

How would they cope with a bunch of yobs? he thought.

Jugs of water and juice covered with muslin stood on the table and there was a wine and a water glass at each place setting. Three bottles of white wine stood in coolers and three bottles of red were at either end of the table.

Six bottles of wine for sixteen people, he thought. *No chance of getting drunk here.*

There were bottles of lager in an ice bucket on the ground well away from the bonfire. His girlfriend raved about the food, but Edwin was too busy trying to work out how he would approach Matthew. At the end of the meal coffee, chocolate mints and brandy, Madeira and port were served.

'Well I don't know,' said Matthew when he talked to him about it after dinner. 'You'll have to ask one of the owners.'

'Do you think they'll consider it? It's a good deal.'

'I'll tell them about it tomorrow.'

'I won't be riding, so I'll be free to tell them all about it.'

His girlfriend was as wholehearted in her praise about the breakfast as she was about everything else. She drew his attention to the fact that the tablecloth was now yellow gingham, and the cutlery was plainer.

Coral put jugs of juice on the table. 'Apple, orange and grapefruit juice. All the fruit's picked from our orchard,' she said proudly. 'Who wants stewed plums, apricots or prunes?'

'This is better than a posh hotel in Sydney,' said his girlfriend.

Others agreed, but Edwin was too anxious about Matthew's response. He hoped he hadn't forgotten to consult Noël.

After breakfast Matthew came up to him. 'They'll see you at eleven. I'll take you over.'

'Thanks. I appreciate it. I'll be in my cabin.'

When Matthew took him into the office Noël, Grace and Juliet still gave no signs that they recognised him. They introduced him to Don who, he was told, was Noël's assistant. Unsurprisingly she seemed to be in charge.

'Is the film historical or contemporary?' she asked.

'Historical.'

'Do you just want the outback location, or houses, sheep, horses and other livestock?'

'The works,' he said, pleased by the questions, which he thought meant she was considering it.

'What type of house were you wanting?'

'Not this homestead – it's too posh and new. Something like one of your cabins would be just right.'

'We don't want to get involved in the film side of things here, however we know someone who might.' She looked at Don who nodded.

'The bloke whose manager I used to be has the ideal property for a historical film. His house is a drop log construction and was built by hand in 1890. Things are too modern on Tordorrach with new water tanks and solar panels all over the place, but the film crew could film there without having to change anything.'

'Interested?' asked Grace.

'I might be. Would he let caravans stay for the duration of the filming?'

'I'm sure he would. We can ask him when we get there. It's about an hour's drive from here – towards Wilcannia,' said Don. 'It's bigger than Tordorrach – one hundred and fifty thousand acres. I can drive you over there this afternoon if you want.'

'Sounds good,' said Edwin.

In contrast to Noël's coolness, the owner of Richmond was pathetically grateful for the opportunity. Edwin wished he'd taken a photo of Oliver Fletcher's face when he told him what the payment would be. He agreed to have caravans for the actors and film crew on site. He said they could stay as long as it took. Don was more cautious and insisted on reading the contract thoroughly before Oliver signed it.

Back at Tordorrach, Edwin went to his cabin, opened his laptop and emailed the good news, along with photographs and the signed contract, to his boss in Sydney. Then he showered and shaved and got dressed and sat on the veranda waiting for his girlfriend to return from the ride.

A man carrying a spade walked in front of his cabin.

'Afternoon,' said Edwin.

The man looked at him, but didn't smile. 'Not riding today?'

'I don't like horses much.' He saw the man's disapproving expressing and added, 'Well they're okay, but I don't like riding them.'

The man's tone was curt when he asked, 'Why come on a riding holiday then?'

'I'm here on business.'

'What sort of business?'

In spite of the man's manner, and sensing that he felt contempt for anyone who couldn't ride, Edwin wanted to dazzle him. 'I'm in films and I'm looking for an outback location.'

The man looked even more unfriendly. 'You should have come here a few years ago,' he said bitterly.

'Oh?'

'I used to own it.' He looked around as if making sure no one was listening. 'That Noël and her cousins bought it. Want a cup of tea or some beer?'

Surprised by the invitation Edwin accepted. The man introduced himself as Seamus. Unsure if Noël was the cause of his ire he decided to probe further. He accepted a beer and they sat at the table on the veranda.

'I used to go out with Noël when we lived in Sydney.'

'Did you now? How interesting. What was she like then?'

Edwin hesitated.

'Haughty? Bossy?' Seamus prompted.

'Yeah. She was gutted when I broke it off with her. Drove me mad. Kept pestering me,' he lied. 'I was glad when she and her cousins went to England. Don't tell anyone. I don't think she recognizes me – I want to keep it that way. She had lots of money – her parents were killed and she inherited the lot – guess she thought that made her attractive.'

Seamus sniggered. 'This is her second marriage. The first husband was rich.'

'Had to pay her off, did he?'

'He died and left her a fortune. I reckon Paul married her for her money.'

Edwin raised his glass. 'Serves her right! Is the marriage happy?'

'Who knows?' Seamus shrugged. 'Who cares?'

There were three of them on the walking tour.

Matthew took them to see the pigs, all of which were wandering about chomping grass or inside their shed sleeping or eating vegetables or fruit.

'Our pigs are like pets,' Matthew said when one ran up to him. He bent down and patted it. 'He doesn't want food, he wants affection. Pigs are intelligent and are one of the most ill-treated animals when it comes to intensive farming. On Tordorrach we have them killed when they are ten months old. Having given them a good life we are not going to chuck them in a lorry and send them on a hellish journey to be slaughtered in pain and terror. We have them killed here. I admit to shedding quite a few tears over it. Noël and I are with them at the end. Yeah, it upsets us, but we owe it to them to be with them at the end and also to make sure their death is pain free.' Another pig ran up to them. 'There are myths about pigs. One is that they are dirty and smelly, but as you can see and smell, they aren't. It's when they are kept in crowded, badly ventilated sheds that they smell. Any questions before we go and visit the sheep?'

'Do you give them names?' asked one of the girls.

'No. That would make it even harder to kill them.'

'There's rabbit on the menu – do you shoot them yourself?'

Matthew nodded. 'Noël and I shoot them. I don't mind admitting that she's a better shot than me.'

Yes, thought Edwin, *I remember her saying she could shoot. I didn't believe her.*

'We mainly shoot kangaroos and rabbits. They're wild and it's less traumatic, because we haven't got a relationship with them and the shooting's done from a distance. We aim for the heart – an instant death.'

In the orchards he said, 'This is Seamus, and he and Xavier, the other gardener, are the reason you have such delicious fruit and vegetables. Seamus will tell you a bit about how they manage the orchards and vegetable gardens.'

'No pesticides,' said Seamus looking at them as if they were armed with cans of pesticides ready to spray them on the trees. 'I check the trunks, limbs and leaves everyday. I pick off any pests with my fingers.'

If he hadn't looked so fierce Edwin would have asked if he ate them, but he thought that rather than taking it as a joke, Seamus would be offended.

'I let the birds do the rest. Birds love insects. In the vegetable gardens it's companion planting. Some plants attract some things and repel others. You've got to know what's what, but I'm too busy to go into all that now.'

What a grump, thought Edwin.

'Thank you, Seamus,' said Matthew.

'I've got a confession to make,' said Edwin as they were walking over to Matthew's house to meet the riders in the group for afternoon tea. 'Before last night, when I had the best pork I've ever tasted, I thought this organic free range stuff was a yarn spun to pacify people who were bothered by meat production, and to stop them going vegetarian.'

'That's mild,' said Matthew. 'A lot of folk think it's a con.'

'Have you got any spare horses? The ones at Richmond are scrawny and don't look as if they could stand to be ridden. This film needs horses.'

'I'll have to ask Mrs Knight, but I doubt she'll want their horses used for filming in case they're ill-treated. That'd be my worry too.'

Matthew was right. Noël refused permission, but sent Don to Richmond with bales of hay and sacks of horse food.

If Noël hadn't been married, Edwin would have reminded her of their past relationship and tried to renew it. In spite of what Seamus had told him he gauged that Paul loved her very much. Seeing them together was hell for him and he was pleased when the week was up and it was time to leave. Back in Sydney in his small rented flat he felt discontented and jealous. He went to his laptop and fired off a review. Two days later, he knew he had been spiteful and foolish, but it was too late to delete his review.

> Good food. Nice cabins, but the set up is funny. A family, consisting of three females – two sisters and their cousin, and their husbands, all live in the one house, which is divided into three apartments. The head of the group is Noël Knight who is married to Paul, a solicitor. She was the one with the money. I heard the gossip that's why he married her. She's not all that good looking so the money must have been the main attraction.

When Matthew read the first paragraph of the review he stormed to his car and drove across to the homestead. The door to the office was open and he went straight in. 'This will be Seamus – sack the –'

'Sit down, Matt,' said Noël. 'I assume this is about the review Edwin wrote.'

'Too right it is. Seamus would have told him that.'

'Probably, but what proof do we have?'

'No one else here would tell him that.'

'I know, but Edwin could have made it up. Seamus is stupid, but is he that stupid?'

Don looked up from his calculator. 'Well, no harm's been done, and some good has come out of it. Oliver's got a good deal, and a lot of much needed money.'

'True,' said Matthew. 'I'll get my son to delete it.'

Noël raised her eyebrows. 'That's not ethical.'

'Writing a pack of lies isn't ethical.'

'I didn't think the reviews could be deleted.'

Matthew laughed. 'My son can hack into most computers.' He looked uncertain. 'Is that okay with you?'

She grinned. 'Sure is. I don't want Paul to see it.' She handed him her phone. 'Ring your son now.'

'And, you are good looking,' he said as he punched in the number. 'Very good looking. And you've got charisma – truck loads of it, hasn't she, Don?'

'She sure has.'

Ω

At the beginning of September, when the season was over, Bill and Linda visited and stayed in one of the cabins. Bill was quiet and introspective. Linda was her usual bubbly self. They stayed for a week and when Noël flew them back to Cobar Bill seemed melancholy. Linda went to work and Noël waited for the bus to Dubbo with Bill.

Troubled by his silence Noël asked, 'Is everything okay?'

He nodded.

'You seem unhappy. Did you enjoy your stay?'

'It was the best holiday I've ever had. It's the thought of going back to work.'

'It can't be that bad, surely?'

'It's tedious. Dreary job. Dreary people.'

When they said goodbye, he hugged her. 'You're the best step-mum anyone could have.'

'I hope you'll come again.'

'I hope so too.'

'Bill seemed miserable,' said Noël when she and Paul were having dinner. 'He said he enjoyed himself, but he didn't look happy.'

'He's had a lot of upheaval. He shares a small flat with Holly – it's crowded, and not what they're used to. She's okay with it, but he's not. But she loves her job and has made lots of friends.'

'It's almost as if he's depressed,' said Noël. 'Has he always been like this?'

'No. He was fine till he left school. Then he was floundering – didn't know what he wanted to do. His results weren't good enough to get a place at uni, but he wasn't despondent about it. He and Holly had their own rooms in our house. We let them have friends sleep over, so he had a great life. His mother going off with my law partner was the worst thing that had happened to him. He can't cope with obstacles and wants everything to be easy. There is a strong streak of benevolence in him. One birthday we sponsored an elephant from a sanctuary in Africa for him – he said it was the best present he'd ever had. We did it every year and I still do. He once told us that he wanted to go and work in this sanctuary, but he's not a traveller – he doesn't want to live anywhere but Australia.'

'Has he investigated working in an animal sanctuary in Australia?'

Paul nodded. 'He applied to four. They all turned him down.'

Chapter 33

October 2015

Coral was coring apples and pushing them over to Mary who chopped them up and put them in the juicer. Mary took a deep breath.

'Are you okay?' Coral asked.

Mary nodded.

Coral was unconvinced. Mary had been pale all morning and, unusually for her, was quiet rather than talkative. 'Why don't you sit down and I'll make you a cup of tea?'

Mary put a handful of apples in the juicer. 'Not enough time.'

'Nonsense. There are no visitors –'

Mary's hand went to the switch then fell away as she staggered and fell to the floor.

Coral tore out of the kitchen. 'Quick, help! Mary's collapsed.'

Only Noël, Grace and Paul were in earshot. They ran into the kitchen. Grace felt for a pulse. Mary was still alive, but her lips were blue and her face grey.

'What would be best?' asked Noël. 'I could fly her into Dubbo, or we can call the Flying Doctor.'

Paul grabbed his satellite phone. 'Flying Doctor. She might have to be taken to Sydney and they've got equipment on board – I think it's a heart attack. Where's Seamus?'

'Probably in the gardens. I'll find him,' offered Grace.

Mary Ryan died in a Sydney hospital three days later. Noël paid for Seamus to fly back to Cobar with her body and told him they would pay for the funeral.

'Whatever you want, Seamus, just tell the undertaker and we will pay.'

Mary's funeral was held in the Catholic Church in Cobar. Although everyone on Tordorrach wanted to attend Seamus requested a private funeral with only family present. 'I don't want all those hypocrites crying and saying how wonderful she was,' he said to Paul.

'That's a bit rough, Seamus. Everyone liked Mary. Their sadness is genuine. They are not hypocrites. If they want to come to her funeral –'

'They are not coming. I don't want you or Noël there either. That's the end of it!'

Paul gave up.

Seamus and his mother and his son and daughter, were the only mourners.

'Why didn't anyone else come?' asked his daughter after the funeral.

'Their employers wouldn't let them have the time off,' replied Seamus, glad his mother was in the kitchen making tea.

'How mean. What sort of people are they?'

He was gratified to finally have someone he could complain to without them jumping to the new owners' defence. 'Selfish. One of them has a plane and they were worried she might mess it up – you know – be sick on it. They wasted valuable time waiting for the Flying Doctor. It's because of them that your mum died. Don't say anything to your gran – she'll get upset.'

He regretted he had lied to her when he received a letter from her four weeks later telling him she had posted a bad review on the *Outback Experience* website. She ended her letter with 'They'll be sorry.'

'And so will I,' he murmured. He started to write her a letter asking her to remove the review, then thought that none of the owners knew his daughter's name. He tore the letter up.

'It's insensitive to talk about this so soon after Mary's death,' Noël said to Coral, 'but we need to find a replacement for her. Do you know of anyone who would be suitable and interested?'

'No, unfortunately. Oh wait. That lassie who was here – the one who had a bossy boyfriend.'

'Zara.'

'That's the one. She helped in the kitchen – she was good. She's got a job in Brisbane. I'm don't know what she does, but she and Vasco email and Skype each other.'

'Good thinking, Coral. I'll talk to Vasco and send her an email.'

Zara started work at Tordorrach three weeks later. She moved into the new staff cabin Noël had ordered for her. Vasco gave her riding lessons. Under his tuition she learnt quickly and became a competent rider.

'Mary was a friend and I miss her,' Coral told Matthew. 'But it's good having a young girl around. And she and Vasco make a nice couple.'

'And you enjoy mothering her,' Matthew said indulgently.

'Noël,' said Don a month after Mary died. 'We've got a bad review.'

She clicked onto the webpage and read the review in disbelief.

The owners of The Outback Experience holidays are lazy, greedy slave drivers. They don't do a thing, just wander about being frivolous and idle. They don't even try to look busy. It's thanks to their slaves that the place is a success.

The food was good – thanks to their slaves. The cabins were clean – thanks to their slaves. The trips were well organised. And not because of the owners who rake in all the money. It's all due to the cooks, gardeners, cleaners and grooms who do all the hard work. The filthy rich owners pretend to be goody goody, but when one of their slaves had a heart attack, they refused to fly her to hospital in their private plane because she might be sick in it. They could have saved her life, but instead they wasted time and called the Flying Doctor. Unsurprisingly she died. They didn't care. They didn't even go to her funeral, or let any of their other slaves attend.

The name of the writer was Breda O'Brien.

'When Mary died the visiting season was over,' said Don.

'A fake review,' said Noël. 'Who would do this?'

'Seamus,' said Don.

She shook her head. 'Seamus hasn't got a computer and wouldn't even know how to turn one on.'

'Breda,' said Don. 'His daughter's name is Breda.'

'We can't prove anything.'

Matthew came into the office. 'You've seen the bad review?'

Noël and Don nodded.

'This will be Seamus's doing,' said Matthew. 'His daughter lives in Perth and her name is Breda.'

'Can you remember her surname?' Don asked.

'No. But I remember hearing that she got married about five years ago. Seamus was fuming because he couldn't afford to go to the wedding. What are we going to do?'

'Sack him,' said Noël.

'I'll second that,' said Matthew.

'Me too,' said Don. 'When?'

'Tomorrow. It's Saturday. Paul will be here. Do you want to come with us, Don?'

'No – it's tempting, but it'd be petty revenge. I'd feel like gloating and that's bad.'

When Noël was angry she became quiet and looked composed. Only Paul knew how enraged she was when, accompanied by

Matthew, they went to see Seamus who was working in the vegetable garden. Ginger was asleep on a pile of weeds.

He heard them approaching and leant on his spade.

'Mr Ryan,' Noël said brusquely.

'What?'

'How is Breda?'

His eyes widened in dismay. He recovered and said, 'Don't know anyone called Breda.'

'Liar,' said Matthew. 'She's your daughter.'

He sighed. 'What of it? If you want this garden weeded stop asking questions that have nothing to do with anything.'

'You were an arrogant dope when you were young, and you're still an arrogant dope.' Noël folded her arms. 'You got your daughter, who had never met any of us, to write a bad review. You can't deny it.'

'I can.'

'You're missing a few brain cells, Seamus,' said Matthew. 'A more intelligent person would have remembered that Breda used to live here and that she got married and moved to Perth. They would have told her to use a false name for her fake review. You told her to lie.'

'I didn't – I swear I didn't.'

'You did. Noël and her family paid for Mary's funeral and offered to pay for the refreshments after the service. You rejected her offer – threw her kindness back in her face. It was you who said you didn't want anyone at the funeral. You're despicable.'

'You're sacked,' Noël said.

Seamus's face lost colour. 'I'm sorry, Mrs Knight.'

'Too late,' she said. 'I want you off this land now.'

'It wasn't like you think. Breda was upset because no one but us was at the funeral. I knew she'd be furious with me if I told her that I wanted it to be private, so I told her that you were all too busy here to come. I didn't tell her to write a review – she did it herself.'

Paul didn't believe him and was thankful that Noël didn't look as if she did either.

'You're still sacked,' she said.

'You can't sack me without notice,' he said with his old belligerence.

'We can. Gross misconduct –'

'You have to pay me two weeks wages in lieu of notice.'

'Only if you have a contract, Mr Ryan. But you don't have a contract, because you refused to sign one – remember? said Noël.'

'Mary had one.'

'She did. But you do not. If you want to take us to court do so.'

'Listen, I can get Breda to delete it.'

'Don't bother,' said Noël. 'Her review is so ludicrous no one will believe it.'

'If that's your attitude, I'll get her to write more bad ones. She can say the food is off and she got food poisoning –'

'Do that and we'll sue for libel,' Noël said calmly. 'And we'll win.'

'Remember what happened last time when you were sued? You lost,' Matthew reminded him. 'Get all your stuff out of your cabin – now. Go and live with your mother.'

'How did you turn out like this, Seamus?' Noël asked as they went to his cabin. 'Bitter, jaundiced – your father wasn't like you and neither was your mother. Juliet and Grace adored your parents. Why are you like this?'

It was clear from his expression that Seamus thought she was softening. 'It was all the bad luck, Mrs Knight. Please give me another chance. I'll make it up to you, I promise.'

'No. You've had enough chances. We are sick of your rudeness and antagonism.'

'And your lies,' Paul added. 'Come to the cabin and get your stuff out.'

When they reached his cabin, Seamus sat on the veranda with his head in his hands. Ginger sat beside him nudging his elbow. Matthew and Paul took all his belongings out of the cabin and put them in his car.

'Do you want the TV, Seamus?' asked Matthew.

'Am I allowed to take it?'

'Yes,' said Noël. 'It was a present to you and Mary. Do you want it?'

He nodded and wiped his eyes.

Paul almost felt sorry for him. 'It's not as if you're going to be homeless,' he said. 'Your mum lives in Cobar.'

Now Seamus was paying the price for his behaviour even Matthew relented. 'You don't have to tell your mum that you've been sacked. Say you left because you wanted to live in the town. Say you've got arthritis or a bad back and the gardening's getting too much for you.' He clapped him on the shoulder. 'Make a new life for yourself in town.'

When Seamus looked up his eyes were red. 'Ginger. Will you let me take Ginger?'

Noël nodded. 'But a two-hour drive in your old banger will upset him. I'll fly him into Cobar for you. Give me your mother's address.'

He picked Ginger up and buried his face in the fur. 'He loves it here. It'd be cruel to take him away.' Tears ran down his face. 'My mum's got a garden, but it's small.'

Paul worried that Noël was going to relent, but she said, 'Tell you what, Seamus, we'll keep an eye on him. He can come to the homestead with us. He'll miss you, but hopefully he'll settle. If he doesn't I'll fly him into Cobar for you. What do you think?'

Seamus nodded. 'Goodbye, Ginger.' He kissed Ginger, put him down and went to his car.

They watched him drive away. Ginger rubbed his head on Matthew's legs.

Paul put his arm around Noël. 'I thought you were going to give him another chance.'

'I nearly did, but I knew that if I had he would be back to his old ways before long.' She picked up Ginger who snuggled contentedly in her arms. 'You're coming to live in the homestead with us.'

'Seamus was a dirty brute – the cabin's filthy,' said Paul.

Noël went inside and wrinkled her nose. 'It stinks.'

'I'll get Coral to clean it,' said Matthew.

'No,' said Noël. 'She's got enough to do.' She put Ginger down. 'Paul and I will do it.'

'I'll help,' said Matthew. 'It won't take long with the three of us. Let's get the windows open – can't stand the pong. The brainless clot didn't even flush the toilet.'

It took longer than they thought. Dishes, pans and cutlery were piled in the sink and the kitchen floor was crusted with dirt and grease. The basin in the shower room was grey rather than white, and the bedlinen was full of Ginger's fur and smelt of sweat.

'I doubt he's cleaned the cabin or changed the sheets since Mary died,' said Paul. He opened a cupboard under the sink and took out detergent, washing up liquid, washing powder, fabric conditioner, furniture polish and an unopened packet of polishing cloths. Noël stripped the bed and she and Matthew took the quilt cover outside and shook it. When she began to put the bed linen in the washing machine Ginger sat on the pillow cases. Noël eased him off, and set the machine to its hottest setting.

Matthew stroked him. 'Funny how Seamus kept the cat clean, but not his cabin.'

By the time the washing machine had finished its cycle the cabin was clean. They hung the bed linen on the rotary clothes line near the cabins. Noël had intended to iron them herself, but they had loaded the iron and ironing board into Seamus's car. When it was dry they took it to the laundry for Olwen to iron.

The next day Noël held an official meeting for the staff to tell them that Seamus had been sacked and the reason why. Their unanimous reaction was relief.

'Did you know the three girls on Tordorrach were Edward Halland's grand-daughters?' Seamus asked his mother.

'Yes, Wendy told me. Didn't you know?'

He shook his head. 'Not till Noël and Paul got married. How would I remember? They left when they were little kids.'

'Didn't you remember their names?'

'I never had anything to do with them.'

'No, I guess not with you being at school most of the time. Anyway, I was so pleased when Wendy told me.'

'Why?'

'They cried and cried when they left; they begged their grandparents to stay, but they'd sold the place to your dad. It was traumatic for them what with their dad dying.'

'And their mother went mad.'

'She didn't go mad. She was okay till she got postnatal depression. When she and Charles first married he taught her to ride and she loved it. She was energetic and always busy. Such a terrible shame that she got postnatal depression. Her daughters were lovely little girls. It was heartrending when they said good-bye to their horses. Even your dad promising he'd look after them and love them made no difference. The poor little mites were inconsolable, which made leaving Tordorrach even harder for their grandparents. Don't you remember?'

Seamus shrugged. 'I was too excited about moving into the homestead. But I do remember the governess crying.'

'Poor Wendy. But she's made a life for herself here. The children at school adore her.' She sighed. 'What a pity you can't work at Tordorrach anymore because of your back. But I do like having you here.'

With Seamus gone the atmosphere on Tordorrach became more relaxed.

'I didn't realise how much his cynicism had affected everyone,' said Grace. Don said that having Seamus so close had been a strain. 'It's good to walk out of my cabin and not see his glares. I could feel his resentment. He seethed whenever he saw me. I'm sure he wished he could thump me.'

Xavier said he could manage on his own till they found a replacement. 'Seamus got everything in great shape – all I have to do is keep it up.'

After a few days of sitting outside Seamus's cabin and mewing, Ginger settled into the homestead.

'He would,' said Friedrich. 'He's got six servants now, rather than one.'

Coral came into the office waving a magazine. 'We've been written up by a food critic in Sydney! A four-page spread with photos!'

I was horrified when I was told to go to this Outback Experience place. I tried to talk my editor out of it. I told her I couldn't ride. She said it didn't matter – I could learn. I said I'd never been to the outback and had no desire to go. That didn't matter either. She told me to look at the website. Although it looked appealing, I still didn't want to go. It was sure to be photo-shopped and the reviews were most likely paid for. I had to be incognito. The thought of having to have riding lessons made me feel ill. She told me to look enthusiastic. That's not easy when you're worried about falling off a horse and breaking your neck. My gloom increased when I discovered I'd have to share a cabin with another single man. Why couldn't it have been an attractive young blonde? I bet he snored. On the plane I tried to work out how I could avoid getting on a horse.

Bad reviews are easier and more fun to write than good ones and I had my one liners ready – rattle on the plate steaks, wichety grubs for breakfast and kangaroo meat with chunks of fur attached to it. I would hate the holiday, but would enjoy writing a vitriolic review. I had my camera ready to take photos of the nauseating food.

The other nine people in the group were excited. My uneasiness grew. When we arrived at Tordorrach, the sight of the cabins dispelled some of my pessimism. The bloke I was sharing with was chatty and already had his eye on one of the girls. I had been so full of trepidation I hadn't even noticed them. We unpacked and walked over to a picturesque courtyard for dinner. The owners ate with us and were interested in our lives. I was posing as a bland public servant.

The food was superb. The presentation wasn't up to much, but when it tastes this good it hardly matters. All the meals were better than anything I've reviewed in five-star hotels. The wines were excellent. For teetotallers there was water, homemade lemonade or fruit juice. I haven't got room to review all the meals, and picking out just one was difficult. So I'll describe the courses I liked best.

The first course was always soup served with wholemeal rolls. My favourite was parsnip. It was tasty, creamy and not too rich. The best main course was duckling with orange sauce. The sauce was piquant and the oranges had been picked from their own trees. The roast potatoes and pumpkin were cooked to perfection. My knife slid through the flesh of the pumpkin as if it were butter.

I had a problem choosing the best dessert, so in the end I went for the most unusual. It was a chocolate and lemon tart. The lemon mousse was deliciously lemony. The dark chocolate topping was decorated with lemon peel strips. Coffee was served with chocolate mints and liqueurs. I chose brandy. By now I had come to expect the best and it was.

My favourite meal was breakfast, because normally I never have time to eat it. The stewed fruit choices were apricots, pears or plums, all from their own orchards. There was apple, apricot or orange juice. However the eggs were cooked they were perfect and accompanied by succulent bacon and grilled tomatoes.

Thankfully, there were two tours of the property. Anxious to get out of riding, I took both. One was a walking tour and the other was a trip in a four-seater plane. During the walking tour we visited the orchards, vegetable gardens, cattle, cow and sheep pastures and the chook houses and pens. Their claim of free-range organic meat, poultry and dairy produce is true. A lovely life and a painless death for the animals is how Matthew, who conducted the tour, described it.

What a holiday it was. The bloke I shared the cabin with didn't snore and he captured a girl. After some persuasion I learnt to ride and surprised myself by how stimulating it was. I had a terrific time, but didn't engage the interest of any of the girls. Maybe next time I come . . .

Chapter 34

Juliet barely managed to conceal her excitement while she and Friedrich waited until Noël had finished entering the wages on the computer. When Noël switched off the computer, Juliet jumped up and ran across the office. 'The most amazing thing.' She thrust a bundle of typewritten pages at Noël.

'What's this?'

'The next bit of the journal. Read it.'

'I haven't got time to read it now.'

'You must. It's only a few pages. I've just typed them out.'

'Why all the excitement?'

Friedrich laughed.

Noël looked exasperated. 'I'm doing the accounts and wages. I haven't got time to read this now.'

'Read it in bed.'

'What's so amazing?'

'Read it. You are not going to believe it!'

Noël looked at Friedrich. 'Is it really that exciting?'

He nodded. 'Oh, yes. And astonishing.'

Yorkshire 1850

My mother heard that I had counteracted her orders.

Predictably she was furious. 'You will regret your actions when the servants rise up against us. They will begin by letting their standards slip. They will become lazy, then insolent. Worse, they will revolt. The French revolution was not that long ago. There will be a guillotine in front of the house and they will all cheer when we are executed.'

I laughed.

'You won't be so cheerful when you are mounting the steps to your death.'

'Tell me, Mama, for I am finding it impossible to understand. Papa's parents were good. How is it that you and Papa were cruel? Did you corrupt him? Was he kind before he married you?'

'You are a fool. They were simpletons.'

'Please answer my question. I wish to be enlightened.'

She looked at me with scorn. 'I hope I die before the peasants start–'

'I hope you die soon, Mama. The servants will eat proper meals. Interfere with my orders and you will be sorry.'

'Those two sluts you have put in one of the guest rooms–'

'They are not sluts - never call them that again.'

She smiled a smile that was not a smile.

At the end of the six-month trial period, Mr Deaville came into my office. He didn't knock. He laid the figures on my desk. He was smiling so I knew the news was bad.

'In compiling the figures I've taken into account the cost of the food given to the workers, the extra cost of lighting, and the wages paid to the extra member of staff needed to prepare the meals,' he said. 'I regret that your predictions were wrong. Profits have decreased, rather than increased.'

I had been so sure that my scheme would work that his words hit me like rocks hurled at my head. 'Are we still making a profit?'

'Of course, but you must now realise that your feeding scheme must cease. It has made the workers sluggish. They are busy thinking about their next free meal instead of concentrating on their work. We can still keep the increased hours, though.'

I loathed his smug expression. 'No,' I said. 'Tomorrow, call a meeting and you can tell them–' I had been going to say that their food breaks would be coming to an end, when I thought of another way to tackle the problem. 'No, I will tell them I will give them one more month for productivity and profits to increase–'

He looked enraged. 'Now listen to me. Your father wanted–'

'What he wanted does not matter. He is dead.'

I made my announcement to the workers the next day. In six months their faces had filled out and they no longer looked pale and exhausted. Until I began to speak they looked happier. When I finished their expressions were bemused.

Immediately after the meeting the foreman hurried up to me as I went to my office. 'Sir, please can I talk to you?'

I showed him into my office and closed the door. Again he refused to sit down and kept looking fearfully at the door. 'It's wrong, Sir,' he whispered. 'The figures are wrong ... they must be. I've kept a record – not written, but in my head.' He saw my expression. 'Sorry, Sir, but I had to speak out.'

'Of course,' I said. 'Please, sit down.'

Reluctantly he pulled out the chair and sat in it as if he expected it to collapse.

I went to the door and locked it. 'Please continue.'

'Production is way up, Sir. And if I'm right then profits must also be up.'

'Yes,' I said softly. 'I was informed that they were down. Someone must have made a mistake. Thank you for alerting me. I will examine the ledgers myself.'

'Please, don't tell–'

'I will keep our conversation confidential. I promise.' I could see that my smile did nothing to reassure him.

'But if I'm wrong, Sir?'

'I will see it as a genuine mistake. As you said, you didn't keep a written record.'

'Will I lose my job?'

'Not while I am the owner of this mill,' I said with more certainty than I felt.

What the foreman said made sense. With the increased hours and healthier workers I had doubted Deaville's figures. Now I was sure that he had not miscalculated. He had lied.

It was three days before I had the opportunity to examine the ledgers. Deaville kept the manager's office locked and I didn't know if there was another key. I could have checked the ledgers in his presence, but he was so devious I wanted to have evidence of his lying before I confronted him. I found a duplicate key on the ring my father had left in my drawer. When Deaville left for the day I watched from the window as he mounted his horse and rode away. Then I went into his office.

The foreman was right. The profits had increased so much that Deaville could not have possibly miscalculated or made a genuine mistake. The cost of the food for the mill workers was minimal, as was the cost of the extra fuel for running the machinery and lighting. The following morning I arrived at the mill early and sat in his office.

His expression when he arrived was accusing. 'What are you doing in here?'

I gestured to the ledgers. 'You lied, Deaville. You are a cheat. You are sacked.'

I had anticipated an argument, but he left without a word. I thought that was the end of it. I should have known better.

To reorganise the office I needed advice. I called the foreman into my office. 'I have to appoint another manager. Would you like the position, Mr Halland?'

'Ah!' exclaimed Noël. She jumped out of bed.

Paul looked startled. 'What?'

She pulled on her dressing gown and ran to the door. 'I'll be back in a minute.' She hurried to Juliet and Friedrich's apartment.

Juliet looked gleeful, when she opened the door and saw Noël. 'You've got to that bit? It's not a common name. Now if it was Holland . . .'

'But our ancestors came out on the first fleet as convicts.'

'You're the mathematician – work it out. Four grandparents, eight great-grandparents, sixteen . . .'

'Okay, okay. How can we find out?'

'Well, I don't want to wreck the surprise.'

'There's another one?'

'Read to the end.'

'Just a second, Juliet.' Noël hurried to the office. Juliet and Friedrich followed. She went to Juliet's desk and pulled the original journal towards her.

'What are you doing?'

She opened the drawer and took out a magnifying glass 'Checking something just to make sure.' She turned the pages of the book and scanned the lines of writing.

'What are you looking for?' asked Friedrich.

'I want to make sure that it is Halland and not Holland.'

Juliet pulled a face. 'I didn't think of that. I could have made a mistake. I'd be so disappointed –'

'Here it is – definitely an 'a'. You were right. It is Halland not Holland. What a coincidence.' She went to the computer. 'We must be able to investigate this.'

'Wait,' said Juliet. 'Wait till you get to the next revelation. Keep reading.'

Chapter 35

He looked startled. 'Sir, I'm not sure I'm capable enough.' His humility made me more certain that I had chosen the right man. 'Mr Halland, you supervise the workers. You are honest and resourceful. You knew the figures were wrong by calculating things in your head. You may think about it, if you wish.'

'Yes, Sir. I will give you my answer tomorrow.'

'I need to ask you a few questions.'

He nodded.

'You may not know the answers, but if not you may be able to tell me who will. Why is there no accountant here?'

'There was one. Deaville sacked him. He said he was slow.'

'Do you know if that was true?'

'It wasn't, but you might dismiss my opinion – he was my cousin. No, he wasn't slow. He was meticulous, careful – he picked things up that another person would have missed – that's why he was sacked.'

'Are you saying ... suggesting ... what are you suggesting?'

'There was ... something going on that shouldn't have been.'

'Please be specific.'

He took a deep breath. 'Mr Deaville was stealing. Not much when your father was alive – but afterwards ...'

'How long have we been without an accountant?'

'My cousin was sacked six months before your father died.'

'Why wasn't he replaced?'

'Mr Deaville said he could do the accounts himself. Your father agreed. He thought it would save money.'

'Did your cousin find another position?'

'Yes, Sir.'

'A pity. I was going to ask if he would like to work here again.'

'I'll ask him, Sir. I'm sure he would. He is unhappy where he is now.'

To my relief Mr Halland accepted the position of manager and his cousin was re-employed as the accountant. A replacement foreman was found from the pool of mill workers. He came highly recommended by Mr Halland.

Just as I was congratulating myself that none of my mother's predictions had come true, Mr Halland hurried into my office with my sister. She was panic stricken and gasping for breath.

I leapt out of my chair. 'Imogen, what's happened?'

'That weasel Deaville. He's always with Mama. I've heard them plotting. I couldn't hear everything they said, but I've been watching. Two hours ago some men arrived. They're going to put you in an insane asylum. The papers are signed. They're waiting for you to come home.'

Mr Halland stood up straight. 'You must stay here, Sir.' He had transformed himself from a nervous and uncertain man into a warrior.

I tried to think of a strategy. 'If I don't arrive home they will come here for me.'

'I will rouse the workers, Sir. They won't let you be taken.'

This was unthinkable. 'No. They will end up with nothing,' I said. 'They might go to jail, or worse they might be hanged.'

'No, Sir. We have to make a stand. We must win. The lives of good people are at stake. First we have to protect you. Go to my house – it's not much–'

'It's better than a lunatic asylum,' I said. 'Imogen, go home. Pretend you've just been riding. You know nothing about this. You have not seen me since this morning when we had breakfast.'

She stared at me in terror. 'She'll beat me. Let me come with you.'

'We can't impose–'

'Yes, Sir, you can. If they come here searching for you, I will say that your sister arrived in a panic and I showed her to your office and you both left shortly after. They'll know that you have escaped.'

'Don't implicate yourself.'

'I won't, Sir. I'll pretend I don't know what's going on.'

He gave me the directions to his house and wrote a note for me to give to his wife. Imogen and I mounted our horses. Mr Halland lived about three miles away from the mill and we found his house easily. It was larger than I expected and set in a clearing in the forest by a stream. We rode over a wooden bridge and were tying our horses to a tree when Mrs Halland came out of the house.

'Are you lost?'

I gave her the note her husband had written.

She looked appalled even before she finished reading it.

'I'm so sorry to intrude.'

She smiled. 'It's no trouble.' She looked at Imogen. 'You look the same age as our daughter. You can share her room.' Then she scrutinised me. 'Andrew has told me all about you. You can share our son's room. Come inside – you are welcome.'

When this is all over, I told myself, I will reward the Hallands.

Andrew came home and I went outside to meet him. 'They came with straightjackets,' he said before he had dismounted from his horse. 'Deaville was with them. I told them that your sister had arrived in a panic and you both left. Deaville was fuming and kept muttering about how you'd escaped. His language when he mentioned your sister was crude. He asked if I had any idea where you were, but I pleaded ignorance and said I thought you had gone home. I have been demoted back to foreman – he has put himself back in the manager's position. I am thankful he didn't dismiss me – I doubt he has any idea that I am colluding with you.'

'I am sorry, I wish I could be optimistic-'

'Sir, the workers are angry. Deaville has already stopped their food. I think they may riot and I will riot with them. Apparently your mother is the owner until you have been found and put away. She has been given power of attorney.'

It wasn't until we were having a dinner of rabbit stew that Imogen provided me with a weapon.

'Deaville and Mama were always sneaking off to her bedroom so they could conspire.' She saw my expression. 'What's wrong?'

'Nothing.' Imogen was too innocent to know the real reason they had gone into our mother's bedroom. 'How often did he visit Mama?' I asked casually.

'All the time.'

'Every day?'

'No, but most days.'

I was careful not to lead her. 'How long has he been visiting her?'

'Ages.'

Andrew and I looked at each other.

'Did he visit her when Papa was alive?'

'Sometimes. Not as often.'

'Was he there at the same time as our father?'

'No. Is it important?'

'Very.'

'You look happy.'

'I am.'

She frowned. 'Why?'

'I'll tell you one day.' For my plan to succeed, I had to know if the servants knew him, so I asked Imogen, 'When Deaville comes to the house, does he come to the front door?'

She frowned. 'I don't think so. He leaves his horse outside if it's not wet, or in the visitors' stables if it is. I've seen him enter through the door leading to the room where Mama writes all her letters.'

'We have to act quickly,' said Andrew.

'The men with Deaville - the ones with the straightjackets - did they go in the same direction as he did?' I asked him.

'No. They were in a carriage. He was on a horse. They went one way and he stayed on to tell us all what would happen in the future. When he left he went towards Shuttleton – to report to your mother, no doubt. But as one of the men got into the carriage I heard him say they'd come back tomorrow. I don't know if he was a doctor.'

'We must be careful. Tomorrow, if Deaville goes towards Shuttleton, come here and tell me.'

He looked apprehensive. 'What are you going to do?'

I didn't want to corrupt my sister or Andrew's daughter so I waited until they had gone to bed. Mrs Halland was washing the dishes while Andrew and I sat at the table with cups of tea.

'Deaville might not visit my mother tomorrow, but as soon as you see him going in that direction tell me. I'll go to the house and challenge her – the both of them. I'll wait until they are in the bedroom, of course.'

I was grateful when Andrew said, 'I'll come with you.'

Chapter 36

One Tuesday evening Paul had just landed the plane and was leaving the hangar when he saw Bill's car driving toward the homestead. When he parked under a tree and got out, Paul walked over to him. 'Bill, what are you doing here? You should have told us you were coming.'

'Dad, can I talk to you?'

Bill's sombre expression and tone alarmed Paul. 'What's wrong? Holly –'

'Holly's fine. Mum's fine. It's about me. Can we go somewhere private?'

Hell, thought Paul. *He's going to tell me he's gay.*

'Of course. Let's go for a walk. Do you fancy going to the billabong?'

Bill nodded and they walked to the billabong in silence. Paul tried to work out what he would say. He hoped he would be able to tone down his reaction and not look disgusted or upset. He felt it was important to be honest but supportive. By the time they reached the billabong twenty minutes later he had it worked out. *Bill, you're my son*, he would say. *I want you to be happy. I admit I'm disappointed, but that's selfishness on my part. I was looking forward to having grandchildren. I'll support you – I want to meet your friend. I hope I'll like him, but if I don't I'll still love you and won't make things uncomfortable for you.*

They stood looking at the water.

'This is difficult for me, Dad . . .'

'Have you done anything illegal?' Paul asked, praying that Bill's news was not even worse than he feared.

'No!'

'Lost your job? Been sacked?'

'No. When Linda and I spent the week here it changed everything for me.'

Paul tried to think what other man could have caused Bill's realisation that he was gay. He'd never thought about it, but he was certain that the groom who assisted Vasco during the rides was heterosexual. He tried to look understanding, but braced himself for Bill's confession.

'I know I'm a disappointment to you.'

'No, Bill, you're not.'

'Holly's got everything sorted out – great job, good at it and gets promoted. Me? I just bumble along not having a clue about what I want to do.'

'You'll find your way one day. I am disappointed, but only because I know you're discontented and restless and there's nothing I can do to help.'

'There is something you can do.'

Here it comes, thought Paul.

'The thing is, Dad, I want to live here.'

'Here? You mean on Tordorrach?'

'Yeah. When you emailed me about Seamus leaving I thought maybe –'

Paul laughed, partly from relief and partly from amusement at his own ludicrous assumptions. Bill had never shown any sign that he was anything other than heterosexual.

Bill looked crestfallen. 'I take it that means you don't want me.'

'You wanting to live here was the last thing I was imagining.'

'I'll do anything that's needed – but if you don't want me I'll understand. You'll have to ask the others – I know that.'

'Won't you miss Sydney?'

Bill smiled. 'You sound like Holly and me when we tried to persuade you not to come to Cobar.'

'I know Linda's here, but –'

'Sydney's changed, Dad. It's edgy. No one's as relaxed. You left Sydney at the right time.'

'When you and Linda were here on holiday you seemed unhappy.'

'Not unhappy. I was in shock. Wanting to live here – I also felt idiotic – I was so antagonistic when Holly and I first came to Cobar, so I didn't know how you'd react when I said I wanted to live here.'

'What made you realise?'

'The first night we were here I woke up – the shutters were open and I could see the stars. I went onto the veranda and I was overcome . . . the air smelt so pure. I've never felt such joy. I knew that I never wanted to go back to Sydney. I was a bit nervous about riding a horse, but it was stimulating even when we were just walking. It was easier than I expected. When I cantered, I wanted to yell I was so exhilarated.'

On the way back to the homestead Paul hoped that Bill's enthusiasm would not wane once he was on Tordorrach. Seamus's cabin was empty and Bill could move into that. 'When you say you'll do anything –'

'Okay, I know I've never done anything with horses or the land, but then neither had you. I can learn. Vasco can teach me to ride and Xavier can teach me about gardening. I'll even wash the dishes and do the ironing.'

Not wanting Bill to feel intimidated by being interviewed by five people, Paul took him into the office. Noël was alone.

'Hello, Bill. I didn't expect to see you – is something wrong?'

'No,' said Paul. 'He's got something to ask you.'

Paul thought Noël would look sceptical, but she said, 'Wonderful, I certainly approve, but I'll have to consult the others.' She stood up. 'Give me a moment.'

Ten minutes later she returned with Juliet, Grace, Friedrich and Guy. 'Welcome to the team. When can you start?'

Bill grinned. 'Thanks. I've got to give two weeks' notice.'

'He can live in Seamus's cabin,' said Noël. 'Do you have to rush back to Sydney?'

'No, I've taken some annual leave.'

'Then stay for dinner and we'll show you your new home. If you like it you can stay there till you go back to Sydney.'

Grace, Juliet and Noël had chosen the furniture in the cabin Seamus and Mary had occupied.

Paul opened the door and showed Bill around. 'What do you think?'

Bill grinned. 'Fabulous, Dad.'

'There's no TV –'

'That's okay – there's not much worth watching on it anyway.'

'There's a cinema in the homestead. When you're in Sydney bring all your DVDs. Most of the ones we've got here are operas.'

In bed that night Paul confessed to Noël that Bill was prone to enthusiasms that died as fast as they began, and he worried that this might be another one. 'I fear that Linda might be the deciding factor. There are no jobs for him in Cobar, but at least he'll be closer to her if he lives on Tordorrach.'

'If it is just another enthusiasm, at least he'll know and so will we.' She kissed him. 'Life is full of false starts. I hope for his sake and ours that he loves it here as much as you do.'

Paul's doubts about his son's dedication were banished when Bill proved himself invaluable and was content with his new life. He loved the cabin, which was bigger than the flat he and Holly had shared. Everyone praised his work and attitude.

'Much better than Seamus,' said Matthew. 'Good worker, willing to learn and we all like him.'

'I'm not as good a gardener.'

'You'll learn.'

Bill looked up from emptying the vegetable and fruit peelings from the homestead kitchen into the wheelbarrow. 'Hi, Dad. Is that the time or are you home early?'

Paul grinned. 'I'm later than usual.'

Bill checked his watch. 'At work I was a clock watcher. As soon as I got to work I couldn't wait for it to be lunchtime. After lunch I wanted it to be going home time. Now I hardly ever look at my watch. But I do look forward to Fridays when you bring Linda here.'

Paul walked with him to the compost heaps.

Bill gestured to the barrow. 'Only a while ago this would have been just a pile of vegetable peelings to me – now there're valuable for compost. I never thought I'd be enthusiastic about vegetable peelings or mucking out the stables.'

They reached the compost heaps and Bill tipped the contents of the barrow on top of one of the heaps and covered it with the sacking. 'Everything's as different as it's possible to be.'

'Yes, I know.'

'Do you?'

Paul smiled. 'The outback is slightly different to Sydney Harbour.'

Bill put the barrow in the shed. 'It's not just the locations, Dad. People are often attracted to the same type of person, but Mum and Noël are nothing alike in either looks or character.'

Bill was right, Paul reflected. Being married to Noël was a complete contrast to being married to Kathryn, who was an excellent cook. In spite of her full-time job she had always had dinner in the oven when Paul got home from work. The only meal Noël managed to prepare was breakfast. Even then the kitchen was strewn with pots, plates and tea-towels when she'd finished. When they were not dining with Juliet, Friedrich, Grace and Guy, Coral cooked their dinner. Kathryn was tidy. Noël left her clothes on the floor when she took them off and the bathroom was a jumble of bottles and towels. She never put the top back on the toothpaste or her toothbrush in its holder. If it hadn't been for Olwen their apartment would have been chaotic. He knew that if they hadn't had someone to tidy up after her, he would have been irritated by her untidiness.

Conversely Noël's desk in the office was tidy and her reference books were arranged neatly on the shelves in alphabetical order, and her organisational skills were exemplary. In some respects Noël and Kathryn were similar. They were good tennis players, they dressed elegantly rather than fashionably, both were interesting conversationalists, loved opera and classical music and they deplored the celebrity culture.

Bill became a competent rider and was good with the horses. He found mucking out the stables and grooming the horses satisfying. He cleaned the tack and helped Xavier in the garden. He and Vasco were the same age and became friends. In the middle of December he announced that he wanted to stay for good. Noël bought him jodhpurs, riding boots and a hat for Christmas. Paul bought him flying lessons.

Ralph was relieved that he was not losing either Paul or Linda. Now he had his pilot's licence Paul flew to Cobar and back to Tordorrach every day during the week. On Friday evenings Linda went to Tordorrach with him and returned on Monday morning.

'The only thing I like about leaving Tordorrach on Mondays,' Linda told him, 'is the plane trip – it's spellbinding.'

'Glad you trust me not to crash,' Paul said.

Ω

Holly had a boyfriend and spent Christmas with his family. Kathryn spent Christmas alone in her flat. She had considered going on a cruise, but recalled the one she had been on with Tim, where most of the passengers had been either couples or young men and women. Not wanting to be viewed as a lone woman desperate for a man, she decided to stay at home. She invited one of the women at work to spend Christmas day with her, but she said she was spending it with her newly widowed sister.

'My life has become barren, routine and lonely,' Kathryn reflected. She loathed living alone, although it was a relief not to be living with Tim. When she bought the flat she had hoped that one of her children, who were always complaining about the tiny flat they shared, would come and live with her, but they turned down her offer.

'I'm sure you'll find another man soon,' Holly had said caustically. 'And we'll be kicked out. At least we're independent. I don't want to depend on anyone else ever again.'

'And if one of us moved in with you the other one would have to find somewhere else to live – the rent on our flat is too much for one,' Bill had said more tactfully. 'But thanks for asking.'

Used to the spacious house in Kirribilli, and Tim's house in Point Piper she felt claustrophobic in the flat with its small rooms and tiny balcony overlooking the sea. She missed the garden, the tennis court and swimming pool, but most of all she missed Paul and the family life they had built together. When she had left Paul she lost all her friends who had liked Paul and disliked Tim. She had a few new friends, but they did not compensate for those she had lost.

It was one of her ex-friends who had told her Tim was seeing other women. 'Girls really – a lot younger than you, Kathryn,' she had said not trying to hide her glee. 'He must have married you so he could get his hands on your money.'

Until Paul and Noël married she had been optimistic that he still loved her in spite of his harsh words when she had arrived unannounced in Cobar. She convinced herself that he was punishing her because he was still humiliated and bitter that she had left him for Tim.

Bill's gift of an exquisite oil painting by Grace cheered her, but his email on Christmas Eve plunged her back into despair.

Hi Mum,

    I've decided to stay on Tordorrach. I don't miss Sydney or the walk to the station and the journey to work on a crowded train. Here I don't have to worry about how I look, or listen to the puerile office gossip. Every morning I get out of bed excited about the day ahead. If I want a piece of fruit I just go to the orchard and pick it. Coral lent me some of her cookbooks and gave me a few cooking lessons.

I haven't done any ironing since I got here. I was prepared to do it, but Olwen, the lovely housekeeper, does it for me. Noël and Dad paid for her and her husband to have solar panels installed on their property for Christmas. Friedrich and Juliet bought her a digital radio. I bought her a coffee-maker. Grace and Guy gave her a puppy because her and her husband's beloved sheepdog died a few weeks ago. She cried when she saw the puppy, was overwhelmed by all the presents and said she didn't deserve them. We all assured her that she did.

Tonight we'll be having dinner with everyone in the courtyard. Coral's made lots of salads and for dessert we're having her ice cream, which is the best I've ever tasted. Tomorrow Noël, Dad and I are having lunch with Grace and Guy in Juliet and Friedrich's apartment. It's Noël's birthday on Christmas Day. I was stuck on what to buy her till I remembered that you and Dad sponsored an elephant for me. So for Christmas I've got her a tiger, and for her birthday an elephant. On Boxing Day I'm going to Cobar to have lunch with Linda and her parents.

How are you spending Christmas?

'Looking forward to going back to work,' whispered Kathryn.

Chapter 37

Yorkshire 1850

ndrew and I had been watching the house for hours. From our location in the bushes we had a good view of my mother's bedroom window. Candles in glass holders stood on the window sill. Deaville's horse was in the stable. The saddle had been removed, which signified that he would stay the night and creep out before the servants woke in the morning. It was after midnight when a silhouette appeared at the window. The candles were extinguished and the curtains closed. The room was dark. Doubts assailed me. Deaville might leave the house before I could catch them together. Not wanting to burst into my mother's bedroom only to find her alone, we waited.

'Sir, I'll watch the stables while you go to the house. If he comes out I'll whistle.'

'He might see you. He's evil enough to attack.'

Andrew went to the nearest tree and climbed up into the branches. 'You've got the candles, holders and the matches, Sir?'

I nodded and walked to the back of the house, avoiding the gravel path. At the servants' door I stuck the candle in the holder, put it on the ground, lit it and cautiously pulled the door open. I crept up the stone staircase. It was colder there than it was outside. I gently pushed the baize door open and entered the area where the main bedrooms were. I reached my mother's door and paused. My heart was pounding. My hopes that I would hear a male voice were in vain. I took a deep breath and twisted the doorknob. It was open. My first piece of luck. Even with my candle the room was dark and the drapes surrounding the bed were tightly closed. I made a barking noise and heard a male voice I recognised.

'What's that? I thought you kept the dogs outside.'

'I do.' There was a shuffling and then the drapes were pulled back and I heard my mother's voice. 'What is that light? Who is there?'

I went into the room, strode to the windows and pulled open the curtains. Moonlight flooded the room. With the flame from the candle in my hand I lit the others on the window sill. 'Good evening, Deaville.'

'You!'

'What are you doing here?' my mother hissed.

'I, as the owner of this house, have every right to be here. What shall I do? Call the servants and let them witness this scene? A respectable widow in bed with a man who was my employee until I sacked him for dishonesty. Or are you going to leave quietly, Deaville? Would you like to go with him, Mama? I won't stop you.'

'Get out of this house. There is an order for you to be locked away in an asylum for the insane.'

'I know.' I put the candle holder on the window sill. 'With me locked away you would become the owner of this house and the mill. But it is not going to-'

She pushed back the blankets. 'Grab him,' she ordered Deaville. 'We will tie him up. We can take him to the asylum tomorrow.'

He sprang out of bed and came towards me. He was taller and heavier than I was, but I had one advantage. I was fully clothed and wore riding boots. He was naked. Before he was close enough to touch me I kicked him as hard as I could in the groin. He yelled and doubled over. I pushed him and he fell to the floor groaning. Then he was quiet and I hoped he had passed out. I ran to the door. 'Help, help!' I yelled, praying that if Deaville was known to any of the servants, they would not recognise him without his clothes on.

My mother jumped out of bed and ran towards me. 'What are you doing?'

I punched her in the face, picked her up and threw her on the bed. 'Mama, I am calling for help. We have an intruder. He assaulted you. I heard your cry and came in.' I hauled Deaville to his feet just as my mother's lady's maid rushed into the room.

'Madame!'

'We have an intruder,' I told her. 'Please, get help.'

She looked at the naked man who was moaning and struggling to free himself from my grip. She ran to the door screaming so loudly I was sure Andrew would be able to hear her. I shoved Deaville back on the floor where he lay cursing. He scrabbled about and managed to get to his knees. When he tried to grab my leg I kicked him in the face.

The first to arrive was a footman. 'Sir!' he shouted when he saw me. 'Are you hurt?'

'No, but my mama is. Tie this man up – he attacked her. We'll take him to the authorities tomorrow.'

'I'll get some rope.'

Blood was running down my mother's face. My signet ring had cut her nose. 'You won't get away with this,' she snarled when the footman ran out. Her lady's maid was still in the corridor screaming.

I strode to the bed and gripped my mother's arms. 'What are you going to tell them, Mama?' I whispered. 'That you are a fornicator, a slut or worse? Was this going on when my father was alive?' I shook her. 'You will say what I tell you to say. I will come back and live in this house and you will be under my authority.' I snatched a diamond necklace from her dressing table and shoved it in the pocket of the trousers Deaville had laid across a chair. 'He tried to rob you.'

The footman returned with three others. They tied Deaville up and carried him down to the cellar. The butler arrived and soothed the hysterical lady's maid. I went back to Andrew and told him what had transpired.

He was astounded. 'When I heard the screaming I thought the worst. I didn't anticipate such a good result.'

'Neither did I. It was only when my mother told him to grab me and tie me up that I had the idea.'

Andrew took my hand and shook it. 'Well done, Sir. You are safe, the mill is safe. The workers are safe.'

'And you are the manager,' I said.

We went over to the stables to our horses. One of the grooms was there. He was in his nightshirt. 'Sir, did I hear screaming or was it foxes?'

'Screaming. We had an intruder. He injured my mother. We tied him up and put him in the cellar. Please go back to bed and do not worry.'

'Shall I take the saddles off the horses?'

'No, I'll do it. Andrew, you can stay here tonight. I'll take you to one of the guest rooms,' I said when the groom had climbed the ladder to his room.

'My wife will worry.'

'If you stay here she will worry over nothing. If you leave here you will be at risk from highwaymen and your horse might stumble in the darkness. You can leave at dawn.'

'Yes, that is sensible. Thank you, Sir.'

As we walked to the house I put my hand on his arm. 'Andrew, I have a request.'

'Sir?'

'We've been through a great deal together. If it had not been for you I would be in the lunatic asylum. I owe you–'

'Please don't think about it.'

'I do think about it. I want you to stop calling me Sir.'

'What shall I call you? Mr Carlyle?'

'At the mill call me Mr Carlyle. At other times call me Adam.'

'Heavens,' exclaimed Noël. 'I suppose I shouldn't be surprised. It's a family name after all.'

'That's not the surprise I was talking about,' said Juliet. 'Read on – just a bit further.'

As I showed Andrew to the guest room, which was for our most important visitors, I asked him, 'Deaville's clothes - should we allow him to get dressed in the morning before we take him?'

'No. The worse he looks at his trial the more believable your story. His clothes will make him appear more respectable.'

Later that morning Deaville was arrested and imprisoned. At his trial he no longer looked commanding. Dressed in prison garb with a bruised face where I had kicked him, his demeanour was defeated and frightened. He was found guilty of assault, attempted rape, and the attempted theft of a valuable necklace. My mother did not defend him. She said what I told her to say. He protested his innocence, but no one believed him. His truthful account of events was dismissed and declared ludicrous. No one believed that a respectable woman who had been recently widowed would take a disgraced employee to her bed. His story that I had put the necklace in his pocket was treated with derision.

When the judge put on his black cap and pronounced the death sentence I justified my actions to allay my guilt. He had stolen money from the mill, and had his theft been discovered and reported to the police he would have been tried and hung anyway. He had plotted with my mother to have me committed to a lunatic asylum. The wretched lives of the mill workers he managed had not affected him. My guilt that I was responsible for his fate lasted until I arrived home. When we got out of the carriage my mother went straight to her rooms. I followed. If she mixed with her friends she might concoct a plausible story and I would still be in danger.

I rang the bell for her maid. 'Mama,' I said solicitously, 'This has been a terrible ordeal for you. You are retiring from society for good. You are moving out of these rooms. Imogen will move into them. Your maid will help you move.'

She took a deep breath, but before she could speak her maid arrived.

'My mother is retiring from society and is moving out of these rooms. Please help her. She won't need many clothes – Imogen can have them.'

My mother gasped.

'Mama, you know it's for the best. This has been torture for you. Come along now, I will help you to your new rooms.'

Her maid was collecting her things and had her back to me. I pulled my mother to her feet and dragged her from the room. Her new rooms were for our less important guests and consisted of a bedroom and dressing room. They were smaller than the sumptuous bedroom she had had since her marriage, but still comfortable. She tried to struggle, but my grip was too firm.

I kept my tone gentle and ignored her groan of distaste when we entered the bedroom. 'Now you have retired from society, you won't need a lady's maid – you can dress and wash yourself and do your own hair. You won't need a boudoir either. Housemaids will bring you food, clean and tidy your rooms, empty your chamber pot, fill your bath and light your fire.'

'There is still an order for your committal to a lunatic asylum, Adam.'

'Thank you for reminding me, Mama.'

Her maid came in with some of her clothes and put them in the dressing-room. I locked the door to my mother's new rooms and followed the lady's maid into the corridor and back into the rooms that would now belong to Imogen.

'My mother will no longer require a lady's maid, but,' I went on quickly when I saw her fearful expression, 'Imogen will. These will be her rooms now. Would you be willing to be her–'

'Oh, yes, Sir, thank you, Sir.'

'Did you like being my mother's lady's maid?'

She looked disconcerted.

'You can be honest with me. I know the servants were treated appallingly and would have not received any reference if they left. I want you to know that if you wish to leave I will give you a reference – a good one. Do you want to leave?'

She beamed. 'Not now, Sir.'

I returned to my mother with a pen, ink and writing paper. I gestured to the desk. 'Sit here. You are going to write a letter.'

She did not move.

'If necessary, I will drag you over. I will be as rough as I need to be.'

She glared at me with venom, got up slowly and sat at the desk.

'Write our address at the top of the letter.'

She did as asked, although as slowly as she dared.

'Now, write this. I will dictate slowly as you seem to have lost some of your wits. "Dear" – now write the names of the doctors. "My son, who was to have been committed to your care, has redeemed himself, as you have no doubt heard. We have reached an understanding, which is agreeable to us both"'

My mother threw down her pen. Ink blots spattered the paper. She raised her hand with the intention of knocking over the ink pot.

I gripped her wrist. 'However long it takes you will write this letter.' I twisted her wrist. She winced in pain. 'Remember, Mama, how you beat me when I was a child for the smallest misdemeanour? Sometimes I had no idea why you were beating me. Understand this – I will beat you – in the same place with the same cane. Unlike you I will not enjoy it, but I will do it if I have to – understand?' I increased my grip on her wrist. She whimpered and nodded. I released her and gave her the pen. I pushed a clean sheet of paper in front of her. 'Write.'

She started to weep.

'You used to beat me when I cried. Fortunately I am not like you. But I will beat you if you refuse to write this letter.'

She took an hour to write it. I put it in the envelope she had addressed. 'Just in case you have any plan to go downstairs and take it out of the box, Mama, I am locking you in your rooms. I will tell the servants that you are frightened of being attacked by another intruder. I warn you that if you cause trouble for me your privileges will be removed.'

'I have no privileges now.'

'You will have someone to bring your food, empty your chamber pot, wash your clothes and clean and tidy your room. Any rebellion on your part and these privileges will be withdrawn until you have learned to behave.'

I don't know if I learned to be cunning, or if necessity made me cunning, or whether it was a trait I had always had, but I began to anticipate my mother's actions and calculate what machinations she might try. Without her maid she would find it difficult to get dressed and impossible to do her hair. I had left her with enough clothes, but none of them were the elaborate dresses she favoured. Imogen took them to the sewing room and asked the seamstress to restyle them for her. My mother's wedding ring was now her only jewellery. I visited her every evening. At first she was aggressive and threatening. When those tactics proved futile, she began to beg and wheedle. That didn't work either, and her growing bewilderment satisfied me. She tried tears. 'Do you find pleasure in torturing me – your own mother?'

'Yes,' I lied. 'You took pleasure in torturing Imogen and me. You would have had me committed to a lunatic asylum. This is my revenge.'

In truth, I found our encounters intolerable. I knew that if I revealed my real feelings she would see this as a weakness and take advantage. The only reason I visited her was to watch her and make sure she was not involved in any plotting.

Chapter 38

January 2016

'Kathryn wants to come and visit Bill. He got an email from her last night,' Paul told Noël as he was getting ready for work.

'That's all right.'

He took a shirt out of the wardrobe. 'Is it?'

'Paul, of course. She is his mother. It's summer. She can stay in one of the cabins. I know you don't want to see her –'

'It's not that.'

'What is it then?'

'Our life here's so perfect. I don't want her causing any disruption.'

'How will she cause disruption?'

Paul went to the mirror and put on his tie. 'I don't know. She could invite Bill to Sydney. Why does she want to come here? I don't trust her.'

'You trusted her once, surely?'

'Yes, but then –'

'She succumbed to temptation. Did Bill seem keen to have her here?'

'Yes.'

'Well, then, she must come. Forbidding her to visit here will cause more disruption than having her stay. Don't force Bill to choose between you.'

'I'm not. I wouldn't.'

She put her arms around him. 'No, but telling Kathryn not to come here will make things awkward for him. His loyalty lies with both of you.'

Kathryn packed for her one week stay on Tordorrach, hoping that she was doing the right thing. She thought about all the things that could turn her visit into a disaster. *What if Noël is cold? What if everyone ignores me?* The thought made her want to email Bill and tell him she was too sick to come, but her desire to see him outweighed her trepidation.

That he now lived on Tordorrach made her understand how much she had failed, not only as a wife but as a mother. Holly rarely visited her and the second bedroom was never used. Bill had uploaded the digital photos of Paul and Noël's wedding on Facebook. She wanted to scroll past them or hide them, but curiosity compelled her to look. Hearing about Noël made her feel even more inferior. Noël's misfortunes had been caused by bad luck and fate. Kathryn's unhappiness was her own fault.

As the bus neared Cobar, Kathryn's nervousness increased. She prayed she would be able to behave with dignity when she saw Paul again, and was introduced to Noël, who, from what she had heard from Holly and Bill, was a paragon. Her amazingly deep blue eyes had been evident in the wedding photographs. She hoped she would find something to dislike about Noël.

Bill met her in Cobar. He looked happy and relaxed. He kissed her and carried her cases to the car. 'You look as if you could do with a good holiday, Mum.'

'Thanks, Bill. Trust you to be so brutally honest.'

'Well you look wound up – fraught. You've lost too much weight.'

'How are the flying lessons going?'

'Really well. Have you . . . got any er –'

'Male admirers?'

He grinned. 'Yeah.'

'Being twice divorced puts them off. And most men – even older ones want someone younger.'

He put her cases in the boot. 'Been to the opera?'

'Once or twice. I hate going alone.'

Bill said nothing. They got into the car. Uncomfortable with the silence she said, 'I saw *Find My Family* – the one about Sylvia Halland. Did she ever make contact?'

'No. And no one who knew her came forward either.'

'Strange. Perhaps she went to New Zealand.'

'It's a mystery,' said Bill. 'And it doesn't look as if it's ever going to be solved.'

'The programme mentioned that she might have returned to Cobar and discovered her husband was dead and Tordorrach had been sold,' Kathryn said as they drove out of Cobar. 'If she knew she was a widow she might have remarried –'

'But someone must know who or where she is,' Bill interrupted. 'Even if she didn't see the programme –'

'I was going to say that she might not have seen the programme because she's no longer in Australia. She could be in America, Canada or even in Europe. If she didn't renew her old passport, which was under her maiden name, she might have applied for a one in her new married name.'

'Friedrich reckons she's got a new family and doesn't want to be found.'

'If that's the case I suppose she'll never come forward – and if she's in another country she'll have no idea her children are looking for her. They were only young when she left, so she probably thinks they've forgotten her. Very sad.'

'Yes.'

'What are the plans when we get to Tordorrach?'

'We're having dinner with everyone tonight. It's too windy to eat in the courtyard, so it'll be in one of the dining rooms.'

'One of the dining rooms. How many are there?'

'Three – four if you count the one off the main kitchen where the visitors eat when it's too windy in the courtyard. I did tell you there are three apartments.'

'I remember. Will your father be there?'

Bill nodded. 'Everyone will be there. You're not going to make a scene, are you?'

'Bill! Do you think I'm a melodramatic idiot?'

'I mean . . . you're not going to cry or anything.'

'No,' she said softly. 'I've done all my crying.'

Kathryn looked at the collection of cabins among bushes and trees. 'What a glorious setting,' she said as Bill took her cases out of the boot.

'You'll notice there aren't any gum trees – there're too much of a fire hazard.'

She followed him up the steps of one of the cabins to a small veranda.

'This is yours for the week,' he said as he opened the door, which led straight into the bedroom. He put her cases near the wardrobe. 'Right, I'll let you settle in. You'll have breakfast with me in my cabin and you'll have dinners with everyone else in the homestead. I'm in the cabin with the garden table and chairs on the veranda. Dinner's at seven. I'll come and get you.'

The cabin smelt of polish, and walls were of rough plaster and painted cream, which made it look like the cabin of an early settler. The floorboards were bare, but varnished. The plain furniture was indigo with worn patches. She thought it was old, but when she opened a drawer in the chest of drawers she saw that they were new, and had been painted to look antique. The room was spacious with a desk, which she put her laptop on, and a chair. A painting she recognised as Grace's hung on the wall over the bed. Although the landscape was different to the one Bill had given for Christmas, Grace's style was distinctive.

She unpacked and hung her clothes in the wardrobe. She had showered that morning, but although Bill's car had air conditioning she was hot and sweaty, so she had another one, surprised by how modern the shower room was. She had envisaged something more primitive. She dried herself, brushed her blonde hair, and put on her dressing gown while she went through her clothes debating what to wear. Not wanting to look as if she was trying to out-glamour Noël she chose a plain white blouse with a

V neck and ruffled collar and pale blue trousers. She put a crystal necklace round her neck. Paul had given it to her one Christmas.

'Would he remember?' she asked herself.

The sun had gone down and the temperature had dropped to a bearable twenty degrees, when she and Bill walked across to the homestead.

'Mum, relax. The tension's coming off you in waves. Noël won't bite and neither will Dad. The only things that bite around here are snakes.'

'Are you trying to calm me down or get me even more wound up?'

'I've been scaring Mum with snake stories,' Bill said as they entered the lounge room in Noël and Paul's apartment.

'Very mean of you, Bill,' said Noël coming forward and holding out her hand. 'Hello, Kathryn.'

Kathryn had been unprepared for Noël's magnetic personality. There was a stillness about her that was unusual given her expressive face. Her eyes were even more vividly blue than in the photographs she had seen on Facebook. Her gaze was sincere, and her voice seductive. 'You're an opera fan too, I believe.' Kathryn liked the way she had immediately begun a conversation of mutual interest. *Like the Queen*, she thought.

Friedrich and Guy introduced themselves.

'My cousins are in the kitchen helping Coral,' said Noël. 'I'm not because I'm hopelessly undomesticated.'

But you can fly a plane, ride a horse and shoot, and you've got Paul, thought Kathryn. *And you're elegant.* She admired Noël's emerald green linen tunic that was belted at the waist, navy trousers and the pearl necklace and earrings that set off the outfit. Given her slender build and delicate wrists her large hands were incongruous, and the magnificent sapphire and emerald engagement ring drew attention to them. She didn't want to look around for Paul, but she wondered where he was and if he was deliberately avoiding her.

'Do you ride?' Noël asked. Kathryn noted the diplomatic way the question was put. Most people would have asked, 'Can you ride?'

She shook her head.

'Would you like to learn, Mum?'

'Well, that might be interesting,' Kathryn said, annoyed with her banal reply.

Paul came into the room with Juliet and Grace. 'Dinner's ready,' he announced.

The dining room was furnished with antique, but plain, furniture. The floorboards shone and the rich green, red and gold Turkish rug was thick. The table was set with a white cloth, the cutlery appeared to be silver, and the glasses were crystal. The beauty of the room was enhanced by vases of colourful flowers on the sideboard, window sills and mantelpiece.

'How lovely,' she said. Bill's look of approval heartened her. 'It's the type of room where I imagine the women should be in evening gowns and tiaras and the men in dinner suits. What gorgeous flowers.'

Noël led her over to a vase. 'Feel them. They're silk. Juliet gets hay fever. And I like to leave flowers outside for the bees and butterflies.'

Bill pulled out a chair for her. She was sitting between Matthew and Xavier and opposite Juliet and Friedrich. Paul was sitting on the same side as she was, but four seats away, making conversation with him impossible. Coral, Olwen and Zara served the first course of iced cucumber soup, and then sat down. That Noël and her cousins were friends with their employees increased her liking and respect for them. Her misgivings that she would feel ill at ease or be an object of curiosity were unfounded. She was included in the conversation, which was mainly about the wildlife and the difficult climate. The food was so delicious she asked Coral for the recipe for the unusual pineapple dessert.

'It's not one of mine,' said Coral. 'It's from a recipe book Zara brought with her.'

'No wonder you're so happy here,' she said to Bill as they walked back to the cabins. 'Such friendly people.'

'If you want riding lessons, Vasco will be happy to teach you – I asked him.'

'He's the groom?'

'Yeah. He and Zara are together. See you in my cabin for breakfast tomorrow.'

'What time?'

'Seven. Bacon and eggs?'

'It's been a long time since I've had that for breakfast.'

'You can have apple, grapefruit, or orange juice. Or stewed plums. Coral juices the apples every morning and gives me a jug whenever I want it.'

'Then I must try that.'

Kathryn was surprised how domesticated Bill had become. His cabin was tidy and clean, and when she arrived the round table, covered with a green gingham cloth, had been set for breakfast. A jug of cloudy apple juice, protected from flies by a muslin cloth weighted with beads, was in the centre, along with jars of marmalade, jam, honey and Vegemite. The windows with fly screens were open and the morning breeze was warm.

Bill sat down and poured apple juice into their glasses. 'I'm pleased you came, Mum.'

'So am I. This juice is delicious.'

'It's good that you and Noël got on okay last night.'

'More than okay. She's an admirable woman. Will I get to meet Linda?'

'She's coming on Friday night. She'll be flying in with Dad. If it's not windy we'll be having a barbie in the courtyard tonight. Matt lights a bonfire and that keeps the mozzies away.'

Kathryn finished her juice. 'I regret messing up my life. I'm sorry that I made you and Holly and Paul unhappy.'

'Yeah, well that's all fine now.' Once Bill would have been embarrassed by her confession, but now he was pragmatic.

'Paul was a great husband. It was my stupidity that wrecked the marriage. I've learned a lesson – too late for me, but can I give you some advice?'

'Go on.' He took their empty glasses over to the sink.

'When you get married always remember my folly if you get tempted to stray. I threw everything away for nothing.'

'Mum, this may seem self-centred, but I've been pondering.' He picked up a frying pan and took butter out of the fridge. 'You were a terrific mother –'

'Until recently.'

'It's our formative years that count. You loved us, disciplined us, taught us to be kind and thoughtful.' He put butter in the frying pan and swirled it round. 'Holly was always going to be okay. She knew what she wanted even when she was little. She worked hard at school and achieved her ambition.' He added two rashers of bacon to the melted butter. 'Me – I was tiresome. A dreamer, with no ambition. I knew what I didn't want to do, but didn't know what I did want to do. I caused you and Dad to worry.'

'And that's all we had to worry about. Some parents had to worry about drugs and wild and illegal behaviour – Paul and I were lucky with you and Holly.'

Bill cracked two eggs into the pan. 'What I'm trying to say is this – if you hadn't made an error of judgement and gone off with Tim, Dad would have never moved to Cobar. He would have never met Noël, and I would have never come to Tordorrach and found out what I wanted to do with my life. I would never have met Linda. So when you think about regrets, remember that it was you who made me find happiness.'

Kathryn left Tordorrach feeling happier than she had when she arrived. Vasco had taught her to ride and, once she got over her initial fear, she found she thoroughly enjoyed it. Noël gave her jodhpurs, riding boots and a hat. Bill told her she looked posh on a horse.

'I won't look posh when I fall off and break something.'

Vasco reassured her. He was an excellent instructor, letting her take her time before proceeding to the next step. She considered joining a riding school when she got back to Sydney. The only thing that marred her visit had been Paul's coolness towards her.

Noël heard raised voices coming from their living room.

'She's not just your ex – you were married for over twenty years,' she heard Bill say. 'You treated her like a complete stranger – you would have been nicer to a complete stranger.'

'Bill –'

'What's wrong with you, Dad? You've found happiness, you're happy, Mum's miserable – yeah go on, say it.'

'Say what?'

'That she deserves it – that it's her own fault! You didn't even ask her how she was! You should have offered to fly her back to Cobar. I would have come with you if you didn't want to be alone with her.'

'It's not my –'

'You made it so obvious you were avoiding her. What's it going to be like when Holly or I get married? Are you going to wreck the day by refusing to come to the wedding?'

Noël stood in the doorway and waited for one of them to notice her. Paul saw her first, then Bill turned round.

She raised her eyebrows. 'Bill, let's go into the courtyard and have some coffee.'

'I'll bring it out,' Paul offered.

They went into the courtyard and sat down.

Noël smiled to lessen the rebuke. 'The first rule when you're having an argument is to let the other person speak. I think your mother enjoyed herself,' she went on when Bill looked shamefaced and said nothing.

He nodded. 'She did. You were nice to her – Dad snubbed her – he acted as if she had leprosy or something. She was a fantastic mother. She never hit or smacked us – she knew how to make a point. One day on my birthday, Dad and Mum took us into Sydney. First we went to the toy department so I could choose what toy I wanted. Holly saw a doll and said she wanted it. When Mum said no, she had a tantrum. Mum quietly told her to stop it and Dad gave her one of his fierce looks. She shut up and sulked for a while. We went to a musical in the afternoon and had dinner afterwards.

'Next day Mum took Holly into the kitchen and filled a glass with water. Then she told Holly that while she wanted a doll many children, not just wanted, but desperately needed, clean water and food. She showed Holly pictures of skeletal children in Africa. Holly never mentioned the doll again. For her next birthday Dad and Mum sponsored a little girl for her. She had other presents too, but this was the one she told everyone about. Every Christmas after that we went to town to buy something for the child. Holly enjoyed that more than receiving presents for herself. In the whole of their marriage Mum made one mistake and Dad can't forgive her. He acts as if she was an abusive, drug-addicted alcoholic.'

'That's the way he is, Bill. When something is over for him then it's finished.'

'His hate is stronger than his love.'

'He doesn't hate her.'

'No, I don't,' said Paul putting a tray with a pot of coffee and mugs on the table. 'Can I join you?'

Noël looked at Bill who nodded.

'I find socialising with her difficult,' said Paul as he poured coffee into their mugs. 'It might be wrong, but I can't help it. It's how I feel. I'm sorry it upset you. Your mother behaved well, which is more than I did.' He smiled. 'I'll try and do better next time.'

'I've just had a thought,' said Bill. 'One of the reasons Mum's unhappy I think, is because she hasn't got a significant man in her life. I reckon she'd be happier if she met someone . . . not to marry, maybe, but to share things with – go to the opera or theatre.' He looked at Noël. 'Do any single older men come on your riding holidays?'

She nodded. 'Sometimes. A widower came last year. I think there've been a few divorcees. Are you thinking your mother might like a riding holiday here?'

'Yeah. Dad?'

'Well . . .'

Noël touched his arm. 'To make everything easier for everyone you and I could go on holiday –'

'Hell,' said Bill. 'I don't want you to feel you have to get away – don't worry. It was just an idea.'

'I'd like to have a holiday in England and show your father Shuttleton Court.'

'But you wouldn't go when the visitors are here.'

'Yes, that's exactly when we would go. All the hard work is before the holidays. During the holidays everything runs smoothly – thanks to all the staff. I'm not indispensable. And Don's so efficient and meticulous I'm almost redundant. And it'll be the spring and summer in England when everything will be open.'

'That's an excellent idea,' said Paul. 'Kathryn will be more relaxed if her moody ex-husband is not hanging around.'

Chapter 39
February 2016

When the bombshell came, Paul reflected that the cliché 'if things seem too good to be true then they probably are,' was right. Their idyll was shattered one morning when two of the workers, who were involved in preparing a piece of land for a quinoa plantation, ran up to the homestead just as Paul was leaving for work.

'We've found a body.'

'What sort of body?' Paul asked, putting down his briefcase. As soon as he'd spoken he realised the question was idiotic. Before the man could reply that it was a dead one he continued, 'I mean is it a skeleton, a recent body, buried, or what?'

'It was buried. It's in a plastic sack thing. The digger split the sack and the body fell out.'

Paul took his satellite phone out of his briefcase and called the police.

Part 3
Sylvia

Chapter 40

Two days after the body had been taken away, a police helicopter arrived with a detective and a forensic pathologist on board. Paul and Matthew took them into the office in the homestead and offered them tea or coffee, which Coral carried in on a tray together with a plate of buttered iced buns.

'It's a female,' said the pathologist when Grace, Juliet, Friedrich and Guy had arrived. 'It's hard to estimate how long she was buried because the body was in a plastic sack and it's partly mummified. She was shot. We've got the bullet. It must have been in her body when she was buried. She was shot in the back – the bullet nicked one of her back ribs.'

'There was a wedding ring on her finger,' said the detective. 'There are initials on it that will help identify her. We are hoping that some of the records of who was employed here still exist. We know you've only just moved here, so I don't expect –'

'We did live here when we were children,' said Juliet.

The detective looked confused. 'But I thought you'd only –'

'Our grandfather owned it.'

'What are the initials on the ring?' Paul asked.

'SD and CH.'

Juliet and Grace looked at each other in horror.

'Oh Christ,' whispered Noël.

'Do you know whose initials?' he asked.

Grace's eyes were wide with shock. 'Our mother. Sylvia. Dale was her maiden name.'

'Our father was Charles Halland,' whispered Juliet.

Paul had assumed the murdered woman was a wife or girlfriend of one of the casual farm labourers or shearers. Now other scenarios sprang into his mind. Had Charles Halland shot his wife to stop her from leaving? Or had his father shot her for the same reason? Were the letters written to Grace, Juliet and their father genuine, or were they forgeries? If they were forgeries who had written them?

He realised that the implications had not yet dawned on Juliet, Grace or Noël, but judging by Friedrich and Guy's expression it had occurred to them. Less sinister options struck him. 'Sylvia might have lost the ring and someone else picked it up,' he said. 'She may have given it away. The body might not be Sylvia's. Just because the ring was hers doesn't mean the body is.'

Noël looked thoughtful. 'That's unlikely, Paul. Why would she give away her wedding ring?

'She was depressed? I'm not sure. It's probably unlikely, but she could have lost it.'

Noël shook her head. 'Not a wedding ring. I never take mine off.'

'Neither do I,' Grace and Juliet said together. Their distressed expressions remained unchanged.

'When was your mother reported as missing?'

'She wasn't,' said Grace. She went on to explain why. 'When we came back here we tried to find her –'

Juliet stood up. 'Wait a sec. I'll get the email the private detective sent us.' She turned on the computer and scrolled down till she found the email.

The detective and pathologist read it in silence.

'If it is your mother, this will explain why he couldn't find any trace of her,' said the detective.

'We'll have to take your DNA,' said the pathologist.

Juliet and Grace nodded and arrangements were made for them to give samples.

When they left Paul rang Ralph and told him the news. 'It's very tense here.'

The following morning was a Saturday. Paul flew into Cobar to see Wendy Jenkins who had been the governess. Grace, Juliet and

Noël wanted to come too, but he persuaded them that she would reveal more if he was by himself.

Not wanting to lull Wendy into thinking it was a social call, he said as soon as she opened the door, 'It will be in the papers soon, but I just wanted you to know that a body has been found on Tordorrach. We're pretty certain that it's Sylvia Halland.'

'Oh Christ.' She let him in and sank into a chair when she reached the lounge.

'Can I ask you a few things before the police come and see you?'

She nodded. 'What . . . how . . . do they know how she died?'

'She was shot.'

Her eyes widened. 'So she came back to Tordorrach and someone murdered her?'

'Perhaps,' he said. 'But it's also possible that she never left.'

'She must have left. Her car was missing.'

'Yes, you're right. I'd forgotten. She did leave, then came back and that's when someone killed her. Although . . . someone could have hidden her car. Did anyone look for it?'

'Not that I can remember. But it wasn't in its usual place, so we assumed she'd taken it. Her clothes were gone, and so were her suitcases. Where would anyone hide it?'

'Tordorrach's seventy thousand acres – there's plenty of room to hide it. Or whoever murdered her might have stolen her car. She was never reported missing so no one would be on the lookout for her car.' Where conversations were concerned Paul had a good memory. He used it now. 'You saw the letters Sylvia wrote to her children and her husband. Did it look like her writing?'

'Yes. Well I assume so. Why?'

'You don't think they were written by someone else?'

'Forged? No. Who would do that?'

'The person who murdered her.'

'Why? Oh I see. So her absence wouldn't be reported to the police.'

'Exactly.'

'I'm not a handwriting expert, and I didn't see much of her writing except on the Christmas and birthday cards she and her husband gave me – I didn't even think that she might not have written them.'

'Were you surprised that she had left?'

Wendy chewed her lip. 'Shocked, but not exactly surprised. The letters were the sort of thing she would have written.'

'It's going to be suspected that her husband shot her because –'

'No! Charles was a kind, gentle man. He loved her – he would never have killed her.' She thought for a moment. 'When he saw the letters he went white. Crying and emotion can be faked, but going white can't be. He was genuinely shocked.'

'Can you think of anyone else who might have –'

'No,' she said vehemently. 'She had no enemies – not many friends, because of her depression, but no enemies. Certainly none that I know of. Her closest friend was Noël's mother.'

'Really?'

'Yes. She was in Sydney University doing mathematics, and Sylvia lived in the same block of flats in Randwick. Sylvia fell off her bike and broke her arm. Noël's mother saw what happened and drove her to the hospital. She waited for her and drove her home and they became friends. It's how Sylvia met Charles.'

'I see. Wendy, the police will ask you all sorts of questions that you won't like, so I'm just forewarning you. One thing they'll ask was if Sylvia was having an affair.'

'Who on earth would she have had an affair with?'

'I don't know. But you were on Tordorrach at the time, so they might ask you if you had any suspicions.'

'She would never have had an affair. She spent most of her time trying to overcome her depression. She was lethargic or crying, but she did have good days – not many, but she made the most of them. On those days I would leave her alone with Grace and Juliet – it was only right that they should experience their mother's love. I suppose it's possible, well it must be possible, that one of the casual station hands – shearers or men who were sometimes hired for odd jobs – developed a passion for her – she was very attractive. Or someone who was a psychopath was hired. How are Grace and Juliet?'

'Upset.'

'Yes,' she said. She went over to a bookcase and picked up a photo. 'I took this on one of Sylvia's good days. As you can see she looks happy and normal. Can I get you a cup of tea – I've just had one but –'

'No thanks.' Paul stood up. 'I hope this will be solved quickly, with minimum distress to Grace and Juliet.'

He was crossing the road outside Wendy Jenkins's house when he remembered that Seamus's mother lived in Cobar. He went to the office and looked her up in the phone book. She lived a short walk away. He now realised he had frequently passed her house. Already the work Seamus had done on her front garden was apparent. Her front lawn was freshly mown and the edges neatly clipped. There were no weeds and new bushes had been planted. There was a bird table near the veranda and the cracked concrete path had been repaired.

He hoped Seamus was not at home, but he opened the door when Paul rang the bell.

'Good afternoon, Seamus.'

He smirked. 'What do you want?'

'Is your mother at home?'

'She's in hospital. Appendicitis. She nearly died.'

'I'm sorry to hear that. I hope she recovers.'

'So you've come to beg me to come back, have you?'

'No. I –'

Seamus slammed the door so hard the dog next door began to bark.

Because it was a murder case, albeit an old one, the results of the DNA test were processed quickly. The police helicopter came to Tordorrach with two detectives. Paul could tell from their expressions what they were going to say.

'I'm sorry to tell you that your DNA shows that the body is that of your mother, but I think you knew that already.'

Grace chewed her lip. 'Yes, but we were hoping . . .'

'We need to ask you some questions.'

Coral hovered in the doorway. 'I saw the helicopter. Can I get you anything?'

'Thanks, Coral,' said Noël. She looked at the detectives. 'Tea or coffee?'

'Coffee for both of us, please.'

'Coral, we'll be in the courtyard,' said Noël, leading the way.

They all sat at one of the cast iron tables.

'What a beautiful garden,' said one of the detectives as he took a pad and pencil out of his briefcase. 'Mrs –'

'Call us Grace and Juliet,' said Grace. 'I'm Grace.' She gestured to Noël. 'This is our cousin Noël. She lived in Sydney when our mother disappeared, but spent her school holidays here.'

He looked at them solemnly. 'I know you were very young, but you might remember something useful. We're waiting for the results to see who owned the revolver from which the bullet was fired. How old were you when your mother supposedly left here?'

'I was five,' said Grace. 'Juliet was three.'

Coral brought out coffee in two cafetières. 'I'll be back in a sec.' She returned with milk and sugar, mugs and a plate piled with biscuits. 'Homemade,' she said.

Noël poured the coffee and handed round the biscuits, which the detectives munched appreciatively.

'Can you recall who worked here at that time?' asked the sergeant, wiping the crumbs from his mouth.

Grace nodded. 'Mr and Mrs Ryan senior – I don't know their Christian names. He was the manager. They lived in the manager's house, but it burnt down some time ago. Their son Seamus was at a boarding school in Sydney. Wendy Jenkins was our governess. There was a gardener – Mr Grey I think his name was. He was old – and is probably dead by now. His wife did the washing and ironing and cleaning for the homestead. The shearers and the seasonal workers came and went.'

'Who actually lived on the property?'

'Our grandparents –'

'Are they still alive?'

'No. Our parents, Miss Jenkins – she lives in Cobar now.'

'Where did she live when she was the governess?'

'In the homestead with us.'

'This homestead?'

'No. The original one is derelict.'

'Our mother wrote us a letter,' said Juliet. 'I'll get it. There's one she wrote to our father as well.'

When Juliet left to find the letters, Paul said to the detectives, 'You might want to get the handwriting analysed – they could be forged. Those letters are the reason Sylvia wasn't reported missing. It could be why whoever murdered her has got away with it for so many years.'

Juliet returned with the letters. 'She didn't put the date on them.'

'Can you remember the approximate date she left?' Paul asked.

'Winter – it was winter.' Grace shook her head. 'It might have been July or June.'

One of the detectives asked for a tissue. Careful not to touch them, he placed the letters in a plastic bag. 'Do you have any other samples of your mother's handwriting?'

'Yes,' said Juliet. 'Christmas and birthday cards to Grace and me, but we also kept the ones she gave our father – it was all we had left of her – and photographs. Do you want them?'

'Yes. We'll return them as soon as they've been analysed. Did your father own a gun or guns?'

'Yes – to kill snakes and if a horse or other animal was injured so badly it had to be shot,' said Grace.

'One of the revolvers was a Colt Metro Mark 3 – .35 calibre,' said Noël.

The detective looked surprised. 'Do you know if any of them are still here?'

She shook her head. 'There are guns here, but we bought them just in case of snakes. I think our grandfather left his here – in the old homestead. He sold the property to the manager Mr Ryan. He's dead, but his son lives in Cobar.'

'Can we have the guns? Just the hand guns.'

'Of course, but they're new. The older ones might still be in the old homestead – do you want to have a look?'

'Yes please.'

'We'll give you the new ones first and then we'll go to the old homestead and see if we can find the old ones.'

He followed Noël to the room where the guns were kept. She unlocked the door and selected the firearms he had requested. He looked at her approvingly. 'It's good to see you keep your firearms locked away securely.'

Noël didn't volunteer that normally at least one gun was kept handy in case of snakes. They had only locked them all away when they heard the police helicopter.

'Is it okay with you if I take the revolver when we go to the old homestead,' she asked. 'We did have cats around, but they are more house and stable cats than feral, so there may be snakes.'

She thought he might query her ability to shoot or remind her that it was against the law to kill snakes, but he nodded and she saw his look of relief.

It took half an hour of searching the old homestead to find the guns and pistols that had belonged to the Hallands.

'Why were they left here?' he asked.

'When the homestead was wrecked, Seamus and his wife moved to a tiny caravan,' said Noël. 'There was hardly enough room for them, let alone guns.'

The detectives left with the weapons and the names and addresses of Seamus and his mother and Wendy Jenkins.

Chapter 41

The news made the Sydney papers. **Bizarre Twist** ran the headline on one. Others, knowing that the dead can't sue, ran a story of the jealous husband murdering his wife when she was going to leave him for another man. To Paul's dismay the atmosphere at Tordorrach had changed from happiness to misery.

'We can't live here anymore,' said Juliet.

'You might not be able to, but I can,' said Grace. 'Stop being so impulsive.'

'Don't make rush decisions,' Paul advised. 'Miss Jenkins thinks one of the casual station hands killed her because he was infatuated with her. She'll tell the police the same thing.'

'How are they going to prove that? Which station hand? There were lots of them. Irresponsible journalists,' stormed Juliet. 'Always after scandal. It should have occurred to them that this man might still be alive and killing women.'

'What do you think, Paul?' asked Grace.

He hesitated. 'Anything's possible.'

Juliet glared at him. 'Even our father murdering her?' She stood up. 'Thanks, Paul!' She ran from the room.

'Juliet is quick to anger,' Friedrich said quietly.

'She always has been,' said Grace.

'I reckon I'd be hostile if someone accused my father of murdering my mother,' Paul said. 'Not that I've made an accusation.' *I just pray that the bullet in Sylvia's body came from a firearm licensed to anyone but Edward or Charles Halland,* he thought.

'Tell Juliet to stop fretting. The marks on the bullet will prove that your father was innocent,' said Noël confidently.

Paul hoped she was right.

Things got worse. The marks on the bullet in Sylvia's body matched the Colt found in the homestead, which had been owned and licensed to Charles Halland. Grace and Juliet were shattered. Noël was disturbed and tried to comfort them.

'But just because the gun was his does not mean that he shot her,' Paul said to them. 'Were there any locks on the doors of the homestead?'

'No. The only unwelcome visitors we had to guard against were snakes, flies and mozzies,' said Grace. 'We kept the fly screen doors closed but not locked.'

'So anyone could have come in at any time?'

'Yes. It was the same in the Ryans' house. I don't think there were any door keys.'

'Were the firearms locked away?'

'I don't know. We were only children. But I guess they were – we never saw them. Well, I didn't . . . Juliet?'

Juliet shook her head.

Paul considered going into Cobar and asking Seamus if he or his father had kept the records of all the permanent staff, seasonal shearers and casual labourers, or if he knew where they were.

'He won't tell you even if he does know,' said Grace. 'Just tell the police and they can search the old homestead. Seamus might even have taken them to his caravan.'

'I don't think so,' said Noël. 'It was small and cramped enough without him piling ledgers all over the place. He probably left them there when he moved into the caravan. Let's take a look.' She saw Paul's reluctance and guessed the reason. 'I'll take a gun just in case there are any snakes.'

Early one morning they all dressed in thick clothing and went to the old homestead. The rooms were full of mouldering furniture and birds' nests. Grace led the way to the room that had been the office. The shelf holding the ledgers had collapsed, and the books were on the floor. While Noël stood by with the revolver Juliet, Guy, Friedrich, Paul and Grace picked up the registers and took them outside.

'Who kept the records?' Paul asked as they walked back to the new homestead.

'I don't know,' said Grace. 'It might have been Mr Ryan senior, or dad could have done them – or our grandparents. I'm not going to open any of these – they've probably got all sorts of creepy crawlies in them. We'll put them in a bin bag.'

Paul emailed the police to say they had the old registers and did they want them. They did, so when he went into Cobar he took them with him.

Ω

Seamus looked helplessly at the mess in the kitchen. In the week since his mother had been rushed to hospital the clean house had become dirty. He had not washed up, vacuumed or put anything away. He had done the washing, but not the ironing. Newspapers littered the lounge. The kitchen stank of old fish and chips and mouldy dishes. His mother was due home in three days, and he knew that instead of resting she would start cleaning. She wouldn't complain or berate him, and that would make him feel more guilty. All his life he had had a woman to look after him; first his mother and then his wife. He was trying to work out what to do when the doorbell rang.

Two men stood behind the fly screen door. 'Seamus Ryan?' said one.

'Yes.'

They showed their badges. 'We are investigating the death of Sylvia Halland and hoped you might know something that would help us.'

Seamus opened the fly screen. 'Come in. Yes, I read in the paper that her body's been found. I was shocked. Everyone thought she'd gone to Sydney.'

Ashamed of the untidy rooms he led them into the lounge. He tossed newspapers off the sofa and chairs and asked them to sit down. 'Sorry about the mess. My mother's in hospital and I've been too worried to do anything.'

Although he was tempted to punish Grace, Juliet and Noël by saying that the accusations the papers were making were probably true, he knew his mother would be upset if she heard about what he'd said. They would be sure to question her when she was well enough. He remembered the kindness of both Edward and Charles Halland, and the generous gifts they had given both him and his parents on birthdays and at Christmas. After Charles had died his parents had lowered the price of Tordorrach so his father could afford to buy it.

'How old were you when Mrs Halland disappeared?'

'Fifteen. I was at school in Sydney – boarding school. My father wrote to me.'

'He was the manager. Is that correct?'

'Yes. He became the owner a few years later when Charles Halland was killed by a snake and his parents sold it and moved away.'

'Mr Ryan, did you ever notice any of the workers – shearers or casual labourers looking at Sylvia in a sexual or nasty way?'

'No.'

'Did you ever notice anything suspicious?'

'No. I was only ever there during the school holidays.'

'Did your father ever mention anything about any of the men that disturbed him?'

'No. I'm sorry. I'm not being much help. But I would like to tell you that what's being suggested in the papers is wrong.'

'Which particular suggestion?'

'That Charles Halland killed his wife.'

'What makes you so sure?'

'He was a good man and so was his father. And Sylvia – well, she was quiet – not the sort to have an affair with anyone.' Suddenly he thought of a way to make life uncomfortable for Matthew. 'I've just remembered something. It might not mean anything, but . . . well my father said that Mr Fulham – that's Matthew's father – he owns Ravenscroft –'

One of the detectives nodded. 'Yes, we've met Matthew.'

'My father said he didn't like the way he looked at Sylvia. She was beautiful. I never saw it – I never had much to do with the Fulhams, but I know it made my father uneasy.' He was about to tell them that his mother was also uneasy, but knew that if they asked her she would deny it.

'Is Mr Fulham senior still alive?'

'No. He died a few years ago.'

'His wife?'

'No. She died about ten years ago – cancer.'

The detectives stood up. 'Thank you for your time, Mr Ryan.'

Seamus went to the front door with them. 'Sorry I couldn't have been more use.' He watched them go down the path. 'See how you cope with them asking about your father, Matthew,' he muttered.

Matthew was at home when the detectives arrived.

'My dad looked at Sylvia in a – who the hell told you that?'

'Sorry, Mr Fulham. It's confidential.'

'Seamus,' said Coral. 'It could only be him. No one else would say anything so untrue.'

'Of course,' said Matthew. 'He's lying. There's always been conflict between me and Seamus. Ask him, Inspector, why he left Tordorrach. He's got a grievance against me. He hates it that I'm the manager.'

'This is his way of getting revenge,' Coral told them.

'Why did he leave Tordorrach, Mr Fulham?'

'He was sacked.'

'By you?'

'No, although I agreed with the decision. The owners sacked him, but I was present. My dad loved my mum, and he would have never looked at any women in the way Seamus is suggesting.'

'Thank you. Before we leave, can we ask you if you ever noticed anything strange? Was anyone looking at Mrs Halland in a way they shouldn't?'

'I was fourteen when Mrs Halland left. I often went to Tordorrach. My parents and the Hallands were friends. I never noticed anyone looking at Mrs Halland in a funny way, but even if they had I would have been too young to realise.'

Seamus was walking back to his mother's house with the flowers and chocolates he had bought to take to the hospital when he saw the two detectives who had interviewed him the day before opening his front gate. Thankful that they had their backs to him he ducked behind a tree. They left after five minutes of knocking and peering through the windows. He regretted he had tried to throw suspicion onto Matthew's father. At the time he hadn't considered that Matthew would know where the accusation had come from.

'The bastard would have told them I got the sack from Tordorrach,' he muttered.

Chapter 42

February 2016

'She came back to Tordorrach and someone murdered her.' The memory came to Paul in the middle of the night. He sat up in bed. 'The governess,' he said aloud. Noël didn't stir. He shook her.

'What?' she murmured.

'The governess.'

She rubbed her eyes. 'What's the time?'

'I don't know. I don't care. I've thought of something.'

She turned on the bedside lamp and looked at the clock. 'It's two o'clock. Couldn't your thoughts have waited till morning?'

He pushed back the quilt. 'No.'

'Where are you going?'

He put on his dressing gown. 'To the study.'

She followed him. He sat at the desk, grabbed a writing pad and took the top off his fountain pen. Whenever he was faced with a puzzle he used a fountain pen. Something about the flow of ink and the way it shone on the paper before it dried helped his deliberations. Noël sat beside him. He wrote 'Wendy Jenkins' on the page.

'Miss Jenkins showed me a photo, but there was another I saw. It was of her, Grace, Juliet and their father. He was a handsome man. She was an attractive young woman.'

'You think Uncle Charles and Miss Jenkins were having an affair?'

'No, although it's possible. But she could have been in love with him.'

'She shot Aunty Sylvia?'

'Is it likely?'

Noël frowned. 'I don't know. I hope not.'

'Did Grace and Juliet ever tell you what they had been doing the day their mother left?'

'No, why?'

'Interesting. I wonder if they remember.'

'Why is that important?'

He wrote '*billabong?*' on the page. 'Because when I first spoke to Wendy Jenkins she told me they'd been at the billabong most of the day, but what if she was lying?'

'But Miss Jenkins and Aunty Sylvia would have to be alone in the house. Uncle Charles and his parents would have had to have been a long way from the house. And how would she have got the body to where it was found?'

'Could Wendy drive?'

'Yes – she had her own car. But she wasn't a hefty woman. She and Aunty Sylvia were about the same size. I doubt she could have dragged or carried her to the car. And there's the time factor. She would have had to have dug a grave. You'll have to put this theory of yours to Grace and Juliet – see what they say.' She yawned. 'Can we go back to bed?'

Paul recalled Miss Jenkins's shock when he told her Sylvia's body had been found. *Was she shocked because it had been found and she would be questioned and suspected?* he wondered.

'Paul's got a theory,' Noël told Grace and Juliet in the morning. 'It's far-fetched and improbable, but you were here and it'd be useful to see what you think.'

Juliet glowered at Paul when she came into the courtyard.

'Stop looking at me as if I'm covered in sewerage,' he said. 'I want this solved as much –'

'You want our father to have done it,' she snapped.

'Sit down, Juliet,' said Friedrich, 'Listen to what Paul has to say.'

They all sat around the table. He'd had time during the hours till morning to think about how Wendy Jenkins could have had the opportunity and the time to murder Sylvia, dig a grave and bury her body.

'Can either of you remember what you were doing on the day your mother disappeared?'

As he'd expected, Juliet, who would have been aged three, didn't know.

Grace took more time to answer. Finally she said, 'I can remember being told that she gone away. Our grandparents were upset and so was our father. They had some letters. I saw our father put them on a shelf. I got out of bed that night and read them.'

'But you can't remember what you were doing before that?'

'No.'

'Were you and Juliet ever away from Miss Jenkins – say at the weekends?'

They looked puzzled.

'I mean did you ever go to neighbouring properties and play with their children?'

'Yes,' said Grace.

'Did Miss Jenkins go with you?'

'She sometimes drove us. Sometimes we walked or rode our bikes or ponies – if it wasn't too hot.'

'Did she stay?'

'No. She came to collect us, or sometimes our grandparents did or our father.'

'Do you know if your mother and Miss Jenkins were ever alone in the house together? Perhaps when your grandparents went into Cobar or Ivanhoe to get supplies?'

'I can't remember,' said Juliet who was looking less sullen. She looked at Grace. 'Can you?'

'No. Are you thinking that Miss Jenkins might have shot our mother?'

'That's my theory, yes.'

'Why?'

'She was in love with, or infatuated with, your father.'

Juliet looked startled. 'Did she tell you that?'

'No, it's all supposition – and, as Noël said improbable . . . the murder bit, not the fact that she was in love with your father.'

'It's possible,' said Guy. 'Just the two women alone in the house.'

'Who went into Cobar to get supplies?' Paul asked. 'Or did you mostly go to Ivanhoe?'

'It depended on what we needed. If it was a big shop we went to Cobar. If it was only a few things we went to Ivanhoe. Sometimes we all went together,' said Grace. 'Sometimes we stayed with Miss Jenkins; sometimes we went with her, sometimes she went alone. She was a lovely governess – we adored her. I don't think she murdered our mother – even if she had been in love with our father.'

'I don't want it to be her,' said Juliet. 'I don't want it to be our father or grandfather. I want it to be one of the casual workers or the shearers, but unless they confess the blame will fall on our father who can't defend himself. It was his gun. She was his wife.'

'They might bring Miss Jenkins into it,' said Grace. 'The papers will say all sorts of things –'

'They'll have to be careful with Miss Jenkins because she's alive. If they're proved wrong she can sue for libel and defamation of character.'

'But how can they be proved wrong?' asked Grace. 'It was ages ago. Who's going to remember? If a shearer or casual worker murdered her, they're not going to confess – they may even be dead themselves.'

'I've just had a thought,' Paul told Noël when she came out of the shower one morning.

'Who's the suspect this time?'

'Still Wendy Jenkins. I agree that my earlier theory was full of holes, but this one –'

Noël unwound the towel from her hair. 'Why are you so fixated on Miss Jenkins?'

He pulled his blue and white striped shirt out of the wardrobe. 'Because she's the only person with a real motive.'

'Hang on. You don't know if she was in love with Uncle Charles. Nobody does. But if she'd killed Aunty Sylvia, wouldn't she try and make it look as if Uncle Charles did it?'

'Not necessarily. Sometimes trying to put the blame on someone else is a sign of guilt. And her affection for Grace, Juliet and you is genuine – she wouldn't want to make any of you suffer.'

'So what's your latest idea?' she asked with a hint of indulgence in her tone and expression.

'Sylvia supposedly left Tordorrach in 1980. Charles died in 1983 – have I got that right?'

Noël took off her dressing gown and dropped it on the bed. 'Supposedly?'

'Since her body was found, we've concluded that she never left here and that whoever murdered her stole her car. But what if Sylvia *did* leave Tordorrach? She went to Sydney and Miss Jenkins and Charles Halland became interested in each other romantically.'

'But the private detective couldn't find any records of Aunty Sylvia being in Sydney.'

'No official records, but maybe she didn't stay long. Think about it this way. What if she was given a new drug or therapy that helped her? Between 1980 when she left and 1983 when her husband died, she came back to Tordorrach.'

Noël was no longer looking sceptical. 'Ah. And by then Miss Jenkins was in love with Uncle Charles.'

'Exactly. One of the first things that Wendy Jenkins said when I told her about Sylvia's body being discovered was, 'She came back to Tordorrach and someone shot her,' or something along those lines.' He went to the mirror and put on his tie. 'Now, there are two possibilities that I can think of – there may be more. Sylvia writes to her husband to tell him she is better and is returning. The letter arrives on a day that Miss Jenkins collected the mail.

She recognises Sylvia's writing and intercepts the letter. From what I've gathered who did what jobs varied – no one person went shopping, so maybe whoever was around collected the mail. Sylvia writes that she is arriving in Cobar by train or plane, gives the date and time, and asks someone to meet her.'

Noël sat at the dressing table and brushed her hair. 'Why not by car? If she went to Sydney, that's how she would have got there.'

'She might have sold it in Sydney – she might have needed money. Cars aren't essential in Sydney like they are here. Miss Jenkins knows that her relationship with Charles will come to an end once Sylvia returns, because he loves his wife. In a carefully thought out plot she digs a grave, lines it with black plastic sacks, and weighs them down with rocks to stop them blowing away.

'The day of Sylvia's arrival, Miss Jenkins goes into Cobar to get supplies. Before she leaves she puts your uncle's revolver under her seat or in her handbag. After buying the supplies she goes to the train station or airport, meets Sylvia and drives her back to Tordorrach. I don't know how she made her get out of the car – maybe she said there was something wrong with the tyre and could Sylvia check it out. Maybe she tells Sylvia that she wants to show her something.'

'Wouldn't Aunty Sylvia be anxious to see her husband and children?'

'Miss Jenkins might have told her that Grace and Juliet were in the bushes waiting to surprise her. They walk to the grave, Miss Jenkins shoots her, gets her into the sack –'

'Why the sack?'

'So dingoes won't smell her and dig her up.'

'Of course. She fills in the grave and goes to the homestead with the supplies, and her relationship with Uncle Charles goes on until he's bitten by a snake,' Noël said slowly. 'Phew! But I still don't want it to be her. If I had been her I would have left Cobar when our grandparents sold Tordorrach – there was always the chance that her body would be discovered sooner rather than later. Why didn't she?'

'I don't know.'

'If I'd been her I would have gone to Sydney or Melbourne where I could have lost myself. If Sylvia's body had been found earlier, say a few years after the Ryan's became the owners, she would have been questioned if she was living in Cobar. If she'd gone away to a big city she might never have been traced – not even by the police.'

'Yes, that's the main flaw in my theory.'

'You said there were two possibilities.'

'Yes. Miss Jenkins is alone in the homestead, or perhaps with Grace and Juliet, when the phone rings. It's Sylvia. Miss Jenkins says the others are all out and Sylvia tells her she's better and is coming home on whatever day. The rest is the same.'

Noël chewed her lip. 'Well I've just thought of something else. What if Aunty Sylvia came back here *after* Charles was killed and my grandparents had already left. She arrived and one of the station hands or casual workers killed her. They can't be sure how long her body's been buried.'

'But the gun belonged to –'

'My grandparents left it here. They wouldn't need a gun in Bowral. Paul, please don't tell the police what you think. There's no proof that Wendy was in love with Uncle Charles. And if she did kill Sylvia it will have been on her conscience. I don't think she's the killer – certainly not the cold calculating murderer you've described. I knew her, you didn't.'

'But you were only a child.'

Chapter 43

The following day they received an email from the detective in charge of the case.

In the course of our investigations we have discovered that Sylvia Halland's car was found in Manly in 1980. It had been vandalised and all the wheels and the number plate were missing. The police identified her as the owner through the engine number. It was towed away. The address on the registration papers was Tordorrach. It was insured for third-party only.

'So she did make it to Sydney,' said Juliet.

Paul emailed the detectives and asked if they had more information about when the car was found.

It was reported, but not by Sylvia Halland. It was parked outside someone's house and they told the police. The date entered in the report is 10th July 1980.

We have just received the result from the handwriting expert. The writing on the Christmas and birthday cards matches the handwriting on the letters Sylvia Halland wrote when she left Tordorrach.

'Strange that she didn't report it,' said Paul. 'If it'd been my car —'
'Not strange when you think about it,' said Grace. 'Our mother didn't think like normal people. She saw her car it had no wheels and no use to anyone. It was ten years old and getting new wheels would cost a lot, and it wasn't comprehensively insured.

She didn't need a car in Sydney. If she lived in Manly where the car was found there were ferries to Sydney and busses.'

Two days later when Paul had left for work, Noël went into the office and downloaded the *Sydney Morning Herald* onto her computer. To her dismay the journalists had made a connection between Sylvia's murder and Wendy Jenkins. They asked questions that damned Wendy without accusing her. Before she had a chance to think, Juliet and Grace came into the office.

'Did Paul do this?' Juliet demanded thrusting her iPad at Noël.

'No, I told him not to.'

'He was the person who dreamed it up. How do you know he didn't?'

Noël picked up the phone and punched in the number. 'Morning, Linda. Could I speak to Paul, please.'

After a brief conversation she said to Juliet and Grace. 'No, he didn't.'

Juliet scowled. 'How do you know he's telling the truth?'

'Juliet, shut up,' said Grace.

'Where did the paper get the photos from?' Juliet asked.

'Do you think Paul's got photos of Wendy's? Think properly, Juliet, before hurling accusations around,' said Noël.

'If Wendy didn't give the papers the photos, how did they get them?' Juliet asked more reasonably.

'The article the papers wrote when we hired the private investigator had photos of Sylvia, and there was one of Wendy, Dad and us,' said Grace. 'That's how they got the photos – we emailed them to them for the article. And Wendy was filmed taking about our mother when they did *Find My Family*. I suppose the journalists think it was a case of female jealousy. Wendy took Mum's place when she left and they've jumped to the conclusion that she was in love with Dad. If our mother returned that would have smashed her hopes of marrying our father. Poor Wendy. Shall we ring her?'

Noël looked at her watch. 'She'll be at school. Ring later.'

Wendy was having her breakfast and reading the *Sydney Morning Herald* on her iPad. When she saw the article she was so upset she couldn't swallow her toast. She spat it out and, fearing she was going to be sick, went to the sink. She stood there trying to quell her panic, but the words, *An attractive young woman. A handsome man whose wife had deserted him,* kept pounding in her brain. *Living in the house together.* She was tempted to ring the school and say she was sick, but thought that would make her seem guilty in the eyes of those who had read the article.

'I'm innocent,' she whispered. 'I must behave as if I haven't seen the article. Or if I have read it, that I think it's journalistic make-believe.'

She pulled her phone out of her bag and was about to send Paul Knight a text but, being married to Noël, he was an interested party so she sent it to Ralph McLachlan instead. She went to the front door and made herself open it. Twisting her lips into a smile that felt fake and probably looked fake, she walked briskly to the school. The people she saw on the way didn't look at her suspiciously. She thought about what the police would do when they saw the article. In the staff room the other teachers acted normally towards her. One said that she was pale and looked at her in concern. She replied she had a headache and was offered painkillers. By lunchtime Ralph McLachlan had still not replied to her text.

He thinks I'm guilty, she thought. *What does Paul think? They must have seen the paper by now.*

By the time the school day ended her head was throbbing. She walked home and felt people were looking at her differently. One woman who always liked to chat crossed the road.

Am I being paranoid? she asked herself.

Her fears were calmed when she saw Seamus's mother who smiled at her.

'Hello, Wendy.'

'How are you, Bernadette? I'm glad to see you're out of hospital.'

'Yes, I'm much better. Are you okay? You look pale.'

She was about to say she had a headache when tears welled.

'Wendy, what's wrong?'

Not wanting to cry in the street she asked, 'Bernadette, have you got a minute?'

'Of course.'

She wiped her eyes. 'Come inside and I'll make some coffee.'

Bernadette followed her into the house.

'You know that Sylvia's body's been found on Tordorrach?' Wendy said when they were in the kitchen.

Bernadette gasped.

'Didn't you know?'

'No, I've been in hospital – Seamus didn't tell me.' She sank onto the sofa.

'She was murdered . . . shot. They're saying I did it – well, not exactly saying – the *Sydney Morning Herald* is insinuating . . . ' She opened her iPad and scrolled to the beginning of the article and handed it to Bernadette who was looking as shocked and as anguished as Wendy felt.

Bernadette read the article and handed the iPad back to Wendy. 'I'm sorry, I can't stay for coffee.' She got up and left.

Wendy put her head in her hands. 'Bernadette thinks I'm guilty – what hope have I got?'

Chapter 44

The following day Paul showed Ralph the article in the *Sydney Morning Herald*.

'I know. Wendy sent me a text. 'I'm going to see her now. She's taken the day off school. Naturally, she's distraught.'

'Will you defend her if she gets arrested?'

'Of course. If the police want to question her I'll be with her. What they've written is rubbish. Wendy Jenkins is incapable of murder – even if she was in love with Charles Halland.'

To Paul's relief Ralph left without asking for his opinion.

Wendy jumped when she heard the doorbell. Terrified that the police had come to arrest her she opened the door. Her heart was beating so fast she thought she would have a heart attack or a stroke. She burst into tears when saw Ralph standing there.

'It's all right, Wendy. Let's sit down and go through everything you can remember. Have you had any breakfast?'

She shook her head. 'I can't eat. I'd be sick.'

'I'll make you some coffee. Believe me, everything's going to be okay.'

She wiped her eyes and followed him into the kitchen. 'Even if they can't prove I did it, I'll have to leave Cobar. Suspicion will be hanging over me.'

Ralph put his hand on her shoulder. 'I'm going to prove you didn't do it.'

For the first time in what seemed like ages she smiled. 'Thank you.'

He made some coffee. 'Can we talk in the kitchen? It's easier for me to write if I'm at a table.'

She cleared a space on the table. Ralph took out his pad and pencil and a rubber and sat down. 'First, I'm going to have to ask you the question the police might ask.'

She shook her head. 'We weren't.'

'You and Charles Halland were not lovers?'

'No. Not before Sylvia left, or after Sylvia left.'

'The police won't stop at that. They'll push and probe.'

She took a sip of coffee. 'I know.'

'As the paper has said, he was a handsome man. You were an attractive young woman. His wife had left him. You lived in the same homestead.'

'With his parents and daughters.'

'Did you get on well with his parents?'

'Very well. They were lovely and treated me like family.'

'Supposing Charles had taken an interest in you after Sylvia left, would they have approved?'

'I think so.'

'Would you have responded to him?'

'Yes.' She smiled. 'I loved him.'

'Ah.'

'The reason nothing happened between us is that he loved Sylvia. He was a faithful man. When Sylvia had her good days he was . . . radiant is the wrong word, but I can't think of a more suitable one . . . euphoric perhaps. Her depression went in cycles and he longed for the good days and dreaded the bad ones. It's not as if she was violent or abusive or anything when she was depressed . . . she just wasn't there is the best way to describe it. She wasn't suicidal either. It was as if her brain had shut down, or her soul had left her body. There was an unspoken agreement between all of us that on her good days he, Sylvia and the children went off together – for a picnic or a ride or even a trip into Cobar. When she left he was devastated. He lived in desperate hope that she would come back. There is no way he could or would have become interested in me or anyone else.'

'He was bitten by the snake three years later, is that right?'

'Yes.'

'That's a long time to grieve, live in hope and have no one to love.'

Wendy took a deep breath. 'I didn't want to get married. My parents' marriage had been miserable. But having lived in the homestead with Charles and having seen how he treated Sylvia and his children . . . if he'd asked me I would have married him. He's the only man I've ever loved, but he never asked or even looked at me as if he wanted to kiss me. His thoughts were with Sylvia. Always with Sylvia.'

'I'm glad you told me. If the police ask, I advise you to tell them. It makes your story believable.'

'You mean it wasn't before?'

'I believed you. But with the slant the paper has put on the story, some people will think otherwise. Now, let's get some dates. Can you remember the exact date Sylvia supposedly left Tordorrach?'

'I'm sorry, I can't.'

'That's okay – it was a long time ago, but I want to try and narrow it down. I'll try some triggers. The year was 1980; is that right?'

'Yes.'

'Was it near anyone's birthday – one of the children's perhaps?'

'Charles's . . . it was a few days after his birthday.'

'Which was when?'

'Seventh of July.'

'Excellent. That fits with the date of the report on her car, which was reported vandalised in Manly on the tenth. So she made it to Sydney.'

The hope that Ralph would be able to prove her innocence died. 'See the difficulty?' she said. 'We know when she left Tordorrach, but we have no idea when she came back. Therefore I have no alibi.'

'Wait. We've only just started. Yes, we have got huge obstacles, but we'll go through everything one by one. According to the private detective there are no records of Sylvia anywhere. Seeing as she went to Sydney that is very odd – unless of course she didn't stay in Sydney long. But he was looking for a missing person who was believed to have vanished voluntarily. He wasn't looking for a murder victim, so perhaps his search was not thorough enough. What did she do when she arrived in Sydney? She must have lived somewhere. Did she get a job? Most importantly, when did she come back to Tordorrach? I'll see if I can find any records of her anywhere in Sydney and I'll start in the Manly area.'

'When she saw her car was vandalised, she might have given up and come straight back home.' Wendy put down her mug. 'I've just thought of something. Noël's mother was her friend. She lived in Sydney. Why didn't she visit her?'

He scribbled on his pad. 'Good point. I'll see if I can follow that one up, although with both of Noël's parents dead it's going to be hard. I'll see if Noël's got any of her mother's diaries or letters. It's a long shot, but worth a try.' He took his phone out of his briefcase. 'I'll ask her now.'

While he was on the phone Wendy prayed Noël would have letters and diaries she could look through.

'She kept the letters, but they are mostly between her parents and Charles when they were on Tordorrach,' said Ralph when he had finished speaking to Noël. 'She'll see if there are any letters from Sylvia, or any mention of her, but she doesn't think so.'

Wendy sighed. 'It's futile.'

'I said I'd prove you are innocent and I will.'

'How?'

'I don't know yet. I'm going to contact the private detective and see if I can get him to look further.'

'Shouldn't the police be doing that?'

'They should, but once they get someone in their sights they get tunnel vision.'

'Me.'

'I doubt they would have suspected you until they saw that rubbish in the paper.'

'Do you think they suspect me now?'

'They might think the insinuations are worth investigating. Wendy, whatever happens, I will defend you.'

Ω

'Paul, Mrs Ryan's here. She wanted to see Uncle Ralph, but he's gone to see Miss Jenkins.'

'Can she make an appointment?'

Linda looked apprehensive. 'She says it's urgent.'

'Show her in,' Paul said, thinking that it was something to do with Seamus. *What the hell's the idiot done now?* he thought.

He could see why Linda had looked perturbed when she brought Bernadette Ryan into his office. She was pale and agitated. She stood in front of his desk wringing her hands. 'It's about the body they've found at Tordorrach – Sylvia's body. I've been in hospital or I would have come earlier. I saw Wendy yesterday – she's upset. The police . . . the papers . . . asking all sorts of questions. She thinks they suspect her.'

'Sit down, Mrs Ryan,' Paul said gently. He was about to ask her if she wanted a cup of tea when Linda, plainly worried about Bernadette Ryan's distress, came in with two mugs and some biscuits. 'There you are,' she said soothingly.

'You were living on Tordorrach at the time, Mrs Ryan. I believe your husband was the manager?'

Bernadette picked up her mug, but her hand was shaking so much she put it down without taking a sip. 'He was a horrible man.'

He thought she meant Charles Halland, until she continued, 'He was always was nice to me when others were around. When it was just me and him . . . beatings. Nothing I ever did pleased him.'

Paul then realised she meant her husband. As he had only ever heard good things about Mr Ryan senior he was sceptical.

'The meals I cooked had too much salt in them, or not enough. The meat was cooked too much, or not enough. Stewed fruit was too sweet or too sour, undercooked or overcooked. He beat me nearly every night. Not where the bruises showed. Everyone thought he was wonderful – all the Hallands, Wendy Jenkins – the shearers, labourers – everybody except me, who knew better.'

Paul wanted information, but to ignore her account of her husband's cruelty would have been callous. 'I see. I'm sorry, Mrs Ryan.'

'I was glad when he died.' Her rant against her dead husband seemed to have soothed her. She picked up her mug and sipped her tea. Her hand was still trembling, but not as badly.

'I can understand that,' he said, hoping that he was not going to be subjected to a long catalogue of the wretched life she had endured. 'The police have all the employment and salary registers. Can you remember the names of any of the shearers or labourers who were employed at the time?'

She looked at him with a blank expression. 'Why?'

'They need to know if anyone saw any of them behaving in a sinister way. Sylvia Halland was murdered. A bullet was found in her body.'

She put her mug down. 'I know. It was me. I shot her,' she said in a dull voice. 'I helped bury her.'

Chapter 45

aul was unable to hide his shock. 'You? Why?'

'I didn't mean to shoot Sylvia. I meant to shoot my husband. They were in our house. He was attacking her.'

'Attacking?'

'Trying to rape her. She was struggling. I aimed the gun at him, but got her instead. If the bullet had hit him it would have been a good shot – right in the back – it must have hit her heart . . . she died quickly. They turned at the wrong time.'

Paul tried to keep his tone conversational while managing to hide his relief that this would quell the rumours. His mind swirled with questions. Sylvia had gone to Sydney. When and why did she return? And why was she in the manager's house? 'Do you know what she was doing in your house?'

'She was going to Cobar.'

'Going to Cobar? But –'

'Her car broke down near our house and she came to ask my husband if he could help get it started. I was washing the kitchen floor. He told me to go to the orchard and pick some apples – he fancied an apple pie that night. He was nice about it, like he was in front of other people. But I had plenty of apples in the larder so I went into the garden instead to pick vegetables. That was near the house. The orchard was a lot further away and I wouldn't have heard Sylvia scream from there. That's why he wanted me to go to the orchard.' Her expression was as lifeless as her voice.

'When I heard her scream I thought there was a snake in the house and that's why I grabbed the gun when I ran back inside. It was Mr Halland's gun – we'd had trouble with snakes – one had got into the house about a month before. It was a King Brown – vicious they are. It nearly bit my husband. I wish it had got him and he'd died, but we were in the kitchen and he chucked a pan of boiling water over it. That's why Mr Halland gave us one of his guns.'

'The police discovered the gun was licensed to Mr Halland,' Paul told her.

'I never thought he'd try and rape Mrs Halland – not his employer's wife.' Tears ran down her face. The blankness left her eyes and anguish replaced it. 'She'd only asked him if he could help her start the car.'

Her mug was empty so Paul went into reception and asked Linda to get some water.

'Shall I get help? What's happened?'

'I'll tell you later. Just get her some water.'

Bernadette's hand was shaking so much, water sloshed out of the glass when he gave it to her.

'We didn't know what to do. I told him I was trying to kill him. I wanted to go to the homestead and tell them, but he stopped me – told me not to be a fool. I helped him bury her that night. He said we had to bury her far away from our house, so if she was ever found they wouldn't connect it to us. We put her in the boot of our car and drove without headlights to a part of the property no one went to much. We put her in bin liners so that dingoes wouldn't get her scent and dig her up.'

'Was your son at home?' Paul asked, wondering if Seamus was complicit even though he would only have been about fifteen years old.

'No. He was at school in Sydney. The little girls – Juliet and Grace – they were somewhere with Wendy Jenkins their governess. I'd seen them earlier – they were going to paint. It was only the next day that we found out that Mrs Halland was leaving for good . . . going to Sydney. We didn't know that at the time. The next day Seamus went –'

'Seamus? You told me he was at school.'

'My husband – his name was Seamus too. It was Wendy who told him that Sylvia had left,' Bernadette continued. 'Seamus had been on the way to the homestead to ask what they wanted him to do with Sylvia's car. He had it all worked out. He thought it would look suspicious if he didn't say something about her car, because it was near our house. He was going to say that he tried to fix the car but couldn't, and that he'd driven her into Cobar in his own car. A while later he came tearing back to our house – in a real state he was – and said that Sylvia had left for good.

'He told me to keep a lookout while he went to her car. He managed to fix it – it only took him fifteen minutes. While I kept watch he drove it to behind our house and covered it with branches. He told me to get over to the homestead and say how sorry I was and all that and offer to help Wendy with the children. We spent that night painting an old sheet in browns and blacks and dark green – camouflage colours. We got her suitcases from the car. We burnt her clothes and put her suitcases under the house.'

Paul recalled that Wendy Jenkins had used the word horrified when she was recounting Mr Ryan's reaction to the news that Sylvia had left Tordorrach for good, but panic stricken would have been a more accurate description.

'We waited in agony for days because we thought the Hallands might decide to go to the police and report her missing. Nothing happened. After that Seamus was much nicer to me – he never hit me again. Maybe it was because I'd tried to kill him and he thought I'd try again.'

Wendy Jenkins thought Bernadette had become more confident because she was helping with Grace and Juliet, which probably fulfilled her maternal instincts, but the main reason was that her husband was no longer beating her, Paul realised.

'What happened to the gun?'

'He gave it back to the Hallands. He didn't want it in our possession if her body was ever found. He told Charles that he'd bought another one. We were bound together by this foul secret.

He told me that if I told anyone about him he'd tell on me, and that it would be worse for me because I'd murdered Mrs Halland, and that I'd be put in jail for life. I told him that I'd been in prison since I'd married him and could cope with being in another sort of prison better than he could. He'd be put in prison too because he was a rapist. They put rapists in prison.'

Paul wondered if she was telling the truth. An alternative version of events struck him. Sylvia Halland and Seamus Ryan senior could have been having an affair. Bernadette could have seen them kissing. Sylvia may have been coming to say goodbye to her lover. Or they could have been going to run away together. Seamus may have kept quiet because of his son, or because his wife had threatened to say he was a rapist.

'I'll go to jail now. I'll confess. I'll tell them everything. Will you tell the police to come here?'

'Mrs Ryan, are you certain your husband was trying to rape her?'

She looked confused. 'What else would he be trying to do? They sure weren't dancing.'

'Could you have mistaken a passionate embrace for something else? Could they have been having an affair?'

'No. He knocked two of her teeth out. Her lip was cut – there was blood all over her mouth. Her blouse was ripped to her waist. She put up a hell of a fight though. His face was so badly scratched he looked as if he'd been attacked by a wildcat, but he had an answer for that. He told people that he'd fallen out of a tree.'

Paul picked up the phone. 'Please give me moment. I need to check something.' He punched in Ralph's number. 'Hi Ralph, are you still with Wendy?'

'Yes.'

'Can I speak to her?'

'Why?' Ralph sounded suspicious. 'What's happened? I don't want you upsetting her more than she's already –'

'Ralph, it's important. Please put her on.'

'Have you got evidence against her?' Ralph snapped.

'No. The opposite. Please, I need her to confirm something.'

'Yes, Paul, what is it?' asked Wendy in a trembling voice.

'Wendy, do you remember seeing Mr Ryan the day after Sylvia disappeared?'

'Yes, he came up to the homestead.'

'If I remember correctly, you told me his face was a mess.'

'Yes, it was.'

'Can you be more specific?'

'He'd fallen out of a tree – it was badly scratched and there was a bruise on his cheekbone. Why?'

'Did you see him fall out of the tree?'

'No. What's this about?'

'How do you know he fell out of a tree?'

'He told me.'

'Wendy, everything's okay, I promise.'

'What's going on, Paul?' asked Ralph.

'Wendy's in the clear. Someone has confessed.'

'Who?'

'I'll tell you later.' Paul disconnected the phone. 'I wish I could spare you this, Mrs Ryan, but I can't keep it quiet. Already there is talk that Charles Halland or his father murdered her. And, as you know, Wendy Jenkins has come under suspicion.'

'That's why I've confessed. Wendy was kind to me – and generous. She could have resented me helping with Grace and Juliet, but she didn't. It didn't make her jealous that they liked me too. I read all these allegations that she and Charles Halland were having an affair, but that's rubbish. Wendy wasn't like that. She didn't ever want to marry.'

'Why not?'

'She told me. Her father made her mother unhappy – he was a bully. Not that he hit her or anything, but they were always fighting. He wouldn't let her work. Wendy said that she wanted the freedom to do what she wanted when she wanted. Her maternal instincts were fulfilled first with being Grace and Juliet's governess and then by her teaching at the kindergarten.' She gave Paul a weak smile. 'I'm seventy. Yes, I know I look more like eighty, but that's what living with a monster did to me. I won't be in jail long before I die. I'm sorry for my son – that's all. This will be hard for him. What are you going to do now?'

He wasn't sure. 'I'll have to inform the police. Can you stay here till Juliet and Grace come? They need to hear this from you. Then we'll work out what to do.'

She nodded. He phoned the Tordorrach homestead. Noël answered. She agreed to fly Juliet and Grace into Cobar.

Chapter 46

Noël, Juliet and Grace arrived forty minutes later. Paul summarised what Bernadette had told him.

Noël was the first to speak. 'Thank you for telling us, Mrs Ryan.'

Grace and Juliet nodded.

'And thank you for trying to help her,' said Grace.

'But her car – it was found in Sydney,' said Juliet. 'How did it get there?'

'My husband didn't want it anywhere near us, so he told Mr Halland that one of his friends in Sydney had died and we were going to the funeral. We left early one morning before it got light – me in Sylvia's car, him in ours. We got to Sydney when it was dark. We parked in a street in Manly. He took the wheels and number plates off her car and fiddled around under the bonnet so it wouldn't start. We put the wheels in the boot of our car and drove back to Tordorrach the next day.' Her smile was bitter. 'Clever he was. He thought of everything.'

Paul never advised his clients to lie, but felt that this was an exception.

'I've got an idea,' he said. 'It's not ethical, but under the circumstances . . . I would suggest, Mrs Ryan, that in your statement to the police, you say that you pointed the gun at your husband to try and stop him, but it went off. Do you know anything about guns?'

'Only that they can kill.'

'Had you ever used one before or since?'

'No.'

'Then the rest of what happened can stand. You accidentally shot Sylvia Halland – and that is the truth. You need say nothing about trying to shoot your husband. Do you agree to that?'

'That's kind of you. Yes.'

He looked at Juliet, Grace and Noël. 'Yes,' they said in unison.

'But perhaps Mrs Ryan could say that she aimed the gun and pulled the trigger with the intention of making her husband stop, and as she knew nothing about guns her aim would be off,' suggested Juliet.

'No. Best keep it simple.'

'But how does a gun go off without you pulling the trigger?'

'It can't,' said Noël. 'But if someone knows nothing about guns they can accidentally pull the trigger. I think that's what Paul means.'

'And it was so long ago,' said Paul. 'Your memory of events could be confused. You'll be convicted of manslaughter, failing to report her death to the police, and helping to bury a body. As you're not a danger to the public I think you'll avoid being sent to jail. And that you confessed willingly, to save another person from being suspected, will go in your favour.' He switched on the computer. 'Give me about ten minutes. I'll type out your statement. The less you have to say when the police arrive, the better.'

'Mrs Ryan, did your husband beat Seamus?' asked Juliet.

'Oh, no. He loved Seamus – he was good to him. And he was good to me in front of him, so Seamus never knew his dad's other side. He was kind to animals too.'

'Yes,' said Grace. 'He told us that riders should never use whips or spurs on horses. And all the dogs adored him. This other aspect of him is unbelievable.'

'It was only me he was cruel to.'

'And our mother,' said Grace.

'She was beautiful,' said Bernadette. 'I don't think he could help himself when she came to ask him for help.'

'Sylvia scratched your husband's face, so his skin should be under her fingernails. It can be tested against your son's DNA.

'So Seamus will have to provide a sample?'

'Yes.'

'He'll refuse.'

'He can't. Otherwise the police might think that you're twisting the truth. They might think that you deliberately killed Sylvia because you caught them kissing and shot her because you were jealous.'

'Seamus loved his dad.' Bernadette covered her face with her hands. 'This will be horrible for him.' Tears ran through her fingers.

Noël put her hand on Bernadette's shoulder. 'Mrs Ryan, if it's any comfort to you, I think we can be certain that your husband would have killed her anyway. Neither of you knew she was leaving, and as he'd injured her in the attack then he would think that she would tell her husband and father-in-law. Not only would he have lost his job and his house, he would have been tried for rape and jailed.'

Bernadette wiped her eyes. 'There's one thing I want you to know. Sylvia had her engagement ring on. He took it off. When we went to Sydney he sold it. However bad he was he was a wonder on the land. He and your grandfather and father got on really well – they had the same ideas. They said that planting trees helped the ecology. My husband bought lots of trees with the money he got from Sylvia's ring. He planted them near our house – a little forest it was. The last time I saw it they'd grown. It's a beautiful place.'

'Yes,' said Noël. 'We take our visitors there. It's one of the places where we break for lunch when the horse treks are on. And some of our wedding photos were taken there.'

Bernadette looked wistful. 'Sylvia's trees . . . that's what I called them. Sylvia's trees.'

Paul finished typing the statement. 'Mrs Ryan, I've kept this brief – just the bare facts. I've left out the fact that your husband was beating you. As he was popular in the district you might not be believed. I've kept it as simple as possible.' He printed out the statement and gave it to her.

She was crying so much she had to keep wiping her eyes. She handed it back to him. 'Yes.'

'You'll remember that you only pointed the gun at him when they question you?'

'Yes.'

'And you don't know what made it go off; you'd never handled a gun before?'

She nodded.

'Is Seamus at home?' he asked.

She pulled another tissue from the box on Paul's desk. 'He should be.'

'I'm sorry, but I have to get him here.' He handed her the phone. Her hands were shaking so much she dropped it. He picked it up. 'What's the number?' When she'd told him, he punched in the numbers and gave Bernadette the phone.

When Seamus arrived his mother was crying. He went and put his arm round her. 'Mum, what's wrong?' He looked at Paul. 'What's happened?'

Paul picked up her statement. 'I'm sorry, Seamus, but you'd better read this.'

When Seamus had finished reading her statement he tore it up. 'Lies. Lies. Why did you make her say this?'

'It's true,' his mother managed to say.

'It can't be. Dad would never –'

'I'm sorry you have to know this, Seamus, but he beat me.'

'No.' He glared at Grace and Juliet. 'What is it about you lot? Can't you face up to the fact that your mother was a slut?'

Juliet leapt forward and slapped Seamus across the face. She was about to rake her nails down his cheek when Paul and Grace grabbed her and pulled her away.

Paul led her to a chair. 'No, Juliet. That is not going to help. Seamus, there is one way to either prove or disprove what your mother has said. According to your mother, Sylvia Halland scratched your father's face. If his skin is found under her fingernails the police will have to take samples of your DNA so it can be matched with the DNA from the skin under her nails.'

'Take it then! It'll prove you lot wrong. You're liars. You refuse to accept that your mother was sex mad.'

'Seamus, stop it,' begged his mother.

Chapter 47

The DNA sample proved that the skin under Sylvia's nails had belonged to Seamus Ryan senior.

'If it hadn't been for the DNA, I would have thought she was lying,' said Grace.

Noël nodded. 'I didn't know him as well as you did, but I always looked forward to seeing him. So did Mum and Dad. It was his charm that hid his . . . evil? Was he evil? Was his charm real? Did he really love us all, or was he pretending?'

'He certainly deceived everyone,' said Paul. 'I've never heard a bad word about him.'

'A wife-beater and a rapist,' said Juliet. Her eyes widened. 'Was our mother his only victim? There could have been others.'

Grace took a deep breath. 'What a terrible thought. There could have been. The women might have thought no one would have believe them if they reported that he raped them.'

'They'd have been right,' said Juliet. 'Even though we've got the evidence we can hardly believe it. Let's ask Miss Jenkins.'

Noël's eyes widened in alarm. 'You think he –'

'No, not Wendy . . . she would never have praised him the way she did. Even if she didn't tell anyone, she would have dropped hints,' said Paul.

'So that's where Seamus gets his character from – I often wondered,' said Noël.

'You think there might have been others?' said Wendy.

'It's possible,' said Paul. 'It's about power. He beat his wife – power. Rape – that's also about power.'

'We were wondering if any of the women . . . not accused, but hinted,' said Grace. 'Or were upset, but wouldn't say why.'

'Not that I can remember. It must have only been Sylvia.'

'He never tried anything with you?' asked Paul.

'No. I was never alone with him, anyway. I was always either with Grace and Juliet or in the homestead with their grandparents. We all ate together. He must have tried to rape Sylvia because he had the chance. They were alone in the house.'

'Not at first – he sent his wife out to the orchard. It was a combination of opportunity and calculation. What other women were on Tordorrach?' asked Paul.

'There was the cook . . . but she was quite old – I can't imagine that she would have aroused any lust in Mr Ryan. There was the cleaner – she was married to one of the stockmen, and I can't remember her ever seeming to be distressed. There were casual cleaners and gardeners. The full-time gardener was married – he and his wife lived in a cottage. I rarely saw her. Now I think about it . . . it was a long time ago . . . I do think it was just Sylvia. She was exquisitely beautiful, but not photogenic. Yes, she looks attractive in the photos, but she was far better in real life – 'drop dead gorgeous' is the modern phrase. And I've just remembered. I was alone with Mr Ryan once – he came to the homestead looking for Charles, but he wasn't there. His parents had gone into Cobar with Sylvia, Grace and Juliet. He didn't try anything, or even act as if he wanted to.'

'Do you think that if Bernadette hadn't shot her he would have killed our mother after he'd raped her?' asked Grace.

'No . . . he wasn't a murderer . . . but that's just my opinion.'

'But he didn't know she was leaving,' said Noël. 'With teeth knocked out and blood and her blouse ripped to –'

'He would have been more likely to have persuaded her that it was her fault – that she provoked him – that she wanted him to have sex with her. That she was just being coy and pretending to be hard to get. He would have had the gall to take her back to the homestead and tell them that she'd had an accident. He was persuasive and charming enough.'

'But wouldn't she have said something?' asked Juliet. 'Accused him?'

'Rape victims often keep it a secret – they feel dirty – ashamed – and he would have foiled her plan to leave. She would worry that no one would believe her. Bernadette never told her son that his father was beating her. Even now that I know the truth I find it hard to believe.'

Ω

Until the results of the DNA were processed, Seamus was convinced that his mother had been blackmailed or bribed into lying about his father. When she maintained her story he decided that the drugs she had been given at the hospital had made her deluded. His memories of his father were all good. He had never been smacked, but when he did something bad enough to warrant punishment he was not allowed to ride or see his horse. He had to stay in the house and do chores such as washing the floor or doing the ironing.

It was his father who had taught him to ride horses and be kind to animals. His mother had seemed happy and his father appeared to treat her well. He called her darling, praised her cooking and his manner towards her was affectionate. The day the DNA results came through, his illusions crumbled. He had to accept that his mother was telling the truth.

'Why? Why did you let him beat you?' Seamus asked.

'I had no choice. Your dad was a strong man –'

'Why did he beat you? What did you do to make him?'

'It wasn't anything that I did wrong, Seamus. It was the way he was. The first time was after you were born and he said you were to be called Seamus – same as him. I never wanted to have two Seamuses in the house, but he insisted. He said the eldest boys in his family were always called Seamus. When I said that they were not called Seamus in my family he hit me. It was such a shock. I couldn't believe it had happened. Up till then I'd been so happy – I loved him so much.

'I always longed for your school holidays because the beatings stopped. It was better than, because he never hit me two weeks before you came home from school so the bruises had time to fade. I suppose he thought I might tell you he beat me and show you the bruises to prove it. He was never violent in front of you. You never knew the truth about your dad.'

'Why did you confess now?'

'Because Wendy Jenkins was under suspicion.'

'So what?'

'Seamus, she's a lovely woman. She's innocent. We're friends.'

'And I'm your son. You didn't think how I'd feel about this?'

'Of course I did. Can't you see that I had to confess?'

'No. They had no proof against Wendy.'

'Suspicion – innuendo – can ruin a person's reputation.'

'What about my reputation? My father's a rapist and my mother's a murderer.'

'What else could I have done?'

'Kept quiet, you stupid woman.' Seamus left the house and went for a walk to try to suppress his rage and torment.

Bernadette knew she should have defied her husband rather than allowing him to persuade her into doing what he wanted.

When the shock of Sylvia's death had diminished he had said, 'You got it wrong. She was upset and I was comforting her. You jumped to the wrong conclusion.' He spoke gently and she realised she was still holding the gun.

'Comforting? Liar. Go on, explain why she's missing two teeth and got blood over her mouth. I know what form your comforting takes.'

'She fell.'

'She didn't. You were trying to rape her and you knocked her teeth out in the process. And what sort of fall ripped her blouse to her waist?'

He smirked. 'No one will believe you. They'll believe me. Who's the one with the gun? Not me. Your fingerprints are all over it – not mine. The police and the Hallands will believe me not you. I'm popular around here – everyone likes me. You'll go to jail for murder. Give me the gun, Bernadette.'

'No.'

'Then put it down and we'll decide what to do.'

'No. We'll go to the homestead and tell them the truth.'

'Sweetheart, there's a much better way. We can pretend this never happened.'

She listened while his outlined his plan. The shame that she had agreed to comply with him stayed with her all her life.

Bernadette picked up the painkillers the hospital had given her and looked at them for a long time. *He's shocked*, she thought. *That's why he's angry. That's why he's blaming me. He'll be reasonable when he's had time to think.*

But when Seamus came home he rebuffed her entreaties. When he had refused to speak to her for five days she found a writing pad and pen.

My darling Seamus,

There is nothing left for me to live for, now I have lost your love. There is a copy of my will lodged with Ralph McLachlan. I have left everything to you. There should be enough money for you to begin a new life. I cashed in my insurance policy and have had everything in my bank account transferred into yours. I pray you will overcome this trauma. Perhaps you should sell the house and move elsewhere. I love you.

Your mother.

She was trembling so much that her writing was like that of much older person.

'But it's readable,' she whispered. She went to the kitchen and filled a glass with water. Seamus was weeding the garden.

She was about to take the first tablet when the doorbell rang. She went down the hall and saw Wendy through the fly screen holding a bunch of flowers and a plastic box.

'Bernadette, thank you.' She held up the box. 'I've made a cake.'

They went into the lounge. Bernadette quickly covered her letter with a magazine. Wendy took the lid off the box and lifted out the cake. Bernadette went into the kitchen, put on the kettle, and got plates and a knife.

'I'm so pleased they haven't jailed you,' Wendy said.

'I'm not allowed to leave Cobar. If I'd had a passport they would have taken it. They were careful – they checked.'

'You could have stayed quiet. It was brave of you to confess.'

'I wouldn't have if the papers hadn't made those allegations against you. Apparently they were saying things about Charlie Halland and his father too.'

Wendy nodded. 'Yes, that was upsetting for Grace and Juliet.' She glanced out the window where Seamus was weeding the garden. 'He's working very hard. How's he taken it?'

Bernadette was tempted to tell the truth, but had no idea how Wendy would react. She was capable of striding outside and berating Seamus, and in his current furious mood he was capable of hitting her. 'Inconsolable.' She made the tea and cut the cake. She ate it mechanically hardly tasting it. She spoke to Wendy only to answer her questions. Her thoughts were about life after death and whether she would be forgiven or cast into hell.

'What do you think happens when we die?'

Wendy looked startled. 'Nothing. There is no heaven or hell or paradise.'

'I hope you're right.'

'Even if there is life after death and a judgement day you'll be forgiven, Bernadette.'

When Wendy left with promises to call again, Bernadette washed up the plates and cups and went back into the lounge. She could see Seamus on his knees clipping the edges of the lawn. She took the first pill and then the second, hoping he would come inside see what she was doing and stop her. He didn't. 'Maybe he wouldn't care,' she muttered as she put the sixth pill in her mouth. 'That would be worse than anything.' She imagined him telling her to hurry and take the lot, rather than calling an ambulance and begging her not to die. When the bottle was empty she sat in a chair and waited.

'I'm sorry, Mr Ryan, your mother didn't make it,' said the doctor.

Seamus wept uncontrollably. He didn't listen to the nurse sitting beside him and talking about bereavement counselling. He didn't see the person who put a mug of coffee in his hand. All he could see were the words his mother had written in her letter to him.

This is all Noël's fault, he thought. *If she hadn't come to Tordorrach, none of this would have happened. Her – with her plans and schemes. She should have told me right from the start that she was a Halland. It's her fault I thought she was English. She sounded English. She acted superior just like the English. Her ancestors were transported just like mine – two of them – not just one. She should hate the English too. How was I supposed to remember Grace and Juliet? They were little girls when they left.*

Paul emailed the Sydney newspapers.

Your story about the murder of Sylvia Halland made serious allegations about Wendy Jenkins that have been proved wrong. Unless you print the truth, and put the story on a prominent page, she will sue.

The Sydney newspapers ran it as their main story complete with photographs and an apology. The local paper's story covered four pages.

When Sylvia's body was released, Grace, Juliet and Noël arranged her funeral.

'We don't want it to be a celebration of her life,' Grace told the vicar. 'What with her depression and death she didn't have much of a life.'

'We'd rather it was a memorial to her, with emphasis on the tragedy of her postnatal depression,' said Juliet.

'No flowers,' said Noël. 'But if anyone wants to give money we'll donate it to a mental health charity.'

The vicar nodded. 'An excellent idea. What hymns would you like?'

'*Love Divine*,' said Grace.

'And *Abide With Me*,' Juliet added. 'We don't want it to be a morbid occasion, but a solemn one.'

All the Tordorrach staff attended and the church was full. Juliet, Grace and Noël all wore navy. The men wore dark suits and ties.

Sylvia was buried in the Cobar cemetery next to her husband. They had ordered a marble headstone.

In Loving Memory Of
Sylvia Halland
1952 – 1980
Beloved wife of Charles
Mother of Grace and Juliet

Chapter 48

Shuttleton Court

March 2016

Noël and Paul went to England for an eight-week holiday at the end of March, a week before the first visitors arrived at Tordorrach. Before going to Yorkshire they spent a week in London and stayed at the Savoy Hotel. Noël took him to her house in South Kensington. He had assumed that, because it was rented out, they would only be able to view it from outside. To his surprise she took him down the steps to the basement where the door was opened by the cook who greeted Noël excitedly. The butler was equally happy to see them.

'Them Americans are away, so I can show you around,' the cook told Paul. 'Then we can have lunch. I've made something special for you.'

After lunch he and Noël went to the Victoria and Albert Museum, and in the evening they went to the opera. The following night they went to Mayfair and had dinner with Grace and Juliet's daughters, who shared the attic flat in Grace and Guy's house that was even larger than Noël's. Four floors were let to a Russian oligarch and his family, while they looked for a house to buy. The cook and housekeeper lived in the basement. Juliet's daughter had had the engagement ring Noël had given her made into a brooch, which she wore on the lapel of her black cashmere jacket. The main topic of conversation was the Referendum in June on whether Britain should leave or stay in the European Union.

Not even the photos or the elaborate wrought iron gates had prepared Paul for the size and splendour of Shuttleton Court. Noël used a key to unlock the gates and he followed her directions and drove the Land Rover they had hired down the winding drive lined with oak trees. They parked in what had once been an enormous barn, between a Jaguar and another Land Rover. Wheeling their cases up to the house took ten minutes. The steps up to the front door were wide and palatial. He looked over the side into the basement area. Ivy grew up the walls and there were six cast-iron tables and chairs.

'The restaurant and bistro,' Noël told him.

'It must be an enormous restaurant.'

Noel took a key out of her coat pocket and put it in the lock of the widest and most elaborate front door Paul had ever seen. 'The kitchens, store rooms and flats for some of the chefs and waiters are down there as well.'

As soon as Noël entered the communal entrance hall she seemed dazed.

'Is it okay to wheel the cases over this?' Paul asked, referring to the cream, terracotta and black encaustic tiled floor.

She nodded.

'Wow. What a staircase.'

When she made no indication that she had heard him he lifted his camera out of its case, thinking that her dreamy expression, which he had never seen before, was just like Grace's. He photographed the floor, the staircase, the chandeliers and the ornate ceiling. Then he pointed the camera at Noël and took her photo. It was spring and the weather was cold. Dressed in a long dark-green coat with a high collar, black boots and a beret she looked as if she had come from a century before. He wore a tweed jacket over a cream shirt, dark brown cords and brogues. The only modern things in the entrance hall were their wheeled suitcases.

'Are you okay, Darling?'

'Adam,' she whispered.

He took her hand. 'If the memories are too sad for you I can book us into a hotel,' he said gently. 'I'm sure Adam's parents will understand.'

She smiled. 'Not my husband. The original Adam – the one who wrote the journal. I can imagine . . . no, I can sense him here all those years ago. I wish I'd read it before we went to Australia. I want to know which room was his and which room was his mother's . . . and Imogen's. Reading his words has brought the past to life. All I knew before was that it had been a happy house and the family were good to the servants – but that wasn't always the case. The way the servants and mill workers were treated went from one extreme to the other. But it was the right way round.'

'How do you mean?'

'Badly treated then well treated. Imagine being well treated and fed and then getting a new owner who took away all your privileges.'

'But according to the journal they had been treated well by Adam's grandparents.'

'Yes, of course. So well treated, to ill treated, and back to being respected and valued.'

'It's the sort of place where you think a butler will appear at any moment,' said Paul.

But instead of a butler a young woman wearing jeans, gumboots and a waxed jacket came bounding down the spectacular staircase. 'Eek! I thought you were ghosts at first. Are you the Aussies?'

'Yes, Paul replied.

'I've heard all about you. Mr and Mrs Carlyle are so excited about your visit. You lived here once, didn't you?' she said to Noël.

'That's right, although mainly at weekends. My husband . . . their son grew up here.'

The young woman reached the bottom step and grinned. 'So you know the way.' She headed for the front door. 'See you later.'

At the top of the staircase Noël turned left. As he followed her down thickly carpeted corridors that went in different directions, Paul said, 'If I wasn't with you I'd need a map to find my way.' The conversion had been so sensitively done that the house didn't look as if it had been divided into apartments. After five minutes they reached a dark oak door with a discreet brass 12 E 1.

'What's the code mean?' he asked as she opened the door.

'Apartment number twelve. East. First floor.'

'I should have packed my compass.'

'Adam and I chose this one because we'd get the morning sun. Juliet and Friedrich were in the west – Juliet's got a passion for sunsets, and Adam's parents are in the south – they like the warmth.'

The inside of the apartment was as splendid as the rest of the house. Royal blue velvet drapes hung at the windows, the furniture was walnut, the chandeliers smaller than the ones in the entrance hall and corridors, and the carpets were luxurious. He thought that even if the rooms were half the size they could still be called large. The walls were half panelled in dark wood and the walls above were painted in a pale chalky blue. A painting of Noël and Adam on their wedding day hung on the wall over the grey marble fireplace. Even without the signature at the bottom he would have recognised it as Grace's work.

Noël had come out of her dreamy state. She opened a door with a flourish. 'The bedroom!'

'Oh yes,' he said softly, gazing at the enormous four poster bed. 'We can have fun in that.'

'I knew you'd like it.'

The velvet drapes surrounding the bed were, like the rest of the upholstery and curtains, royal blue. 'This should be called the blue apartment. It's opulent, but in a strange way it's homely. Did you feel overwhelmed when you first lived here?'

'We never really lived here – we came at weekends and holidays. But you're right. In spite of the grandeur I felt at ease. Adam's parents were welcoming, so that helped Juliet and me to settle in.'

Paul went to the window that overlooked a knot garden planted with tulips. Beyond that was a woodland.

'That'll be a haze of bluebells in another month,' Noël told him.

To the right he saw a lake and to the left was a wall covered in wisteria. 'I would have chosen this apartment for the view alone. What's behind the wall?'

'An orchard. Mainly apples, plums and pears. And there are greenhouses.' She took his hand. 'I'll show you the rest.'

A bottle of champagne and a card stood on the table in the kitchen.

'Did you ever cook in here?'

She giggled. 'Rarely. I did warn Adam that I was a hopeless cook, but he didn't believe me till he saw me in action and tasted the results. We ate mostly in the bistro or restaurant, or with Juliet and Friedrich or Adam's parents. When friends from London came to visit the cooks always sent something up from the kitchens.' Noël picked up the card and read it aloud. 'Welcome to you both. Come and see us when you are ready. Love Arthur and Jennifer.'

At his and Noël's wedding Paul had addressed them as Mr and Mrs Carlyle. Noël had called them Mum and Dad. 'Adam's parents?'

'Yes.' She took his hand. 'Let's go and see them.'

That evening they all ate in the restaurant, which had white table linen, silver cutlery and white china with a blue and gold rim. There were displays of white and yellow flowers.

'There must be a wedding tomorrow,' said Noël.

The head waiter hurried over to greet Noël. 'So good to see you again. We've all missed you.'

Paul was surprised to find that the menu was exclusively British.

'That's its major selling point,' said Noël. 'Plus the organic, free-range meat, poultry and dairy. There are very few places that serve only British food. The bistro does Italian and Greek as well as British.'

Paul ordered fillet steak with a mushroom sauce, which he found delicious. 'I feel as if I'm eating Coral's cooking – it's just as good.'

The next morning after breakfast, which they ate in the bistro, Noël took Paul outside to explore.

'The grounds must cost a fortune to maintain,' he said as he saw gardeners pulling up weeds and mowing the lawns.

'That's why the service charges are so steep, but it's also a wedding venue. People can get married in the nearby church, but if they don't want to they can get married in what used to be the ballroom. I'll take you there later.'

'Does that bring in much income?'

'Yes. There're at least two weddings a week on average. The money is put in a communal pot and goes towards the service charges. If there is any excess, which isn't often, it's carried forward to the following year in case there's a shortfall.'

'Do they always have the reception in the restaurant?'

'Usually. So that brings in lots of money. Their friends and relations are often so impressed that they come back regularly to the restaurant or bistro. And the single wedding guests frequently decide to get married here. The restaurant and bistro are always full in the evenings. You have to book for the restaurant, but not for the bistro.

'Now I want to orientate myself back to 1850 and find where Adam and Andrew waited to trap his mother with Deaville.' She pulled a sheaf of papers, that Juliet had printed out for her, from her jacket pocket. 'He walked to the back of the house avoiding the gravel path. At the servants' door . . .'

'Were his mother's rooms at the front, back or side of the house?'

'He doesn't say.' She gave him the pages.

'Andrew climbed up a tree.'

Noël grimaced. 'Which tree? Could be anywhere.'

'His mother's rooms would be the best in the house, wouldn't they?'

'Yes, but there are so many major rooms. Important guests had to have principal rooms, and the views, from whatever window, are all sensational. When I was reading the journal at Tordorrach, I kept trying to work out the exact locations Adam mentioned, but I couldn't. I thought actually being here would make it easier, but it's not. The gravel paths are still here and so are the trees.'

'Wait, said Paul. 'It would have to have been a mature tree for Andrew to climb up into the branches. It was a hundred and sixty six years ago, so –'

'It could have died or been chopped down.'

'Or it could still be here and even bigger.'

'Along with all the others. I wish he'd specified what it was. It could have been an oak, a chestnut –'

Paul laughed. 'He had no idea that someone in 2016 would want to follow his footsteps. Anyway it's not that important, is it?'

'Yes, Andrew might be an ancestor of mine. And because I've had an idea. It's all in my head, but it's growing. Two apartments, mine and Juliet and Friedrich's, are holiday lets. People who want to holiday in this sort of place are usually interested in history. What if we printed out a précis of Adam's story?'

'Why just for people on holiday? People who own or rent apartments in places like this would be interested in the history too. Adam's story's got what readers like – conflict and the struggle between good and evil.'

'Do you think it's an interesting idea?'

'It's an excellent idea. Why do accountants have a reputation for being dull?'

Noël laughed. 'It's a traditional label. Juliet hasn't finished typing it out yet, so I haven't read the whole thing, but so far it's riveting. And it might tell us why or how the Hallands, if they are our Hallands, ended up in Australia.'

He took her hand. 'Come on, Sherlock, let's see if we can work out the location of that tree and the evil mother's bedroom.' He studied the pages. 'The directions are all here. He went through the servant's door and crept up the stone staircase.'

Noël looked at the pages. 'But . . . Adam pushed open the baize door and entered the area where the main bedrooms were. Bedrooms plural.'

'How many apartments in each wing?'

'It varies. There are eight in the east wing – four on the ground floor and four on the first. But in 1850 the bedrooms would have all been on the first floor. The rooms on the ground floor would have been reception rooms.'

'Is there still a billiard room?'

'Not where the original one was, but there is one in the basement.'

After a few days at Shuttleton Court, Paul was mystified. He understood Noël's reasons for moving to Australia, but not Juliet's or Grace's and certainly not Guy and Friedrich's. Their London houses in Mayfair and Victoria were not only superbly located they were also beautifully furnished and spacious. They had live-in staff, leaving them free to pursue their art, photography, architecture and management of the art gallery. Juliet and Friedrich's apartment at Shuttleton Court, where they had spent weekends, was larger than Noël's because Grace and Guy usually came with them.

He sought the most tactful way to question Noël one afternoon when they were having a picnic in one of the woods. The early April sun was warm and they found a picnic table in a patch of sun. They had bought butter, cheese, ham that came from the Shuttleton pigs, granary bread and apples from the farm shop. Noël was always greeted warmly and told how much she was missed.

'How could Juliet and Grace swap this for Australia? And how did they persuade Friedrich and Guy to move? This is idyllic. I would have thought that an urbane man like Guy would have wanted to rush back to London at the earliest opportunity, but he's settled in at Tordorrach as if he was born to outback living.'

Noël poured their wine into glasses. 'Guy thrives on challenges. He and their daughter were having a lot of disputes over what pictures should be exhibited in the gallery. Guy doesn't like abstract art, but his daughter loves it and argued that both should be exhibited. Just before we saw that Tordorrach was for sale Guy let her have her way. He was stunned, and also chastened, when the first set of abstract art she exhibited was a success. As for Friedrich, the chance to design a property from scratch, rather than converting mansions like this and posh London houses into apartments, was too exciting to ignore. Juliet, Grace and me? Yes England's wonderful and we love it, but Tordorrach is our spiritual home.'

Paul tore a piece of bread from the loaf. 'Would you have moved to Australia if it hadn't been for Tordorrach?'

'No. It's only when I found it was for sale that we started talking about it. The decision took a year – we didn't rush into it.'

He leant forward and kissed her. 'Thank God it was for sale.'

Ω

Paul and Noël posted photos of Shuttleton Court and the Yorkshire countryside on Facebook. Linda was in raptures, especially when Bill showed her his father's email one Friday night when they had just got into bed.

The apartments belonging to Noël and Juliet and Friedrich are holiday lets. Would you and Linda like to come here for a holiday when there are no bookings – usually in winter, early spring and late autumn? Staying in the apartment would cost you nothing.

'Oh, yes,' said Linda. 'It's magnificent Let's go. We both get four weeks holiday.'

Bill grinned. 'I feel I'm on permanent holiday here.'

'But you work hard.'

'I know. But it still feels like a holiday – doing things I love. Gardening and horses have become my hobbies.'

Linda looked dismayed. 'You don't want us to go?'

He put his arm around her. 'Did I say that?'

'You don't seem all that enthusiastic.'

'I am. I was just mulling over something.'

'What?'

'Shall we go there for our honeymoon?'

She pulled herself out of his arms. 'Is that a marriage proposal?'

Daunted by her grave expression, he tried to think of something witty to say to ease the pain of her refusal, but before he could speak she grabbed his hands and gripped them hard. 'Because if it is . . . the answer is yes.'

Bill had worried that without Noël around Juliet and Grace would be unable to cope, but as Noël had foreseen, everything went smoothly. Grace pulled herself out of her dreaminess, and Juliet became almost as efficient as Noël. Kathryn came for a holiday during the week Bill had informed her there would be two single men – one was Kathryn's age and the other seven years older. He was pleased that she was far more relaxed now that his father was not present.

He and Xavier were kept busy in the gardens and orchards, but they ate with the visitors every night. Not wanting to hamper his mother's chances of a blossoming relationship he always chose a seat away from her. The two men seemed promising. The older one was a widower with three children, the other was divorced and had a daughter.

Aware that his mother felt rejected by Holly, he wanted her to feel special. One night when all the visitors had gone to bed he asked her to stay at the table in the courtyard so they could chat. He and Linda sat opposite her. The candles were still alight and the dying embers of the bonfire glowed.

'Why are you both so solemn?'

'We haven't told anyone else yet,' said Linda, taking Bill's hand.

'Mum, we wanted you to be the first to know. We're getting married.'

Kathryn burst into tears. She reached out and put her hand on Linda's arm. 'Wonderful!' She wiped her eyes. 'I'm crying because I'm thrilled and touched.'

Part 4
Retribution

Chapter 49

August 2016

Five months after his mother's death Seamus was still haunted by grief and remorse. He tried to work off his grief by working frantically hard. He painted the exterior of the house, kept the garden immaculate, and gave himself a routine for keeping the house tidy and clean. Breakfast was the only meal he ate at home. For lunch he bought sandwiches and for dinner he went to cafes. His mother's house had no mortgage. He bought a new car with the money she had left him, invested the rest, and was able to live on the interest. Every month he went to the cemetery and laid flowers on her grave. The drought had broken and the grass was green.

'Noël has all the luck,' he muttered. 'The water tanks at Tordorrach will be full, there'll be plenty of grass for the cows, horses and sheep. Why couldn't the drought have broken when I was the owner?'

When he returned home he began to tidy the shed. His mother had rarely gone into it and Seamus had filled it with tools, cans of paint, brushes, a lawn mower, watering cans and a hose that was long enough to reach the end of the garden. When he saw what looked like a coil of rope he tensed. He knew the snake was hibernating, but he backed away. His axe was hanging on the wall of the shed. He took it down. He found a pair of thick gauntlet gardening gloves and pulled them on.

It was almost spring, and the snake might be coming out of hibernation and be alert enough to bite him. Not wanting to risk it, he tried to see where the head of the deadly King Brown was.

He had just seen it and raised his axe when the idea struck him. He lowered the axe. He went inside and pulled freezer blocks out of the fridge. Carefully putting them near the snake he went into town and bought a large wicker picnic basket. Back in the shed he pulled on the gardening gloves. Ready to drop the snake if it moved, he picked it up, put it in the picnic basket, shut the lid and secured it with the toggles.

He laughed. 'Here's a present for you, Noël.'

For days he tried to devise the perfect murder. First he wrote placating letters to Grace, Juliet and Noël.

10th August 2016

Dear Grace and Juliet,

Please forgive my behaviour. I was shocked and upset. Before guilt and grief drove her to take her own life, my mother finally convinced me that my father was not the charming man he seemed. He beat her regularly, but never while I was home. It is taking me time to come to terms with this dreadful revelation, as I am sure you will understand.

I am so sorry that his actions led to your mother's death.

I hope all is well at Tordorrach.

Seamus

Dear Noël,

I have written to Grace and Juliet apologising for my behaviour, and I know that I also owe you and Paul an apology.

Seamus

He put his house on the market. 'When the snake bites Noël, I'll have to escape so I have to move away,' he said to himself. 'Sydney's the best place to get lost in. There must be lots of Ryans there. I won't buy a place – I'll rent.'

His house sold quickly. People who came to view it were impressed by the garden and the size, although they all said it needed a new bathroom and kitchen. He went to Sydney, but the rental for even a small flat was extortionate. He caught a train to Melbourne where the rents were more affordable, although still expensive. He found a flat to rent in Elsternwick. It was small and only had one bedroom, but until he was sure he had escaped detection it was all he needed. He arranged to move in when the sale of his house was complete in the middle of November. The flat was furnished, which was perfect for Seamus. He went to a second-hand furniture shop in Cobar and arranged for them to take his furniture the day before he left his house. He hadn't expected it to be worth much and was surprised by the amount the owner of the shop offered.

'Going anywhere nice, Seamus?'

'Brisbane,' he lied. 'I wanted to stay here, but . . .'

'I understand. Terrible thing to happen. Good luck. Hope all goes well.'

'No one will know me there. I can . . .'

'Yeah, I know. Start again.'

When the warmer weather came he put freezer packs on the basket to keep the snake drowsy. He kept it alive by opening the lid slightly and pushing pieces of meat through the gap. He let it come out of hibernation every few days so it could eat. He kept it moist by spraying a thin mist of water from the hose through the wicker. When it began to hiss and move around he piled the freezer packs on top. He watched and listened and was able to estimate how long it took for it to come out of hibernation.

He thought about all the possible scenarios. His car was new so people at Tordorrach would not know who was visiting Tordorrach until he got out. If he was lucky he would find Noël alone, but he doubted that would happen given that six people lived in the homestead and Coral would most likely be in the kitchen. 'Even if there are lots of people around, once the snake rears up there will be panic and I can escape,' he said to himself. 'Their attention will be on the snake and Noël.'

Ω

Paul woke and sleepily ran his hand over Noël's abdomen. He was surprised to feel a faint flutter. He pushed back the quilt, pulled up her nightdress and stared. 'When,' he whispered in her ear, 'were you going to tell me?'

'What?' she murmured. 'Is it time to get up?'

'This. Or are you putting on weight because you're contented?'

'I don't know . . . let me sleep.'

He kissed her. 'Tired, putting on weight – you haven't been sick though.'

She opened her eyes. 'Why should I be sick?'

'Pregnant women often are.'

She sat up and stared at him. 'I'm not pregnant.'

'I think you are.'

'I can't be.'

'Why not?'

'I've never been . . . I'm too old.'

'Have your periods stopped?'

'Yes, but they've always been erratic. I lost a lot of weight when Adam's cancer was diagnosed and after he died. I'm putting on weight because I'm happy and contented.'

He took her in his arms and kissed her. 'We'll make an appointment with the doctor. I'm sure they will agree with me.'

'I told you,' said Paul when a scan showed that Noël was twenty-one weeks pregnant. 'You are happy about it, aren't you?' he asked anxiously as they walked to Cobar airport.

'Oh, yes . . . just . . . I don't know . . .'

The news stunned her. She and Adam had been married for fifteen years and nothing had ever happened. Tests had showed that Adam had a low sperm count. Noël had hidden her disappointment. 'We've got each other,' she'd consoled him. Instead of having children of their own they lavished affection on their nieces. When Adam died Noël's sense of loss was acute. She had cursed the fate that had prevented them from having children and the pancreatic cancer that had taken Adam from her.

As they flew back to Tordorrach she started to think about what could go wrong. By the time they landed she was planning the nursery. They told Grace and Juliet first.

'Boy or girl?' Juliet asked excitedly.

Noël shook her head. 'I didn't want to know.'

'Neither did I,' said Paul.

Grace began a painting for the nursery and Juliet was thrilled about all the baby photos she intended to take.

'Darling, if the baby's a boy, would you like to call him Adam?'

Noël looked thoughtful. 'No.'

'I wouldn't mind – I'd be happy. Adam's a good name.'

She put her arms around him. 'Let's call him something for himself.'

'What was your father's name?'

'Giuseppe.'

'Oh.'

'Shall we call him that?'

'Well . . . '

She nudged him. 'Only joking.'

'You want to wait till he's born?'

She nodded. 'We'll see what suits him. The same if it's a girl. A name for themselves – not after anyone – something unique to them.'

It was months since Noël had read the journal. Now that the mystery of Sylvia's disappearance was solved, and her mind kept wandering when she tried to do the accounts, she began reading it again. Don scolded her when she arrived in the office and told her she must rest. 'You're on maternity leave. If I need you

I'll ask,' he said. 'How about we meet every evening and go through things?'

Noël agreed.

Shuttleton Court 1851

'Mama,' I said solicitously, 'Victor Deaville was hung yesterday morning. I know you have been worried that he might escape, but you no longer have to fear him. He is dead and cannot harm you.'

Her expression did not change. I had wondered if she would feel sorrow, but realised that to her Deaville had been nothing more than a way to help her get rid of me.

When our year of mourning for my father was over, people visited my mother. Instead of letting the butler or one of the footmen take the visiting cards to her, I took the visitors up to her rooms myself. They waited in the corridor and I left the door ajar so they could hear our exchange.

'Mama, Lord and Lady so-and-so are here, would you like to see them?'

'No, I wouldn't,' she would snap, unaware that they were in the next room. 'Tell them to go away.'

It wasn't that she didn't want to see visitors; it was because she no longer had fine clothes or jewellery and her hair was untidy. Soon word of her rudeness circulated and visitors stopped calling.

Secure in my position, I told her all the things I had done. 'The maids' attic rooms have been painted and they have curtains and new sheets and thick blankets on their beds and rugs on the floor. I've had new uniforms made for them – two for winter and two for summer. The laundry, scullery and kitchen maids have goose fat for their hands.'

Unable to bear anymore she put her hands over her ears. I pulled them away. 'They eat the same as we do. They are happy. They smile at me because they like me and they curtsy because they respect me. Did they ever smile at you, Mama?'

'You care for the servants more than you care for me.'

'Yes, I do.'

'You will regret this, Adam.'

'When will I regret it?'

'When you have no money left. When you have thrown it all away on the low-class scum.'

I pretended to consider this. 'But, Mama, now you are not spending vast amounts on clothes and jewels and entertaining, I have more money than I had a year ago.' I looked at the clock on her mantelpiece. 'Ah, I must leave you. I am interviewing two gentlemen for the teaching post in the school I have reopened. Imogen's governess will be teaching the youngest children.' I saw her expression of fury as I left the room.

Freed from our mother's dominance and cruelty, Imogen flourished. She put on weight and gained an air of authority. I consulted her about the running of the household.

'Should we keep the cook and the housekeeper or sack them?' I asked her as we were breakfasting one morning.

She went to the sideboard and piled her plate with scrambled eggs and toast while she considered it. 'Were they willingly cruel to the maids or was it all because of our mother?'

'I think there is a lot of cruelty in both of them,' I said. 'They ate well – it would have been easy for them to have increased the food given to the servants under them. Yes, they were frightened of our mother, but the estate has enough food for everyone to be well fed. Our mother need never have known who was eating what. The accounts were nothing to do with her – the estate manager handled them. He is a decent chap.'

Imogen returned to the table. 'Sack them.'

'I want to, but would they spread rumours of my insanity to their next employer? Now I am turning my back on conventional society and breaking my engagement I will have powerful enemies. My fiancée's family are noble. Impoverished, but with influential friends and relations.'

She chewed her lip. 'Would giving them good references prevent them making trouble? You don't have to tell them why you're dismissing them – you can be gentle and say you are reducing the household. Sound regretful. Pay them off. Who would you put in their place?'

'I'll promote one of the kitchen maids to cook and one of the housemaids to housekeeper.'

'It will have to be someone literate,' she said. 'And I think there is an assistant cook.'

Noël fell asleep. Paul woke her when he got home from work, removed the manuscript, and put a tray on the bed.

'Coral's made you a cheese and tomato omelette.'

'This is ridiculous,' she said. 'I feel so useless and lazy.'

He kissed her. 'Obey your body.'

'I used to read three books a week. Now I fall asleep after a few pages.'

Chapter 50

Although Noël would rather have stayed in bed late, she made the effort to get up early and get dressed as though she was going to work. Everyone waited on her, and although irritated by her own lack of energy, she was grateful for their concern and assistance. 'Some women work right up to the day before the birth,' she told Juliet. 'Why can't I?'

'Just accept it. It's the way you are. You're older than most pregnant women, and when you're not pregnant you are full of energy,' she said. She pulled two chairs into the spring sun on the veranda. 'Sit down, start reading and I'll make some coffee.'

Shuttleton Court 1851

Imogen was right. Getting rid of the cook and the housekeeper was painless. First I tackled the housekeeper. Two days later I dealt with the cook. I explained that now my father was dead and my mother had retired from society we would have no more lavish dinners or parties. I gave them excellent references and money in lieu of notice. I told them this was so they could start looking for positions immediately without the responsibility of work. I knew they had families they could stay with so they would not be homeless, and told them to contact me if they were having problems finding work. I never heard from either of them again.

The assistant cook became the cook and the senior housemaid became the housekeeper. Imogen and I agreed to cut down on the amount of food we ate at breakfast and dinner. 'Just stewed fruit, eggs and toast and tea for breakfast,' I told the new cook. 'And three courses for dinner – soup, a roast and vegetables, and a pudding. No cheese course, just brandy for me and a pot of chocolate for Miss Carlyle. 'Give the menu to her to approve in the morning. She will give you advance notice when we have guests.' I was about to end the meeting with her when I thought of something. 'What time do you and the other servants have their dinner?'

'Usually eleven, sometimes midnight.'

'In future you will eat first. Imogen and I will dine at seven. Will that suit you?'

'Oh, yes, Sir. Thank you, Sir.'

In spite of her youth Imogen did an excellent job of replacing our mother. The only thing we agreed with our mother about was the preference for English rather than French food, which made the task of the cook and her assistants easier.

Extricating myself from my engagement was more problematic. Now our period of mourning was over the family began calling and tried to arrange a date. I had hoped that rumours of my mother's rudeness would put them off, but they were desperate for our money. I knew that if I broke the engagement they would sue for breach of promise and their family connection with minor royalty would help them get as much money as possible.

'I'm sorry to have to tell you,' I told the family, 'that my mother is...' I hesitated as if I was reluctant to use the words mad or insane, but they came to that conclusion when they saw my embarrassment.

'Yes, we have heard,' said her father impatiently. 'But she can be kept out of sight. She need not come to the wedding. People will understand – she has retired from society.'

Feeling trapped I said, 'It grieves me that she will not be part of something so important. Our wedding will be a lavish event. What are we to tell people?'

'That she is ill.'

I was groping for a response when Imogen, who was going to be a bridesmaid, said, 'It is far worse than that.' She looked at me. 'I'm sorry, Adam, but you have to tell them.' She put her hand on my arm. 'I know you want to keep it secret, but we have to tell the truth.'

I lowered my head as if distressed, and hoped that Imogen would continue as I had no idea what she had in mind.

'Our mother is...'

'What?' snapped the father.

Imogen wiped her eyes. 'She makes a lot of... noise,' she whispered.

'What sort of noise?'

'Screaming,' I said. 'Imogen, I wish you hadn't –'

'She is violent,' continued Imogen. 'She has injured so many maids we can't get anyone to look after her. She deliberately ... soils herself. We have to clean up after her.' Her face lit up and she looked at my fiancée. 'After you and Adam marry, you can help me look after her.'

'No, she will not!' said her mother.

I hoped they would storm out, but her father said, 'Get her locked up. Put her in a lunatic asylum.'

Imogen covered her face with her hands and said through a storm of weeping, 'We couldn't do that to our mother. This is her home. She would die in an asylum.'

Her weeping turned into hysteria. Their expressions were disgusted.

I drew her father aside. 'Insanity runs in the family,' I said softly.

Finally they left. Tears of laughter ran down Imogen's face.

Over dinner one evening, Imogen said, 'I want to do something useful.'

'What sort of thing?'

'I don't know. I only know that I despise the social gatherings Mama had. If the school needed teachers I could work there.'

'Would you like to do that?'

'Yes, but they have got teachers. Does my governess need help?'

'Let's ask her. As well as teaching the youngest ones reading and writing and arithmetic, she takes the needlework classes.'

The governess was delighted to have Imogen's help and Imogen enjoyed teaching and felt fulfilled.

'I've been thinking about what to do with Mama's jewels,' she said one day. 'If we sold some of them we would get a fortune.'

I had forgotten about them, and thought of all the things we could do with the money. Instead of repairing some of the workers' cottages we could demolish them and build new ones. We could build new lodgings for the gardeners and furnish them with beds, thick blankets and proper mattresses.

We went to Imogen's rooms and she opened the safe. Inside were ropes of pearls, pearl chokers, six tiaras set with rubies, sapphires, emeralds and diamonds, twenty necklaces, twenty-five bracelets, thirty brooches and fifteen rings. She selected a beautiful diamond ring, which was less ostentatious than the rest. 'You could give this to your fiancée,' she said with a sly smile. 'When you get one.'

'I think that's my ring,' Noël said to Juliet. 'Adam did say it was a family heirloom.

Imogen selected the simpler pieces of jewellery, which were far more attractive than the rest of the flamboyant and gaudy collection. She held up a diamond ring surrounded by rubies. 'It will be nice to give this to a daughter on a special birthday, if either of us ever have daughters,' she said.

Juliet looked at her engagement ring. 'This is definitely the same one. Rings like this are unusual – it's more often a ruby surrounded by diamonds not a diamond surrounded by rubies.'

I picked up a ruby and diamond tiara. 'You could wear this on your wedding day.'

'You will let me marry whoever I want?' she asked anxiously.

'Yes. And I will marry who I want.'

Shuttleton Court became serene. The servants were healthy, well fed and happy. We stopped the segregation of males and females at meal times. If an unmarried maid became pregnant we looked after her instead of dismissing her as my parents had done. Romance flourished. In the second year of my ownership there were five weddings. Two of our footmen married our maids and one of the coachmen married our assistant cook. Two of our scullery maids married grooms. We attended every wedding, hosted a wedding breakfast and gave them practical gifts. When they had a baby we gave them baby clothes and a cradle and increased their wages.

The Halland family were frequent dinner guests and Imogen became close friends with their daughter.

'She's so much nicer than those ghastly girls Mama made me mix with.'

It was Andrew who prevented me from making some reckless mistakes. I had banned hunting on my land and stopped going to church. I didn't believe in God or heaven or hell and had no intention of being hypocritical.

'Adam, you made a lot of enemies when you forbade the hunt to cross your land. The gentry were prepared to accept that you gave up hunting yourself, but this has incensed them. You need all the support from the church you can get. Go to church every Sunday. Open the fêtes and donate money. You don't know how many people know that your mother tried to get you committed to a lunatic asylum – your neighbours are powerful and could damage you.'

What Andrew said was wise. I went to church, which had a new vicar. I invited him and his wife to dinner. Imogen and I supported his charities. We donated money to the church when its roof was damaged by a storm. I was surprised to find that I liked him and his wife. I had been bored by the sermons preached by the sanctimonious old vicar and I had been prepared to think of other things during the new vicar's sermons, but they were short, interesting and relevant. He spoke about goodness in this life and said very little about the afterlife, which made me think that perhaps he didn't believe in it either, and had chosen to be a vicar so he could help people unfortunate enough to be born into poverty.

Our servants all attended church on Sundays. Half of them went to the morning service and the other half went to evensong. After the service we all went to the servants hall and had morning tea or supper. The vicar and his family came to lunch. The local workhouse was his major charity.

'I don't give them money – to make sure it's the inmates who get the help, not the people who run it. I suspect that money would go into the pockets of the administrators. I buy soap and blankets and my wife makes clothes for the children and plain dresses for the women.'

'I would be happy to donate bolts of cotton. Just let me know how many you need. And I'll donate food – we've got plenty in the kitchen garden and the orchard. Please come and help yourself – take anything you need. I'll let the gardeners know.'

Imogen asked if she could accompany the vicar on a visit. She came home with a newborn baby. Fighting back tears she said, 'Her mother died having her.'

I was about to suggest that we put the baby in our old nursery, when she said, 'The head gardener's baby was stillborn three days ago. Can we give her this one?'

I looked at the tiny infant, and doubted it would live long enough to give the gardener's wife any solace. 'She may not want it.'

'But it was her firstborn.'

'She might not want a replacement.'

'It's not a replacement – hers was a boy. This is a girl.'

'Let us ask her,' said the vicar.

The three of us walked to the cottage. She was in the kitchen. Her face was pale and she looked desperately unhappy. There were damp patches on her chest. She had milk and I hoped she would want to give it to an infant that was not her own. When the vicar explained the reason for our visit, she smiled, reached out her arms to Imogen and took the baby. The gardener and his wife named her Imogen. In spite of my pessimistic prognosis the infant thrived and was christened in the church.

You wouldn't be able to do that now, Noël thought. *There'd be social workers and health visitors everywhere. Reports as to the suitability of the adopters and their home, forms to fill in and criminal record checks.*

This gave Imogen an idea. We visited the workhouse with the vicar and spoke to the midwife.

'What happens to the babies whose mothers die in childbirth?' Imogen asked.

'They usually die too,' she replied disinterestedly.

'But what if they survive?' I asked.

She shrugged. 'They go to the orphanage. But not many survive.'

'Can you notify me when a woman dies and her infant survives?' asked the vicar.

She looked mystified.

'My sister and I are willing to give the motherless children a home and an education.'

In the first year, three infant girls and one boy from the workhouse came to Shuttleton Court. We added cots to the old nursery, where the infants were fed, bathed and dressed in clean clothes. We employed a nanny to take care of them. She was compassionate and approved of our venture, unlike many of our neighbours who decried what they thought was our stupidity. They wrote letters entreating us to tell them that the rumours were untrue, and informed us that we would be infested with lice if we continued to provide shelter to workhouse brats. We took delight in replying, and giving them a lecture about Christian principles, charity and kindness. Just to infuriate them even more we quoted from the New Testament.

It took me three years to complete all my projects. The roofs of the cottages were repaired and broken glass in the windows replaced. Others were demolished and new ones built. The gardeners had a new weatherproof barn with windows to let in the light and thick curtains to keep out the cold. The mattresses and blankets were new and they were on beds not the floor. All the old mattresses and blankets were taken to the kennels for the dogs. Our gamekeeper was in charge of the gun room, and the breeding of pheasants and grouse, but there were no shooting parties. The birds, deer, rabbits and hares were shot to order only by the gamekeeper. If fifteen pheasants were required by the cook then only fifteen were shot. Instead of sharing a crowded cold dormitory the maids now slept two to a room with comfortable beds and mattresses.

Knowing how much my mother hated hearing about all the improvements I was making, I kept her informed. She complained that she could hear babies crying and was horrified when I told her what Imogen and I were doing.

'You are bringing them up as members of this family?'

'No, Mama. We are making sure they are well fed, clothed and educated. They will train as servants when they are old enough. The boys will be taught to ride, look after horses and gardening and the girls will learn cooking, cleaning and sewing.'

'Well, that's a relief. I thought you had gone completely mad – it would be just like you to adopt them and give the bastards our name.'

To incense her further I told her about our plans for the brighter ones, who we decided to help release from a life of servitude if that was their wish.

'We will set some up in business as dressmakers,' I told her, relishing her furious expression. 'We will help them to get a little shop. If they are good at baking they could have a bread and cake shop. The boys could be butchers or grocers. Imogen and I must give them opportunities to be independent and rule their own lives. Not all of them will want to – some will prefer to stay here.' I left before she could respond.

A month later I made a mistake that could have been disastrous.

Chapter 51

'Hell, what now?' said Noël. She picked up her cup and drank the last of her coffee.

Juliet looked over her shoulder. 'Oh, yes – that bit. His mother was such an evil witch I would have been tempted to stick a knife in her heart or poison her food.'

When I went into her rooms one evening my mother was in bed groaning and clutching her stomach.

'Send for the doctor,' she begged. 'I am in terrible pain.'

I told one of the coachmen to get the doctor. When he arrived three hours later my mother pointed at me. 'He is trying to murder me.'

The doctor stared at me in shock.

'No. Mama, why are you saying this?'

'He is insane. I tried to have him committed, but he was too clever for me.'

'Excuse me, Doctor,' I said. 'We need a witness.' My heart was pounding as I left the room. I found the maid who looked after her and asked her to come to my mother's rooms. 'My mother is accusing me of trying to murder her.'

She gasped and we entered the room.

'Doctor, this is my mother's maid. Mama, repeat your accusations.'

She looked wary.

'Your mistress tells me that her son is trying to kill her,' the doctor said, sounding helpless.

'Madame, no. He is good to you!'

'I have not retired from society – he forced me.'

The doctor looked more confident. 'Madame, it is rumoured that you refuse to see anyone who calls.'

'Because he keeps me locked away.'

I turned to the maid. 'For her own safety. She is terrified of being attacked by another intruder.'

'Yes, Sir. I've heard that Madame is frightened.' She turned to the doctor. 'I've seen Mr Carlyle bringing visitors to her room, but she refuses to see them.'

'Do you think I am insane?' I asked her.

'No, Mr Carlyle. You are kind and generous,' she said sincerely.

'Have you ever heard me speak roughly to Madame?'

She shook her head. 'No, Sir.'

The doctor left the room and the maid and I followed. I smiled at her. 'Thank you. I am sorry to have interrupted your work. You may go now.'

The doctor took a deep breath. 'Your mother is plainly still tormented by your father's death and the unfortunate events with the burglar.' He hesitated. 'Do you think ... suspect that he dishonoured her?'

'I hope not, but it is possible,' I said slowly. 'He was naked and that was plainly his intent, but whether I arrived in time ... I have no way of telling. It was too delicate a subject to mention and my mother was distraught.'

'If he did, then that would unbalance her mind even more,' said the doctor.

I tried to look grim, but I nearly laughed with relief that her plot had failed.

'I will give her laudanum; that should bring her some peace,' said the doctor.

I led him outside and shook his hand. 'Thank you, Doctor. My coachman will drive you home. Is it possible for him to collect the laudanum from you tonight?'

'Certainly. As soon as he returns give her some. I will write the dosage down.'

I went inside and poured myself a brandy. When Imogen came into the dining room I told her what had happened.

'We will have to be more careful,' she said.

We went into our mother's room. 'From today you will make your own bed and clean this room yourself,' I said. 'A housemaid will empty your chamber pot. I will bring your food. Your door will remain locked. I don't want you wandering around the house alone. You might fall down the stairs or get up to mischief. I warned you, Mama. Try anything like that again and I will have you committed.'

'How can you do this to me – your own mother?'

'You were going to do it to me, Mama.'

'The doctor thinks you are deranged,' said Imogen with a smirk.

I nodded. 'It will be easy to have you incarcerated. So no more tricks, or you will be sent to a place far worse than this.'

Imogen put her billiard cue in the rack. She looked pensive. I asked her if there was anything wrong.

'Yes. These animals.' She gestured to the tiger skin rugs. 'Can we get rid of them?'

'How? Put them in the attic?'

'Sell them and use the money for something good. They make me feel guilty. Beautiful creatures killed for their skin, just so we could use them as decoration.' She looked at the head of a stag on the wall. 'How could anyone shoot that for fun?'

I agreed with her, but thanks to Andrew's warnings about my recklessness, I had become more cautious. 'We can sell them,' I said. 'But never say anything against the hunters. Our neighbours hate us enough already. This might convince them to move against us.'

'I will keep quiet about my feelings,' she said solemnly.

I contacted a taxidermy shop in Leeds, and the owner came to look at what we had. He offered me a lot more than I was expecting.

'Why are you selling such a wonderful collection,' he asked.

'We need the money,' I lied.

Dozens of glass cases containing foxes, fish and exotic birds were removed. The tiger, cheetah, puma and leopard skins were all rolled up and carried outside to the carriages. All the stag and deer heads were carefully taken down from the walls.

Inevitably there was some damage to the walls, which the maintenance men repaired and repainted.

We put the money into a retirement fund for our servants and mill workers. When our butler turned sixty we had a party for him in the servants' hall. Although he had wanted to continue working he had arthritis and was happy when we'd told him six months earlier that he and his wife could live in their cottage for life. He trained one of the older footmen to take his place. My parents had never acknowledged the birthdays or retirement of any of our servants, and this was the first retirement since I had become the owner. I abhor long speeches so kept it brief.

'In gratitude for your dedicated service, I present you with this,' I announced, handing him a scroll.

He undid the ribbon and opened it. He read it and looked at me in astonishment.

'What is it?' asked his wife.

He was so overcome he was unable to speak.

'The deeds to your cottage,' I said. 'You now own it.'

Imogen and I did not tell our mother, but she found out.

'This is preposterous,' she said. 'Before long the servants will own more than we do.'

'Than I do, you mean,' I said with a smirk that I knew would infuriate her.

'They will turn against you. Don't think they will show you any gratitude.'

'On the contrary, Mama,' said Imogen. 'It will make the servants more loyal and give them something to strive for. Their hard work will be rewarded. Idle servants will be sacked, demoted or have their wages reduced until they improve. Although none of the servants are idle. You are the only idle person in this household.'

'They will become idle with you feeble pair managing things. You have lost what little sense you had. Imogen, you look like a servant, dressed like that. No man will want to marry you – no one decent that is.'

'I would rather look like a servant than a whore, which is what you frequently looked like.'

'She looks nothing like a servant,' I argued. 'Servants don't wear velvet, silk or lace, or pearls or diamond brooches.'

Imogen did a pirouette, and the skirt of her emerald green velvet dress swirled. 'Do you recognise this, Mama? I had it altered to my own taste. More demure – less vulgar.'

'How dare you?'

'Do keep quiet,' said Imogen. 'You are not only unintelligent; you are tedious.'

Our mother's expression made us laugh.

'Curse you both,' she snarled as we left her room.

Imogen spun round and made the sign of the cross. 'To ward off evil,' she whispered. Then she giggled and joined me in the corridor.

'It wasn't that disastrous,' said Noël. 'He managed to convince the doctor.'

'It would have been if the doctor had believed his mother,' said Juliet. He would have got Adam put in the lunatic asylum.'

Chapter 52

January 2017

Seamus put freezer packs in the boot of his car and placed the basket on top. The snake was moving and trying to get out of its prison. He quickly piled more freezer packs on top. He drove out of Cobar with the image of Noël opening the basket and the snake rearing up and biting her on the neck or face. He checked his watch. The timing had to be right. He wanted the snake to be active enough to bite Noël but not so energetic that it hissed and alerted her to its presence. The thought of things that could go wrong made his heart pound. To calm himself he turned on the radio, but Donald Trump's speech about his forthcoming inauguration and what he would do when he was president made him more agitated. He switched to a station that was playing music.

Half an hour away from Tordorrach he stopped the car. He removed all the freezer packs and put them on the back seat. He turned off the air conditioner. It was so hot that sweat was pouring from him when he reached Tordorrach. As he drove through the gates he saw that in spite of the scorching heat the grass that had sprung up in the winter and spring was green. He wiped the sweat from his face and drove up to the homestead. He swore when he saw Matthew walking towards him. His expression was friendly until Seamus got out of the car, then he frowned and folded his arms.

'Hello, Matt.'

'What are you doing here, Seamus?' His tone was not as hostile as he expected, but it wasn't welcoming either.

Disguising his hatred and nerves and trying to sound humble, Seamus said, 'I've come to apologise to –'

'They got your letters. Took you long enough.'

'I want to do this in person. I'm a lot of things and I've made a lot of mistakes, but I'm not a coward. When I know I've done something wrong I say I'm sorry. I want to make peace.' He went to the boot and opened it, praying that the snake would not start writhing and hissing. 'I've got some presents . . . my mother suggested it before she . . .'

'Yes,' said Matthew. 'I heard about that. I'm sorry.'

Thankful that the snake was quiet, Seamus picked up the basket. 'It's just a little gift for the New Year – wine and chocolates.'

'I can give it to them.'

'I want to do this myself. I understand that Grace and Juliet won't want to see me, but was hoping Noël . . .'

Matthew seemed doubtful, but then said, 'Okay, come with me. She's in the office with Paul.'

The last two words were emphasized. *Thinks I'm like my dad*, he thought.

He hoped that Matthew would show him into the office and leave, but he said, 'Wait here – I'll ask her if she wants to see you.'

Seconds later Matthew opened the door and gestured Seamus inside. He was alarmed when, instead of leaving, Matthew stood in the doorway. *It's too late to back out now*, he thought, surprised to see that Noël was heavily pregnant. She was wearing a white smocked sundress. *Plenty of bare flesh for the snake to sink its fangs into*, he thought. 'Mrs Knight, I'm sorry.'

'Thank you. We got your letters. I'm sorry about your mother.'

'This is just a little something – wine, chocolates, biscuits. If I'd known I would have got something for the baby – congratulations.' He put the basket down on the desk in front of her and stepped back to be near the door.

Noël pulled out the toggles. Seamus heard the hiss and hoped no one else had. It hissed again. Paul's warning was too late. The lid rose and the snake reared up. Seamus laughed. Paul was behind the basket. He kicked it at Seamus. Matt and Paul grabbed Noël and dragged her from the room. Paul pulled the door shut trapping Seamus inside. He tried to open it, but Matt and Paul managed to keep it shut.

'Turn the air conditioning down as cold as it'll go!' screamed Noël.

Coral came dashing down the hallway. 'What's happened?'

'Seamus's in there with a King Brown.'

'Help!' shouted Seamus. 'Let me out!'

Noël was breathing heavily. 'I think I'm in labour.'

Paul let go of the door handle to support her, but the door began to inch open, so he had to renew his grip. Coral put her arm around Noël. A blast of cold air told them that someone had heard Noël's instruction.

Juliet came running out of her apartment. 'What's wrong?'

'I've been bitten!' yelled Seamus.

'Good,' said Matthew.

'What's happened?' demanded Juliet.

Paul's satellite phone was in the office with Seamus.

Matthew's was clipped to his belt. Coral grabbed it and punched in the emergency number. 'We've got a King Brown in the house – it's bitten a man. It's in a closed room. The man is too – he brought the snake with him – he tried to murder one of the owners.' As she gave the location Noël groaned. 'And we've got a woman in labour – she's thirty-seven weeks.' She looked at the puddle on the floor. 'Her waters have broken. She's the one he tried to murder. Yes, we've got a runway. Thanks.' She disconnected the call. 'The Flying Doctor's being called and they're bringing someone to catch the snake and make sure it's a King Brown so they can tell the hospital to have the right antivenin ready.'

'Let's hope Seamus dies before he gets the stuff,' said Paul.

Bill was cleaning out the horses' water troughs when he heard the plane. He went outside and watched it land and taxi towards the homestead. When he saw that it was the Flying Doctor he dropped the brush and ran towards it. By the time he was halfway there, the ambulance men had disappeared into the homestead. Minutes later the men reappeared with Noël in a wheelchair, and a man he'd never seen before on a stretcher. His father was beside Noël holding her hand. Matthew, Juliet, Grace, Coral, Friedrich and Guy were close behind. He ran faster, but not fast enough. The plane took off with his father on board. His heart pounded with fear.

Matthew hurried toward him. 'Noël's in labour and Seamus has been bitten by a snake – I think he's dead or dying. If he's not dead he will be by the time they get to Dubbo.'

'Seamus?' said Bill when he had recovered his breath.

'The bloke who used to own this place.'

'What was he doing here? Wasn't he sacked?'

'He tried to kill Noël.' He put his hand on Bill's shoulder. 'She's okay. How about you fly the plane to Dubbo?

Bill shook his head. 'I've never flown solo – Noël or Dad have always been with me.'

'Okay. I'll drive you. We'll be there in four hours. Let's get some water.'

'No, I want to –'

'Bill, going anywhere in the outback without water is dangerous,' Matthew said sternly.

'Yeah. Sorry. I should know that.'

Coral gave them bottles of water for their journey and shoved a tin of biscuits at them. She would have made them sandwiches, but Matthew said there was no time. They had just got into the car when the police helicopter arrived.

At Dubbo Seamus was taken to one part of the hospital and Noël was rushed into the labour ward. Paul went with her and held her hand while she was hooked up to monitors.

'Mr Knight, we're going to have to do a caesarean,' said one of the nurses after three hours. 'The doctor's on his way.'

Paul was ushered outside into the waiting area.

Bill arrived thirty minutes later. 'Matt drove me. He told me all about it.'

Paul was too distraught to speak.

'Seamus is dead? Matt said he reckoned he was. The snake bit him. You look bad. Let me get you some coffee.'

'She's dying.'

Bill put his arm round his father. 'Oh, Dad. No. Christ. Did the snake bite her? Matt said –'

'I don't think so.'

'Then how come she's dying?'

'She's having a caesarean.'

'Why? What did they say?'

'Nothing . . . just got me out of there.'

'Dad, did they say she was dying?'

'No.'

'What makes you think she is?'

'She's pale – white . . . in agony. She's too old for this. The nurses looked worried. When your mother had you and Holly it was – easy – well, easier than this.'

Bill stood up. 'I'll go and find someone.'

'No. Stay with me – please.'

'Dad, caesareans are normal. I'm sure she'll be okay.'

Paul put his head in his hands. 'But this is a country hospital – she should be in Sydney.'

A doctor appeared. 'Congratulations, Mr Knight, you've got a son.'

Paul jumped up. 'Noël?'

'She's sleeping off the anaesthetic.'

When Noël and the baby came home from hospital with Paul they found the baby's room painted pale blue and the windows hung with the blue and white gingham curtains Coral had made. Grace's three watercolours depicting nursery rhymes hung on the walls. The white cot was made up with matching bed linen and a china mobile of blue teddy bears with red ribbons round their necks hung over the cot.

'Do you like it?' asked Bill. 'Matt and I painted it.'

Noël gave him a hug. 'Thank you, Bill, it's lovely. Where's Matt?'

'In the kitchen trying to help Coral cook a celebration dinner – but I think he's getting in her way more than helping.'

Chapter 53

Paul knew the police would have probing questions, but was too overwhelmed by the birth of his son and the attempted murder of Noël to prepare himself and Matthew. The detectives who had investigated Sylvia's murder arrived two days after Noël and the baby came home. Matthew was at his house. When he heard the helicopter he drove to the homestead. Paul was baffled by the detectives' attitude. Neither of them mentioned Noël or the baby and they looked grim when they asked to see the room where Seamus had given the basket containing the snake to Noël. Coral brought in a jug of iced water, coffee, tea and sandwiches.

'Why did you shut Seamus Ryan in here with the snake?' asked one of the detectives.

'He was trying to murder my wife and unborn child.'

'You were both in here with him?'

'Yeah,' said Matthew.

One of the detectives poured out two glasses of water. 'Two men. Why didn't you overpower him?'

'We had to get my wife and ourselves out of the room away from the snake.'

'You knew it was a King Brown?'

Matthew nodded.

'How did you know?'

'I've lived in the outback all my life. Knowing what's a venomous snake and what isn't can mean you live or die.'

'Why didn't you let Seamus Ryan out and leave the snake in here?'

'The safety of a murderer wasn't our first priority,' Matthew snapped. 'Seamus Ryan was the one with the snake.'

'It bit him instead of my wife. His own actions, not ours, caused his death,' said Paul.

'Mr Ryan isn't dead,' the younger detective said with a note of satisfaction in his tone.

Paul saw that Matthew was as astonished as he was.

'He isn't?' said Matthew. 'He looked dead to me. How did he survive the bite of a King Brown?'

'He wasn't bitten. He had a heart attack,' said the inspector.

Paul shook his head in disbelief. 'But he said the snake had bitten him.'

'It tried. Mr Ryan thought it had, which probably caused his heart attack. It only made a tiny puncture mark. It was very sick. When the environmental agency took it to the wildlife sanctuary they had to destroy it. It had been kept in enforced hibernation for too long at much colder temperatures than usual. Mr Ryan's heart attack was serious, but he's recovering well. We have your statement, Mr Fulham. It was made the next day, but we understand things were chaotic.' He handed the statement to Matthew. 'Please read it through to refresh your memory.'

I heard Seamus Ryan arrive, Matthew's statement began. *I didn't know it was him at first, because he had a new car. His old car was a rust bucket and it made a hell of a racket. I knew his mum had committed suicide so that's why I didn't order him off the property. He was haggard.*

I asked him why he was here.

He looked jittery — sounded it too. Said he was sorry and all that rubbish. He told me he'd brought wine and chocolates for Grace, Juliet and Noël. I saw a lot of freezer packs and assumed that they were to stop the chocolates melting. He was different — not arrogant like he used to be. I thought he must have had counselling.

I almost believed him, but in the back of my mind there was a niggling of doubt. He insisted on seeing Noël. He said he wanted to give the hamper to her personally and tell her how sorry he was. He said he was many things, but he wasn't a coward. So I took him to the office where I knew Noël and Paul were doing the accounts. Noël's assistant had the flu. My concern that he might be like his dad and try and rape her was quelled by knowing that Paul was with her. But just in case Paul might have left the office, I went inside with Seamus and stood in the doorway. It was lucky that the snake was still a bit groggy or it would have bitten Noël. Paul and I managed to pull her out of the way. We got outside the office. Seamus kept trying to pull the door open. Paul and I kept it shut. He said he'd been bitten, and Noël went into labour. My wife rang the emergency number.

'Yeah,' said Matthew. 'That's how it happened.'

'Is there anything you'd like to add?'

Matthew handed the statement back to the inspector. 'No.'

'Mr Ryan's version of events contradicts yours, Mr Fulham.'

The detectives curt tones and attitude were aggravating Paul. 'Contradicts? How?' he snapped.

'According to him, you all lured him here and it was you and Mr and Mrs Knight who gave him the basket with the snake inside, telling him that it was a present and you were sorry about his mother.'

Paul was too stunned to speak.

'You can't believe that,' said Matthew so quietly Paul hardly heard him.

'His claims have to be investigated.'

Matthew took a deep breath. 'We never wanted to see him again – none of us here.'

The detective looked dubious. 'Why would Mr Ryan want to kill Mrs Knight?'

To give himself time to answer Paul poured himself a cup of tea. 'Lots of reasons. He was jealous. Noël and her cousins had turned Tordorrach into a thriving business. He had failed – worse than failed. He'd let a prosperous station die and a beautiful homestead go to wrack and ruin. And she sacked him.'

The detective referred to his notebook. 'He says that you wanted revenge because his mother killed Sylvia Halland. He says that he wrote Mrs Knight and her cousins Grace and Juliet letters of apology – did you receive them?'

'Yes.'

'After you received them you wrote to Seamus and invited him here?'

'No. And this is vague,' said Paul. 'Who wrote the letter inviting him here?'

'He didn't say – he is still in a serious condition and – '

'When he recovers sufficiently, please get a statement from him stating specifics. Who supposedly wrote this letter? When did he receive it? And, most importantly, get him to give you this letter – he won't be able to because it doesn't exist. Now, if you have no further questions I have a wife and baby son to attend to. Next time you come, please tell us in advance and I'll have my solicitor here.'

The older detective looked antagonistic. 'I thought you were a solicitor, Mr Knight.'

'I am, but I've had a turbulent week and feel too shattered to think clearly.'

The other detective looked at Matthew. 'You had a grievance against Mr Ryan. He told us that your father looked at Sylvia Halland in a sinister way.'

'I thought you believed me when I told you Seamus was seeking revenge against me because I was the manager here and I witnessed Mrs Knight sacking him,' Matthew retorted.

'Just one thing more, if we may?'

Paul nodded and resisted the temptation to tell him to hurry up.

'In your statement, Mr Fulham, you said you saw that Seamus had a lot of freezer packs. You thought they were to stop the chocolates melting.'

'Yeah, that's right.'

'If the freezer packs were cold the snake would have been in hibernation. But you said it reared up at Noël Knight.'

'They were on the back seat. In my statement I didn't think to say where they were. The basket with the snake in it was in the boot.'

'You were suspicious, yet you took him into the office to see Noël. Why?'

'I felt a bit . . . only a bit – sorry for him. I was cynical enough to think he wanted his job back and that this was his way of doing it. I never suspected he had a snake in the basket.'

'You knew his mother was dead so you would have known he'd inherited her house and her money, so why would he want his old job back?'

'I didn't know he'd inherited her money. I never saw him again after he left here – after he was sacked. How would I know he'd inherited her money? I didn't know much about her. I didn't know she had any money or owned the house she lived in.'

'But she and her husband once owned Tordorrach. You must have known that.'

'I did. But by the time Noël and her cousins bought it, the place was in a bad way. Seamus was heavily in debt . . . I had no idea how much money his mother had.'

'Did you find the freezer packs in Mr Ryan's car?' asked Paul.

'Yes.'

'Well then – you said the wildlife sanctuary said the snake had been kept at much colder temperatures than usual.'

'We did ask Mr Ryan about that. He said he had freezer packs because he had brought you wine and chocolates – it was a hot day so it's logical that he would want to keep the chocolates from melting. We have a problem here, Mr Knight. You say that Seamus Ryan tried to kill your wife. Seamus Ryan says that you, your wife, Matthew Fulham, Grace and Guy Ashcroft and Juliet and Friedrich Reinhardt tried to kill him. It is our job to find out who is telling the truth. If we failed to investigate Mr Ryan's allegations we would be poor detectives. If you cooperate we can solve the case quickly. Please ring your solicitor and ask him to come here now. If he can't we'll get a duty solicitor.'

'It will take him two hours to get here,' protested Paul.

'We can wait.'

'Hang on,' said Matthew. 'When we escaped from this room, Noël shouted for someone to get the air conditioning turned to its coldest setting. Someone – I don't know who, heard her and did it. If we were trying to murder Seamus why would we do that? We were out of danger. It was Seamus who was shut in here with the snake.'

'That's right,' said Paul. 'By the time the Flying Doctor and the environmental agency bloke arrived it was so cold in here we were shivering. If you ring them they will confirm how cold it was and prove that we are telling the truth. And I believe that the snake had gone into hibernation again. Have you still got the basket?'

The detectives looked blank.

'Seamus Ryan brought the snake here in a picnic basket,' said Paul keeping the contempt out of his tone. 'It's not in our office, so I assume that either the police or the environment agency bloke took it away. When you find it, check it for evidence that a snake had been inside. Then check it for Seamus Ryan's fingerprints. Only Noël touched the basket. If you haven't lost it you should find Seamus Ryan's prints all over it and perhaps his DNA. I hope you haven't lost that vital piece of evidence.' It was with difficulty that he stopped himself from calling them inept fools.

'When did you last see the basket, Mr Knight?'

'I don't know. It was pandemonium here. I went in the Flying Doctor plane with my wife, and stayed in a hotel in Dubbo until she and our baby came home from hospital two days ago. Now I suggest you locate the basket and do the necessary tests.'

The detectives left.

Seamus had gained some time and prayed he would be well enough to escape from the hospital before the police came to arrest him.

I'll catch the coach to Cobar and get my money, he thought. *Then I'll catch the coach back to Dubbo and book a plane to Melbourne.*

His chest still ached, but he found it easier to breathe. He closed his eyes and drifted into sleep. When he woke there were two detectives by his bed. The basket containing the snake had been found and tested.

'Your DNA and that of the snake was all over the basket. Your fingerprints were on the straps securing it. There was only one print from Noël Knight, your intended victim.'

'They wiped them off,' said Seamus 'And they must have missed one of hers. They tried to kill me. I never tried to kill any of them.'

The detectives shook their heads and handcuffed his left hand to the bed.

Chapter 54

Yorkshire 1853

Imogen and I were relieved when our mother died. The maid who brought her breakfast looked serious, but not upset, when she told us that she was unable to wake her. There was an empty bottle of Laudanum on her bedside table.

'A broken heart,' the doctor said when he arrived. 'I'm afraid it was suicide.'

Behaving like a grieving son, I said, 'Could it have been accidental? Perhaps she forgot she had taken one dose and took another?'

'No. There's too much gone. She would have survived a double dose – even a triple one.'

'She won't be buried in consecrated ground,' Imogen said, her voice quivering with what sounded like grief, but what I suspected was suppressed laughter.

The doctor patted her shoulder. 'I'll put accidental on the certificate.'

I visualised my mother taking the laudanum triumphant that she would get her revenge. I was sorry that she would never know she had failed. Her funeral was attended only by myself and Imogen. She was buried in the churchyard. There is no memorial plaque in the church and no headstone on her grave. We didn't want her immortalised in marble or brass. The only indication that she and my father existed are their portraits in the house. They were a good looking couple and the artist was skilled. In her portrait my mother was arranging flowers. In his, my father was on his horse. That is the only reason I left them hanging and did not burn them. But

I did remove the small plaque on the frames giving their names. My descendants will look at them and wonder who they were, and never know that their good looks concealed the evil of their souls.

'Friedrich and Adam always wondered about those portraits,' said Noël. 'All the others in the house have a little plaque on the frame with the name of the artist and the person or people.'

'Are they still in the house?' Paul asked.

'Yes, they're in Juliet and Friedrich's apartment.'

A week after her death our mother's evil returned to haunt us. After Deaville's trial I had dispensed with her solicitor and now used the brother of our estate manager. When a footman told me that my mother's solicitor wanted to see me urgently, I said I would see him in my office.

I'd always disliked him and when he was shown into my office, I made no effort to hide my distaste. He made no effort to hide his triumph.

'Adam.'

'Mr Carlyle to you.'

'As your mother's solicitor–'

'You are not her solicitor. You no longer have any business with this family.'

'Oh, but I do, Adam,' he said with deliberate insolence. Without being asked he sat down. He took out a letter and waved it. 'This letter is from your mother. The doctor found it under her bedclothes. It was addressed to me.'

My heart pounded.

'You say I am no longer your solicitor. This letter will change your mind.' He removed the pages from the envelope and unfolded them. 'I will read it to you.'

'I'm capable of reading it myself.'

He chuckled. 'Oh no. It's not leaving my possession.'

I shrugged to disguise my fear. Even though I was dreading the worst I was unprepared for the contents.

He cleared his throat and began to read. 'My son Adam, in collusion with my daughter Imogen, is trying to murder me. He is insane, but cunning. When my husband passed away Victor Deaville helped me manage the household. Adam resented this and worked against him. One evening, when Mr Deaville was here explaining the household accounts to me, my son burst into the drawing room brandishing a pistol. He made us go to my rooms and forced Mr Deaville to undress. Then he turned on me and told me if I did not undress and get into my nightgown he would shoot me. Unable to resist I complied. He then attacked Mr Deaville and called for help. When I attempted to stop him he punched me in the face and threw me on the bed. My injuries were caused by my son, not Mr Deaville. To ensure Mr Deaville's arrest, Adam planted one of my diamond necklaces in Mr Deaville's pocket. He told the footmen, the butler and my lady's maid that Mr Deaville was an intruder and had tried to rob me.

I committed perjury because my son told me he would lock me in the cellars and torture me unless I lied to the court and the officials. He is guilty of murdering an innocent man who was helping me manage the household accounts. I urge you to contact the authorities and arrest my son. His motive for murder was because I knew he was insane, and, with the help of Mr Deaville, was trying to get him committed to an asylum for the insane. After Mr Deaville's conviction, my son moved me to these rooms, which he kept locked. He forbade me to have visitors and made me write to the doctors at the asylum cancelling the order for him to be incarcerated. Please inform the authorities–'

I had heard enough. 'What do you want?'

'That's better, Adam. You are finally being sensible. I want you to reinstate me as your solicitor. Now that's not difficult, is it?'

'It's blackmail.'

He looked hurt. 'No. An exchange of favours. The alternative is you being charged with murdering your mother.'

'Blackmail. Were you at Deaville's trial?'

'Alas, I was in Italy at the time.'

'Then I will summarise what took place. If you don't believe me you can check the court records. At his trial Deaville stated that he and my mother were lovers and that I had found them in bed together and that I had attacked him and deposited the diamond necklace in the pocket of his coat. If my mother's version of events is true, why didn't Deaville use that as his defence?' I saw to my satisfaction that his triumphant expression had faded.

'Did my mother write that letter or did you?'

He looked outraged. 'Are you accusing me–'

'Yes, I'm accusing you of attempted blackmail and forgery.'

'This letter was written by your mother. The doctor will confirm it.'

'He will confirm that a letter addressed to you was found on her person, but while the envelope was written by her, was the letter also written by her? Or did you write it?'

Although I had demolished his blackmail attempt, I had to end this forever. No one else must see the letter, which in spite of what I had implied, I knew was genuine. I rang the bell. When a footman arrived I asked him to find my sister. She appeared ten minutes later. Turning my back on the solicitor, I mouthed. 'Distract him.'

She responded by falling at my feet and groaning. As the solicitor jumped up I snatched the letter, screwed it up and flung it on the fire. 'Get out of this house. Never come back. If you do I'll have you arrested for trespass. I'll show you out.'

To complete his humiliation I ushered him to one of the servants' doors and shoved him outside.

When all the improvements had been made, my life became more routine and I had free time. I had been aware of Gertrude, Imogen's governess, for a long time before I began to court her. She was intelligent, kind and attractive. When she said she would marry me I gave her the diamond engagement ring

Imogen had kept. We married in 1854. It caused a furore, but neither of us cared.

To my delight, when Imogen was seventeen she and Andrew's son James began courting. They married in 1855 and moved into the east wing.

Noël stared at the page. 'Imogen married a Halland! Our families were connected all those years ago.' She looked at Juliet. 'Do you think it's the same Halland?'

Juliet went to the computer. 'I've been checking out web pages. There's a births, deaths and marriages register. It's tedious going through, but I've found that Adam and Gertrude had nine children. Imogen's husband was James Andrew Halland. Luckily all the first sons and daughters are named after their grandparents with their parents' name the second name.'

'But what about the Hallands? When did they come to Australia?'

'I don't know. I checked the census records, but found nothing in the 1901 census. But in 1900 the death register records all the four children of Elizabeth and Thomas Halland dying within weeks of each other from scarlet fever.'

'Oh, Christ,' said Noël. 'How tragic. So the line died out? They can't be our Hallands.'

'They might be. In 1900 Elizabeth was twenty-seven and Thomas was twenty- nine. They were still young enough to have more children, but there's no record of any more births.'

'What about death records?'

Juliet shook her head. 'Nothing there either. It's my guess that they came to Australia.'

'Shipping records?'

'Ah.' Juliet found a website, paid the subscription charges, and quickly found their names. 'They arrived in Sydney,' she said excitedly. 'In 1901.'

'But why choose the outback?'

'Clean, remote, far away from any diseases. Let's check the registry of births, deaths and marriages.' Juliet typed *NSW births, deaths and marriages* and clicked on family history and births when the page appeared. 'We don't want to put in too much information – it slows down the search.' She typed Halland in the surname and Elizabeth in the mother's name. 'What date period will we enter?'

'Make it as wide as possible.'

Juliet entered 1901 to 1910. Seconds later five births came up. All were for the district of Cobar.

'That's them,' whispered Noël. 'Children of Elizabeth and Thomas. Three daughters and two sons.' She looked at the last page of Adam's journal. 'Is this where it ends? Maybe there's another journal. I'll e-mail Adam's parents – they might be able to find it.'

Juliet counted the remaining pages. 'There are seventeen more pages, all blank – he wouldn't have started another volume before finishing this one.'

'It must be strange being a writer,' mused Noël. 'Conflict and drama – you've got to have them. I guess it all went well after their mother died. The source of trouble was gone. Narrator Adam would have been dead by 1900 when tragedy struck.'

'Not necessarily. He started the journal in 1850 when his father died. He was twenty, so he'd be seventy in 1900. He could have been dead, but maybe he found the deaths of the children too traumatic to write about. Or he could have had arthritis and found writing difficult and painful.'

'Deaths,' said Noël. 'Check the British death register.'

'Ah,' said Juliet a few minutes later. 'He died the same year.'

Noël stared at the last page. 'So this is where it ends,' she murmured.

'His journal yes, but not his influence,' said Juliet. 'It's there for all to see. The cosy cottages. And there's my daughter – she's his descendant. Adam – the original one – lives on in her. And Grace's daughter and your son are his descendants too – through Imogen.'

'Did you feel anything weird when Friedrich and Adam took you all out to dinner the first time?' Paul asked Noël when she told him.

'Not weird, but we got on so well it's as if we'd known each other for years. We had opera in common and we talked about that, so I guess I assumed that's why we had such rapport. There were no uncomfortable silences – we just chatted and had fun.'

'Apart from opera what did you talk about?'

'They told us about Shuttleton and their parents and we told them about Tordorrach – so although both places were different we had the love of the land and horses in common. And Friedrich, Adam and I could shoot.'

'How did you feel when you first went to Shuttleton?'

'It felt right. Immediately I felt I belonged, even though I'd never lived in such a huge place before. I didn't feel overawed. Do you believe there is such a thing as ancestral memory?'

'Who knows? It's possible, but impossible to prove. Imogen and her husband moved into the east wing. You and Adam chose your apartment in the east wing. Did you choose it together, or was it more Adam's preference?'

'We looked at all of them – Juliet and Friedrich were with us. Friedrich knew he wanted their apartment to be in the west wing – he and Juliet have got a thing about sunsets.'

'A lot of families had to give up their huge mansions after the world wars because of taxes. Places like that must have been a nightmare to run, especially when people didn't want to go into service anymore. How did the Carlyles survive?'

'They made an absolute fortune during both world wars – the mills churned out cloth for uniforms, bandages and tents. After the wars most of the surviving men returned to Shuttleton to work, because the living conditions were good and the family treated them well. Some of the female servants went into nursing, but a lot of them returned to Shuttleton. Anyone who was wounded was allowed to live there and paid a pension. There is a story that during the First World War the family bought cars and hid their horses so they wouldn't be commandeered.'

'Were they conscientious objectors?'

'No. They just loved their horses and didn't want them to suffer. In the Second World War, Adam and Friedrich's grandfather was in the Air Force, and their grandmother was an ambulance driver.'

Their baby cried and they went to his room. Paul lifted him out of his cot. 'Hello, Baby.'

'What have we done, Paul?'

'Done?'

Noël stroked the baby's head. 'This is a terrible world and we've brought a baby into it. America's got a lunatic, misogynist president. God know what will happen now. He's dangerous.'

The baby wailed.

'He's not hungry – he probably needs changing,' said Noël.

Paul put him on the changing table. 'When are we going to find a name for you? We can't keep calling you Baby.'

'You were right,' said Noël taking a clean nappy out of the drawer. 'Your first suggestion. We should call him Adam . . . not after my husband, but after the original Adam.'

'What changed your mind?'

'His integrity, courage and kindness. My husband was a good man too, but he didn't have the obstacles the first Adam had to face.

Paul took off the nappy. 'But the Adam in the journal did send an innocent man to his death.'

'Not innocent. Deaville was a malicious, scheming man who would have been hanged anyway if his theft from the mill had been discovered. And he was conspiring with Adam's mother to have him put in a lunatic asylum. The original Adam was brought up to be cruel, insensitive and money orientated. He fought all that and improved the lives of his servants and mill workers. In doing so he took a huge risk, but he disregarded the danger and the condemnation of his peers. And so did Imogen.'

Paul kissed the baby's tiny hands. 'Hello, Adam.'

I am indebted to the Bloodhound Books team especially:
Betsy Reavley
Fred Freeman
Sumaria Wilson
Heather Fitt

Special thanks to:
Michael and Sally Bannister for their generosity when I visited
Cobar in 2014.
Justin Conroy for his advice about planes.

In loving memory of:
Ethel Curnow née Stephen
Carlyle Stephen
Grace Vincent née Holland
Jack Holland